1-25

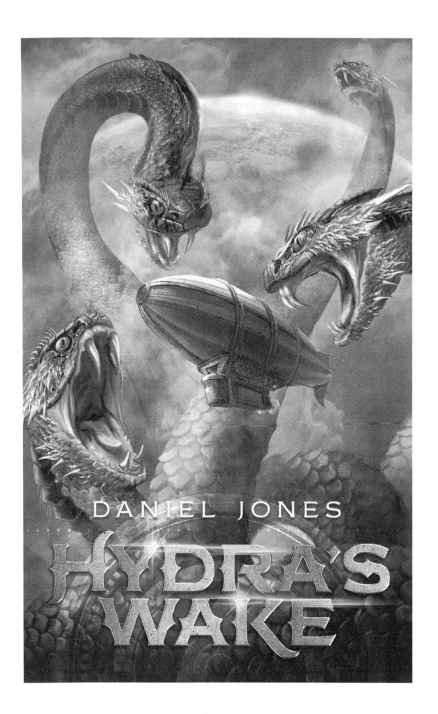

DANIEL JONES

HYDRA'S WAKE

II

HYDRA'S WAKE

Daniel Jones

Daniel Jones

IT IS TIME
FOR A WILD
RIDE!

For more information, please contact Daniel Jones via admin@creatureauthor.com

FIRST EDITION

Library of Congress Data
Library of Congress Control Number: 2022901329
Amazon Identifier
Hardcover ISBN: 9798759782964

Cover design by Ivan Zanchetta & Bookcoversart.com
Printed in the United States of America

CONTENTS

PROLOGUE:
THE WORLD OF
YERAPUTS

"They say the universe is full of places with different shapes and stories. And where we live is one of the more unique places. Can anyone tell me how Yeraputs was formed?" Jessie asks the room full of young kids. A bunch of hands shoot into the air, and the room fills with *ooh ooh's* and *pick me's*. "Yes, you there in the middle." It's exciting to see the energy from this school group.

"Heart smashed into Shell a long time ago, making Yeraputs a twin planet world," the young boy answers full of energy.

Jessie is somewhat surprised by such a specific answer, it's as though children are getting smarter every year they come in for a tour. "Well done! That's right. Heart was a drifting planet that smashed into Shell, but in a special way that made Shell a little like a cradle for Heart." Jessie does her best to match their energy. "Does anyone know why we can fly from Heart to Shell and back?"

"Because they share an atmosphere. We can breathe air all the way." A student blurts this out before anyone else has a chance.

"And do you know what the space of atmosphere between the planets is called?" she follows up. Not many hands go up this time, so she picks the one closest to her. "Go for it."

"The Tradewinds. It's always windy there because Shell and Heart spin different ways, and gravity goes up and down between them," the kid answers with certainty.

"You're correct," says a man wearing a green shirt and blue jeans.

"Look who's here, everyone! This is my boss. He owns the whole company. Everyone say hi to Mr. Whip." Jessie puts him in the spotlight.

He laughs and waves at the students in the tour group as he receives the universal reply of Hi Mr. Whip from the kids and their teachers. "Is everyone having fun so far?" They all say yes, but the reply is a little lackluster. "Well, tell you kids what. We're about to load some cargo onto our best airship. Follow me to a viewing area, and everyone can come watch."

Jessie chuckles as the group gets very excited. She pulls Rogue aside while the teachers try to settle the kids down. "You sure know how to get them all riled up."

"Just make sure they stay in the observation area please. It's the cargo from the Mining Conglomerate."

"That cargo? The fragile cargo?" She comes up with a creative way to describe it.

"Very," he replies with a smile. "Mason's still in the hospital, so I'll be flying by myself. As usual, you're in charge of operations and whatnot till I get back. I shouldn't be more than a week, week and a half."

"Do you have enough supplies on board?"

"Just stocked up with all the food and whatnot I'll need. Gonna make it a multi-leg journey, since there's a lot of transportation work that needs to be done on Outer Shell. Cities there are getting bigger by the day."

One of the kids comes up to them. "Does it take a long time to fly there?"

"Not at all. In fact, you know the big holes in Shell that you can see through?" he asks the kid.

"Yeah," he replies, now nervous.

"Well, those are so big, there's a lot of space to fly all the way through Shell. You can fly to the other side of Shell faster than you can fly to the other side of Heart. Isn't that neat?"

"Whoa," the whole class responds since they quiet while listening to the conversation.

"Do you fly the airships yourself?" another kid asks.

"As often as I can. I love flying. It's why I started this delivery company."

"Why airships and not airplanes?" another kid asks.

"Airplanes are the coolest machines to fly, but they're expensive and not the best for cargo when the gravity flips in the Tradewinds. My dirigibles are more stable and secure for carrying cargo. But I'll tell you a small secret. I have small airplanes on every ship. If there's a problem, those small airplanes will allow me to get off the ship safely before it crashes. Or if I want a little fun while taking a break, I can always take them out for a spin." His joke makes a few of the teachers' chuckle. "Follow me to our observation area!"

Jessie brings up the rear as Rogue takes them down a long hallway leading to the skyport. From the observation area, everyone looks out at a large dirigible with a group of people loading crates into the hold. The kids are enthralled and make all sorts of observations about how big and cool the dirigible looks.

"Pretty soon, I'll be taking off in that ship, so hang around and watch the launch. Then Miss Jessie will take you on a tour of the second ship over there."

Jessie follows him up to the exit. "Is there anything on the books I need to know about while you're out?"

"Everything is on automatic schedules and recurring orders. No surprises this time, I promise."

Jessie leans against the wall, crossing her arms and smirking.

He chuckles. "Come on, you practically run the place these days. I couldn't ask for a better operations leader in the whole city. I left everything on your desk."

1: LANDING IN A GHOST TOWN

Rogue Whip wakes up and finds himself on the ground. The freezing cold dirt does nothing to hide the throbbing pain throughout his entire body. After a few moments, his head stops spinning and he can see he's in a forest. A line of trees in front of him is knocked down and crushed. There's debris all around him and bits of metal and cloth are draped on what's left of the trees. Once he gains his bearings, he realizes that his dirigible has crashed.

When he takes a look behind him, he can see that the cargo hold is gone, but the majority of his cabin is intact. His mind races with questions. But for now, all he can remember is how the winds across the inner Shell were more turbulent than anything he's ever experienced before.

More of his memory returns and he recalls when the wind shears blew past the dirigible. They felt like a current of fast-moving air waves, shaking hard enough to make his cargo unstable. His only choice was to descend into the forest. After that it gets more difficult for him to remember.

He doesn't know where he crashed. Is he on Heart or Shell? If he's on Shell, he knows waiting for a rescue is an unreliable plan since most of Shell's terrain makes rescues difficult. He tilts his head back to the cabin and focuses on thinking about reaching the charts inside. If he can get to them he'll be able to figure out where exactly he is.

His first attempt to get up proves difficult. The pain throughout his body is excruciating. All he can do is tense his muscles, not move them. After a few painful attempts, he forces himself to sit up and screams. His body is sorer than he's ever felt it before. Once the sensation becomes manageable, he checks himself over. None of his bones appear to be broken, and he doesn't notice any bleeding.

One thing that does stand out to him is that his emergency vest deployed and is ripped apart from the airbags expanding. He's glad he invested in one, which likely explains how he survived such a hard landing.

Next, he spots his helmet, which landed about ten feet away. To knock that off his head, the landing had to hit harder than he first realized. He brushes off the dirt from his dark-green company shirt and the front of his blue jeans. Out of frustration, he rips off the vest and throws it into the bushes as hard he can. This reminds him of how much pain he is in, and he screams.

"Goddamm!"

He forces himself to focus on reaching a first aid kit. *I know I have one in the cabin, which has a pain wipe injector. Ok, come on, you got this, you gotta reach the cockpit. But damn my body is wrecked.*

After several failed attempts to get up, he decides to lie still and breathe. *Too much. Too painful. I can hardly feel anything from the waist down that isn't throbbing.* The pain needs to subside before he can get up.

The area is peaceful and quiet, aside from the faint sound of crackling flames. Then it occurs to him: *I can't stay still! What if the forest is on fire? I need to run.* He forces himself to sit up again and searches for the source of the sound. He finds no signs of flames, and despite the faint smell, he can't locate where the smoke is coming from.

The extra time staying down allows him to regain more control of his body. After a few more attempts, he manages to stand. While the level of pain he feels is manageable, he still screams in agony. "Ah, damn!"

From a standing position, he sees more of the wreckage and his surroundings. Turns out he's on the crest of a hill that slopes downward in front of him.

And when he turns around, he realizes the crash site is on the edge of a cliff. *Half of my dirigible is on the top of the cliff, and it's safe to say the other half landed at the bottom. What kind of twisted luck is that?* He walks step by agonizing step over to the ledge.

Sure enough, when he takes a look down the cliff, his ship's cargo hold and engine room are being consumed by flames several hundred feet below. *Ok, the engine blew up and fell way down there. That's fine. I can't shake the sense of dread about the payload... what was it? I can't remember, I can't think straight.* He returns his attention to the cabin, which, despite its unorthodox landing, is intact and only a little banged up, though most of the glass is gone.

Rogue climbs into the flight deck through the front, finding everything is thrown everywhere. "Man, what a wreck." The first aid kit catches his eye. It's still in its bracket on the wall. "I'll call that a break. At least I have medicine and food." Rogue tries to sound triumphant to reassure himself. He grabs the kit and sits in the pilot's chair. After clearing the console, he places his kit where a map would be, opens it up and finds everything intact. *Good, this is perfect.*

Next, he retrieves the white metal tube labeled PAIN WIPE in bold, blue, blocky letters. This is a medical concoction used to block pain sensors for a little while. Only to be used when there are no other options, and no means of getting help. Because it masks the presence of serious injuries, which can result in a failure to address real problems, or seek emergency attention, which may result in death.

After struggling to open the tube, he pulls the device out. A syringe mounted on a black, cloth, arm-length sleeve. The purpose is to help users with little medical experience perform a proper injection. After putting it on and using the injector Rogue's stomach churns. He always has a mild reaction to these things.

The sensation soon subsides, and this allows him to focus. *In times like this, I am so glad I am a scout. I'd be useless otherwise. Wow, today's modern medicine works like a charm. Take a few deep breaths; keep the blood flowing.*

After controlling his breathing, he looks around at the mess. "Ok, the maps flew off the console. Wonderful," he groans, taking the injection sleeve off and throwing it against the wall of the cabin in frustration. His flight and flow charts are mixed in with the debris. The charts he picks up off the floor are all for Shell, which means all those for Heart are currently tucked away. *Screw me! Am I stuck on inner Shell? Yeah, no way I'm on Heart.* This isn't the outcome he hoped for.

"It's okay, I got this," he tries to convince himself. "Not like I'm dead. Not yet."

He spots a chart still clamped nearby. "Ok, that's progress." He forces a more confident tone. *Ah, right, before it became a ride from hell, I was updating this thing. I remember making some marks after I saw the tip of Mount Hade.* He walks over, brushes the shattered glass and dirt off carefully and inspects it. The first thing he identifies is a long cliff face on the north side of the map. "The Deep Forest Province. I must be on these Backfin Cliffs. Now I need to check outside and find Mount Hade. I can figure this out from there. Where's my compass?"

He steps outside with a compass. Looking south, he finds the cone shaped mountain with tall thin needle peaks soaring high in the distance. Mount Hade is the signature landmark for the forest. Those who navigate the Tradewinds are familiar with this lone mountain. At the base is a wide, perfect cone, like a volcano. The center consists of towering thin peaks, like pillars made from a different kind of rock protruding thousands of feet above the rest. "I am where I suspected

I was. That's definitely a sign of progress."

That also brings with it the bad news. *Chances are I am well over a thousand miles in any direction from potential rescue. There may be a handful of mining camps are in the area. Doesn't help me at all though, because this time of year they'll be empty. Nearest city would to the north, way north. Of all the places to be, this forest is famous for thick fog and violent wildlife. It's official, I've crashed into hell. Oh wait. I could've just looked up and seen Heart and realize I'm on Shell. How badly did I hit my head?*

Rogue doesn't keep weapons on board since he never has to deal with aggressive wildlife, or any real wilderness survival gear. Which is going to be a problem since on the inner side of Shell, nights and daily eclipses can become freezing. Dawn is visible for now, though soon Heart will be casting a shadow of darkness over the area.

With his fears confirmed he walks back inside the cabin, taking a closer look at the map on the wall. *How screwed am I?* There appears to be a nearby railway line used by the miners. "Well, this gives me two possible directions to follow."

He measures the distance from the crash site to the tracks. It's close to twenty miles or so. *Over this terrible terrain, it might take me a day to cross in my current condition. Then, it's a matter of either following it down to a closed mining site, or to what is likely the major mining hub. Wait, Edgar's Hub, Ok, maybe I'm not that stranded.*

He measures the distance out on the accompanying map he located on the floor. The mining hub is around seven hundred and sixty miles away. The closest mining camp is about one hundred and twenty miles following the line through winding mountains. *I'd rather try to take a safe way down the cliff, and travel only forty miles. Never realized how big the Forest is.* "The mining camp means shelter and a chance of finding a way to communicate. Camp Tor," Rogue reads out loud, after giving it some thought. The map also shows two runways at the site. "If I still have the bailing plane, I can make that."

He looks around again. "Ok, if I go to Tor, what do I need to be aware of?" He starts opening cabinets on the Flying Deck wall looking for a Shell bestiary. Someone had given it to him as a gift. Once again, it's going to come in handy, and once he finds it, he takes it into his personal quarters in the back of the cabin.

He uses the bestiary frequently because Shell's diverse wildlife includes a lot of dangerous, carnivorous avian species. The information provides a great guide for dealing with airborne threats using methods that don't rely on aggression. *Around here I'm a tasty snack. For what though? That is the question.*

He catches the reflection of his face in the mirror on the wall and is surprised to find himself covered in several good bruises, as opposed to major lacerations or other damage. *Right, first thing is first. Check out my condition.* He takes his shirt off to check over his body. He looks a bit off color, indicating he must've been in the dirt for a while during the cold morning. His arms are covered in small scrapes and major bruises from rolling across the ground on landing.

He is a six-foot-tall dirigible pilot who deals with heavy loads, giving him a fit, muscular build. He isn't a body builder, but he's proud of his bulging arms and powerful legs. Which, of course, comes with the job, and he keeps himself in shape to handle his cargo with ease. "Waste of time they said. Well, these muscles may be why I endured the crash so well." He mocks his other pilots as he grabs a new shirt and puts it on. The shirt features his company's logo embroidered on the shoulder. ROGUE WHIP'S TRADEWINDS CROSSING.

He returns his attention to the bestiary and after flipping through the pages, he finds the section on the Deep Forest Province. Tor Valley Biome.

"Don't think anything small is a major threat." Going down the list, he picks out only carnivores known to eat people and identifies sixteen. The valley is home to two apex predators. "Harpy bear, over two hundred feet tall, resembles a bear in appearance, shocker. They walk on all four limbs and have a thick coat of massive feathers and bony plates of ivory. They roam the forest and hunt at night. Four of them of significant size are found in the province. Only one shows a tendency to roam into Tor Valley, usually to fight the other apex predator for territory. Read about the Tor hydra for details. It goes on about neat lifestyle stuff that I don't care about." After seeing the word hydra, he leans back and sighs.

"A hydra? Here? No way!" he exclaims in surprise and dread. He's heard the rumors about people who fall into a coma after getting close to any of those. There are stories and legends about something called the hydra's wake. Well, they're more than stories, but there aren't any survivors of hydra's wake who can give actual accounts of what it is. *Guess I'm in the right spot to figure out if that's all true or not.*

He flips a few pages further and finds the entry on the local hydra.

"This author's knowledge of hydras is limited. This super-massive animal features many trademark traits not found amongst other animals. The most famous is the ability to regenerate two heads for each one lost. It boasts a dense, almost impenetrable reptilian skin, with bony armor covering most of the body. We do know it prefers to hunt using an airborne toxin designed to disorient its prey. This is the second famous trait, what we call hydra's wake. Humans experience this in the forms of hallucinations and other effects, though details are sparse and there aren't any historical records of survivors who have experienced it. My team and I are unable to verify this firsthand out of safety concerns. The hydra's wake is the most dangerous hunting technique used by any animal on record." Rogue tries to recall what he's heard about the hydra's wake, then he continues reading.

"Suffice to say, for survival, avoid the beast's territories at all costs. They are the utmost apex predator in Yeraputs. We do know the hydras hibernate according to a specific schedule. Observations over centuries have revealed a strict and predictable hibernation cycle. This allows us to predict with certainty when they are active or hibernating. We hope one day to be able to surviving being close enough to one to study it better. With our current technology, it is not possible sans death or permanent coma." Rogue arrives at the end of the section. "That's all? Not a lot to go on." The next page shows an archon. *So that's why the mines stay empty for so long. Who knew? Mining Season is during hydra sleeping season.*

He continues to read about the rest. *Archons? They aren't dangerous, I see them every day in the Tradewinds; they're cute flying cats. Though, to be fair, I wouldn't exactly pet one.* He goes further down the list. "Greater talon eagles. Flying there is looking a little less like a great plan. Big spider, bigger spider, note to self, don't go into the forest itself. But tyros and maulers? Those might be a problem." His concern grows as he flips through the pages.

"The tyro is a larger carnivore with reptilian skin of various colors, found all across Inner Shell. The defining feature is an enormous skull with a maw full of three rows of teeth. Powerful leg muscles allow them to run and jump great distances. They can run up to seventy miles an hour in clear open fields. An adult will stand around fifteen feet tall and be close to thirty feet long. It is worth noting their intelligence and preference for hunting in pairs. They live in small social groups of multiple families, defending territory as a pack." *That would be a nasty thing to meet. Hope I don't have the pleasure.*

He remembers hearing about Maulers before in a menagerie on Heart. "Maulers are uncommon, although found everywhere on Yeraputs. They are half the size of an average human and come in several varieties. For this entry we will discuss those found in Inner

Shell. In the wilds, their fierce attitude makes them dangerous. They show little regard for their own safety when engaging territorial intruders. Their maws have small teeth, which are inefficient in combat. They rely on sharp talons on their hands and feet when hunting or fighting. They will attack an intruder's extremities. By staying persistent with quick in and out attacks, they prefer to wait for the intruder or prey to die from blood loss."

A noise from outside distracts Rogue. Keeping quiet, he moves to the flight deck and checks out the area, but doesn't see anything at first. He turns around to head back to the Personal Quarters when loud chirping breaks his attention and sends a shiver up his spine. Rogue looks over his shoulder and spots a mauler inspecting the wreckage. This is a big one too, and its presence gives Rogue and overwhelming sense of dread. *It's not scared of the debris. I hope it didn't have a nest or home that got crushed on my way down.*

His stomach growls, getting the Mauler's attention. In an instant, it looks up at the deck, locking eyes with the human. *Not good.* Nothing but clear space stands between the vicious mauler and Rogue. *I need something, anything, to be between me and that thing now.*

Ok, let's not panic, let's stay calm and assess the situation. A dangerous carnivore small enough to jump in here, and I'm betting he's too hungry to just walk away. Ah, wait. The console, the bird cage! If this thing's battery still works, I can lower that. At least I'll have something between us that can buy me a little time to figure this out. The mauler stays still, staring at him.

The controls are to my right, that's away from it, which is good. Maybe the backing away will buy some time while it decides how to attack me. I don't know, but let's try it. Rogue takes a step to the side and hears a shrill hissing sound.

He keeps his movements steady and calm. *Almost there, only a few steps further.* By the time he reaches the pilot's chair, the animal lowers its torso, ready to pounce. Rogue presses the button to lower the bird cage that protects the decks from bird strikes during flight.

A wire lattice rolls down from the lip of the outer cabin, guided down along the dirigible frame to the floor. The sudden motor noise and movement attracts the mauler's curiosity. It seems comfortable with the mechanical sounds at first. But the clamping noise indicating the cage is secure startles them both.

The Mauler hisses when it realizes the cage prevents it from attacking, but then resumes its inspection of the rest of the wreckage.

Rogue sits down. Smoke from the fire at the base of the cliffs is getting thicker, but the mauler doesn't appear concerned.

While it continues to sniff the ground, Rogue spots something surprising on the mauler's neck. *Is that a collar? Is it possible scavengers are nearby who witnessed the crash? That explains it's comfort around manmade stuff.* The mauler picks up Rogue's pilot helmet and takes off into the bushes. *Wait hold up! Maulers don't grab things like that unless they're trained. Right? And the collar? Am I not alone out here? I don't like this one bit.*

After a moment spent assessing the situation, his gut tells him to leave. "Camp Tor or bust." He grabs his backpack from the front of the cabin, hurries to the back room, fills it with food, the first aid kit, and clothes. When he finishes, he opens the back door leading to the observation deck, and a wave of relief hits him.

His small airplane, designed for emergency ditching, has survived. The easy part will be launching off the wrecked cabin, getting into the air. His plane is pointing toward the edge of the cliff and, out of sheer luck, none of the dirigible's balloon cloth is in the way.

The airplane has a single huge propeller in the rear and a kite style wing on top. Its range is limited to a hundred miles or so with space for two people, or one person and a person-sized load of cargo. Rogue gathers all the remaining supplies he has on hand, and prepares the launch mechanism. *On a positive note, flying to this place while I still have daylight is a bonus.* "I hope no one hears this." Something in the back of his mind is telling him whoever is nearby is probably not friendly.

After a few short moments, Rogue launches himself off the cliff side and flies upwards. Turns out his crash left a larger path of destruction than he first thought. The trail of destroyed trees and scraped land stretches for half a mile at least. *A nine million copper fire. That's a lot of cash down the drain. Damn, it's gonna take me all year to replace that one dirigible, and that's only if I'm lucky.*

He turns his sights towards Camp Tor, and follows the map. After a short ten-minute flight, he finds the camp at the other end of the valley at the base of the cliffs. Rogue thinks, for a moment, that he has overshot the mining camp; the place he's approaching is the size of a small town, with over a dozen buildings.

An array of rail tracks line the ground like walkways. The place is larger than Rogue expected. *Whoa, the airfield is a full airstrip with tarmac!* "Perfect! Talk about catching a break!" He breathes a sigh of relief.

Rogue makes a smooth landing. To his right, he can see the entire valley, which has a central lake and a river leading into the forest. He is thankful to see nothing other than grazing animals in the distance. *So far, so good. No monsters and no new problems. That's a gorgeous valley though.*

He gets out of the plane and heads to the airstrip station. There appears to be a reception area and inside where a door sign reads LOBBY. He walks around to the other side of the building and reads LOUNGE printed on a door. He checks inside, and indeed, within is a fancy looking lounge. Behind him he notes the crane structures over the rail lines next to the platforms. They resemble those uses at his skyport in Acinvar.

He returns to the door marked LOBBY and tries to open it. To his surprise, the door opens without creaking. *Who leaves a building unlocked like this? Oh well, maybe they left in a hurry? Everything is covered in thick dust it smells musty in here.*

"Man, this room is filthy." He blows dust off a nearby table then turns his attention to the reception desk. On top of the desk is a piece of paper with a handwritten note:
IF YOU FIND YOURSELF STRANDED, FEEL FREE TO CAMP IN THIS BUILDING. BE MINDFUL OF THE LOCAL WILDLIFE, THE NEXT MINING SEASON, WHICH IS IN AUG. STAY ALIVE UNTIL THEN. ROOM KEYS ARE BEHIND THE RECEPTION COUNTER. IF YOU GET BORED, THERE ARE THINGS TO DO AROUND HERE. (WE WILL EVEN PAY YOU FOR YOUR TROUBLE!)

August? That's a long wait. Okay, it's May now. The food I brought with me will last a week or so; I'll have to ration what I have and find a way to be creative, I guess. Let's take this one hour at a time for now. A solid room helps, and Rogue appreciates the humor in doing off-season work for some spare change. *Not the worst idea ever. Might even make enough to afford a trip back to Heart.*

He goes around the counter and finds the keys laid out. All are present. It appears as though he's alone for now, so he grabs the first one and walks down the hallway to a door on the left with the same number as the key. The door is also unlocked when Rogue tries to open it. *It's odd that nothing got locked up when they evacuated.*

Inside, the room has a typical apartment set-up. A desk near the door with a chair. A table with another piece of paper on top, and a king-size bed with folded blankets. Rogue takes a few steps in. To his right is the cooking area, with a basic wood stove, and a stocked pantry with dry foods. "Do people wind up getting stranded here often?" he wonders out loud. To his immediate left is a lavatory.

The whole place is neat and tidy, and the windows with curtains provide an incredible view over the airstrip and valley. There is a clear view of a variety of animals grazing in the fields and visiting the river running through. "I crash landed into a much-needed vacation."

This is really something. I didn't think the mining camps did this for people. It's super generous.

Now, feeling a little more secure, he takes a moment to contemplate the cost of the crash.

So, my fleet is running on automatic orders for a few months. But I won't be able to make any new income. And I know Jessie can run things in my stead until I return for as long as it takes. He hates the idea of losing his company because of this crash.

Just sitting in the silence is meditative. *They better not declare me dead. That would be such a headache. Ugh! Just thinking of the reports and apologizing to the vendors. The stress that will put on everyone back home. My reputation will sink. This is giving me a migraine.* He goes outside to collect his belongings. "Business needs to wait. I gotta focus on myself for now."

He sets his stuff down on the floor across from the bed and tries to relax by sitting in the chair and leaning back, but finds himself growing more restless by the second. *Dammit, I can't sit still.* He decides to go back to the reception desk, where he recalls seeing a map, and do some exploring of Camp Tor. He takes the map down from the wall and waves it around to shake the dust off.

Cliffs to the north and the valley to the south. The row of buildings closest to Backfin Cliffs are all BARRACKS. The cliff shows a break where the rail line leaves camp, going toward the primary railroad line. Near the primary line somebody wrote VERY RUGGED HILLS. Turns out the camp has two mines, a PHOSPHORUS MINE, and a GEMSTONE MINE.

Another set of tracks leads into the phosphorus mine. The tracks split in two directions, one leading to the loading bay at the STATION, and one next to the REFINERY. In the center of the camp is RUBY WELL. North of the entrance to the phosphorous mine is a GENERAL STORE, a MAINTENANCE SHOP, and, adjacent to the airstrip is an OFFICE.

In the opposite direction from the general store is a POWER PLANT. Another trail heads east from the Ruby Well. Rogue follows with his finger past the refinery along the cliffs in the direction of the crash site. The gemstone mine can be found there, along with another path to a SKYPORT.

"They have another skyport here?" He didn't see anything on top of those cliffs when he circled around to get a better angle on the tarmac. He goes to the door between the lobby and the lounge, which is better kept up, then heads for the door going outside. From his vantage point he is quick to appreciate how everything is accurate and as described on the map.

He walks over to see the Ruby Well, which is a plain brick circle about four feet high and ten feet wide. The well goes down further than Rogue can see, and pipes on the side run the length of the well. At the surface, the pipes feed into a rusty box with several more pipes leading into the ground.

Rogue admires the sight, while reflecting on how outdated even his company's office is by comparison. *They must have running water in these buildings. This place is more advanced than half the cities I can think of. Heck not even all of Acinvar has that. These miners don't fool around. They make sure they have the best stuff.*

Rogue walks to the closest barracks and enters. Inside it's an open floor plan, with bunk beds lined up in neat uniform rows. The outer walls have full wall windows, and the view is unhindered all-around camp. The windows have shutters that extend down from the ceiling. In the center of the room is a common area with desks, tables, shelves with books, and couches. At the back of the building, the wall facing the cliff is solid and is where the showers and lavatories are located.

Something stands out to Rogue as he explores. *So, they have advanced plumbing, reliable power, but they live like sardines in a can. All crammed together like some boarding school or military unit. That would grow old on me real fast.*

From the barracks, he heads towards the refinery. The larger, warehouse-style building is made with as much window as solid wall. A very different style from the buildings on Heart. There are a lot huge machines inside, which he assumes are for processing phosphorus. Several bay doors are on the end of the building closest to the airstrip and station. And there are stairs heading to an upper floor that is concealed by a section of solid wall.

"What is it with all the transparency around here?" *I guess privacy is only for guests in the station and the office. That, or architects on Shell are super proud of their glass work. I'm all for natural lighting, but this is too much.*

He enters through the double doors at the front of the refinery. The floor is marked with bright painted paths, with green for safe areas, and red for work zones. The place is covered with obsessive signage about wearing protective equipment. Other notices promote only using the machines you have training on, and a variety of other safety warnings.

To his left is a collection of chairs and desks resembling a roll call and assignment area. Beyond that are the stairs to the mezzanine. To the right is an open stretch leading to the loading bay and the rail line.

Ahead are all sorts of machines. He doesn't know what they do, aside from the obvious task of refining phosphorus. "This is a much more intense process than I would have guessed." The equipment and furniture are all covered in a thin layer of dust. *You'd think they would cover these things. Doing so would prevent a ton of cleaning that needs to be done when they come back.*

He inspects the nearest one and brushes dust off the machine's label.

"A particle sifter?" he glances at a control panel and sees a series of levers with different colors and shapes. "Guess it's easy to use when you get trained on it."

He heads up to the second floor, where he discovers a tight-knit array of writing desks. *This must be where the whole operation is managed.* He reads some papers left out on the desks. Each one is covered with a clutter of handwritten charts, numbers, and notes. He finds an executive-style desk adjacent to a closed office with a massive book labeled MASTER COPY OF RECORDS. His curiosity leads him to open to the bookmark. "Oh cool; let's see how much Camp Tor made last season." He combs through the chart.

"I'm going to need to look into this business. Seven hundred million coppers!? In a few months? It would take me way too many years to do the same! He does a double take, admiring the numbers. After skimming several pages, he closes the book and puts it back to look for any notes like the one he read in the lobby but finds nothing. He decides to check out the office and general store next.

Upon leaving the refinery, he feels a tremor, like something colossal hitting the ground in the distance. The silence in the air feels chilling. Even more unsettling is that the only sound he hears is his footsteps. *Am I going deaf from the crash? No, I can hear my footsteps on the rubble. Something isn't right.* No wind, no birds. Nothing makes any sound around him.

"Ok, that's terrifying." He feels uneasy and rushes back to the station making as little noise as possible. Once he is inside the lounge, the tremors grow stronger, as though the source is moving closer. Rogue acts fast, closing the door. This produces a strange mechanical noise, which he ignores for the moment. He glances out through the window to look around camp.

The tremors continue to intensify with each passing one as whatever is causing it gets closer. He still doesn't hear anything, and the silence is deafening. After waiting a moment with nothing changing, Rogue returns to his room and through the window he sees what's causing the tremors.

The gargantuan hydra with four heads is devouring several of the animals in the field. None of them react to the hydra's presence. It is an eerie sight, with the hydra just walking up to everything and eating without effort. The hydra is larger than he imagined possible. The enormous creature is several miles away, and yet it's like watching an elephant only a couple dozen feet away. Nothing he's seen before comes anywhere close to the size of the creature before him, and the Bestiary didn't do it justice.

Its scales are a vibrant orange and black. Two massive legs bulge with muscle, and each neck is double the length of its body. The heads appear similar to a snake's head. The closest thing to come to mind is a viper's head. A thick, sail-like tail, twice as long as its necks waves around. Bony patches line its entire body, and some giant plates protrude from its shoulders.

He closes the window curtains and locks the door. This triggers the mechanism from earlier again inside the walls, and the room suddenly feels pressurized. After the adrenaline rush begins to pass, Rogue realizes the pain wipe is starting to wear off and his body is aching again. The pressure in the building, making his ears pop, is not helping either. Rogue takes a moment to lie on the bed, close his eyes, and take a nap.

While Rogue sleeps peacefully, two men search the wreckage.

One is an elderly man wearing a dark-blue suit of the finest wool, complete with silver trimming and blue-diamond cuff links, as well as a few other minor adornments. Complete with polished black dress shoes and a matching bowler hat. This is the sadistic torturer Lord Albert Richtoff.

The other is a mercenary named Hunter Smith. Lord Albert hires him when going on manhunts that require a specialist in locating government spies. Hunter is wearing beige canvas pants with brown combat boots, a pale-yellow leather jacket, and a faded red shirt. In his thirties, he's a bit taller than average, with a fit build. A long scar on his neck complements his rugged and grizzled appearance. His weapon of choice is a custom-made shotgun.

"Do you think he managed to survive that?" Hunter peers down the cliff at the remains of the cargo hold.

"Must I be the observant one? This cannot be more clear. The emergency plane is missing. The bird cage is in use but shows no damage. So much as a single tree impact would have left significant damage, thus I wager it deployed after the crash. All personal items, first aid kits, and supplies on board are missing. I am certain no one stayed here. This leaves no doubt about his survival." Albert speaks with the demeanor of a frustrated inspector as he leaves the cabin wreckage with a displeased grimace.

"So, he managed to ditch. That's a problem." Hunter returns his attention to the cabin half of the wreckage. The mauler with a collar drops the helmet where it was found. Hunter digs into his pocket, reaching for a treat to give it.

"His emergency plane can't go far under its own power. If he ditched while in the sky gap, he would have managed to get back to Heart. Which adds a serious complication to the plan," Hunter continues.

"As I stated regarding the bird cage, I do not think he ditched in mid-air." Albert is confident in his statement. "The inside is a mess, but too much is missing for anyone to gather in a turbulent free-fall situation."

"Then it's likely he ran to a nearby mining camp," Hunter deduces with a grin.

"I do not know. They are without a doubt abandoned during this time of year. I fail to imagine he will find anything more than a shelter to die of hunger in." Albert holds his hand up to his chin and gives the situation some thought.

"Then he may have gone high and glided as far as he could towards the mining hub to the west. Such a feat is doable, as he's a well-trained pilot," Hunter proclaims.

Albert does not enjoy the idea, though Hunter might be right. A spy of such caliber is indeed capable of pulling off the difficult feat. "He enjoyed a full morning's head start. I need the fool brought to me alive to answer me for what he has committed. With insatiable eagerness I await his agony and suffering." The two men walk down the hill towards a clearing. At their landing site, awaiting their return, are the helicopters they came in. They are experimental military models that have been remodeled for Albert's luxury.

"Return to Heart, and I will cover the mining hub and do what I can to locate and bring him to you," Hunter suggests to Albert, hoping he'll take it. He's not a fan of working with the psychopath, but the money Albert pays is enough to make him look the other way most of the time.

"Take a sweep of the closest mining camps as well. I do not wish to overlook the possibility. If he chose to go to the mining hub you will find evidence and witnesses. The man will pay in agony, blood, humiliation, and death." Albert is almost rambling. He doesn't want Rogue Whip to roll over and die. He wants to be the one to control the murder, in as slow, painful, and torturous a method as he can imagine.

The moment they reach the clearing, Hunter waves his hand in a circular motion. The pilot of the furthest helicopter waves back and begins flight checks. Both pilots wear light blue and silver flight suits, a signature of Albert's personal staff. As soon as Hunter approaches, he and his pilot get into the cockpit and begin to take off.

"I'll have him at the manor by the end of the day," Hunter shouts over the noise of the engine.

"I will endure the agony and await your return." Albert's response is a mixture of dismissive, bored, and angry as he waves at Hunter as he heads off.

"Empty handed?" the pilot asks Hunter after securing the cockpit.

"He ditched. We gotta search the nearby camps and the mining hub." Hunter explains.

"On our way down, I spotted an airstrip at Camp Tor, forty miles down the cliffs to the west." The pilot puts the idea out for Hunter. "When we're up high enough tell me if you can see anything on its airstrip, and we'll come back and signal Albert."

"I hope so, to make everyone's lives easier," Hunter says with a resigned smile. The shorter this trip is, the better.

Albert waits for Hunter to be well on his way before approaching his personal ride. He opens the central door on the side to reveal a guard with a weapon pointed at a woman in restraints. "What a shame. Your father continues to evade us and forces me to endure the emotion of disappointment. Does he have any idea how rude he is being by evading my capture? I would love to be rid of you both, so eager am I to be able to begin our session of quality fun." His voice is like an angry yet bored king. In a fit of rage, he enters compartment and stomps on her stomach several times.

The gag in her mouth prevents her from making any sound. All she can do is try to inhale after the impacts knocking the breath out of her.

"I forbid you to die yet, so I suppose we have to keep you alive somehow," Albert says, stepping out. Then he glances up at the guard. "I am certain the mauler's leftovers will suffice to keep her going. She only needs to survive a few more days at the most."

The guard nods as Albert closes the door and heads to the front with the pilot. The pilot secured the pet mauler into its cage at the back of the helicopter while Albert paid his victim a visit.

"Where to?" the pilot asks.

"I suppose we must return to Heart. This trip is turning out to be disappointing. I despise wasting money on mercenary services."

"On the upside, we performed a successful weapons test." Albert's pilot uses an encouraging tone and smiles.

"Ah, I did forget the test we were doing on the side during this trip. Yes, the weapon works to great effect, as planned. I suppose I have no choice but to look forward to some decent military sales from today's events." Albert's tone lightens at the topic of the weapon test.

Albert stares down at his fancy dress suit. "Oh dear, I seem to have dropped a cuff link somewhere." He mutters, sounding disgruntled. "I suppose you are right about me wearing this into the wilds."

The pilot chuckles as he searches around the cockpit for Albert's cuff link. "It'll be all smiles from here, My Lord."

"Must I blow your insignificant brains out?" Albert is furious and everything about his body language shows how frustrated he is.

"No sir; your suit has endured enough woes today. At the very least the blue diamond and pure silver will stand out brighter with less soiling. In addition, blood is difficult to get out of fine wool." his pilot says, once he finds the cuff link on the floor near Albert's seat. He hands it to him.

"Indeed." Albert puts his cuff link back on. "Alright, I am only missing what has escaped my hands for now. Take me home and keep her ready for some traveling."

"Can do, will do, My lord." The pilot fires the helicopter up, looking up to adjust some instruments above his head. After making the adjustments he spots signals coming from Hunter's helicopter. "Sir, they are signaling us."

Albert glances up to find the other helicopter is signaling with a flag to follow them. "Follow them with haste now," Albert demands, his face is turning beet red from his anger.

The pilot takes off and follows the first helicopter.

Together they move west, towards a nearby mining camp. Hunter and his pilot had used a telescope to spot Rogue's escape plane on the runway.

"Where are they taking us?" Albert inquires to himself out loud.

The helicopter Hunter is in starts to descend.

"If I have to guess, it would be the runway with the emergency lander," His pilot suggests.

"Did we not pass this place on the way in?" Albert's tone grows impatient as he examines the area.

"Aye we did. We were so focused on the flames from the crash I guess only one of us had the wherewithal to search elsewhere," the pilot replies.

"Indeed," Albert says with a smile. The top wing of the airplane is beige with a green-and-blue logo. ROGUE WHIP'S TRADEWINDS CROSSING. "I do savor a fun chase at times. Makes the soul relish and take further delight in the joys to come."

The two helicopters land near the airplane. A very thin layer of pale blue mist, covering the ground, is kicked up by the rotors and forms a haze around them.

Hunter steps out and takes a look around with some confusion. "Why in the blazes would Rogue have come here?" He checks his shotgun and primes it. Behind him Albert's helicopter also lands.

Albert steps out, kicking the pavement to shake dirt off his shoes, and stares at the mining camp with a degree of surprise. "This should not pose much challenge." Even his tone matches Hunter's confusion.

"It's odd." Hunter scratches his head. "Why an abandoned mining camp like this? I mean, he's not incompetent, so I wonder what made this better than other options in his mind."

"As commoner filth would say, don't know, don't care. Do your job, capture him and bring him here." Albert opens the side cabin to the middle of his helicopter again. "Mack, I should like for you to assist with canvasing the area. She will not be going anywhere."

The guard nods and steps out. Mack is wearing a bright-yellow shirt with black pants and carries an oversize revolver. His slick black hair matches the color and gloss of his sunglasses. He takes them off while staring out at the camp with some confusion. "I'll search for tracks."

Albert grabs the woman by the ankles and throws her to the ground. Violently, he drags her across the tarmac to the mud at the side of the runway away from the helicopters. "You stay there!" he shouts at the woman while stomping on her stomach. Next, he kicks her over and jumps on her head, burying her face in the mud. "Ah, yes, much-needed stress relief."

Hunter walks up to the platform where the station should be. Charred remains and a barely standing wooden skeleton is all they see. "These buildings are burnt to a crisp. Must've been ages ago," Hunter observes aloud.

"Yes, do be careful to make sure these ruins do not collapse upon you. You dying makes getting a refund from you difficult, should you fail me." Albert walks towards the office building. It is the only one with solid uncharred wood for half of the exterior. The ashes from the fire seem to have vanished many years ago. Albert takes care as he walks around to the missing side, to find the interior ruins are bare and hollow.

"This doesn't make sense." Mack says, looking at Hunter while he kneels over the footprints in the mud.

"No, it doesn't. Almost like a trap," Hunter acknowledges.

"What is it?" Albert demands.

"His footprints are fresh, from the airstrip to this platform. We can tell that he walked back to the plane, and over here is another trail to the platform. Beyond the platform in any other direction there's nothing in the mud. Almost like he left no tracks. This mud is thick enough to-"

"I get the point." Albert cuts him off. The frustration building inside him again. He turns, looks out over the valley, and a sense of dread passes through him. "Gents, I suggest, with the strongest possible terms, that we locate solid shelter." He struggles to keep calm but the panic in his voice alarms Hunter and Mack.

Hunter glances behind him and lays eyes on the four headed hydra in the distance. The sight surprises him so much he stumbles backwards. He waves at the pilots and motions for them to come over while holding a finger to his mouth telling them to be silent.

After the pilots walk over and catch a sight of the hydra, they exchange glances. This is now a serious problem, since there's no chance they can take off in time to escape the animal. The sound of their engines will surely attract its attention and it'll be on top of them before they get off the ground. Albert catches up to the group as quietly as he can. "What are the chances the mine entrance is open and can hold up till the monster wanders off?" Albert keeps his voice as quiet as possible.

"We have to move, now." Hunter says.

Mack starts to walk over to the woman.

"Leave the trash. This is a big enough problem. Let us not add to our troubles for the moment." Albert insists, though saying the words pains him deep in his soul.

Mack rejoins the group as they tread through the mud to try to find the mine entrance. They reach the center of the mining camp, next to a well. A wooden post with CAMP TOR at the top bears signs and arrows pointing to the nearby charred buildings. The office, station, barracks, store, church, power plant, refinery, and two mines are all listed.

"A phosphorus mine and a gemstone mine." Albert reads aloud, exchanging glances with the others. "Well, this place burned to the ground. A mine once full of flammable minerals does not sound like an ideal place to be after any fire."

A tremor shakes the ground as the hydra takes a step. "Underground at all sounds terrible," Hunter says. "Yet I agree, the Gemstone Mine is best. We have to make it half a mile that way."

The group heads off towards to the entrance. As they walk, Albert keeps watching behind them with each tremor, to make sure the hydra doesn't spot them. They manage to reach the edge of the camp before they hear the mauler shriek.

"What the blazes? Please no." Albert closes his eyes for a moment and frowns as the five of them turn to look towards the airstrip.

The mauler lowers itself, preparing a pounce on the woman. Before it does, an even louder, deeper roar erupts from the valley. Then it looks over and notices the hydra's heads staring straight at it.

"How did it break free of the cage in the helicopter?" Hunter asks with a mix of frustration and confusion.

"Doesn't matter. We need to run before we attract attention to ourselves." Mack says as its heads are facing in the camp's general direction.

They begin running towards the gemstone mines. The ground shakes with every step the hydra takes. After a couple of minutes, they find another sign pointing toward a path to a crevice between large boulders, going into the cliff face.

Albert's mauler runs off towards the forest and finds a burrow beneath a tree not too far from the airstrip.

The hydra investigates the trees for a minute and sniffs around, trying to find the snack. The four heads are enormous. A helicopter could fit into any one of the mouths. It locates the mauler hiding under a tree but isn't going to knock the tree over to get it. Also, it avoids modifying the environment to avoid scaring off prey. One of the heads notices the vehicles and scans the camp for any new activity.

The five men study it from behind the boulders as the

gargantuan creature moves without making a sound. Then it begins to walk away, a tremor vibrating the ground with each step. Albert lets out a sigh of relief, just as one of the hydra heads looks toward the airstrip, then turns around its gaze locks directly on the humans. The motion is repeated by the other three heads.

The group scrambles further into the crevice, as they continue to retreat, they find themselves in a small clearing in front of the entrance of the mine and run inside as fast as they can. After getting about fifty feet in, they check behind them and see the hydra. It already has one of its heads at the entrance, but it's too large to come after them.

Albert releases another long sigh. He feels relief and disbelief, followed by anger. "If you wander off and let us go, there is a tasty snack all tied up by our machines which you can have." Albert shouts at the hydra while it roars.

"Sir, let's not push our luck," Mack suggests as he reaches into his jacket and pulls out a pocket-sized crank light and starts winding it to turn it on. Inside, everything appears to be in fair shape. The support structures are intact, and even made with fresh, new wood. "It will be dark soon because of the daily eclipse, and I have a feeling we'll be freezing in here."

"Hey, what are your names again?" Hunter asks the pilots.

"I'm Dusty, he's Ned," the pilot for Albert's helicopter replies.

"You two will help me find firewood further down the mine shaft." Hunter commands.

Dusty is a little heavier set than the average person, standing 5'8", in his fifties, with thin brown hair. A real bodyguard type. Ned is younger, in his early thirties, thinner than average, and stands only 5'1". He keeps his curly hair dyed blonde.

Dusty and Ned both nod and follow Hunter down the shaft.

"Have you ever seen one before?" Hunter's voice shakes with fear after the encounter with the hydra.

"A hydra? No. I know for a fact only about a half dozen of them exist," Dusty answers.

"Can't say I have either," Hunter adds looking back as Albert and Mack gawk at the entrance. "Well, I can guess why hydras are the most dangerous creature in Yeraputs."

2: NO LONGER ALONE

Rogue awakens to a darkened room. He gets up and remembers that a massive hydra is outside. He opens the curtain to find that Heart's shadow has darkened Inner Shell. "Daily eclipses are neat and all, but sheesh," he exclaims, before noticing the two helicopters next to his airplane. "The hell?"

Rogue walks toward the lobby. The first thing that he notices is the lights are on. *The map did say there's a power plant, but I can't understand how this place has power with everyone gone.* He approaches the room with caution and peers inside. To his relief, the only noticeable difference is a little dust shaken off the fixtures because of the tremors earlier. With nothing else out of place, he exits the building to find out who landed, but doesn't see anyone around.

A strong breeze makes the cold air feel painful. "Oh man, this is way crazy cold." Rogue is hit by a gust of frozen air and starts shivering. He did not bring cold weather gear with him. The tarmac is lit up by the station's lights, so at least he can see everything. All of the markings on the helicopters are foreign, and there isn't anything about them that he is familiar with. Walking up to the helicopters, he puts his hand over the engine compartment. Still a little warm to the touch, which means these landed a few hours ago.

Rogue looks around, and spots a naked woman tied up in the mud. "Am I seeing things?" He is convinced he is hallucinating but runs toward her. She is covered with bruises all over her stomach and face. Her hair is thick and knotted. A tube-like gag is in her mouth, and her arms and legs are bound behind her with thin cables meant to cut if she resists too much.

The right side of her face and right arm are covered with scrape marks. She appears to have been dragged over sharp rocks not long ago. Or he realizes, along the rough edge of the tarmac. Rogue touches her to check if she is alive. She is freezing cold, but her chest is rising and falling. She is breathing and alive.

A surge of urgency rushes into him. He does not hesitate to pick her up and carry her to his room. He places her on the bed, and searches the kitchen for a knife with which to cut her bindings. After cutting off the wires, he pulls the gag out of her mouth, which causes her to vomit. Rogue holds her on her side until he's certain she's finished vomiting.

I gotta warm her up. He fires up the wood stove to generate as much warmth in the room as possible. He returns to the bedside and finds something better mounted on the wall. "Electric heating?" He says with relief and excitement.

He turns the heater on to the highest setting and finds the light switch for the room by the door.

Ignoring the bruises and scrapes, Rogue's jaw drops after he takes a better look at the woman. She has fair skin, dark red hair, and the face of an angel. He looks out at the helicopters again. *Her body is thin, really thin, whoever did this to her probably also starved her as close to death as they could. What the hell is going on here? Ok, stop and think, this woman was obviously going to be left for dead. But why isn't anyone else around?* The thoughts soon change to panic at seeing the growing blood stain on the sheets. He notices for the first time that her forearm is bleeding from having a deep laceration. Her blood is also on his shirt from carrying her inside.

"Oh, that's a problem." He acts on instinct and digs into his first aid kit, rummaging for stuff to clean, clot, and close the wound. He had forgotten that he has laceration wraps and is excited to find them. This is another advanced new medical product Rogue bought. They are long elastic wraps with a biological serum designed to rapidly heal the flesh. The serum cleans the body of common toxins and infections and stimulates cell mitosis to go into overdrive for rapid recovery.

He needs to open the wound to check for anything foreign inside that must be removed before applying the wrap. "This might hurt like hell in a second, so please forgive me," he said to her even though she is still unconscious. *Wait a minute. I better use a pain wipe.* He grabs one, leaving one in the kit, and uses the injection on the woman's other arm. Next, he returns to the bleeding wound and opens it up with his fingers. Inside he finds something black and slimy squirming around.

A common mud leech.

"Great, a slimy flesh-eating bug," Rogue observes aloud. *That's a real nasty problem. I gotta pull it out and hope it didn't start laying eggs.* He checks the first aid kit, but doesn't find anything capable of grabbing the slimy-bodied leech. So he searches the kitchen and finds some tongs. *Not the best option, but I don't have a better one. This will have to work before the damn bug starts burrowing up into her torso, which is what they do.*

He also grabs a knife, putting the blade on the wood stove to heat it up. *Hot knives are the easiest way to kill those things, so they don't flop around and bite anyone again. Learned that trick when one tried to dig into my leg as a kid.* The memory pops into his head, and he is confident he remembers what to do.

Rogue reopens her bleeding wound, sliding the tongs in. The intruder squirms around, evading him with ease using its slime coating and the slippery blood. Rather than delving deeper into her arm, it flops out of the woman's arm, landing on the bed. *Well, that was simple, and this is disgusting.*

He secures the leech with the tongs, setting it down on the nearby table. He then grabs the hot knife and starts cutting apart the deadly parasite. After slicing the bug up into a few pieces as he remembers doing from his youth, he fills a glass with water. He needs to wash out her blood, which is now mixed with leech slime, hoping he doesn't find any eggs.

He moves her so he can hold her arm over the side of the bed as he pours the water in. As he uses a slow and controlled flow, rinsing away the contaminated blood and watches tiny black beads coming out. They are leech eggs, and he makes sure to get them all. No eggs come out the second time, but the blood is making him nauseous, so he stops.

How long was she outside in that freezing mud? How long did I sleep? Did they land right after I went down for my nap? This is a surreal encounter. He double checks the wound and is relieved to find he cleared all the eggs out.

With everything clear he administers the serum and begins applying the wrap. *Please, please don't bleed out on me.* He wants to ask her so many questions. Like, why was she in the mud? Who did this to her, and are they in danger?

After he finishes up, Rogue goes into the next room and takes the new blanket and bed sheets. He changes out the bloody ones and puts her in the clean bed. He takes the old sheets and tosses them into the other room, also grabbing another sheet to mop up the blood and vomit in his room.

With the woman now resting on a clean bed, he walks out to the lobby area. He sits in the chair for about an hour staring into space. *Come on Rogue, you gotta think clearly. Stop and assess. Who did that to the woman, and why? What are they here for? I gotta go find some answers.* Then he gets up and decides to resume exploring the mining camp. When he stands, he tears his pants. "Well, of course, what else is going to happen today?" Dropping his hands to his sides and slouching as he speaks.

He returns to the room; happy he brought spare clothes, and changes into a pair of blue canvas pants, a white button-up shirt, and fresh socks. The room is sweltering hot now, so he puts out the wood stove, but keeps the electric heater on.

Back in the lobby, he discovers the chair he used is back in place under a table, but he doesn't recall moving anything. He looks around, but can't tell if anything else is different, then heads for the door to take a better look at the helicopters. As soon as he is outside, the sounds of nocturnal birds chirping and hooting fill the air. *The hydra has left the area. Fantastic, makes exploring much easier.* He starts walking across the platform.

After taking a few steps, he trips on something. To his surprise, he recognizes the collar from the mauler at the crash site earlier. Or, at least, a similar one. Nearby is a long smear of blood along the tarmac leading out to the valley. *The hydra must've caught itself a snack. And it's possible that's what happened to whoever these belonged to. I need to watch myself out here.*

He approaches the nearest helicopter, glances inside the cockpit, and pounds on the canopy in frustration. They both use unique activation plates to start up. *Damnit, no doubt the pilots would keep these on their person if they're competent.*

Rogue kicks the side of one. "Of course, these are high end models." The chances of escaping in them drops to zero. *And the hydra leaving means it had no reason to stay, which I'm sure means the plates will be hydra poop. Assuming they're not dissolved by the stomach acid first. These models have Yensi military tech, I can see those magnetic gears under the blades, damn things won't turn without being unlocked. The reality is, I won't be able to hijack them, at least at this point.*

After walking towards the far end of the platform, he decides to check out the rest of the camp, despite the freezing air. Lights outside some buildings are turned on; the station, refinery, office, general store, and a few outdoor workstations are lit brightly. Half of the barracks and maintenance shop are dark. The inconsistency strikes Rogue as odd.

There are also several fresh human footsteps in the mud. Rogue is glad he's not doing this when the hydra is in camp. Upon closer inspection, he can find five different sets. They all lead in one direction, which, looking at the signpost by the Ruby Well, heads towards the gemstone mine. *Ok, so, note to self: they are hiding in the mines. I'll no doubt have to avoid them until I can learn more details.*

The power plant being operational makes him curious, so he crosses over to a bulky wooden building with no windows. He finds a door and tries opening it, encountering resistance. The door is hard to open, but like everything else so far, is unlocked. Once Rogue gets inside, he is greeted by several giant vats covering the floor and several paths leading underground. He walks over to a nearby table and picks up several papers. The heading on them reads GEOTHERMAL STATION.

"Ah, so they managed to make geothermal power work here. Unlimited energy, courtesy of a half-destroyed planet," he said with an awe inspired tone. *This is next gen stuff here. I've heard rumors of these things, but they don't work well on Heart. The electricity these places can produce will one day make steam power completely obsolete.* He reads some gauges near a desk labeled CONTROLS watching while the readings on the gauges fluctuate within the green zone margins. Everything appears to be running as expected, within the parameters. "I have no idea what all this stuff does, but this is pretty cool."

This place is technologically on a whole different level than most of Yeraputs. Plentiful electricity is a rare luxury just about everywhere else. *Hell, with the battery powered electrics I've seen, this is becoming more of a reality with each year. Gotta say though, it's so cool to see this operation at work.*

But this is top of the line, fresh out of the invention works, expensive stuff. How can they afford this stuff? Oh, wait, that's right, they pull in an insane amount of money every season. And Rogue is well aware of the price tag for some of those luxuries as he uses them in his fleet's upgrades.

Before he resumes exploring the place, a thought crosses his mind that makes him feel guilty. *What am I doing? I patched that woman up and left her. Guess it's a good thing I'm not a doctor, heh. Hey stranger, what an impressive bloody wound you got. Here's a band aid! Then never follow up with the patient. Yeah, that would go over well. I should go back and keep an eye on her, so I can ask her things when she wakes up.*

Also, I need to wait for the eclipse to end before I do anything brash. Come on Rogue, critical thinking needed here. Remember your situational awareness. He leaves the power plant and hurries back towards the station.

Entering through the lounge, he takes a moment to examine the racks behind the bar, stocked full of wines, ales, and mead. The room uses soft lighting and fine luxury couches, and tables for billiards. The whole setup reminds Rogue of something like a fancy casino. *I think this makes sense though. The miners do need a place like this for some down time.*

Unlike the lobby, nothing in the lounge is covered in layers of dust. The air also tastes fresher to breathe. *The air quality difference is odd. Chalk that up to the weird stuff around here, I guess.*

When he enters the room, the woman is sitting up on the bed. She turns her head to face him when he enters. Her mixed expressions of shock and surprise resemble those on Rogue.

"You're awake. That's great news." He's excited to see that she's awake, but has to stop himself from bombarding her with questions, keeping in mind how he found her.

She brings her knees to her chest and holds them tight. She faces away from him and starts shivering under the blanket. This new stranger's presence terrifies her, and she seems confused about how she ended up in this room.

"No, it's ok, please relax. I promise you, you're safe here. I found you lying in the mud outside. You were tied up, frozen, and getting eaten by a mud leech. So, I brought you in here and put the bandage on your arm. I also cranked up the heat to make sure you didn't freeze to death."

Her eyes move to her arm, then back to him. She still clings to her legs, rolled in a tight ball. Rogue shuts the door. She flinches at the sound, shutting her eyes and mouth tight, expecting to be beaten, or grabbed, or used in some inhumane way. But nothing is happening to her, yet.

How is the sound of a door closing so scary? She's not shivering because she's cold. That's pure terror. I need to prove I'm not dangerous. He walks to the desk chair and sits down. "Are you alright?" In the instant he asks the question he feels silly. *I realize she isn't alright, but I gotta break the ice somehow.*

She stares at him, confusion and fear are apparent in her expression and body language is. Her eyes pierce his as she studies him.

Ok, that was a stupid question. Rogue is unsure if she did not understand him, or if she is injured in some way that renders her unable to speak. "Can you speak?"

She shakes her head no.

"Oh, I'm sorry." Rogue gets an idea and goes to the kitchen to make some tea for them. "My name is Rogue Whip."

The woman's eyes widen in disbelief, and her reaction is one of complete shock. She lets go of her knees and her jaw drops.

Rogue's back is still turned towards her as he puts the teapot on the wood stove. "I own a transportation fleet, and earlier today I crashed not too far away, and used my escape plane to come here. But I'm from Acinvar; on Heart."

The woman has vivid flashbacks from the helicopter, watching out the side window with Mack's hand on the back of her head and a gun shoved into her neck.

"Keep your eyes open now as we blow your dear, loving father out of the sky," Albert said, with great enthusiasm and a smile from ear to ear.

The second helicopter was equipped with a new weapon that fired intense blasts of air in a pinpoint direction. The weapon proved effective over the distance of a mile, and punctured most dirigible cloths in their tests. This was the first time the weapon was being used in a test run in real conditions inside the Tradewinds.

The weapon let out a small flash from the firing mechanism. All she could do was observe as the wave of air moving fast through the thin clouds, blowing them apart like a wind shear, until the blast hit the dirigible and sliced the cloth open. They all watch as the dirigible appeared unaffected except for the cargo hold snapping from the frame.

After Rogue's dirigible began descending to Shell, it started to heave from side to side and became increasingly unstable with each sway. The deflating vehicle began an inevitable barrel roll while plummeting towards the ground. A thick layer of storm clouds blocked the view of where the crash happened.

"My Lord, we must wait for the storm to pass before we can land, otherwise, we will become a crash site with him," the pilot called out to Albert.

"I agree, and I am not without all mercy. Some extra time will give this pathetic trash time to fear and mourn for her father." Albert is overjoyed. "Signal Gort and Westly to wait at the manor."

After she finishes replaying the memory in her head, she stares at Rogue with an expression of complete surprise. His back is still turned to her while he continues preparing the tea. She lets go of her knees and starts to draw in deep and heavy breaths. A knot grows inside her chest, and she is overwhelmed with a wide range of emotions. She is thankful that her father is not here, but she also fears this new man. If he learns about the mistake, how will he react?

Rogue hears her breathing hard and turns around to look at her. "Are you having trouble breathing?"

She continues staring at him with a freaked-out expression. When she realizes what he asked her, she takes a deep breath then shakes her head no.

"Are you in any physical pain?" Another ridiculous question. As soon as he finishes speaking, he remembers injecting her with a pain wipe. She is unlikely to feel much of anything. *I stink at this today. Think before speaking you idiot.*

She shakes her head no again.

"Are you scared?" is the next question out of his mouth. *Alright, now I'm asking better questions.*

She nods this time and locks eyes with him.

Rogue can feel the fear coming from her eyes. The terror is evident from before but feels so strong he can almost experience her fear himself. "The people who tied you up?"

She freezes for a moment, then she gives a single slow nod.

"I wish I could ask you who did this to you, who you are, and, well, I have so many questions for you. This is a mining camp on Shell, Camp Tor, and until we showed up, the place was abandoned," Rogue continues, but the woman starts to ignore him. "I'm going to find something to write with and write on."

She again replies by shaking her head no.

"Do you know how to write?"

Again, she shakes her head no.

"I can teach you," Rogue offers but before he can finish speaking, she raises her hand, signaling for him to stop. "Ok, umm. Well at the least would you like cream or sugar in your tea?"

After a long pause during which she stares into space, she faces him and nods.

"Would you like both?"

She nods, then again stares into space. Her demeanor changes from fear and confusion to something else.

Rogue opens the drawer labeled SPICES. The drawer is full and well stocked, and he finds plenty of sugar. There is also cream in an ice box that runs on electricity. And several other cooking provisions. No meat though. Everything in the pantry appears to be sacks of dried fruits and vegetables. There are also cans of various goods and spices, and jars with varieties of rice, beans, and pasta.

The water boils after a few minutes, and he uses tea pouches from his personal kit. One thing about his travels is he enjoys doing a delivery route for a luxury tea company. And they spoil their routine transporters with amazing tea. Now seems like an appropriate time to use some.

The woman sits on the bed watching Rogue. So many emotions are swirling in her head. She doesn't know how to make sense of everything that's happening. Then her stomach growls loud enough for him to hear.

Rogue laughs when he hears her. *That broke this dark silence. Now I'm kinda hungry myself. Let's check out what we got to fix the hunger problem.* He returns to the pantry. After rummaging through canisters, he discovers a glass and rubber-sealed breadbox, which is filled with several rolls and a section full of cheese wheels. He pulls out a roll of bread and checks for mold. When he doesn't find any, he walks over and hands the roll to her.

She glares at the bread as he offers it to her. Her eyes move from him to the food and to her bandaged arm. This is the first time in so long that anyone has treated her with kindness. Before her is the first real bite of food she can eat in longer than she is able to remember. After all that time, the whole idea of eating food is almost new to her.

The idea someone might do anything other than humiliate her for being mute, or take advantage of her attractive body upon first meeting her is new. Only for a short moment does she want to trust someone new. She looks apprehensive and remains motionless, staring at her hands with a blank expression on her face.

Rogue turns around to fetch her a glass of cool water while the tea brews. When he turns back, he realizes she hasn't taken a bite. *I can't shake the feeling she wasn't meant to survive whatever happened out there. An abuse victim, that much is obvious, but who did that to her and why? What did she go through to where taking a simple bite of bread is such a scary thing? She doesn't trust anything, and I'm willing to bet she can't trust me yet.*

He's struggling with how to handle the situation. *Is she a slave? Prisoner? Did they bring her here to torture her? None of this is making sense.* The questions keep flying through Rogue's mind, faster than he can keep track of them. He is, pure and simple, not someone who is prepared for handling something like this.

She finally takes a tiny bite of the bread, which turns out to be a little stale and crunchy, but the flavor is overwhelming to her. She stares down at the roll in awe and her hands shakes. After the momentary pause she devours the entire roll, until she starts choking from the dry bread getting caught in her throat.

Rogue hurries from the kitchen to the bedside before she

can choke. He hands her the glass, and the water does the trick, clearing her throat. *Whoa, I can't eat that fast. What the hell? She's starving.* "Take it easy, there's no need to rush, and we have plenty. Here, I'll bring you some more." As he gets up, she looks him in the eye again. All he does is smile back at her.

He gives her a few more rolls and she continues to devour them, but at a more normal and less frantic pace. She stops for a moment and takes in the sensation of having real food in her stomach. While eating the roll, she lets the blanket fall to the bed but doesn't react.

Rogue wants to say something about her exposure but decides to let her enjoy the meal in peace and returns his attention to the tea. He leaves the bedside and walks by the table, spotting the piece of paper on top and picking it up to read the message.

A NOTE TO THOSE OF YOU FREELOADERS STAYING IN THIS ROOM. WE DO ASK YOU TO CHECK THE REFINERY FOR A FULL LIST OF WHAT WE CAN PAY YOU FOR WHILE YOU ARE OTHERWISE FREELOADING OFF OUR CAMP. THE PHOSPHORUS MINE IS UNSTABLE AND MUST BE AVOIDED FOR SAFETY REASONS! BUT THE GEMSTONE MINE, IS A DIFFERENT STORY. YOU LIKE SHINY THINGS, RIGHT? WELL, ONCE YOU ARE BORED AND NOT STARVING, START WORKING.

Rogue decides that while mining for diamonds and rubies or whatever does sound like fun, this mystery woman is a bigger issue.

As he puts the paper down, he eyes the dead leech still on the table. *Ah, yeah, should get rid of the leech, I guess.* Using the tongs, he puts the sliced leech bits on the paper and opens the window to throw the leech out. Then he drops the knife and tongs onto a wash table in the kitchen.

The woman finishes the rolls and brushes the crumbs off the blanket. She watches Rogue pour their tea, inspecting everything he does with intense focus.

Rogue brings the tea over and hands her a big cup and a small tray with the cream and sugar. "This tea is from Elvador. They make the best tea on Yeraputs. My company does a few runs for them every year, and they treat me well for my services."

She doesn't care what Elvador is, but as soon as she takes a sip she sits still, stunned by the luxury. The tea is smooth, bold, and more than good. The expression on her face doesn't surprise Rogue. This is without a doubt the best cup of tea she's ever enjoyed in her life. Her reaction to the bread and tea makes Rogue wonder what she went through if regular food elicits such a reaction.

Rogue smiles as she eases up and relaxes a little. "It's incredible what a little food can do," he says under his breath. Then he takes a sip from his cup. *Oh, yes, this is what I need. I should've done this the moment I landed. This helps with the nerves.* He blocks everything else out for a brief moment.

The woman glances over, finding him sitting still with his eyes closed. He is bruised all over. This man is the Rogue Whip Albert's men shot down. He is bigger than most of Albert's bodyguards. Stronger looking too. A business owner with muscles, who is kind. He's too nice to be real in her mind. She apprehensively returns her stare down at her tea takes another sip.

As he finishes his cup, he looks over and sees her savoring every sip. The blanket is still at her waist, and she isn't covering up. "I'm going to try to find some clothes for you."

The words coming out of his mouth capture her full attention. In Albert's possession, she forgot that women wear clothes. This Rogue Whip isn't some trick Albert sent to further torture her. This guy is something different altogether. She just stares at him, nods, and returns to the bliss she is finding in the tea. Then she starts crying.

Her nightmare is over. The torture, humiliation, daily routines of hell, constant beating, the pain, suffering, and incessant abuse, is over. She is rescued, although she doesn't understand how she got in this room or this bed. Her hand trembles. She's unable to hold her tea steady, puts the cup down, before crying into the blanket. She's allowed to cry now, which is more than she had the right to do since her kidnapping. And what they did to her mother at the time. The moment was too much for her.

Rogue leaves the room and pulls out the map he found earlier. *I should check out the general store by the power plant. If they don't have anything I can always try raiding the barracks for uniforms or something. The store is near the phosphorus mine entrance by the train tracks going into the station. Ok, that's an easy ask. All I gotta do is follow the track line.*

He walks out of the station. The sky is getting darker as the eclipse grows deeper. Which also means it will be noon soon, and daylight is still a few hours away. He follows the rail until he approaches the general store. The lights inside are dim, but turned on. The plant produces a deep humming noise, and steam starts pouring from the smokestack. Rogue ignores the humming, assuming it is part of a normal automated process.

When he gets closer to the store, however, he finds the door at some point has been torn off. The damage appears to be recent. The door and wood splinters from the frame are still on the floor. *Someone was desperate to get in here.* He walks inside, locates light switches near the door, and flips every switch to turn the lights on.

The shelves are stripped of most of their products. He walks around until he comes across an aisle full of clothes. Most of them are reflective yellow and flat gray mining jumpsuits. *I guess I won't find the uniforms in the barracks. These don't look bad. At least to my eyes anyway, but what do I know about women's clothing or fashion? Also, it looks like only the food aisles got raided. Strange way to clear out inventory.*

There are some pants in denim and other durable materials around, but they all have various sizes. Rogue glances them over and is unsure about what to grab her, because she is thinner than most women. *A jumpsuit would be the best option, and she can adjust it as she needs to. If she hates it, I can always bring her here.* So, he grabs a few of them. The shoes are all similar black safety boots made from leather hide and metal plates; he grabs a pair he guesses will fit.

Getting clothes for women sure is a stressful thing. I suppose that's why they shop like crazy for them. Hell, I can't decide what to give her that won't fall off or not make any sense. Fashion still matters, right? A few aisles down he spots some respirator masks used for going into the deep portions of the mines. He decides on grabbing several of those as well. *The hydra's wake thing is some kind of air toxin, right? Maybe the filters in these can help keep us safe?*

Rogue returns to the room to find the woman is asleep on the bed. Her empty cup of tea is on the nightstand. She is curled up tightly in the sheets. He sets the pile of clothes down on the chair next to her. His body is still sore from the wreck, so he decides to lie down on the other side of the bed on top of the blanket. "What a bizarre day," he says to himself out loud and closes his eyes to try taking another nap.

Ned and Dusty leave the group to explore a shaft Dusty spotted on the map identifying a possible storage facility. Hunter has a fire going, and the electric lights have activated on their own. Lord Albert seems to like the idea of stealing gemstones to salvage the trip, at least from a financial perspective.

"The lights in here work? How interesting." Ned can't help wondering aloud.

"If I have to guess," says Dusty, "they have some sort of power plant on the outskirts of the mine. Here on Shell they use geothermal plants, so maybe one of those is still working. On a more important note, how much do you think they left here?"

"The gems? I have no clue," Ned answers. "They probably abandoned a few crates' worth, I'm sure."

The two reach a T-junction. The sign indicates going to the right SHAFT EXIT TO SURFACE, and to the left SORTING AND STORAGE CHAMBER.

"Are we seeing this right, a storage and an exit?" Dusty asks.

"Sure looks to be the case to me. Why?"

"We can fill the rides with the gems and leave before the rest of them learn we're gone. We'll be rich enough to live our lives in peace and comfort. No more dealing with that sick bastard Lord Assface." Dusty makes no effort to hide his disgust.

Ned shakes his head. "Let's assume you can sneak by them. What about the hydra?"

"We'll play this by ear, kiddo. All I know is the bastard is a high paying disgusting creature. The pay is great, the job is easy, but the rest isn't something anyone sane tolerates."

Ned nods in agreement. "Yeah, you're right, but every time anyone considers leaving, they either find a bonus or vanish."

"I remember the guy who used to pilot him vanished. Got a little too frisky with a victim, and Albert wasn't willing to share. Think he and the victim shared the same fate that day, but I don't know for certain. One day, out of the blue I got promoted from driving around his spoiled little brat to being his top pilot."

"Wasn't it Edgar who was his primary pilot before you?" Ned is sure he remembers the person but asks to pass the time.

"Yeah. Now you mention it, Edgar was his name. Poor old fool. Dude was older than Albert. Serves him his whole life. Steps out of line once and we never hear from him again."

The two men come to a large chamber. The wooden floors are similar to what they have found in all of the major chambers they have come across so far. This time the walls are made of wood too. The miners built a huge room inside this chamber.

"This must be the sort and storage facility we're looking for." Dusty rubs his hands together and grins from ear to ear.

"If any one of them followed us we'll both be dead just based on your thoughts, so have some discretion." Ned suggests.

"Hey now, I been waiting a while to escape that bastard's shadow alive." Dusty starts looking among the crates in the center of the room, finding tools inside them.

Ned finds a sliding door and pulls it open. Inside is a workshop where miners cut the gemstones. "We're getting there," Ned calls out to Dusty.

"What ya find?" Dusty comes over. "These are some professional jeweler toys."

They leave the room and walk to the next sliding door. Inside they find several crates labeled COMMERCIAL POOR.

"Let's see if anything is inside them, then go looking for the best stuff." Dusty's excitement is growing by the second.

Ned grabs a crowbar, and they open the first box. It's loaded with several raw gemstones of all colors. "Man, if it wasn't for the box saying poor on the outside, I'd be hauling ass," Ned comments before he can control himself.

"Hah, there's a bit of rebel in you after all." Dusty walks deeper into the room and soon discovers a few crates marked as CUSTOM GOOD. "I smell a potential jackpot!" He proceeds to pull one of them out and set it to the side. Before opening it, he notices a massive, locked crate built into the mine wall, almost like a safe. "And this must be the shiny golden ticket. Hey, help me out and find something to cut a lock over here!"

"Would a key work?" Ned picks up a ring of keys from next to the door. He throws the keys to Dusty.

Dusty misses the catch and picks the keys off the floor. "I'd say too easy if that's the case; but eh, let's try them." He tries the first key, which does not go in all the way. He follows up with the second key, which goes in perfectly and turns. The lock comes undone. "I'm feeling so giddy, I tell ya."

Ned keeps checking over his shoulder as Dusty opens the container and pulls out two wooden trunks labeled the FINEST BATCHES. "Safe to say these are the ones we're after."

"Here, I'll take one, you take the other; these things weigh hundreds of pounds. They're heavy."

"Two hundred pounds of the finest quality gems! How many millions of coppers? Okay, fine, your point stands. Let's abandon the group and leave them here to rot and die," Ned says. "Can't believe I'm a sellout."

"This ain't no sellout. This is a lottery on steroids," Dusty corrects Ned with a grin.

Ned grabs one of the trunks. Lifting it is a real challenge. "Jeez."

"Here, this one is a fair bit lighter." Dusty puts his down and grabs the crate Ned is unable to lift.

Ned lifts the other one. It is lighter, but still heavy to him. At least he can lift this one and walk with it. "This is crazy, I'm going to need to take some breaks."

"We'll cut through the forest around to the airstrip." Dusty sounds confident.

The two of them head towards the exit shaft. About an hour passes before they reach the helicopters and load the crates into the one Ned was flying.

"Hey, when we fire this thing up, how will we stop them from coming after us? The engine takes a lot of time to warm up. The others will come over here and start shooting at us before we're airborne. And this place is freezing out here." Ned states the obvious but he needs the details of a realistic escape plan.

"I was thinking about something on the way over," Dusty says. "We're going to bury them with a cave in. We found a small box of dynamite when we were looking for firewood. So, we'll go back in, make some small talk to throw them off, do another round, and grab the dynamite. Light the fuse at the entrance when they aren't suspecting anything, and run like hell, get our asses skyward. If we time everything right, we can turn the engines on when the explosion goes off. Maximize the time we need before the hydra comes back and attacks us."

"Wasn't there an airplane over there earlier?" Ned is thrown off by the missing plane because the sound of it taking off should have been a hydra magnet. But they haven't felt any tremors for some time.

"Yeah, why?" Dusty speaks before looking in the direction of the plane. To his surprise Rogue's plane is, in fact, gone. "That Rogue Whip fella must've figured Albert is chasing him and run away. And we're leaving Albert here. I guess it's the cherry on top to know we will smite Albert by taking his last victim out of his reach." They head towards the well and follow the trail back to the mine entrance. They spot Mack walking toward them, and he's alone. Both of them hide behind some bushes and watch as Mack walks over to the airstrip. Once there, he appears to be panicking. Then he runs further down the platform to the station ruins, and picks something up off the ground. The mauler's collar. He looks out over the valley and kicks at the ground.

"What's his deal?" Ned gives Dusty a sideways glance.

"No idea. It's like he's freaking out. Something is off." Dusty considers that the missing plane is news Mack won't be eager to give Albert, given how he will react to Rogue Whip's escaping.

Mack heads back toward the mine, scratching his head,

checking over his shoulder every few steps. Both pilots follow along from a distance.

Mack stops at the entrance, dreading what he is about to say. "It sure didn't stick around long." Mack says toward Albert.

"So, the hydra did wander off then?" Albert throws a piece of wood into the fire he and Hunter built.

"Yeah, ate your pets on the way out." Mack answers with a shaky voice as he hands the mauler's collar to Albert. "Found this on the platform by the airstrip and a trail of blood to go with. Girl is gone too. There's a hole in the mud where you left her."

"What are you not telling me?" Albert picks up on Mack's lack of enthusiasm and the fearful expression on his face.

"The helicopters and airplane are all gone."

"What?!" Hunter shouts, sounding alarmed. "We would've heard the helicopters taking off."

"Do not you dare speak those words to me. Especially if you find this to be a sick joke!" Albert explodes with a sudden burst of anger. He shifted instantly from mellow and bored to extreme and passionate rage.

"No jokes, My Lord. Come see for yourself." Mack hopes Albert can maintain control over himself to think through the situation.

The look in Mack's eye tells Albert he indeed is not joking. "Ned and Dusty have betrayed us then."

Ned and Dusty walk in. "This mine has several entrances." Ned calls out.

Albert is confused, if the helicopters are gone, how is Ned and Dusty still here?

Hunter shakes his head in disbelief. "Was gonna ask how the hell you two slipped out."

"What did you two do to those helicopters? Answer me now or perish!" Albert screams at the top of his lungs.

The pilots pick up on his tone.

"Not a damn thing! They're on the tarmac where we left them!" Dusty shoots back.

"Liars! They are gone!" Mack yells.

Dusty and Ned glance at each other. "We secured the ignition plates. That's not possible you know!" Ned shouts back at them.

Dusty whispers to Ned so the others don't hear them. "Didn't we just load one up with treasure before Mack came out?"

"Bullshit! I was at the bloody airstrip! You two did something to them!" Mack shouts.

"Yes, we did. The hell is he going on about? He was right next to them." Ned answers Dusty while Mack is busy shouting. The three others are clearly distressed, with Albert looking red enough to light the entire mine.

"ENOUGH!" Albert bellows, loud enough for his voice to echo through the mine several times. After a moment passes, he calms down and tries to regain his composure. "Ned, Dusty, I demand you escort us all to the vehicles. I will execute the liar on the tarmac."

"So much for the plan." Dusty gives his response to Ned in a hushed voice.

"I need to look for myself. Mack, if I do not find your humor appropriate, you will take the place of Rogue Whip, do you understand?" Albert scrambles to his feet and approaches the entrance to the mine.

"I don't know what those damn pilots did, but I'm not lying. You two better be ready to fill that shoe." Mack is fuming mad himself now.

The two pilots turn around, sliding through the crevice again, and walk over toward the airstrip. The others coming behind them. When they get within sight of the helicopters, the pilots shake their heads. "They're right there on the airstrip where we left them. The airplane is gone though." Ned confirms.

After a moment of silence Ned and Dusty turn around to find the rest of the group isn't around them anymore. "Well, that's strange." Dusty looks in all directions.

"They were right behind us, right?" Ned keeps his voice quiet so only Dusty can hear him.

"Wait a sec, aren't the buildings supposed to be burned to the frames?" Dusty feels as though he might be going crazy. A few of buildings look unaffected by the fire and are lit up with electric lights.

"I mean, there was a hydra terrifying the crap out of us. It's possible we didn't pay attention." Ned heads over to the helicopters, then he stops and feels the left side of his jacket. "Hey Dusty, you got your plate?"

Dusty laughs. "Are you serious? Are you that dumb?" He reaches into his jacket's left pocket and finds it empty. "What the?"

Ned nods. "I don't think we dropped them, but we're not going anywhere if we don't find those."

"Oh, we'll be going somewhere. Six feet under; courtesy of Albert and gang." Dusty can't speak without stuttering between the cold air and the fear of Albert's wrath as he heads in the direction of the mine.

"Fair point." Ned says as he follows.

They reach the rock crevice near the mine but there is no sign of the others. "Are they having a laugh at our expense?" Dusty says as he faces Ned in panic and disbelief.

"I don't think so." Ned's tone is more skeptical. "They can't possibly have found out about our plan. Did they?"

"Where did those incompetent fools disappear off to so damn fast?" Albert is searching in all directions, but they get to the airstrip only to find an empty tarmac.

"I'd wager wherever they hid the helicopters," Mack motions with his hand, indicating the empty airstrip, with the plane and the helicopters gone. "Told you!"

"I do not believe this! They lied, the both of them. No, the three of them. Rogue Whip must be responsible for this!" Albert grows more frantic by the second.

Hunter looks out at the airstrip and sees the airplane still there but keeps quiet. He listens to Mack and Albert both saying their helicopters and Rogue's plane are missing. The pilots saw both helicopters but no plane, while he is staring at only the plane.

Albert and Mack give Hunter bewildered looks.

"What in the dear sweet world are you so calm and quiet about? Have we gone mad?" Albert rants like a lunatic.

"Are we seeing different things?" Mack can't help but note how Hunter isn't freaking out.

"I believe so, Mack." Hunter steps on the tarmac where he knew a helicopter was once parked.

"Well, enlighten me to your version of this infernal hallucination." Albert insists, in a somewhat calmer tone.

"Honestly, I see Rogue's plane, but not our helicopters," Hunter reveals. "And I don't think we are all going mad."

Albert gazes out at the valley as he ponders. In an instant his demeanor changes as though he is enlightened by a revelation. "Wait, yes, of course. Hydras emit a hallucinogen used to deceive and confuse their prey, do they not?"

Hunter nods. "Yeah, I believe I read that in a book somewhere."

Mack forces out a laugh. "Oh great. That's just *perfect!*" The sense of dread is too much, so he stops laughing, but he comes up with an idea. "So, wait. What if they're still here? We should be able to physically bump into them."

"Worth a shot. I'll guide you to the plane." Hunter is surprised he didn't think of the idea himself. He guides Mack and Albert to the plane. Hunter stops in front of the plane and grabs the wing. It feels real enough. "Here's the wing."

Mack tries to grab near the spot Hunter indicates, but there's nothing there.

Hunter witnesses Mack's hand go through the wing. "Ok, I'm the one hallucinating." He smacks it hard. His hand hurts as though he hit the real thing too hard, making a clanging noise.

"I heard the bang. You hit the plane. I do not see it, but I did hear that," Albert says, his tone now analytical and curious.

"That's messed up." Mack's tone matches his alarmed expression. Hunter punches the wing a second time and, while Albert and Mack do not see the plane, they hear the banging sounds.

"So, Hunter is not hallucinating. The plane is somehow corporeal and there for him. There is more at work here than we assume." Albert says, thinking aloud.

"If that's the case, we're now facing a situation where we have too many possibilities. Rogue Whip could still be here, and I think he is." Hunter brings up the idea for the sake of keeping Albert's explosive emotions and whims in check.

"Never you mind such trivial problems. This whole experience is ruined and has soured my taste for destroying them. The bastard is a spy, and he stole information that shut down my operations in an entire ocean. So be it. May they all die as if the likes of time does not acknowledge their presence. The hydra delivers me a minor justice eating Rogue Whip's daughter. Though I now wish I took my personal revenge by destroying her myself. Nothing puts a damper on a long-awaited torture session more than getting caught in paranormal nuisances." Albert looks up at heart and shakes his head.

Mack and Hunter exchange glances. Albert never gives up hunting people like this.

"Fair enough then. How do we leave?" Mack takes a moment to glance over the darkened valley.

"I should like to do so in some form other than walking. We need to find the pilots and find the corporeal version of where the helicopters exist, and leave." Albert understands accomplishing this will not be a simple task.

"Ya know, I never spent any actual time on Shell," Ned says, as the two pilots walk through the crevice.

"I like the outer side of Shell. They got some gorgeous beaches there," Dusty replies.

They reach the entrance of the mine. "I don't think we should enter through there." Ned says.

"Got a funny feeling or something?" Dusty asked.

"Something's not right," Ned answers. "I can't put my finger on what. And I'm not just talking about the three murderous assholes playing hide-and-seek, that's getting beneath my skin."

Dusty peeks down the mine shaft. There is an unnatural darkness inside. "How about we stay out of the mines and find a different way out of here?" he suggests.

"I like your plan, Dusty."

They back away, returning to the crevice between the rocks leading back to the forest. As they get to the halfway point, they feel colder air pouring down on them and look up. They don't see anything above them aside from the Heart Eclipse; dots of lights from airships moving like stars, and open sky.

"That was weird, like a bucket of ice got poured on us," Dusty says breaking the momentary silence.

"I guess this is why these lucrative mine camps are abandoned most of the year," Ned suggests.

"If we escape this with our lives then I'm taking ya to the best beach I can think of. And we'll take a vacation for as long as we need," Dusty says, trying not to think about the current situation. The two men move forward.

"Sounds perfect. Heart is gorgeous from this view. You got the city lights dotting the horizon, the Tradewinds traffic looking like slow shooting stars. Also, there's this gorgeous eclipse halo," Ned says, taking the sight in.

"It's a beautiful view; I'll give it that." Dusty agrees.

A deep sounding hoo-hah comes from the forest causing Ned and Dusty to stop. "Isn't that one of them scary giant hawks?" Ned whispers to Dusty.

"Step with care, let's not draw attention to ourselves. I'd like to not die to some hungry creature that thinks we're prey." Dusty keeps his voice as low and quiet as he can. He forgets the name of the forest they are in, but he's familiar with the fact that it's home to more than its fair share of creatures capable of feasting on humans.

After a slow walk, they approach one of the solid buildings and rush inside.

"That's a bit of decent luck for a change, right?" Ned asks.

"I'll take a rickety shack at this point, but at least this is a step in the right direction." Dusty is relieved not to be hiding in a mine with something that causes tremors every time it walks.

They glance around. The building has an open floor, with no indoor walls, and is filled with rows of beds. In the center are a few tables in a common area with couches. "Gotta be staff quarters for the miners." Ned states aloud. "Reminds me of my army days."

Dusty walks over to some beds and comes up on a piece of paper with something written on it. "Hey Ned, found a note for us." Dusty holds it up.

"What?" Ned comes over out of curiosity. Dusty hands him the note which reads:

NOTHING'S REAL AND EVERYTHING'S REAL. THIS DAMN PHENOMENON IS CALLED THE HYDRA'S WAKE. IF YOU FIND YOURSELF HALLUCINATING HEAD TO THE POOL AT THE BOTTOM OF THE CRYSTAL CAVE. THE WATER HAS SOMETHING IN IT THAT WILL CLEAR THE TOXINS FROM YOUR BREATHING FOR A SHORT TIME.

"I don't recall anything about a crystal cave anywhere," Dusty points out, when Ned looks up.

"I wonder if some modern medicine can do the same thing."

"Sounds reasonable. A pain wipe is a neural inhibitor. Might do something. Course, there's always breathing the clean air from scuba diving tanks. We have both on the helicopters."

"We should wait until daylight comes, then make a run for the med kits."

"I agree. In the meantime, grab a seat and let's wait this thing out."

"A seat? What, you suck at billiards or something?" Ned points at a billiards table in the common area.

"Oh, I didn't see the table before. Well in that case you're gonna get your ass beat, boy." Dusty heads over to the table.

"The view of him is a disturbing sight, floating in the middle of the air." Albert comments on Hunter sitting in the plane, though he and Mack only see him in mid-air, like he is hovering.

"Yeah, man, climb down and let's figure out where the pilots went," Mack pleads. "So, what is happening to us again?"

"I think it's part of the hallucinations caused by the hydra toxin." Hunter has done some studies on apex predators and is familiar with the hydra's wake. "I've read stories where people become really disoriented and out of sorts. Hydras are rare. Who would think we would ever see one alive?"

"Must be why they can eat everything in sight. Explains how they grow so massive," Mack deduces.

"I wish I knew how long these hallucinations will persist, and these paranormal effects will last. This toxin, hydra's wake, there should be some way to cure or rid our bodies of it." Albert suggests.

"Back up a bit, I think it's time you mention more on this Rogue Whip character. Now that we're stuck in a crazy dream together, I gotta ask. The hell are we hunting him down for exactly?" Hunter asks.

Albert turns to face the two of them as they stare at him. "Fine, if only to pass the time, I suppose."

A deep hoo-hah comes from the forest off to the side in the distance. All three men are quick to look in the direction of the noise.

"It can wait. We need to find cover," Mack says.

"Damn, why this particular forest of all the places on Inner Shell?" Albert scans the sky above him to locate the deadly bird of prey, but with the eclipse he can't see well.

"Weapons at the ready, gents," Hunter says as he hops off the plane and shoulders the shotgun he carries with him.

Mack grabs the revolver from his holster. "True, that's something we can take down."

Albert darts his eyes around, looking for anything that will work as a shelter. There are no decent options nearby. "I insist we go back to the mine."

"Agreed. Let's move," says Mack.

"I got point, you got rear." Hunter orders, while taking the lead.

Rogue wakes up to sunlight pouring in through the window. He feels like he has been sleeping in an odd position only to wake up on the ground, again. He sits up and looks at the bed. The woman is glaring at him with an angry expression.

"I'm sorry, did I do something bad?" He is still waking up, but her body language alarms him and works better than coffee.

She doesn't move a muscle and only continues to glare with intense anger.

Rogue stretches to loosen up and sees the pile of jumpers he brought thrown across the room. "Oh, did none of them fit?" he asks her. *I mean, at least she won't be naked anymore.*

She gives a silent sigh. Her facial expression makes clear the jumpsuit fashion is not the problem. In fact, she is wearing one.

"Is it because I was laying on the bed?" Rogue asks trying to figure out what is making her so angry.

Before he knows what hit him, the woman gets to her knees and delivers a strong haymaker punch right into his crotch. The last thing she remembers is falling asleep, and then she wakes up still naked right next to him. She is angry and still feels vulnerable.

Rogue lets out a long, high-pitched scream as he falls back to the floor. After a few moments, regaining his bearings, he tries to sit up. *Damn, this chick has some incredible muscle power. That hurt worse than the crash.* "You could have just woken me up and pointed at the chair or something," he says trying to ignore the throbbing pain.

She crosses her arms and gives him a glare that is universally understood with two sarcastic words. Oh Really?

"I'm sorry if I did anything wrong," Rogue says.

She remains motionless. Her body had moved before she could think by throwing that punch. It was the first time she had landed a good hit on anyone in. While she is now sure he didn't deserve it, she also wants to defend herself and retains an unapologetic expression.

"Did I try anything bad? Aside from lying in bed next to you?"

She shakes her head no.

Rogue gets up. "Ok, please forgive me. I will do right by you next time. I'm sorry." He pretends the punch doesn't hurt as much as it does. *Damn, that still hurts. Girl got me good.* He limps over to the chair and sits down. Once the pain subsides, he faces her and shakes his head. "You're right, I should've given you more space. I can't imagine what you've endured. So hey, while you rest, I'm going to explore Camp Tor while we have direct daylight."

She nods and tries to stand. But she is unable to. After a few tries she gets up and stumbles. Rogue manages to catch her before she hits the floor. He lifts her up and puts her back on the bed. She's upset that she can't walk yet.

Rogue goes to the kitchen, fills a pitcher with water and brings it to the nightstand by the bed, with a cup. "You were lying in the cold mud for several hours by the time I found you. You were hypothermic and had a mud leech eating into your arm. I used a pain wipe, and a laceration wrap after getting the leech out of your arm. You need to rest a while longer. I'll be back in a bit. And I promise you'll be safe here. I'll lock the door."

She reluctantly nods. Her body language makes it clear how

frustrated she is with her situation.

He grabs one of the masks as he leaves the room, locking up behind him as promised.

After he walks out, she pokes her arm on the bandage, which stings. Pain wipes make people feel nothing, so he could've done anything to her, and she wouldn't be aware. The consideration makes her mad, but the stinging pain in her arm gives her pause. She touches the bruises on her stomach, legs, and arms. Each time, she feels some pain, and numbness. She admits to herself that he is right. She needs more rest.

Before Rogue leaves the station, he puts the mask on. He spots a thin layer of mist hovering above the ground by a few inches. *That's an interesting mist. If you didn't look straight down close enough, it would go overlooked.* Bending over to examine the mist hurts. Standing up straight, he leans up against the wall. "Dear gods, it still hurts. Way too painful."

After he takes some slow steps, the throbbing pain begins to subside. "Damn, I guess this must be what they mean by fiery redheads." He walks over to the sign by the Ruby Well and contemplates what to check out next. "Camp Tor. The station is a luxury stay complete with damsels in distress to be a hero for. I do not recommend the local wildlife, though." Rogue is trying to unwind. He glances over at the office building and heads towards it.

Let's try to find some answers about this hydra first. That's the biggest threat in the whole area. The office front door is the first door he finds locked. So he starts to circle the building, finding an unlocked door at the back. Inside the room is dark, with black metal covering the walls. The word SECURITY is written in bright yellow letters above the inner doorway.

Ok, this is a good start, I think. Not a very secure security office, but whatever. I'm only stranded here after crash landing, not exactly an expected guest. A door to the right with a complex lock bears the word ARMORY. *Now that will help if the people that woman was with show up.* Another door ahead leads towards the front of the office.

As he heads for the door, a billboard catches his eye, right behind the security desk. There is a picture of the hydra on it and a warning. "Well, well, what do we have here?" He reads the paper.
THE HYDRA'S DORMANT PERIOD IS FOUR MONTHS. WHEN AWAKE IT RESIDES IN THE FOREST USING TOR VALLEY AS A GAME TRAIL. AT THE TIME OF THIS WRITING THE HYDRA HAS FOUR HEADS AND EMITS A NASTY TOXIN CALLED HYDRA'S WAKE. IF YOU SEE THIS CREATURE, RUN TO AN ENCLOSED SPACE.

ALL KNOWN ANTI HALLUCINOGENS ARE INEFFECTIVE. THE EFFECTS OF THE HYDRA'S WAKE ARE PERMANENT. FILTERS ON MASKS WILL PROVIDE PROTECTION FOR A FEW DAYS, BUT WE RECOMMEND NOT EXCEEDING A SINGLE MASK'S USE BEYOND A FULL DAY. BE WARNED THEY WILL GET CLOGGED IF THE TOXIC MIST IS TOO THICK.

Rogue gulps. "So do not breathe in the presence of a nearby giant scary monster." He glances at a file on the desk.

UNKNOWN METAL IN PHOSPHOROUS MINE

This catches Rogue's attention. He sits down and opens the file to read more. Skipping past parts about who filled out the paperwork, and the time and date he turns to the short paragraph on the details page.

MINERS IN FACE EIGHTEEN HAVE RUN INTO WHAT IS BEST DESCRIBED AS AN UNUSUAL METAL WALL. THE METAL BEARS A PHYSICAL RESEMBLANCE TO ALUMINUM, ALTHOUGH IT IS FAR DENSER AND IMPERVIOUS TO OUR WEAPONS AND TOOLS. WE CANNOT EXTRACT A SIZABLE SAMPLE, OR SCRATCH OR DENT THE THING FOR THAT MATTER. BECAUSE OF THE LACK OF KNOWLEDGE, WE ARE CLOSING THE PHOSPHOROUS MINE UNTIL NEXT SEASON FOR EXPERT ANALYSIS.

I'll have to visit this thing for myself. This sounds interesting. He closes the file and resumes walking to the front of the office. This door is also locked. "Odd. They allow me to come in here, and see what I assume is classified stuff, and the possibility of opening the weapons room. Yet the oh-so-important paperwork is all locked up. That or some dumb ass forgot to lock the security door on the way out."

He exits the building, wondering where to go next. While heading toward the refinery hoping to find more information there, he sees three men walking over to the well from the direction of the gemstone mines. One is dressed for an executive ball, in a dress suit sporting silver adornments and blue-diamond jewelry. The other two are dressed like typical thugs or mercenaries. One is carrying a customized shotgun, and the other is armed with a ReelGun revolver. *Oh great, mercenaries from Heart. This keeps getting better and better.*

3: THE ANCIENT HYDRA

Rogue sidesteps to move out of their way. To his surprise, they walk by him. They don't notice his presence. Then before he can control himself, he calls out. "Hey, excuse me!" The group doesn't respond as he tries to gain their attention by shouting at them. He notices that the one without a weapon in the expensive suit is clutching his arm. *Um, what the hell? Did they not see or hear me? How strange?*

"Can we at least talk about what happened in the mines?" Mack insists.

"We were ambushed by tons of dead people. What is there to discuss?" Hunter shoots back in an angry tone. His face is dark red, and his veins are popping out of his arms and neck.

Rogue overhears them and decides to catch up and walk next to them. "Hey, guys." They still don't react to him. *Ok, they are either amazing at ignoring people, or they can't tell I'm here.*

"Those things were not dead, you fool, they were moving," Albert chimes in, but his voice sounds weak. "The dead do not move."

"Our bullets went through them. We burned through a ton of ammo. We wasted every shot. They had to be hallucinations." Mack's suggestion is unconvincing.

Albert stops to turn around. "Does this look like a hallucination to you!?" He screams at the top of his lungs and waves the arm he is clutching at them, revealing a serious wound. The flesh is shredded as if from a severe bite by an animal.

Rogue makes a mental note that the mangled bite looks infected. *That's some massive discoloring.* "What the hell?" Rogue looks in the direction of the mine they came out of.

"We came here with five of us, seven if you include the pet and the dead weight. We're dealing with some wacky-ass stuff. We need to calm down." Mack retorts.

"No! If I am to die like this, I want to put an end to that Lotus Island bastard Rogue Whip. That ignorant, disrespectful, foolish military spy will pay for his treachery! A year of tracking him down. I will make him pay oh so dearly if I ever catch him." Albert points his finger at Mack and Hunter.

Rogue walks right up to Albert's face and takes a serious look at him. "I've never met you. And I am sure as hell not a spy." His blood boils, and he is overwhelmed with anger and hatred. "And you are the one who tortured the poor woman!"

"So that's what this is all about? The fiasco from the Lotus Islands last year? The woman from your chopper, she's Rogue's daughter from the botched revenge mission, isn't she?" Hunter shouts.

"You really didn't recognize her? Worse yet, you're only figuring this out now?" Mack gives Hunter a sideways glance.

"Can you forget them and focus on the real important stuff such as, oh, I don't know, say, the hydra? Those zombies? The fact that we don't have a ride home?" Hunter shouts.

"Important? Nothing is more important than ensuring Rogue Whip dies here!" Albert retorts.

Rogue can no longer hold himself back after hearing this. "Not if I kill you first!" He grabs Albert by the throat and tries to choke him to death, but his efforts are doing nothing. He squeezes as hard as he can but fails to press into Albert's neck.

Albert feels a vice grip around his neck and tries to grab at whatever is wrapped around it. "What is this?" he demands.

Mack and Hunter stand by, watching Albert grasp at the empty air at his throat.

"What are you doing? If you're faking this I swear to the gods..." Hunter had hoped leaving the mine would end the paranormal experiences.

"Is something strangling him?" Mack suggests as the two exchange glances and began searching around. "No offense mate, but with shit this weird, we ain't helping."

I've never killed anyone before but you're evil and you don't have any idea I'm here. Guess I can pull off a perfect murder. Rogue tries squeezing with every ounce of his strength.

"I can't move!" Albert calls out.

Rogue is getting frustrated. For a dirigible pilot he keeps himself in excellent shape. Crushing this guy's neck should be simple. *What the hell is going on here? I can't crush him, and his neck isn't squeezing.*

Albert's eyes widen, and he gazes straight into Rogue's hateful stare. He catches a quick glimmer of Rogue. "Ghost!"

"What?" Mack and Hunter speak in unison.

"I am unsure. The apparition lasted only for a brief second." Albert begins to breathe harder, and then, when he realizes he isn't choking and manages to calm down.

"Is it Rogue Whip?" Hunter asked.

"No, I am afraid not. He is a mountain of muscle and far too young. Spirit, please release me." Albert calls out in a pleading tone.

"You think the guy we shot down is behind this?" Mack challenges Hunter.

"Well, you got me. At this point I'm rolling with the whole everything is possible gig." Hunter makes a strong point.

"Wait, those weren't wind shears? You shot me down!?" Rogue stops strangling him. Now full of rage on his own behalf, he draws back his arm, clenches his fist and launches as hard a haymaker as he can into Albert's face, knocking Albert back off his feet and to the ground.

"What the hell!?" Mack and Hunter both back up a few feet.

"Albert! Lord Albert!" Hunter is cautious while approaching him. "Dammit. He's knocked out cold."

"By what?" Mack spins around, looking in all directions, finding they are alone for now. "And why isn't it screwing with us?"

"Shut up and don't give the ghost any bright ideas. If he or she hates Lord Albert Richtoff, so be it." Hunter isn't worried about Albert dying at all.

"Alright, but we need to find a way to deal with the laceration or he'll bleed out." Mack rushes over to Albert's side. "I'll make a fire so we can brand the wound closed."

An idea pops into Rogue's head, and he walks over to Albert, and tries to stomp on his wounded arm, but to no avail. He ends up stomping through the arm and hitting the ground. "Well, you lucky turd," Rogue says. *Strange, my foot went through him, his arm is directly through my leg. What the hell is going on? Wait a minute, this silence again.* An eerie silence catches his attention; it feels the same as before, when the hydra first appeared. Not chancing being out in the open, Rogue runs for the station.

"Hey, Mack, stop and listen, will you?" Hunter is getting an uneasy feeling.

"What?"

"The silence. Like nature just stopped." Hunter glances up and around.

Mack stops to listen. Indeed, nature is silent. "The damn thing is back."

Rogue returns to the room and peers cautiously out of the

windows, making sure they are secure and closed tight.

The woman gives him a surprised expression, like he is crazy.

"A hydra is coming. A massive one with a huge problem." Rogue states, waiting for the first tremor to come.

Given the woman's expression, she doesn't know what he's talking about.

"Mega monster with powerful bad magic powers and likes to eat people," Rogue says, and no sooner than when he finishes speaking they feel a small tremor.

"Well, hey now, a building, staff barracks," Hunter points out. The two of them pick up the unconscious Albert and run for the building.

The tremors continue, getting stronger each time.

Albert starts to come to as they enter the barracks. "Did anyone remember to flip off the conductor of the train?"

"Sorry My Lord, the blasted hydra is coming back. We're out of time." Hunter said.

Albert groans as the blood loss starts to take its toll.

"Hold still. I hope this thing works." Mack returns with a first aid kit he found near the door next to a fire kit. "Found a can of clotting foam. While this isn't as effective as the new laceration tape stuff, I've used these on myself a time or two, and they do the job."

Hunter holds Albert down and pins his arm. "Hey, buddy, this is going to hurt like being on the receiving end of one of your play sessions."

"Did you just call me buddy?" Albert sputters.

"Ready?" Hunter secures Albert's arm tightly in his grip.

"For what? Unhand me, you brutes!" Albert tries to force Hunter off him, but to no avail. Mack opens the wound and pours the foam in. Albert scream in pain at the top of his lungs. After a few seconds the pain intensifies, and Albert gets louder.

They squint under the impact of the earsplitting screaming coming from Albert. "Why don't you tell the damned thing where we are?" Hunter thinks hiding in here isn't the best plan. They're sitting ducks, just waiting for the hydra to smash the building down and munch on them.

Albert passes out again. "Thank all of the gods he's out." Mack says, looking up to find the hydra's heads are outside the window. It scans the room, then moves to the next one. Mack ducks down.

"Stay still; don't move. It's looking for us through the windows." He whispers.

"Ned, the hydra is back, searching one of the burned down frames for something." Dusty said while looking outside.

Ned comes over. Sure enough it's acting as if an actual building is there. "I wonder if that's a solid building and if it's possible someone is inside."

"Would explain its attention," Dusty agrees.

"I find it bizarre how an animal is making us lose our minds," Ned comments.

"I find it disgusting; you're merely referring to the monster from hell as an ordinary animal." Dusty gives him an agitated glance.

"Well, I can't say I'm enjoying its effects, but hydras are just oversize animals."

"You're kidding me. Ned, check out what's on the ground near the well." Dusty discovers the two bronze plates not far from the Well.

"The hell?" Ned says when he spots them. "That's absurd No way they fell out of our jackets."

"With how this day is turning out, I'm glad they're not in the mine. I can use the bushes between here and them as cover, and grab them. Then we can leave when this thing walks off again." Dusty searches for a way outside without opening the front door.

"Why not just wait for the hydra to leave?"

"And risk a chance of the plates getting stomped on and broken?"

"I'll be honest, I've no faith in this idea of yours. But do what you want."

"Oh, thanks for the vote of confidence, pal." Dusty spots an open window, and moves towards it. He checks over his shoulder, finding that Ned hasn't moved from the spot. "Would be nice if you could help out, but fine." He sighs with disappointment, shakes his head and opens the window a little further up. It moves silently, to Dusty's relief.

He slips through, crouches, and races to the nearest hedge bush being sure to not make any sound.

Ned is watching him reach front hedges unnoticed. "Dammit, he'll need a backup plan." He works up some courage, then, he moves to the opposite end of the building. If he needs to distract the monster, pounding on a window might work. He reaches the corner and glances outside. Dusty is halfway to the well, moving with a surprising demonstration of stealth. The hydra begins releasing something like a thick blue steam off its body. "Oh no, more of this crap."

Soon the entire area is coated in a thin, pale-blue mist which settles on the ground and becomes almost invisible. Dusty is feeling lightheaded by the time he reaches the well. When he kneels over to grab the plate, his hand goes right through it. He can't believe it. The plate is right in front of his face, but he can't pick it up.

After several frantic attempts, his hand is stabbed. Dusty uses every ounce of his strength and willpower not to make a sound. Then he lifts the throbbing hand up to discover that a huge scorpion stung him. He grabs the scorpion with his other hand, yanking the stinger out and throwing it away. He is overcome with fear that he might draw the hydra's attention.

To his relief, no audible sound comes when the scorpion lands. The silence of nature becomes deafening, and he can hear his heartbeat. He sits against the well, hiding out of sight. As he inspects his hand, his stomach growls loud enough for everyone to hear. He can feel his insides move as his body made more uncontrollable gurgling noises that echo around the camp.

One of the eyes on the head closest to Dusty glances over towards the well. These humans are an elusive lot, and it decides to act as if the human by the well is invisible. But the eye focuses on the well making sure not to move its head from where Albert's group is hiding. The corners of the lips on the head lift a little, imitating a contented smile.

Rogue is watching the whole thing from the window in the lounge area of the station wearing a better air mask that he found in an emergency fire kit. *The way this building reacts to the mist means the tremors activate a mechanism sealing the building. Should be safe, but still, this stuff is scary.*

Luckily, the pilot he's watching does reveal to him where the helicopter plates are. "Thank you for showing me the way out of here." The guy by the well grabs his stomach, reacting to something, and Rogue sees the hydra bat an eye in the man's direction, without moving the head or giving any other sign of reacting, but somehow it knows he's there. *Hang on, a smile? No way, the damned hydra is smiling on purpose, that guy's dead.*

Dusty peeks over to check if the hydra is aware of him. To his relief, it remains focused on the empty space within the charred wooden framework. He tries to grab the other plate by crawling over and putting his hand out, hoping to feel metal in his fingers. This time he succeeds in picking it up. He holds the ignition plate close to him and returns to hiding behind the well.

Ned sees Dusty grab their ticket home and jumps for joy. "Hot damn, this is working. Dude has balls."

Rogue pays close attention to the narrowing eyes following Dusty when he goes for the muddy plate. *Shit, he got one. And I think the moment he leaves his hiding place; he'll be done for. This hydra is a master of patience; he doesn't move, and is an expert at playing possum. How smart is this animal?*

Dusty starts returning to Ned, using the same path he took to reach the well. He gets to halfway between the well and the next bush when a growl breaks the silence. All four heads are turning his way, focusing on Dusty with a menacing grin on each face.

"Oh no!" Ned starts pounding on the wall. None of the heads move in response. "Hey! Over here, four face!" His cries are ignored.

"I'm right. Played the patience game until he got too far into the open to escape." Rogue mutters to himself. *And those facial expressions during the attack. Readable emotions. This isn't any ordinary animal. This one's smart enough to play games.*

Dusty lifts the plate and throws it as hard as he can as the first head starts to lunge at him. After throwing the ignition plate towards the barracks, he dives into the mud. The first head passes above him and misses, but the second one grabs him by the back of the leg.

Lifting him up, and just as fast, opens its mouth at a better angle for swallowing the human. After the jaws snap shut, the bronze plate crashes through a window of the barracks where Ned is.

Ned keeps pounding on the window in shock. "No! Dusty!"

The hydra inspects the building with one head, seeing Ned still pounding frantically on the window. It's satisfied at seeing the human acting senselessly and decides to walk away.

"I swear that was an attack just now. Someone became a snack." Mack peers out a window next to the door of their building.

"Better not be one of our pilots." Hunter is still trying to stabilize Albert.

The only remnants of Dusty are a trail of blood and a severed hand with a timepiece still on the wrist.

"I can't tell, but when the coast is clear I'll go take a look. I can see a giant pool of fresh blood. Damn thing swallowed them up and squeezed them dry in the process," Mack says as the shaking from the retreating hydra weakens.

Rogue goes to the lobby to find where the hydra has wandered off to. Somehow the beast has vanished. So, instead, he keeps track of how hard the thuds are, gauging how far away the sneaky hydra is going, he suspects it will stay close. While focusing on the tremors stop instead of fading, proving that the hydra is staying somewhere nearby.

"It's going to make a game of finishing us off," he thinks out loud. "Like a bored person, that Hydra finds this is a way to entertain itself." The implications of the level of intelligence demonstrated terrifies Rogue. They're dealing with something very different from any other animal. This one understands the concept of sport.

But while the Hydra is out of camp playing hide-and-seek, Rogue decides to retrieve the second helicopter plate. *This monster is staying too close for me to be able to just start up a helicopter and take off. Maybe at some point I'll get the time.* But for now, the first step in the plan is to recover the ignition plate and match which of the helicopters the plate goes to.

Ok, so the bad guys survived their encounter when they first landed. Either they got lucky, or this hydra enjoys every moment of the chase. We aren't much of a snack, but we warrant attention. Albert and his lackeys are in the barracks closest to the Refinery. And another is still in the other barracks, the guy pounding on the windows was trying to be a distraction. Earlier they said they had five people, so now there are four left. That's important to know. Everything indicates these are dangerous people.

He figures they are pinned down just as he is, but they are scattered. If he isn't careful, they will kill him. They did worse to the woman. But as dangerous as the group of men is, this intelligent hydra by far is the biggest threat. *This is odd, why are they split up like that. In any case, I haven't revealed myself to anyone dangerous. I also don't know if the hydra realizes I am here or not but I need to make sure I avoid getting caught.*

As Rogue continues to assess the situation, another fact comes to mind. *The woman survived when the hydra first visited camp. Maybe she was ignored on purpose for some bizarre reason. Or because she was covered in mud, she was camouflaged and managed to stay unseen. Gotta take this slow. This thing is meticulous and can hide from sight. Hard to believe an animal that size can vanish. Although, soon hiding won't be an issue. Actual nighttime is coming soon enough.*

Rogue leaves the station and runs over to the well finding a scorpion nest near the second plate. "That's pleasant." He grabs the plate and inspects the notches and holes looking for damage. It appears fine to him, so he heads over to the airstrip to figure out which of the two helicopters this plate works on.

Ned sits in the corner of the building staring into space, tears running down his face. Dusty was his brother-in-law. What is he going to tell his sister? He closes his eyes and pounds on the floor. "Dammit you asshole."

"I'm going to go check how much fuel is in the airplane. Keep an eye on him." Hunter says as he walks towards the door, unable to sit still.

"I don't think that's a good idea. The hydra hasn't left the area, it only walked far enough to be out of sight. The tremors stopped but didn't fade out. And besides, none of us want to breathe in any more of the hydra's wake crap." Mack looks up to see Hunter grab the shotgun.

"We've gotten ourselves pinned down several times now. We hid from a giant carnivorous bird and got attacked by what I can only describe as zombies in the mine. I will be checking the fuel level of the plane, and I'm leaving your asses here." Hunter is quick to aim his shotgun at Mack.

"Fine, I ain't stopping ya. Do me a favor and drop the shotgun when you die, please. Don't let it go with ya into the stomach of anything." Mack decides to let Hunter leave. If Mack dies, no one will be on Albert's side in this mess. He has no intention of betraying his boss.

Hunter walks out the door, and finds that the well has vanished. He checks behind him, and the building he just left is the same charred frame as the rest of them. "Bullshit!" Out of frustration he rushes over to the airstrip, only to discover that the airplane is gone. He stops and takes a breath. "Of course, this would happen the instant I start to lose my head!"

Rogue leaves the cockpit of the helicopter matching the plate he grabbed. When he turns around, one of the mercenaries is standing nearby on the tarmac. "Oh great." *This guy is pissed off. Why hasn't he shot at me yet?*

"Well, I'm not going back into the blasted gemstone mine." Hunter says, spitting on the ground. He storms off towards the gap in the cliffs, following the rail line out of camp.

Rogue realizes he's still invisible to the mercenary, so he decides to follow him. He catches up and walks with him. "So, has the asswipe keeled over yet?" He asks Hunter, knowing Hunter can't interact with him.

"Real funny," Hunter complains to himself.

Rogue stops for a second in surprise. Did the man hear him?

"Hydra's wake legend and bullshit. Ok, so we're gonna waste my near infinite wealth on getting petty revenge. All because he got careless and tried to screw with the wrong nation. Of course, spies will be part of their retaliation. So, he tries to get petty revenge using his daughter as a lure. I ought to put a few slugs in that bastard's sick skull," Hunter mumbles on.

Hold up, is the woman Albert's daughter? No wait, Albert said earlier the woman is Rogue Whip the spy's daughter. This is some messed up stuff going on around here. Rogue thought and keeps up when he realizes Hunter is rambling on with useful information. "So, what are you guys?" He hopes an answer to his question will come next.

"Come to think of it, if he didn't pay as well as he does, I'd have done him in a while ago. And collected any number of the bounties on his head." Hunter stops after following the rail track for a moment. He glances over and stares at the giant opening to the phosphorus mine. "Ah hell, aside from the smell, the shafts are massive and less spooky looking. How bad can this mine be?"

Rogue stares down the enormous mine entrance. The train tracks lead to a rail car loading platform not far down the shaft. Three sets of rail tracks leave the entrance and joins the primary line leading to a switch track going towards the Refinery. "Oh right, Face Eighteen." Rogue says aloud, meaning to only think it in his head.

Hunter gets a chill down his neck. He could swear he heard someone say something. "Face Eighteen?"

Rogue gives Hunter a concerned glance. Somehow the man hears him now, but he merely shoulders the shotgun like a soldier and moves forward. Rogue lets a little distance grow between them. *Too close. I shouldn't speak out loud again.*

Hunter reaches the platform inside, finding a map of the entire mine used for assigning miners to faces. Face Eighteen is scribbled with marks and partially scratched out.

Rogue finds breathing in the mask difficult, as if its clogged, and takes it off. Glancing at the filter, finds it full of wake toxin residue. The wind seems to have cleared the wake from Camp, so he tosses the mask aside and follows Hunter to the platform. Rogue studies the map. *Face Eighteen isn't far from here if I'm reading this map correctly.* "So, go down three levels and walk to the second shaft to the right." He speaks out loud again without thinking.

Hunter overhears Rogue talking and spins around to find Rogue standing not far behind him. "What the hell?"

Rogue gawks at Hunter only to realize by the expression on his face, that Rogue's cover from the hydra's wake is over. "Hello." *Ah, crap. Busted.*

"Who are you? Tell me or I'll blow you to pieces!" Hunter points his shotgun straight at Rogue.

Rogue is quick on his feet and decides to use the delusions in a risky gambit. *These guys have been hallucinating all day long, seeing who knows what. Let's try an old scout skit that might work here.* "Who would you like me to be? But please, be aware I'm only a figment of your imagination."

Hunter lowers his weapon. "So, these damned hallucinations can talk now?" Given everything they witnessed happen in the other mine, Hunter considers it could be possible.

Did not expect that would be so easy. Alright let's see how far I can push this. Rogue spreads his arms and shrugs. "Would seem to be the case."

"The last time we hallucinated other people they tried to kill us." Hunter puts his hand back on his weapon.

"Different mine, different experience." Rogue is quick to reply with a calm tone.

"Right." Hunter starts to turn around. "On second thought, can you stay in front of me? If you would be so kind."

If doing so keeps you from shooting me, that's simple enough. Rogue moves to stand next to the map. "So, this Face Eighteen. What will you find?"

"Would you happen to know why they scribbled the location over?" Hunter asked.

"Oh, you would love to learn why. If you were a betting man, you might say something it is important. Including a potential security-related secret." Rogue said turning to check the map. "The legend down in the corner uses indicators for things like cave-ins; nothing, however, explains the scribbling. Therefore, the scribbling is related to a different matter altogether."

"Stop talking like Albert," Hunter shouts.

"Relax, he will get what's coming to him. I mean, let's be honest here, you have a hydra running loose and every time Albert is visible, it wants a juicy piece of him." Saying this might be the make or break moment of the plan. *I suspect this guy isn't on the same page as the evil bastard. He's coming off as a total traitor, so I can use this juicy detail to my advantage.*

"Hey, now you're on to something." Hunter said.

"Well, we should discover what this secret is, and talk about how you're gonna string him up like a snack for our hydra buddy and let him die." Rogue walks over to the elevators.

"No, I won't put any real effort into destroying him. That's too much like what he would do to someone else. I'd rather have the pleasure of killing him myself. With a bullet through the head." Hunter's tone is full of aggravation. He's hoping Albert perishes.

"Quick and simple. Effective too, but does he deserve a quiet end?" Rogue is thankful he's finding a way to keep the charade going while getting more information.

Hunter takes another glance at the map. "The exact opposite of how he murders others. Simple, unoriginal, boring, and rather uneventful. I'd wager his soul would be tortured to learn how dull his end will be." Hunter savors the idea.

"You're right. Makes a lot of sense now." Rogue does his best to play along.

"So, you're a figment of my imagination, eh?" Hunter sounds exhausted.

"Yep. Everything happening here is going to stay between you and you." Rogue tries not to smile much. *This is an incredible plan. So glad I came up with this.*

"Funny." Hunter shakes his head and contemplates why he's enduring this hallucination, of all things. "So, do we share memories or something?"

"I'm afraid I can't recall anything aside from showing up behind you a mere moment ago," Rogue replies.

"Alright; I'd prefer you didn't spout anything from my past." Hunter is relieved the hallucination won't be guilt tripping him. He glances towards the entrance of the mine, making sure he's not being followed.

"You coming or what?" Rogue regrets speaking so soon, fearing he has blown his cover. *I can't believe I just did that.*

"Yeah, yeah, I'm making sure Mack doesn't try anything stupid. The loyal lackey has a revolver modified for long range. I didn't leave him on nice terms and need to keep my eyes open over my back." Hunter follows and, when they get to the elevators, opens the one that goes to the third level down. Both of them step on. "Do you have a name?" Hunter wants to test this apparition, as he pulls on the brake lever and pushes on the rope control lever.

"I don't think so. Why not give me one?" Rogue notices the shotgun is missing its safety mechanism and tries not to react.

"Figgy works for me. This better not be some sort of trap." Hunter adjusts the levers a little.

Figgy? Really? Well, I'll play along. "I hope not, because I'm here to make a discovery. I don't have time for setting traps in my short life."

"Your short life. Interesting way to put it." Hunter starts chuckling. Rogue tries his best to match the chuckle, but soon goes silent. "But you're right. Or I guess I'm right. I'm right? Right?"

"You're always right." Rogue nods along. *Ok, this is crazy; I'm starting to feel a bit unhinged.*

Hunter spots the sign to start braking and does so. "Ah crap, which way from here? I didn't study the map."

"Yes, you did; you go straight and take the second right, past those barricades ahead. You said so yourself. Well, projected through me. First thing out of my mouth. I remember that, but because you made me."

"How long am I stuck with you?" Hunter feels as if he's dealing with an annoying sibling.

Rogue raises his eyebrows up. "Somewhere you've read the hydra's wake legend. And now you are living this legend. Unlike a bad dream, though, you can't wake up from this."

"You know what? Forget I asked. Bloody hydra." Hunter opens the elevator. Rogue steps off first and makes sure to keep some distance between them as he leads the way. These shafts are impressive and well-maintained. And they installed electric lighting going throughout the mine.

"The Chamber of Secrets awaits at Face Eighteen." Rogue motions in the direction of the shaft on the right. An unguarded security checkpoint is easy for them to walk through.

"Figgy, you're annoying me, so shut up." Hunter retorts. "Good lord; I guess I can be an annoying pain in the neck."

"You're the voice of reason in the group. You should speak up more often." Rogue's creativity is working so far.

Hunter nods. "What did I tell you? Ah damn, you're spot on though. Yeah, I gotta admit, all too often when they go out on the deep end, while I end up being the guy who pulls em out."

They walk down the shaft heading towards Face Eighteen. After a while they arrived in a massive chamber.

"You weren't kidding when you said chamber." Hunter is surprised by how much has been excavated to create the chamber. While the room isn't big, the area around the mysterious wall is cleared out.

"You surprise yourself sometimes with what you guess." Rogue reflects the surprised tone Hunter uses. "And here you are, the mystery revealed." Several electric lights are operating and shining on the bizarre metal.

"The hell is this?" Hunter wonders.

Rogue places his hand on the metal. "Solid metal. I've never felt anything so strange to the touch."

Hunter pokes the metal. It's the smoothest surface he's ever touched, perfectly flat. But also, warm, and like being close to a ball of static electricity. The hair on their heads and arms stand up.

"Try shooting it." Rogue steps to the side and examines the wall further.

"Yeah, I thought about that. But, at the same time, I don't think I should."

"Ricochet and kill yourself because that's how your luck is today?"

"Ah hell, you actually are a piece of my damned imagination."

Rogue finds a tiny groove. He puts his hand on the groove, and feels a flap of metal, almost like a handle. He pulls on the flap, and the entire wall shakes a little. The flap forms an indentation. They hear hissing air as what appears to be a doorway opens next to him.

"What the hell?" Hunter aims his shotgun at the sudden movement. Inside the doorway a light shines brightly, making the chamber almost as bright as daylight. "No way am I going inside." Hunter shakes his head while backing up.

Rogue shoots a glance at him. "I guess this is where I leave you. It's been fun." He enters, taking the opportunity to escape from Hunter. *I was running out of ideas to keep that charade going. Glad he's a coward.* The door slides closed and transforms into a wall behind him.

Hunter turns around, looking down the eerie mine shaft. The unsettling silence following Rogue's departure unnerves him. "Figgy? Hey, man, this isn't funny." he calls out. After a few more moments he runs back towards the elevator. "I need to get outta here."

Rogue sits down. "Damn, I actually pulled that off. I need a moment before moving on." He may have trapped himself in here but for now he's happy not to be killed by the mercenary. After taking a while to catch his breath, he takes in his new surroundings. The floor and ceiling are emitting a bright, pale-orange light. The walls are smooth, reflective, and shiny.

He walks along the endless corridor for about an hour until he comes upon a transparent wall. The barrier's material resembles glass but it isn't. As he gets closer, the barrier lifts to clear the way. *What the hell did I walk into? Curiosity may kill the cat this time.*

Now he's nervous and sweaty. The air is too warm. Something feels dark in here. Not evil, but a deeper, darker sensation, as if nothing but pure emptiness is ahead. But he continues walking down the hallway. *The way out is sealed off behind me. It's not like I can exactly turn back now.*

A wall of bright-green light beams form and begin running the length of the corridor towards Rogue. Before he can react, the light passes through him and continues until reaching the transparent door behind him. Then the beams vanish, reappear, and move in reverse, passing through him a second time. Rogue freezes for a moment, not understanding what has just happened. The walls form blue moving arrows, telling him to keep moving forward. "Ok, this is terrifying. Guess I'm expected now." He keeps walking forward, moving at a slow and cautious pace.

After a while, when nothing happens, he picks up the pace a little. If only because now he's becoming a little claustrophobic because of the lack of visual variation in the corridor as he continues forward. After walking several miles, he finally arrives at the end, finding a more obvious door on the left. When he approaches it, the door slides into the ceiling with a hiss of air, like the one when he first opened the wall.

The room he enters is unlike anything he's ever seen before. The walls before him are made of transparent material, like the door halfway along the passage he came from. And it is very high, overlooking an underground valley. In the center a massive light on the ceiling resembles a fake sun.

The walls and ceiling of the massive area are constructed of the same metallic material as the outside wall. He looks down at the valley itself, stretching on for miles, as far as the eye can see. And the room is tall, at least a mile high. The largest cities in Yeraputs could fit many times over in here and still leave room to spare.

"Someone built this place?" He's in awe at the sheer size of the building. "What is this place?"

"Someone. Person. Built. Constructed. This. Identifier. Place. Location. What. Inquiry initiator. Is. Terminology. This. Analysis. Place. In progress?" His own voice echoes around him, but it is not an echo.

"Hello?" The sudden speech breaking the silence causes Rogue to jump. *What the hell?*

"Hello?" Again, his voice projects back to him. He can't tell where the voice is coming from.

Rogue glances behind him to find the door to the corridor is shut. "Who is there?"

"Human." The pitch and tone sound mechanical.

"Human?" He examines the room, looking for the source but can't find anything.

"You?" This time the word matches his exact voice.

"Yes, I am human." *Hold up, am I affected? These are delusions, right?*

"No need to worry about hydra toxins. You are safe here." The new tone changes to sound more mechanical and refined.

Rogue steps back as a pole rises from the platform he's standing on.

"Place your hand on top." The tone is demanding.

"You can't ask politely?" Rogue says as he follows the directions given to him.

"Forgive me. Your language is new to me. I did my best to learn from the scans I took of your mind when you arrived." The pitch changes many times during the sentence.

Rogue is sweating and feels much more unsettled. "Well, you're doing great for your first time." He finds that staying calm is difficult. The pole under his hand warms up and gets hot before becoming cold again.

"I can guarantee you are unaffected. I am unable to detect any signs of the hydra's toxins in your biological systems." This time it sounds like a whole new person, with no pitch or tonal problems.

How does this machine know that? Did the pole just take a sample of my blood or something? He didn't feel anything poke into him. But before he can speak again, he sees something is moving around the field below him, another hydra. This one is smaller and only has one head. "So, where am I?"

"A containment center."

"For what? Hydras?" Rogue has shivers going down his spine as he spots many more in the valley. The one on the surface is causing enough problems, and this place has hundreds, maybe thousands of them.

"Yes."

This container spells doom for humanity. After a moment of silence and watching the hydra, Rogue says, "Can you elaborate further please?"

"I am pleased to do so. This facility's purpose and design is to contain specimens of multiple hydra species. These hydras, as you identify them, are weapons, bio engineered for wars once waged on planet Norgut."

"Norgut? Isn't that the planet that predates the twin worlds?" The word is familiar, but he hasn't used it since back in his schooldays.

"I appreciate your educated intellect, though your original pronunciation is off."

He forces a chuckle. Whatever is talking to him is developing a sense of sarcasm. "These days we call this planet Shell." *Ok, so I found a box full of death monsters. Doesn't mean I should panic, right? Stay calm, find out where this conversation goes. Maybe learn a few things I can use to escape.*

"Indeed. Please allow me to provide a simplified explanation. When the former dominant race of Norgut ventured to other worlds, they sealed their weapons in containers like this one. Their purpose is to prevent the incoming collision from opening these facilities. The intention was to give life from the new world a chance to survive. Humans at the time were an isolated and advanced civilization on the stray planet Yeraputs when the worlds collided. The collision appears to set your species backwards, in terms of technological advancement, although your race has survived. Due to the unique cosmic nature of the impact, life indeed survived as predicted. This is delightful news."

That's a ton of information to spit out all at once. "Where did the inhabitants of Norgut go?"

"Unknown to us."

"Okay, so what are you, if you don't mind me asking?"

"I'm sorry, you do not possess terminology for what I am. The closest in your language is a mechanical being with the ability to imitate sentience."

"So, you are artificial and intelligent."

"That is a more elegant way to explain my being. I am more or less an artificial intelligent machine. Clever human. Your presence, and what information I can gather from you, force me to ask a question. Are these creatures on the surface?"

So, this place can read my mind in here, but has no idea what goes on outside. "Yes, but only a few of them. They are rare, and not many people who witness them are able to talk about the encounter."

"If I display them can you identify the one currently loose in the area? I am unable to learn such information directly from your thoughts."

"Sure. Does having four heads matter at all? Or is the whole cut-one-off-two-will-grow thing accurate?"

"Irrelevant to species, accurate as described, and unfortunate. The more heads they grow, the more powerful the creatures become."

Rogue's surprise grows as several species of hydra-like creatures are now displayed on the transparent wall in front of him. "There are this many types?" He can't believe his eyes.

"Nineteen species of this weapon are successful creations. Touch the one most closely resembling those on the surface, please."

Rogue searches for the orange-and-black blotches pattern. When he spots the one from outside, he placed a hand over the image.

"Are you certain?"

"Positive. The skin pattern is unmistakable." He checks the others again to be sure and none of them feature the color orange. "This one emits a blue mist, or I'm guessing that's what I found earlier, what we call a hydra's wake, which, you already figured out, I guess. The toxin does all sorts of unusual things to us humans."

"This is most troubling."

"So, you said these containers are for hydras and you mentioned weapons. Are the hydras themselves weapons?"

"Indeed they are."

This is unreal. The implications of everything here is crazy. "And I assume from your reaction the hydra outside is an advanced version of these weapons?" *The concept is terrifying to him.*

"Well, yes, in fact among the more advanced. Its intelligence rivals that of the former dominant species and it has many other abilities. Only a small number were able to survive their creation. They are so dangerous their makers sealed them in a container all to themselves. Your news brings to a close the peculiar mystery about the Gaean Center losing contact during the planetary impact. I assumed, and am proven incorrect in this assumption, the containment center was ejected into empty space."

He listens carefully to every word the AI says. "So, when the planets collided, the container they were in became compromised and broke open."

"A least likely scenario which the evidence provided by you supports to be true."

"Can you help us kill them off?" He figures this is worth a shot since they're the most dangerous of them all.

"I do not have the power to do so."

Ok, he doesn't, but the way he worded the response gives me an idea. "Does such power still exist on the planet?"

"Yes, such weapons do exist. Although, I caution you before asking to seek out those weapons."

Rogue stops for a moment, and gives thought to the warning. "I think I understand. If we unlock whatever power is capable of destroying these hydras, one can assume the weapons may become a worse problem than the hydras."

"I appreciate your understanding."

This is insane. This whole place is unbelievable. This is real, right? "If I got in here, what will stop other people from approaching?" As he speaks, he realizes he doesn't have a way out, but will deal with leaving later.

"I will scan them for their intentions and only allow those I deem worthy of learning certain knowledge inside. I selected you based on the fact you have no interest in anything other than to satisfy a curiosity. One who wishes only to learn will always be welcome."

Oh yeah, I did come down here from the start with nothing more than curiosity. Before learning that this secret can wipe out humanity. His eyes follow one of the Hydras below him wandering around. "What's to stop me from talking about this place when I am outside?"

"The Gaean Hydra with four heads on the surface is an overwhelming obstacle. Afterward, nothing. This knowledge is yours to do with as you determine. I will not hinder you."

"So, you're not concerned if this container or the others are going to be discovered." *Talk about the greatest archaeological find in the whole history of Yeraputs.*

"Our discovery is inevitable; this is an acceptable truth. At least now we understand your most current language to communicate with, should such an occasion happen in the future."

Rogue returns his focus to the transparent wall, where the image becomes enlarged. "Gaean hydra. How can they be killed?"

"Your intentions are confrontational now?"

"My intentions are to either overcome the monster or escape its territory. I intend to survive." *Being trapped here for the rest of my life isn't what I have planned. This AI thing knows a lot, and can read my mind somehow. Whatever. I just need the knowledge to leave. Hydra dead or alive doesn't matter.*

"An appropriate response. My records indicate multiple vulnerabilities, including asphyxiation, very specific diseases, and prolonged exposure to intense fire. Excessive physical impacts damaging the primary body if severe enough to break through the thick armor is another option. Between the two legs is the best approach for this."

"So the easiest way would be to lure it into a forest and burn the whole area out. Or crush it with a massive landslide." *Both of those things are impossible to control. A fluke of nature is required.*

"A forest will fail to burn at the required temperatures. Special weaponry is required. The main body possesses a bony armor under its primary layer of skin designed to nullify moderate impacts. Any projectile required to penetrate hydra skin must be moving at tremendous speeds. My scans of your current understanding of modern warfare in technological terms shows your species possesses inadequate weaponry, for either kinetic impact or energy production."

"Explains why I can't think of ever hearing about anyone managing to kill one." Rogue's head is starting to ache. His situation is looking hopeless, but somehow they need to figure out how to deal with the hydra. *Hold on, we don't necessarily gotta kill it to escape the valley alive, right?*

An idea pops into his mind. "Hey, wait, what if we lured the one outside in here somehow? Can we find a way to do that? I understand how incredibly intelligent they are, but at the same time they can become bored. And from what I've seen today, the one around here is having fun with a game of hunting us down. With your help we can set up decoys leading into the container here. And I'm sure you would love to have a specimen of their species to study and observe."

The response comes after several minutes of silence. "I find the idea delightful and appealing. Under the limits set by my creators, I should not allow this to happen. But by your logic concerning the secret of this container, who is to stop me?"

Rogue is excited. "You are awesome!" *About time I heard some good news.*

"Except for the fact this container possesses an unbreakable seal, with no accessible entrance through which any specimen can leave or enter. You will need to use the transportation method used to bring the current specimens here. The transportation method is to alter the creature's physical state so that it may be dismantled, transferred on a particle level, and reassembled."

Say what now? His expression becomes blank. "How do you dismantle a hydra?"

"Your technology is insufficient for this. I do not have knowledge of if such technology still available in the surrounding area. And to move a creature of such size requires a device capable of encompassing the creature to begin with. I am afraid you will not be able to carry one out of here."

"So, I'm back to square one." Rogue sounds defeated. *This is just grand. Dandy all the way.*

"You are beyond your first step as you attained knowledge."

"Fine, I'm at square two." *I'm talking to a machine alright. Super literal jerk.*

"The gaean hydras are roughly two hundred thousand of your years old. They have learned much in their time."

Oh sure, make this sound more impossible, why not. Rogue begins pacing the room. "Shame they can't develop age related illnesses." *Come on, give me something I can use to help leave the valley!*

"I cannot anticipate when such ailments will occur. Your distress is understandable."

He stops pacing and stares out into the underground valley.

"I do have something I want to give you. In theory, I can provide immunity from the hydra's wake to assist you."

"You can do what now?" He can't believe his ears. "An immunity from hydra's wake? That's a perfect solution."

"Obviously, this is untested in humans. Yet I do believe your DNA is capable of successful alteration to create such an effect."

"How does this immunity work?"

"Genetic modification of course, in the simplest terms. The process will require an oral ingestion."

"So, I gotta eat or drink something?" He scans the room for anything new.

"Which would you prefer?"

"Drink, please. No chewing, and being able to chug it down fast sounds more doable." *Hope I don't have to walk to the other end of this place to receive this.*

After a few minutes of silence, a section of the wall behind him opens up. A panel moves out of a dark space containing a vial which is smaller than he expects. "This should do."

Whoa, incredible. That's easy! This makes escaping doable. Oh, wait, the woman, I need to help her out too. "Can you make another one for another person please?"

"Is this human near the container?"

Rogue thinks of the woman in the room at the station. Then he remembers Albert's gang. He needs to return to her, so she does not end up back in their hands, if they somehow manage to find her. Or if she tries leaving and runs into the hydra.

But before he can speak a new panel comes out with another vial. "This second one will be appropriate for the woman you show concern for. Please do not mix them. Doing so will result in permanent adverse and irreversible side effects."

Rogue does not hesitate in swallowing the first one. The liquid is bland and flavorless aside from a bitter metallic aftertaste. "That should make keeping them straight simple."

"Indeed. Please take hold of the additional vial. I will arrange for your relocation. Please know you are welcome to revisit at any time. I enjoyed your company Rogue Whip, and I wish you the best of luck."

Rogue grabs the second vial, and suddenly becomes drowsy and unable to move. Soon he blacks out.

Albert wakes up next to Mack, who has been watching over him. "Ugh, that bastard."

"I fixed your arm," Mack interrupts him.

Albert lifts his arm and inspects the bandages. "So, he did. No matter, I still wish to tear his guts out and hang him with them for the severe pain he inflicted upon me."

"You show no mercy, eh?" Mack is glad Albert is awake again. "And forgive me, but I said I fixed you up. Hunter left to steal the plane, though he hasn't run away yet. The pressure and unusual circumstance have him turning against us."

"Never show mercy to anyone for any reason. Otherwise, you lose your spot at the top of the food chain." Albert groans as he speaks. He sits up and looks around. "Did the foul beast leave yet?"

"No, the hydra is still lurking nearby. The monster is smart, visiting every few hours to inspect the camp for changes, as if waiting for us to come out and be easy prey. This hydra shows incredible intelligence. Seems careful to not step on the rail tracks or touch the buildings. I'm not entirely sure why it does that though."

"For the time being, I could care less. Have we found the pilots?" Albert asked.

"Dusty got himself eaten. Found his hand and timepiece." Mack holds up Dusty's wristwatch and gives it to Albert.

"Unfortunate. He was a decent man. The smoothest flying pilot I could afford." Compliments coming from Albert, about anyone, are rare. "And what of Ned?"

"Haven't seen him since we got separated."

"Where has the blasted mercenary gone off to then?"

"He's been hiding in one of the ruins near the phosphorus mine. Hydra chased him inside on its latest patrol."

"Also unfortunate for me. Have we located Rogue Whip?"

"No, and if he's still here then it's a safe bet to say his daughter may still be alive too. It leaves massive pools of blood where it eats victims. I remember there wasn't one where you left her this morning."

"I tire of the hydra's wake and the level of incompetence displayed by my men, save for you." Albert brushes dust off his suit. "We need to find them and dispose of them in a manner befitting their inhumane crimes."

Mack rolls his eyes. The reasonable Albert has vanished, and the cruel Albert is back to his old self. "You know what, given the way things are going for us, our priority should be escaping this cursed valley. I'll walk if need be. We'll have to follow the rail line to the hub." Mack tries to make Albert focus on their survival.

"Are you mad? Much as I agree with you on the major point,

such a journey will take weeks. You lack the ammunition for us to hunt and the equipment to survive, let alone travel any significant distance in this forest." Albert argues. "To this point I accept this as a challenge we have no answer for yet. In the meantime, I would like to do something within my grasp. Torturing a group of meat bags to the delight of our local monster sounds like fun. I shall set up a rotisserie, skewer them alive and cook them for the beast."

"While your plan does sound like loads of fun, I'd like to focus on the survival bit. So, if you'll be so kind, leave such ideas in your head for you to relish. Helps keep my head clear, so I can warn you of appropriate danger, which is beneficial to us both. You won't be able to cook anyone if you're dead." Mack says. If for no other reason than to shut the old geezer up since he is going off the rails again.

Albert, for a moment, wears a hurt expression on his face but decides to let his guard do what guards do. "What time is it if you have an idea?"

"Dusty's timepiece broke during the attack, I guess sometime in the middle of the night or early morning now." Mack gives his best educated guess.

"I say, I do not recognize what that is." Albert is looking out the window, changing the topic.

A four-legged bird-like creature is sniffing the ground. Only the outline is visible near the edge of the forest bordering the camp. As the creature comes closer to camp, Albert can see that the head resembles something like a cat.

"Wow, an archon. I'm guessing the pools of blood from your pet and Dusty attracted its attention," Mack answers. "Those are very rare."

"The reputation of this forest is to make the rare a rather common sight." Albert takes a moment to admire the creature.

"True, Deep Forest is famous for that. Rare predators of all sorts call this place home. Hence, the reason it's so far from any actual civilization."

The two men study the archon's movements. Soon the creature walks over to where Dusty was eaten. The fresh blood has indeed attracted the curious creature into camp. It's covered in thick brown feathers, its head is a golden yellow, and it has a long thin tail.

"Watching this creature pressures me to ask how nature evolved such an animal." Albert finds the thought helps him keep his mind off the excruciating pain in his arm.

"Truly, natural evolution created an interesting design." Mack agrees.

The two continue watching from the window when they hear another hoo-hah.

"Well, the other threat is back." Albert said.

"Must have a nest nearby," Mack adds.

"That is not good for us." Albert shifts his focus from the animal and inspects the bandages around his arm.

"Or it." Mack grins while the animal turns around with its head held high and began unfolding its wings. The look in its eye resembles that of a cat on the hunt.

Albert keeps watching as the archon prepares to take off. "Beautiful, even in darkness." The flapping from the wings is silent as the mighty predator takes flight. Once out of sight, a huge bellowing roar comes from the far distance. "What in the world? Another monster?" The roar repeats a second time. It is not from a hydra.

"I do not know." Mack says. "Those horrific sounds are coming from somewhere out in the valley."

Ned stares out the window. He can't see anything beyond the airstrip, but the sounds are clearly from two giants in a fight. The ground shakes several times as roars come from the darkness of the night. No doubt the Hydra is involved in a rumble with something else.

"Well, well, well, check out who I found." Hunter comes up behind Ned without making a sound, causing Ned to jump.

"Hey, man." Ned replies.

"You hanging in there?" Hunter puts a hand on Ned's shoulder. He knows Ned was close to Dusty.

"In general, no," Ned answers with a grim tone.

"Given the circumstances?"

"Oh, I'm just dandy." Ned's sarcasm needs work.

"So, I gotta ask, what did Dusty think he was doing?"

Ned glances back at him, then shakes his head and takes a deep breath. "The ignition plates somehow fell out of our pockets over by the well. Without them, the helicopters aren't going anywhere." He glances down at the one Dusty threw to him. "Dusty went to grab them and threw this one through a window right as he went."

Hunter sees the plate is mangled and bent in a corner. "What the hell bent a thick bronze plate?"

"Came like this. He died all for nothing. If I bend this part back, I'll ruin the notches and this piece of junk will still be useless. A few hours ago, I had the balls to go searching for the second one, but it's gone."

"Damn shame. I'm sorry, man." Hunter does his best to comfort Ned.

"Yep."

"So, listen, can we escape on the airplane to somewhere the hydra may not follow?" Hunter thinks the idea of escaping might help.

"Assuming we can survive long enough to start the engine and take off to the air. Thing is, we need two minutes from ignition to take off. Guess another minute to fly beyond its reach. Go straight up and see how far we can glide the thing. Maybe reach the gravity gap with the Tradewinds and be able to glide to Heart. Long shots all around. We'll need to refuel as well. I don't trust how much is in the reserve. Also, I would want to expand the tank and maximize the fuel we have to make sure we can finish a flight to Heart." Ned's voice is calculated, analytical. It sounds as though he is thinking of how to set his plan in motion.

"You say that with a lot of confidence, as if you've been working on this plan for a while."

"Yeah, the plane phased in for me and I took a solid look. The piece of trash is only a ditching glider with a pipsqueak motor," Ned continues. "But the wing is sturdy and can handle some upgrades, and I can make them happen if we can find a tool shop or repair area here. Distracting the hydra aside, the plan is doable."

"Well, I got a thought on how to distract the hydra for at least three minutes." Hunter says, matching Ned's tone.

"Enlighten me."

"We can bank on another fight like this one, or we can offer up Albert as a sacrificial lamb on the other side of the valley."

"Avoiding the topic of ramifications of the second option, how in the hell do you intend to pull off doing something most hit men consider impossible?" Ned likes the idea of offing Albert, but he never considered trying something so daring.

"No clue, but he's the easiest one to overpower physically right now. His arm got torn up in the mine and he nearly bled out. If we can separate him from Mack, I can drag him to the valley and leave him for dead like an angry noisy dinner bell."

Ned nods his head in agreement. "Getting him and Mack apart is a challenge. But that's a suicide mission given Albert is a madman. And I hardly suspect he's unarmed."

Hunter checks out the window. "Hey now, I see the refinery.

Can we take the plane inside to make the modifications?"

Ned's jaw drops when he raises his head up. "Hey, I can see it too. Yeah, if we carry the plane in, the rest is easy."

"The plane can't possibly weigh more than we can lift, right?"

"No way. It's very lightweight."

"Let's go while the hydra's is busy. If we're lucky, we can finish and take off before this fight ends."

They walk to the front of the barracks. Hunter searches around to make sure nothing else is waiting for them. "We're clear for now."

They head for the airstrip. Trying not to fall every time the ground shakes. "What the hell can go toe-to-toe with that thing?" Ned asks in a bewildered voice.

"In this forest, quite a number of monsters. But the hydra is the only one using tricks like the damned hydra's wake. The harpy bears are the best known competitor, but I can think of a few others. It may surprise you to know, it's not the biggest animal here." The Deep Forest is home to a number of behemoths capable of outclassing hydras for size. This hydra is proving to be the nastiest to come across, though.

"I still see the plane," Ned comments with excitement.

"I do too. Gotta say, I read that Inner Shell gets cold, but this is freezing insanity," Hunter adds. The two men run to the plane.

"See the helicopters?" Ned asks.

"Who cares if we can't use them." Hunter blurts out, even though he does see them.

"Well," Ned starts to say, but decides to keep the part about the gems to himself for now.

They reach the plane and grab the bars connecting the carriage to the wing.

"One, two, three." Together they lift Rogue's plane with ease.

"Didn't expect any airplane to be this light." Hunter trips when a tremor causes him to lose his footing.

"Surprised this thing didn't blow away in the wind," Ned says as they carry the plane to the refinery at a brisk walking pace, trying not to trip at each irregular tremor.

"We should have everything we need in the refinery." Hunter asserts.

"Everything but fuel, yeah," Ned answers. "We'll need to siphon some from a helicopter when we can reach one."

Rogue wakes up in the lounge of the station. "How'd I return here?" He finds the metal vial in his hand. "Oh, right."

He heads for the room. The door is wide open and the smell of burned food lingers. *Ugh, smells like my dorm back when I was in school and had no idea how to cook.* He finds the woman closing the window. "Hey, I'm back."

The woman makes eye contact with him and points out towards the valley, where distant roaring is coming from. Strong tremors hit every few seconds from the fight between two enormous animals.

"If I have to guess, the hydra is fighting something."

Her expression tells him she wants to learn more about what's going on outside.

She nods and stares out of the window again.

"In the meantime, I found an antidote to stop the toxic mist from the hydra, called hydra's wake. This will give you immunity against the toxin. I drank mine when I found it and walked through the mist unharmed. The miners kept some for emergencies." Rogue shows her the vial. *Not everything is true. But I can't say here, have some special medicine I got from an ancient building. Given what she's been through.*

She stares at the vial nervously and hesitates for a short moment but takes it from him. She sniffs the top and peers into the liquid, which is clear. After her inspection, she drinks the contents and starts coughing. After a second, she sits down, the grimace on her face making it clear she doesn't like the aftertaste.

Hey, she trusted me. I'd call that a major development. Rogue takes the plate from his pants pocket and sets it down on the table, thankful the notches and holes are still in perfect condition. "We need to think of a way to distract the hydra long enough to take off in a helicopter. Then we both can escape this hell of a camp safe and sound."

She switches glances between him and the plate with a confused expression.

"This hydra is fast and can cross the valley in less than a few minutes. The helicopters and the little plane outside will make enough noise to gain its attention. And that's not a good thing. Somehow, we'll figure out how to make sure we have enough time to start the engine and fly out of its reach. The only alternative is to try to walk out of here, through the Deep Forest Province."

At the mention of Deep Forest, her confusion turns into concern.

"This is Camp Tor. We're at the base of the Backfin Cliffs next to Tor Valley," Rogue elaborates.

She nods along.

Rogue lets out a deep breath. He walks over to the kitchen to find what she burned. Some rice grains in a ceramic pot. "Here, let me make a new batch for us." He grabs another pot and the bag of rice she left on the counter. "I ran into Albert and some of his men."

She locks up at hearing the name and starts to breathe heavily again. Her body begins shaking uncontrollably.

"They can't see me because they're all affected by the hydra's wake. But I learned where the mix up is. They confused me for your father," he says. *Uh oh. I should've kept my mouth shut.*

She grabs her legs and pulls them close to her chest.

He sits next to her. "He's not going to come after you ever again. I promise. Breathe deep, close your eyes, then look at me." After a moment she locks her eyes with his. Tears form in hers. "You have my word. He can't find you here."

Her lips tremble as she tries to control her breathing. The stare coming from her is intense and full of emotion.

Moving slowly, he wipes the tears off her face. When he touches her, she shudders, but then keeps watching as he wipes them away. "I want you to hold me to this promise, ok?"

She closes her eyes and puts her hand on his. She nods in agreement and wipes the rest of her tears away herself. Something about him helps her feel at ease. Only heroes in bedtime stories say the kinds of things he just did. But the way he said them makes her want to believe him.

It's crazy how strong this woman is. Not only her body, although her face, her hand, and her punch from earlier make me think an army was required to kidnap her. But her spirit. There's a fire in those eyes. She's incredible.

"The mercenaries said your old man is some sort of military spy. And they are chasing him, right?"

Again, she nods.

"That's incredible. I could never handle being a spy. I normally run from fights, and I've never had to survive like this before. Anyways, we need to work together to find a way out of this place and get you back home safe."

She shakes her head no.

"No, you don't want to go home?"

She nods her head.

"Because of your father?"

She first nods, and then switches to shaking no.

"Albert?"

She only nods once this time.

"Well, I don't like him. Not one bit. Dude is messed up in the head. To be honest, I would take him out if I could, he's the first person I've met that I've wanted to hurt. When I ran into him, I actually tried. Grabbed his neck and tried breaking it. The damned hydra's toxin affected us, and I guess I couldn't interact with them. Turns out this whole thing is one hydra-sized mistake. But I'm ok with it, really. Had they gone after your father for real, you'd be worse off, and if me getting shot down is part of saving your life, well then, I'm glad it happened."

Her face shows she wants to ask so many questions and say a lot of things.

He looks at her with an expression of forced confidence. But she can clearly tell how nervous he is. "For what it's worth, I'll do everything I can to help you out of here. And if Albert is a concern, I'll find a way to deal with him."

She sits motionless wondering why he cares so much?

"So, you don't want to go home. Are you married? Have you been?"

The sudden shift throws her off, and she shakes her head no.

"I assume no kids of your own?"

Her confused expression gives him the answer, but she shakes no again.

"When this is all over, do you have somewhere I can take you?"

Another no.

Great, I can't leave her on her own. Being mute is a curse, one I. Well, probably best to keep parts of my past buried. I'm changing. Rogue starts cooking the new batch of rice. "We'll fix that when we're safe. Would you like anything to go with the rice?"

She gets up and walks over with a bad limp. Then from the pantry she pulls out a canister containing gravy mix and holds it towards him. He smiles and nods. She stands next to him while he prepares the rice and gravy. "After this we might as well get some shut-eye until dawn."

After the food is ready Rogue overhears voices outside the window. Two of Albert's men, one of them the man Rogue tricked earlier, are running towards Rogue's plane. The fight in the distance is still going on. Rogue watches them pick up the plane and run off the airstrip. "What the hell are they doing to my plane?" he mentions out loud.

The woman taps his shoulder and points to the chair.

"If they're doing something to my plane so they can leave, that's important to know."

She gives him an angry glare, causing him to stop and pay attention to her. She lifts her hands making an upside down V with her left hand, using the fingers on her right hand to flick in between the V shape, and wobbles the hand down.

Rogue doesn't hesitate and sits down. She hit him once before, and he isn't about to give her a reason to punch him again.

She walks over and locks the door, sitting on the bed while the two eat the food.

"Sorry, I've been walking out on you a lot today. But after everything you've been through, I assumed you may have wanted a quiet spot to yourself," he says with a sheepish expression.

She rolls her eyes at him and shakes her head.

"Guess when we check out more tomorrow, you're coming with." *I don't blame her in the least, I get cranky from bed rest. But if this Albert guy finds her it will be a huge problem. Oh well, we'll cross that bridge when we run into him.*

She nods.

"That settles it," Rogue affirms. When they finish their meal, the roars are louder from outside, but the ground shakes less. "Guess the hydra is the winner."

4: SOULS OF THE FAULTLESS

Mack glances outside as Ned and Hunter are walking next to each other. All he sees is air, but they are carrying something. "Hey Albert." He turns around to find Albert asleep on one of the nearby bunks. "That's fine by me," Mack says to himself as he leaves the building. Now he can see the airplane they are carrying to the refinery.

He walks towards them and hits what seems to be an invisible wall blocking half of the camp, bumping into the wall hard enough to fall backwards.

Someone laughs behind him. "Oh man, that is rich." The voice sounds like ten of the same man speaking all at once, with an echo.

"Who's there?" Mack jumps back up and searches around.

"Oh, it doesn't matter, but you should understand I'm harmless. Stuck here, same as you lot. The hydra's wake is quite the phenomenon. Sadly for you, you can hear me, so the only hope for you is to soon pass into this dimension."

"What the hell?" Mack can't see anyone.

"Calm down. You haven't gotten eaten yet. Though, to be honest, you may want to consider the option. I am. Well, was. Until you guys showed up."

Mack pulls his revolver out. "Show yourself."

"I don't know how to. I'm standing to your left. Now I'm behind you. If you can't find me then too bad. Put the gun down before you hurt yourself, please."

After scanning the area again, Mack puts away his gun. He feels around, but all he can find is the long invisible wall he bumped into.

"What's in front of you is some sort of dimensional barrier, surrounding parts of the gemstone mine. And there's a reason for it. Come on and I'll tell ya everything I know."

Mack begins to panic, pounding on the wall. "What's going on? What the hell?"

"Ok, here's the deal. This is a lot to explain, and I've been trying to chat with any of you for a while now. You're clearly the first person to be able to hear me. So, yay, I guess. But can you stop acting like a bat-shit-crazy lunatic?"

Mack tries to calm down. This new turn of events has made

him snap and whoever is with him is right. "Yeah, I think I got control of myself again. Who are you and how long have you been here?"

"The start of the season, or beforehand. I don't remember because time moves differently for me. I think. Feels like several months of time were skipped for me. Anyways, you can call me Joe."

"Since at least last off-season?" While the cold air is biting, this new person is giving him shivers.

"Yeah, turns out escaping the toxic hydra's wake isn't possible. As you descend into madness, it manages to merge you into an alternate reality. If you resist, you stay on this side. If you succumb, well, you end up like the souls gathered in the gemstone mine."

"Zombies?" The revelation catches Mack's full attention. "This leads to becoming a zombie?"

"This is a lot more complicated than that. But let's go somewhere safer to talk. The fight between the hydra and the harpy bear is finished. Ended in a draw. That bear has been trying to take the hydra's valley for a while now. I hope the bear didn't add another head, though our local hydra will have a nice prime number of heads, and that's cool. Anyways, the safest place to chat where both of us can be out of sight is in the phosphorus mine."

With nothing to lose, Mack hurries towards the huge opening of the mine. "How deep are we going in?"

"Far enough to make this hydra lose interest. Inside is a loading platform. Pass through and keep walking until you reach a chamber with running water. We can talk there." Joe keeps his voice slow and clear for the directions.

The eerie silence returns, but at least the ground isn't shaking. He runs towards the entrance. Once inside, he keeps going straight, passing the platform, and follows the shaft. It goes farther than he expects, but it isn't long before he hears the sound of rushing water in the distance. The dirt floor transitions into wood after he passes a mine-cart station. The major equipment is locked away and stored in the walls. Mack continues to follow the shaft until a railing appears, and the water is louder. When he reaches the first major chamber, the sound fills the room. "Running water? More like an underground river."

"Same difference, honestly." This time, Joe's voice is much clearer and comes with no echo.

"I hope hearing you better isn't a direct sign of what you were saying earlier."

"I don't think so. But from where I am, I can see in the dark. Handy when the sun only shines a fraction of the time here."

"That's how you can tell what the hydra fought in the dark of night." Mack raises his eyebrows and looks for something to sit on. "Ok, so what gives?"

"This is going to be a bit of a mouthful so give me the time to explain this all in one go. Afterward, we can dissect everything for you." Joe coughs to clear his throat.

"Shoot; I'm all ears." Mack sits on a nearby crate.

"Well, as you figured out by now, the toxin called hydra's wake is a nasty thing used to completely disorient its prey. The effects are different depending on the specific individual hydra from which they originate. And this one's nasty effects alter reality almost in a dimensional sense. Things phase in and out and, well, you experienced a fair amount of the paranormal stuff yourself. The point is, this will keep going until you either succumb to the toxin, and become, what my best guess is, one of its puppets. Those zombies you mentioned. They hide in the altered reality in the gemstone mines looking to add more to their ranks. Anyone affected by the wake can interact with them and vice versa. But they will only aim to kill. You still with me, buddy?"

"Yeah, I follow. This is a lot to take in, and sounds very fantastic, but I'm following ya." Mack hangs on every word that Joe is telling him. This toxin is, apparently, far more dangerous than he imagined.

"Cool. If you fight to stay yourself, you turn into what I think I am now. Which is someone stuck in normal reality, but only those under the toxin's effects can, in varying degrees, contact me. And again, the same in reverse; I can't do anything to those unaffected. I can see the real world change around me, and things at random will disappear and reappear at random. Feels like being a ghost. No need to eat or drink, which is kinda cool. Oh, and critical detail here. If you wander too far from the hydra you become exhausted and eventually find yourself unable to move at all unless the behemoth moves closer to you. Can't escape the damned titan of misery and suffering."

"I guess you tried to figure out how to escape."

"But the water only works if you manage to breathe in no more than a breath of the stuff. When the mist hit me, I was hyperventilating from a fear of something, don't really remember what, and well, my fate got sealed before I stood a chance. The next thing I know it feels like several months have passed and I'm invisible to everything. The constant headache hurts too."

"Are you alone or are others stuck with you in the altered reality?"

"Well, not until recently. Before you guys showed up my buddy decided to try the zombie gig. It's heart wrenching and, if you hadn't come, I'd have done so myself by now."

"So, this is your life. Hallucinating non-stop. Existing to suffer, cut off from the world, and eventually dying from the hydra." Speaking the words aloud, Mack grows tense.

"Hey, I've been unable to speak to anyone new in half a year, I think. Cut me some slack. But yeah, that's how this goes." Joe's tone grows solemn, as he realizes the news isn't pleasant.

A sense of dread fills Mack as he leans up against the rail, watching the river pass beneath the platform. A grim thought passes through his head, and he pulls out his ReelGun revolver and glances down at the silver barrel and onyx grip handle. "I don't like what you said one bit."

"Well, if someone warned me, I would've wished they'd told me straight up. That way nothing is a surprise."

The dread turns into spite as Mack spins the wheel on the revolver. "I don't know what lies ahead of me, but I do own this, and I own my life. I have no intention letting some hydra control when I go."

"How do you plan to ensure that, might I ask?"

Mack gazes around and lets out a small chuckle as he realizes Joe isn't reacting to the gun. "I'll control my own way out."

"You're not likely going to do that." Joe can see his revolver but unless Mack uses it soon, his fate is up to this hydra.

"Have you tried to leave this place? If you've been here since the miners were here?" The question pops into Mack's head, and he needs to ask.

"I will cut you off. I hitched a ride on the first train out. Got a little past the halfway point to the Mining Hub when I discovered I'm unable to move. And I sensed myself fading off physically, mentally. All things I am, as best I can tell, started to vanish. All I managed to do is roll off the train. One day the hydra wakes up, does its patrol thing, and gets closer; I could feel myself come back. I ran like hell to be nearby so I could exist. I'm still only a snack, but as long as I follow the rules of staying hidden, I stay alive. Were it not for my buddy, I'd have become hydra kibble already. I do know that leaving the hydra's reach makes a victim's body go back to the normal reality, but in a never waking coma. I wanted to avoid that fate since well, I'm attached to living my life actively." Joe is rambling.

Mack listens to every word. "Joe If I ever find you, I'll put you out of your misery on your own terms."

"I'd love to let you try. I can't use my weapon on myself." Joe drops the sarcasm and sounds solemn. "That's awfully kind of you, though."

"This is a living nightmare. So you're armed? With what, if you don't mind me asking?"

"An old Pyrecone. Which is useless here, because hydras are fireproof and too damn smart. I'll even go as far as to say they're smarter than we are." Joe sounds drained.

"Yeah, we've learned the damned thing is a sneaky son of a bitch."

After a long pause Joe asks another question. "Did you go into the station?"

At first Mack has no clue what Joe is referring to before he remembers the signpost by the well indicating one exists. "The camp station?"

"Yeah."

"No, the building never materialized for us."

"You guys must've flown through its toxin. Well, the station is a terrifying set up. Luring people into a false sense of security when they are stranded and try to come here to regroup. Somehow the monster uses those zombies to prepare the station's hotel after everyone leaves. Fills all the rooms with food and supplies, clean sheets, everything you can imagine. Makes most luxury hotels on Heart look like a cheap mess. Then they leave notes to lure those people to work in the mines for free gemstones or use the refinery. The people do so and make noise, letting the hydra learn of their presence. Next it comes over and does its thing."

"Has anyone else been here before us? Since the miners left, I mean."

"I've witnessed several people die since it woke up this time around. My buddy and I tried to leave notes where we could, to warn of the hydra's wake and to escape before they are killed. But that's all been in vain since the stuff we leave is only visible to people once they're under the toxin's influence and it's already too late. But for you guys, when that little airplane came, it attracted the hydra here without the need of waiting for someone to try working the mines. There are several mining camps that it visits along the entire valley. To make sure people keep taking refuge, it takes great care in not disrupting any of them. And its zombies will even fix its accidents when needed. You'd think the Mining Conglomerate actually pays the hydra as an employee for how much effort it puts into maintaining their stuff."

"I'm guessing the miners have a way of knowing when this thing's hibernation cycle is?" Mack doesn't know much about hydras in general.

"Yeah, the hibernation is as predictable as the sunrise. This hydra goes down and wakes up within specific weeks of the year, so predicting when it hibernates and becomes safe for people is the easy part. And you can bet they make sure they're gone well before it's due to wake up."

The ground shakes a few times, followed by the regular footstep tremors. "What happens if you manage to kill the bloody hydra?"

"Now, that is what my motivation for sticking around has been. Though after the first few months of this I realized killing anything so massive is nothing short of impossible." Joe recalls his efforts using mining dynamite.

"Yeah, we did shoot down a cargo dirigible which was carrying several tons of Hexogen. Even though the wreck caught fire, I can't imagine the explosives went up. There isn't any crater to indicate a blast." Mack remembers only an isolated fire at the base of the cliff, not a massive crater.

"You shot down a dirigible carrying Hexogen. Who pissed you off?"

Mack chuckles. "Let's just say my boss is a notorious bad guy who is used by governments and elites to do dirty work. There are no shortage of people we hunt down. That's the short version. Trust me when I say my boss, Lord Albert, is not someone you want to befriend. He makes this hydra seem tame."

"That is important to know." Joe sounds hesitant. "I don't think I've seen who you're chasing yet."

"He might not be under the hydra's wake enough. The dude is a big shot military spy. I'm starting to wonder if he lured us here knowing the hydra would make his life simpler." Mack now considers the possibility.

"Oh my sweet jewels! That would be so brilliant of him. Using a hydra to kill enemies on purpose would be such a cool story. Except for your gang of course. If that's the case, y'all are screwed. Which is kinda funny for me but sad for you guys. You know, I'm sorry if I'm coming off as awkward."

Mack laughs. "You really have been lonely. No worries, friend. Although I suggest you stay away from Albert. Anyway, we used a new air cannon to shoot the dirigible down; new high tech crap that takes advantage of the Tradewinds."

"I don't know what to make of y'all but sounds like fun. Where is the crash site?"

"I'd say roughly forty miles away, or so. Backfin Cliffs." Mack said, realizing his memory is awesome for once, which surprises him.

"And you said this wreckage has a few tons of the stuff?"

"Manifest from the target said ten tons."

"That's a huge bomb. I have so many questions, but I also don't want to ask them. Hey, level with me, are you part of a criminal gang or organization?"

"Yes, I am, a personal bodyguard of Lord Albert Richtoff. As I said, our business is doing bad things to people at the request of people who need to stay clean. What if we get the hydra over a bomb, detonating the thing at the right moment?"

"Well, only one way to find out. But you should move this bomb to a place where you can position it for a better detonation. Do I have to join you guys or die?"

Mack laughs again. "Like I said, keep clear of Albert, he's not someone you want to be close to."

"Interesting. Alright, back to bombing hydras."

"Yeah, getting a hydra to hug a cliff doesn't seem plausible. We'd require a way to transport the material, make this bomb, and lure the beast out to our trap." Mack looks around the darkened chamber as the lights flicker from a strong tremor.

"Well, regarding transport of super heavy things, I can think of a way. But the best way to lure the hydra would be to put someone out in the valley to get their attention. Do that right and you can have it walk onto the bomb. So, pick someone on your team that you don't want to go home with."

Mack considers Joe's suggestion, but there's a problem.

"We're talking about transporting ten tons of high explosives, and you make transportation sound like the easiest part of the gig?"

"There's a short-range dirigible in the launch bay in the skyport that's in the cliffs. Moves slow and quiet, and it's kinda small. It can't fly above the Shell's atmosphere and cross the gap to Heart. Useless for a practical escape. But it can carry a heavy payload."

Mack's jaw drops a little. If this guy is telling the truth, then moving a bomb won't be a problem. Assuming they can interact with the ship.

"The upper most chamber of the gemstone mine is a retrofitted miniature skyport used between the camps." Joe says. "But, as you may have discovered, a bunch of, uh, you said zombies, guess that's easier to say than altered puppet souls, right? Yeah, so a zombie horde is on the way inside. And a hyper-intelligent super predator hunting you down for the thrill is outside. Oh, and this doesn't include an army of nasty animals who will think you're intruding in the forest. And that's not even mentioning the barrier you got flattened by."

Mack crosses his legs and thinks for a moment. "If I can reach any of the others, they can start to make this whole thing happen."

"Your pals ran into the refinery, right? This camp has a local network of telegraphs connecting the major buildings and mines. You should be able to send messages to them without alerting the hydra. It's somewhere over here. Do you understand Morse Code?"

Rogue starts to lock the doors to the station when, in the lobby, a tapping sound, similar to a telegraph, breaks the silence. *What now? New things are getting under my skin.*

The woman points towards a spot behind the reception desk.

"Someone is really going for it," Rogue says as he walks over. He yawns. "So much for catching some shut-eye." The clicks have short and long pauses between them. *Morse Code?*

Ned and Hunter glance up when the sound of metal tapping echoes in the refinery, which turns out to be a giant empty warehouse.

"What the hell? Morse Code?" Ned recognizes the pattern of the tapping noise.

"Where's the noise coming from?" Hunter searches around for the source.

"Sounds like a telegraph up on the landing!" The two head over to the stairs and the tapping becomes clearer. "Yeah, it's definitely from up there."

When they reach the second floor, they discover several desks lined up, covered in piles of dusty papers. "This is creepsville to the max."

Hunter walks past a few desks and finds the telegraph machine kicking up a dust cloud a little further away. "Found our telegraph. I have no clue how to translate this stuff though."

Ned comes over. "Attention refinery." he relays at the end of the transmission.

"The refinery?" Rogue translates out loud and glances at the woman. "Someone's asking for the refinery."

The woman can't believe her ears. He can translate the tapping. She searches some drawers on the desk and finds a piece of paper and a writing device.

"Ah perfect. Thank you." Rogue smiles at her and finds she is more surprised than anything else. *Huh, wonder what's on her mind? The apprehension is gone.*

Hunter sits on a nearby desk as Ned replies: COPY. GO.

Mack taps in: WHO?

"Man, you guys really don't trust each other, do you?" Joe laughs at Mack's caution.

"In case you forgot, we're here to hunt down another person. And if I contact the wrong person by mistake that probably won't end so well." Mack replies, doing his best to ignore Joe.

"It won't end well regardless, so what's the difference?" Joe shoots back.

"Yes indeed, who are you guys?" Rogue eavesdrops.

"What if it's Rogue Whip?" Hunter urges Ned to be cautious.

"At this point, what's the harm? Might be better off on his side." The idea doesn't bother Ned much to Hunter's relief as he taps: NED. YOU?

"Ned? Thank god." Mack responds with: MACK.

"So, he's not the spy you're looking for?" Joe is unable to contain his curiosity.

"No, he's one of our pilots." Mack pays attention as the telegraph comes back with: ALBERT?

"Are you going to round everyone up?" Joe is excited at the prospect of meeting more new people.

"Yes, everyone except our boss. He needs to rest because he's in bad shape." Mack taps in: NO.

Hunter stands next to him as Ned writes out the letters. "Well, that's a relief. And, for the record, I agree. If we run into Rogue, we switch sides."

"Hang on," Ned says, "more is coming in."

COME TO PHOS MINE, Rogue writes down. "Oh wonderful. That place again?" He looks at the woman. "Sounds like they're gathering in the phosphorus mine. I need to find out what they're up to."

The woman nods and waves for him to go. She takes a seat and starts shaking.

"You gonna be ok staying in here until I come back?"

She shakes her head no, but, being honest with herself, she still has trouble walking. Getting from the room to the lounge took far more effort than she thought it would. Walking as far as the mine would be too difficult.

"Ok, well if you see me coming, please unlock a door for me."

She nods. Asking her to be his lookout at least gives her something to feel important about.

Rogue walks over and waits by the door. After a moment, the two men emerge from the refinery, heading to the phosphorus mine. "I know one of them is Hunter. The other guy must be Ned." A tapping on his shoulder makes him glance over his shoulder. He turns to find the woman on her feet again. "What's up?"

She holds a knife up near her throat and moves in a slicing motion across her neck and points at the mine.

"What?" The sight surprises him before he figures out the intended message. "You're asking me to murder them?"

She shakes her head no, followed by nodding yes. She needs to say something, and she starts tapping the knife on the wall.

"Kill? You want me to kill one of them?" *Only one of them?* "Wait, hold up. You understand Morse Code, but can't read or write?" *What the hell? Are you kidding me? Is this a common thing among mute folk?*

She nods with a sheepish expression. Not everyone realizes she's trying to communicate, and fewer still can translate her tapping. And here is this stranger, who happens to understand the code. What god made this happen?

"Ok, umm, the one named Hunter?"

She shakes her head no and starts tapping on the wall again.

"You want me to kill the guy named Mack."

She nods once, angry, with tears flowing from her eyes. The raw anger coming from her shifts to pain.

Her pain is so deep, raw, and mixed. "I'll deal with Mack." He takes the knife, and she gives him a hug. "I will make sure you never see him again."

The force with which she wraps her arms around him is incredible. How strong she is catches Rogue off guard. She's crushing his spine, and he can't breathe. *What did this girl do with her body? She's got some serious muscle. Never mind the hydra eating me. She'll kill me by asphyxiation if she doesn't let go soon. My body still hurts like hell from the crash landing.*

He's never murdered anyone before but her reaction gives him a sense that he needs to do this for her. "It will be alright," Rogue says with as much assurance as possible. *What the hell is happening to me? I've never been ok with the idea of killing anyone before. But first I was ok with killing Albert, now I'm ok with doing in his crew too. I almost feel that avenging this woman is something I am responsible for.*

"So, what happens if we can't see him?" Hunter glances behind them as they enter the phosphorus mine. The hydra's tremors aren't too strong, so they head to the mine.

"Let's find out before asking what ifs." The possibility didn't occur to Ned, and he hopes they won't have any problems.

"You two took your sweet ass time," Mack says.

"You can see us?" Hunter is relieved.

"Yeah, come on this way." Mack ushers them in.

Rogue manages to pass the loading platform when a tremor shakes in the ground. *Took longer than I expected to start moving again.*

Mack introduces Joe, though only Mack and Ned can hear him. Rogue and Hunter see and hear nothing.

Rogue stays behind some barrels near the entrance to the chamber, listening to them talk about Rogue's cargo and how making a bomb from the Hexogen might be the best chance to kill the hydra. *All things considered, this is a brilliant plan, I have to admit. Wait, Hexogen is super explosive. Oh shit, how in the hell did I survive the crash again?*

Rogue thinks about how lucky he was the cargo didn't go off. *Oh, wait, yeah, It's encased in those giant container things with tubes inside. Stuff won't explode unless exposed to anything hotter than lit thermite.*

"So, we have to go through the zombie caves to reach the highest part of the mine. This takes us to a skyport where a dirigible is. Then fly over the forest twice and somehow set up a massive trap for the damned hydra." Ned sums up.

"I know who to use as bait." This is a perfect way to off Albert in Hunter's mind.

"Rogue Whip." Mack says with a smirk.

"Albert," Hunter says at the same time.

"What the hell is wrong with you?" Mack is bewildered by Hunter's suggestion.

"Are you an idiot? Albert is the only one who is injured, noisy, and makes a great lure." Hunter argues.

"That's treason! Do you have any idea what you're saying?" He shouts at the top of his lungs, resisting the urge to shoot Hunter where he stands.

"Well, I won't help with this plan if we don't use Albert, and besides, we haven't seen Rogue Whip once since we've been here. I'm willing to bet he isn't even in the camp anymore. Simply put, we can't use someone we can't catch for the bait." A solemn silence follows Hunter's argument.

"So, when the going gets too tough, you back out on your employers, hope they die so you can back out of a job refund free? Is that how you roll?" The idea of betraying Albert is infuriating to Mack, and all he can do is shout at this mercenary.

"This isn't a normal situation by any stretch." While Hunter knows Mack is loyal to a fault, this is pushing reason past the limit. "Unlike you, I am a freelance mercenary, and this job went sideways the moment we landed. It's not in my contract to pull your asses out of this. Unless you can pay way more." Now he can't hold himself back as the blood in his veins begins to boil.

"Ned? Albert needs a little help here, please." Somehow Mack manages to change tone in the hopes Ned will back him up on this point. He tries to keep calm.

"I'm thinking Albert for the same reasons. But if we do run into Rogue, I'll switch my vote." Ned puts an arm between them and looks Mack in the eye. "Fighting each other won't help us, and we gotta do what we can, using only what the situation allows."

The wind is taken out of Mack's sails by Ned's words. "I can't believe this!"

"Believe what you wish. We're getting out of here, and if killing Albert is required, I'll be alright. Only means less evil is in this universe anyways." The comment is rude, but Hunter feels the need to get in Mack's face.

For a moment Mack paces around them, scratching his head. "Traitors, the both of you!"

"Mack, let Albert go. This sucks, but we don't have the power to do otherwise, except for volunteering to die, and I ain't going to do that. No way. And neither should you, for that matter. And we aren't strong enough to make Hunter be bait." Ned tries to reason with him.

Mack stops pacing and puts his hands on his knees as he hunches over. "Every man for himself now, huh?"

"You want to stay here and die? You're of course free to make that choice. But, if you band with us, we'll get you out." Hunter lays down the ultimatum.

"How do we want to deal with the zombies?" Ned changes the subject, attempting to ease the tension in the room.

"Bypass them. Go around and locate an easy way up cliff and rappel down to the chamber. If we can find a way to scale up to the top." Moving to the new topic puts Hunter at ease.

"Talk about a hell of a hike," Joe proclaims. "Nearest way up those cliffs is about fifty miles down the tracks."

Mack shakes his head. "Fine. If you assholes think you can betray him and live, fine."

"You'll survive too, if that counts for anything." Ned says, trying to reassure Mack.

"I can't say that's likely the case. Albert is. Well, you. Ah, shit, I can't process this now. Anyhow, our ghost buddy says getting up the cliff will be quite a walk before you reach the pathway leading up." The concept of being independent is new, and Mack speaks as if he lacks a voice of his own.

"Not exactly," Ned replies. "When Dusty and I did our exploring, we found a rickety old bridge. It's broken down but is in the middle of unfinished repairs. If we can bridge the ravine, we hike up the path without entering the mine. On the other side we could see a tall structure a little further past the ravine."

"I'm shocked." Joe's voice sounds enthusiastic. "I remember the ravine bridges collapsed, and they fixed the one inside the mine, but I thought they decided not to fix the outside one because of how soon the hydra's dormant time was ending."

"What do we need to finish the repairs?" Focusing on being objective is all Mack can do.

"Well, we didn't get a detailed look. We'll have to wait until daylight to find out," Ned answers.

Hunter leers at Mack. "You ran into a wall keeping you away from the gemstone mine, right? Makes you useless for now. While we figure out getting to the dirigible, you can search for a spot where we can plant this bomb. Also, you can say you're not as involved to ease your conscious if need be."

"Fine, I'll explore the valley and look for a ravine nearby or something." Mack's tone is growing more impersonal.

"We should head back to the refinery." Ned says to Hunter.

Ned sees Mack reaching for his gun as Hunter turns his back. Mack grabs his revolver and for a second aims at Hunter's head. Before Ned says anything, he turns to Ned and lets out a sigh. "Here, if you run into those zombies you'll need this. I don't have any sane reasons for carrying a gun at the moment."

Mack hands Ned his weapon.

Ned nods and takes the revolver. The look in Mack's eye worries Ned. Handing him the gun isn't to help Ned, but to stop Mack. "We'll be back before dawn to go over more details."

"Go away." Mack is thinking of what to do as the others leave.

Rogue waits until the two men have left the mine and brandishes the knife he took from the woman. His blood boils with anger. This will be the first time he's murdered anyone, but he finds himself at peace with the idea. "Mack, I can't imagine what you did to that woman, but you die here."

Mack does not respond to what Rogue shouts at him and begins pacing again. "I can't believe this."

"Man, you guys are so touchy-feely with each other, no one would think how you talk sounds harsh." Joe's says sarcastically.

"I should've shot him. Them." Mack throws his arms up and kicks the ground.

"You'd be very dead, not like either way makes a difference." Joe has no sympathy for him.

Mack sits down and scratches his head. "Killing Albert doesn't sound easy because killing him is *not* easy. He's smart; keeps a unique weapon on him, which makes fighting him upfront suicidal; in fact, doing so is almost impossible. Both of those goons will die before they lay a hand on Albert."

Rogue stops to eavesdrop further, since the details sound important.

"What kind of weapon would be too dangerous for a group of mercenaries to handle?" Joe's curiosity keeps the conversation going.

"I can't remember the name of the weapon off the top of my head, but he uses a thin, flexible sword. Can make the blade move almost like a whip one second and the next he can make it move like a solid sword or a soft rope."

"Sounds like Albert carries an urumi. Odd choice of weapon," Rogue mutters to himself.

Mack gets up. "I need to warn Albert. No way am I letting them kill my lord."

Rogue makes his move, Coming out from behind the barrels, he rushes at Mack. *Now or never!*

"Hey, Mack! Watch out! A flying knife is heading your way! Eleven o' clock!" Joe's voice calls out.

Mack stops to find what Joe is seeing but doesn't see anything. "What are you talking about?"

Rogue puts the knife against Mack's neck. In this moment, Mack stares straight into his eyes. "What the?" he says as Rogue slits Mack's throat. *Wow, I cut through his neck easier than I imagined.*

Mack catches sight of Rogue Whip, but the blood drains from his body before he can react. Darkness soon follows.

Rogue turns around to find the entry of the mine is now blocked. After a moment he can focus better and finds the hydra has one of its heads in as far as the loading platform, sniffing the air. *So much for not confronting the literal demon.* Rogue drags the body towards it. The monster's eyes stay fixated on Rogue as he approaches.

"Somehow I bet you can understand me," Rogue says. "I am not your enemy. This man did bad things to a friend of mine." Rogue carries the corpse until he's halfway to the entrance. He throws Mack's body close to the head and backs away.

The curious hydra sniffs Mack, then raises its head up to the ceiling and growls. This human has taken liberty to end the life of another in its presence. For the hydra, there is no greater crime than to rob it of a kill. It bears its teeth at the human.

The hair on the back of Rogue's neck stands up when he realizes the head can still go deeper into the mine. He sprints deeper down the shaft as the hydra's head lunges at him and follows him as deep as its neck will go with its mouth agape. After Rogue is out of reach, the angry hydra unleashes an ear shattering roar. Rogue can tell from its eyes that the creature is pissed. It retracts its head, eating Mack on the way out.

Rogue sits down and catches his breath. "That was dumb," he says to himself. After a few moments, the tremors indicate the hydra is leaving, Rogue heads down to the containment facility. *I should ask that machine thing if this crazy plan will work. And I need to stop by the general store for new clothes that aren't soaked in blood.*

Hunter peeks out the window of the refinery as the hydra rushes by without generating strong tremors. "It's terrifying how the monster can move without making a sound, especially given how massive it is."

Ned glances around at the reports and papers on the desks. "This place makes no sense."

"What do you mean?"

"These papers are all written in a language I've never seen before," Ned replies. "A while ago, before we went to the mine, I could read them like normal. How did the writing change to a whole different language?"

Hunter glances over at the papers near him. "They look fine to me, bud. Stuff about rock cores, gem quality, and other mining garbage."

Ned closes his eyes and backs away from the desk. "So, do you think this plan will work?"

"You're talking about a crazy amount of high explosives. And that's not doing it justice. I can't say I recall hearing a hydra getting taken down. But at the same time, I can't say I've ever heard of anything surviving sitting on a bomb that massive going off. The worst case scenario is we get an eight headed hydra waiting for us." Hunter takes a moment to fathom what an explosion so massive can do.

"I can't fathom that," Ned said with a nervous chuckle.

Hunter leans up against the wall with his arms crossed. "I'm having a difficult time digesting everything Mack told us."

"The zombies?" Ned asks.

"Yeah." Hunter starts pacing.

"When they attacked you guys, I wasn't around to see them. I kinda think I can navigate the mine to the top," Ned comments after an awkward silence.

"You're more than welcome to try." The choice between traversing a scary mine and avoiding the hydra or make a lot of noise attracting attention repairing the bridge isn't fun.

Ned stares down at the weapon Mack gave him. "I can't help but wonder if having weapons has anything to do with how the toxin affects people."

"What do ya mean?" Hunter gives him a curious glance.

"The hydra may choose to affect those who have weapons in specific ways. Might be a factor is all I am saying."

The idea makes sense, so Hunter shrugs. "Eh, screw it. Let's leave our weapons here and see what happens."

Rogue reaches the metal wall in Face Eighteen and searches for the groove from earlier. "I remember it is around here." He says to himself.

"Hello again." The AI's voice comes from the wall, making Rogue jump.

Rogue is unable to figure out where the voice is coming from but decides it doesn't matter. *Wait, I don't have to run all the way to the room this time?* "I have a question for you regarding defeating this hydra."

"Ambitious goal. I will answer as well as I can."

"Would the explosive Hexogen, in a huge quantity, be able to do the job? If we get the hydra to stand over the bomb in a trap. Say around ten tons worth, twenty thousand pounds."

"Allow me to dig through the scans of your memory to decipher this." The AI's voice now carries emotions.

"Take as much time as you wish." *This thing sounds more human every time we talk.*

"Kind of you. I understand Hexogen is a rather interesting chemical compound, trinitro triazinane. Possesses astounding potential for use as an explosive. In the quantity you're inquiring, the result is a significant kinetic energy release. Your knowledge of chemistry, as you call the science, is enough for me to simulate. Allow me a short moment."

Rogue nods and sits on a nearby rock. He drops the bloody knife after he realizes he's still holding it. "That was oddly thrilling."

"I'm sorry?" The AI tries to convey curiosity.

"I did something I don't want to have to do in my life ever again." Rogue takes the time to contemplate his first murder. "I'd like to focus on the larger task: dealing with the hydra."

"Moments ago, you committed a murder; your first. Thrilling, you said?"

"Well, if you scan the details out of my brain you can see why I did." *Well, the conjecture is a matter of my opinion.*

"I would advise use of the word evil," the AI corrects. "From a morality standpoint I cannot and will not judge your action. I would like to express my sympathy to your logic, and commend you for the act of heroism."

"You're awesome." The response makes Rogue chuckle. *Heroism? Ok. I don't think what I did was heroic. The machine is picking up on some human behaviors now. Next will be profanity and slang.*

"Thank you. I've finished my simulations, and they are showing your bomb will not kill the gaean hydra. Yet, you would succeed in delivering a permanent injury. If you focus the blast on the body's center of mass, you will have a probable opportunity to amputate one of its two legs. Such injury would be severe enough to alter the hydra's mobility and require a long time for it to recover, leaving it vulnerable to some other wildlife in the local area. I imagine a few of the more territorial larger beasts would be able to finish the attempt to kill the specimen."

Rogue's face lights up with a smile. He's relieved.

"I gather from your vitals this response pleases you. Do you have such material on hand?"

"I happen to have the material nearby. A crash site forty miles away." Rogue brings the image of the wreck to his mind.

"Impressive. I will have to observe the area for results. Do your best not to die because I like you."

"Thank you. Will do." Rogue runs back up the shaft towards the surface.

Ned and Hunter make their way down the gemstone mine shaft. Hunter holds a lantern since the lights are out in some stretches of the mine.

"So, the map in the first chamber said the elevator up is on the far side of the Stanley Pit," Ned said.

"We got about halfway before getting up to our necks in living hell," Hunter recalls from the earlier encounter.

As the two walk, everything is dead silent. Out of nowhere a crashing sound comes from behind them. They jump and spin around. The sound of chains scraping the wooden floor is approaching them. "Well, that's not a good sign," Ned says with a shaky voice.

A second set of chains starts dragging on the floor, from the direction in which they are going.

They face forward again, Hunter flashes the lantern along the shaft in both directions, but nothing appears to have changed.

Ned is motionless and terrified.

Hunter manages to take another step towards the Stanley Pit. Still, nothing happens except for the scraping sounds of an iron chain being dragged. The scraping is getting fainter.

"I don't see what fell behind us." Ned looks over his shoulder.

"Well, seeing nothing is a good sign for now." Hunter lets out a sigh of relief at the calm silence inside the mine. "You may be right about the whole carrying a weapon bit."

The two men take small steps, moving closer to the pit. After a few moments of silence, they resume walking at a regular pace.

"Those souls are being tortured through no fault of their own. I can't imagine the pain the one guy Mack was talking about endured." Hunter says to break the eerie silence.

"I don't think we should talk. If we are in their presence, let's at the very least respect their souls," Ned suggests.

They spot something small on the floor in the distance. "Oh, don't tell me that's what I think that is." Hunter's voice is trembling in fear.

"Stop talking and keep going," Ned replies, though he's freaking out at the sight of the chained cuffs lying in the middle of the ground ahead of them.

They run past the cuffs and stop when a shadow forms on the wall. They turn around and find they are alone. No one is behind them forming the shadow. Looking around, they only see a shadow of the man, but not the man.

They continue forward, careful not to make a sound. Shadow after shadow appears on the walls as they walk through the shaft. They are coming up on the chamber where Hunter first encountered the zombies. The chamber contains exits to two different shafts. Ned pulls out the map. "Left to the Stanley Pit."

"The room does not agree." Hunter says. All the shadows raise their arms and point to the right.

Ned double checks his map. He's certain he copied the path

correctly.

"Let's not anger them." Hunter suggests, and approaches the exit on the right.

Ned follows along, maintaining a slow pace. The electricity comes on, and the lights shine bright, blinding them for a second.

Hunter dims the lamp to conserve fuel. They stare as more shadows point further ahead.

The shaft takes a sharp turn, and they exercise caution when they approach. Looking around the corner they see they've arrived at the base of a makeshift stairway leading up several flights to a platform and another chamber. The sound of chains scraping on wood returns.

"Let's go find what they are trying to show us." Hunter climbs the stairs with Ned following close behind him. "Bud, too close," Hunter says, glancing back at Ned who is right up on him.

"Sorry, I'm terrified out of my wits here," Ned replies.

The laughter of an erratic crowd fills the air for a short moment.

Ned is embarrassed and gives Hunter space.

Metal clanging starts behind them. They step aside as two cuffs with no chain come out of the stone wall and begins running up the stairs toward them. They get up against the rail and wait as the cuffs pass them and continue up until they stop at the top.

Hunter is trying not to hyperventilate and shoots a glance at Ned when he can control his breathing.

Ned shakes his head no, with fear in his eyes.

Hunter squints down at the mine shaft where they have come from. Letting out a sigh, knowing he has no choice, he continues up the steps.

Ned's whole body shivers in fear, and he reluctantly follows. This time everything is silent. Not even their own footsteps make any noise.

Hunter gawks down at his feet. He stomps as hard as he can, but makes no noise.

Ned catches on to the lack of sound and tries to speak, but the words won't come out. He can't move his lips except to breathe.

Hunter shares the sensation, but his gut feeling is to follow through. He continues up to the top, he stops. In front of him is an incredible and unexpected sight. He peers down at Ned, who hasn't moved and waves for him to come up.

If it wasn't for the look of awe all over Hunter's face, Ned wouldn't have budged. But he slowly goes up to see what the deal is.

Hunter waits for Ned and they stare at the chamber they entered.

"Whoa," Ned says with awe.

"I know, right?" Hunter can't help but smile at the sight.

"Wow, what a gorgeous view. This isn't so bad," Ned continues.

Before them is a giant chamber with massive columns of crystals. The wooden platform extends across the entire chamber. Electric lights are positioned to make the crystals appear as though they are glowing brilliantly. They are around fifty feet tall, going into the ceiling.

A hand lands on Hunter's right shoulder and Ned's left, causing them to jump. They check behind them, only to discover a tall Shadow Figure. This being is twice their height, like a free roaming shade in a dark cloak made of smoke. Moving with a cold silence, the figure passes between them.

The figure evaporates away after taking a few steps forward. Then the lights on the walls fade. Once they turn off, the lights illuminating the crystals start to dim until they go dark. A moment passes before a shaft at the end of the room lights up.

"To the lake of your dreams." Is whispered by many different voices inside their heads.

"Guess our tour isn't over yet," Ned mutters.

"Nope. Let's move faster. Acting like chickens may amuse them, but I don't want to run their patience thin." Hunter walks towards the lit shaft.

Ned follows him, complacently.

In an instant, the air in the chamber becomes colder than ice. They stop when they walk into an invisible barrier. The shadows reappear on the wall ahead of them pointing down the shaft but lower their arms when the men bump into the barrier.

"Come to us," the voices again whisper in their heads.

Ned tries to walk down the barrier looking for a way around but can't. "How?"

"We will make you come." This time the whispers are only heard in Ned's head.

"What is going on here?" Ned asks.

"I guess we can't go farther?" Hunter heads in the other direction feeling for a way through but doesn't find one.

The lights come back on and the shadows vanish. The air stops freezing but the barrier remains.

"Watch that be a shortcut." Hunter sarcastically remarks.

"No, I think that way leads to the active gemstone faces, and

I could swear I heard something about a lake." Ned comments as he stares at the shaft. "Let's head back down to the lower chamber and take the other shaft to the Stanley Pit and make a run for the dirigible."

They walk back to the stairs and find a thick layer of dust on the wood now.

At the platform up top the shadow figure looms, watching them leave.

Hunter runs his hand across the railing and admires the dust accumulation on his hand "That's-"

"An awesome sign." Ned says cutting Hunter off.

"What do you think that was all about?" Hunter looks back at the crystals.

"I can't even guess. Paranormal and trans dimensional stuff is beyond my comprehending." Ned replies. They head back down the stairs, this time hearing their footsteps like normal. They backtrack to the Y-junction chamber, discovering a bunch of mining tools lying against one of the walls. The room appears more normal than before.

"Now, this is more like it." A normal-looking room is a welcome sight to Hunter.

They walk down the route leading towards Stanley Pit. Lights in the mine shaft shake and then flicker.

"Must be on the move again." Hunter thinks the tremor is coming from somewhere closer than the camp. The hydra might be on the cliff now.

"I'm sure the mine will hold up," Ned replies, as he checks the ceiling, and hoping it won't cave in on them.

A dark spot on the floor speeds past them swiftly going towards the Stanley Pit. The spot is followed by what seems like thousands. The spots move way too fast to keep track of. They vanish around the bend in the path before Ned or Hunter can successfully follow one. After a few moments, they stop coming.

Ned and Hunter keep looking back and forth. The shaft seems clear and empty. "We're alive, unharmed, and so far, no zombies," Ned proclaims, trying to focus on tuning the surrounding events out, but they're difficult to ignore.

Hunter nods. "Yeah, the sooner we get there, the better, so we can leave," He says with nervous tension.

A song echoes through the mine in whispering voices. "Yes, the quicker you go, the faster you can depart," the shadows' voices sing.

Ned shuts his eyes as the shadows on the wall begin depicting people carrying chests and throwing gems up in the air like excited miners getting rich.

Hunter's view is different. His shadows remain motionless when they reappear on the walls.

"On expeditious legs you run, the easier you can die." The voices grow angry as they sing the next verse and continue, "With haste you use, the closer you die."

"That was Dusty's stupid idea!" Ned shouts and keeps his eyes closed, collapsing to the ground.

"What was Dusty's idea?" Hunter sits next to him.

"The sooner you arrive here, the swifter this will end. The fastest you are there, the better you perish." The shadows' voices deepen as they speak faster and make less sense. The singing is debilitating and annoying.

"Ok, the song is getting old now." Hunter comments.

"Now you are here! Next you will be dead!" Now these voices are shouting as the last verse is sung without a tune.

"Ned, are you alright?"

Ned shakes his head. "They've been watching us the whole time. They know everything about us." He rambles.

"Come on, on your feet." Hunter lifts him up. "We're not far, we got this."

Ned nods. "Yeah."

They continue to walk further down the shaft.

"Stop that now! Stop that please! Stop that song!" The voices adopt a childish tone and sing to a nursery rhyme tune, mocking Hunter's thoughts. After singing the same thing a few times, the shadows vanish again.

"I didn't say anything out loud!" While the words were in Hunter's head, he knows he never said them out loud.

"They making fun of you too?" Ned glances at Hunter finding he's agitated.

Hunter shakes his head. "They're going to make this a long walk."

Ned nods. "Like you said, we got this."

"No, you don't, you pantsless prick!" The now demonic voices chime only for Hunter's ears.

Hunter checks to find he is still wearing his pants. "Now they are being straight up rude."

Ned chuckles, although he is completely terrified. The overwhelming fear is making him feel numb to everything now. "Well, as long as we keep our heads on, we'll leave here alive."

Hunter stops moving as the shadows line the wall again. They raise their arms to their heads as if they are about to tear them off to mock what Ned said. Only for them to simply pat their heads and vanish.

Hunter starts to jog along the shaft. "Hey, I'm getting sick of this place."

Ned sprints to catch up.

When they turn the corner, they find more shadows waiting on the walls. They stand motionless in the shapes of different people. Men, women, and children are all depicted as mere outlined shadows.

Ned and Hunter don't speak a word as they jog through, quietly observing each shadow they pass. They assume these must be those poor unfortunate souls, those who succumbed to the toxins of the hydra's wake before the hydra got the chance to eat them. They walk for hours before reaching the end of the mine shaft.

The light of predawn comes through the window. Rogue is awake and takes a moment to admire Crystal. *A new day and I'm still in this room with this babe. So yesterday was real and this is happening. I can feel every bruise and bump on my body. Every muscle is sore and every bone aches. I need a hospital, and so does she. We gotta reach the skyport and escape the valley.*

Turns out, while she can't read or write, she does understand Morse Code. Her first job was translating live political speeches via telegraph for the media. Rogue also got her name, and an apology for punching him.

Before waking her up, Rogue opens the first aid kit to put new bandaging on her arm. When he unwraps the laceration wrap, he can see the wound is closed and healing. *The gel stuff these wraps come with is amazing.* After he finishes with the new bandages, he gets brave and shakes her side; she stays asleep, so he pinches her, rushing off the bed to grab something off the table as she wakes up, yawns, and stretches.

She rubs her eyes and smiles when she sees him looking at her. She waves hi.

"Hey, I went for a visit to the maintenance shop while you slept. Made you this." He hands her a little metal box with a long flap and an open end. A clicker. He made them in scouts to use for orientation and survival exercises.

She stares at the gift and a huge smile crosses her face. She snatches it from his hand, and presses the flap, making a crisp loud clicking noise. She presses several times and waves her arms and legs around like an excited child. YAY! she clicks. I TALK WOO! She kicks her legs with excitement and an ear-to-ear smile grows on her face.

Rogue smiles. "I'm happy you like the clicker."

I LOVE IT! she clicks back. She then inspects the device. The craftsmanship isn't perfect, but he did make the box by hand. She's used these before, but they were always stolen by bullies. While they're cheap to buy, finding them requires going to stores where lots of men shop, often leading to her getting harassed. But he crafted this himself to give her a voice of her own. This is way better than tapping on the table or wall.

"We're going to go to the top of the gemstone mine, to a skyport. Inside is a dirigible we can leave in. While it's useless for getting to Heart, we can take it and fly to the Mine Colony Hub," Rogue says. *Really what we should be doing is running away and let these pathetic criminals suffer their fates here.*

Crystal nods, gets out of the bed, and tosses on some boots he grabbed for her from the general store since the first pair he brought didn't fit. When they are ready, they head out.

Rogue grabs the map from the lobby, and they search around for any sign of the local hydra. They find the wounded hydra laying down in the center of the valley on the far side. With the dim light from predawn he can see giant claw marks from whatever it fought earlier. "The hydra sure did take a pounding. Those marks on its leg, man that's gotta hurt." *Whoa, incredible. I can't imagine how intense their fight was.*

She looks out the window to see for herself, then heads towards the lounge side. LEGS WORK BETTER! she clicks with a smile. Today is a new day, and the long conversation she had with Rogue last night helped make her feel better. As he slept, she spent the whole night thinking of the good things in her life from before she got kidnapped. As the sun rises into the sky, she makes a commitment to herself to reclaim who she is. In her head she tells herself she won't be defeated.

Rogue pays attention to her walking, distracted by how she makes the jumpsuit fashionable and attractive. "Well, let me know if you need any help on the way." *Gotta say, she's different today, like all the weight is off her chest. Her smile is like no other.* When they leave the station to their surprise, Albert is standing next to the well. Before he can stop her, she grabs the nearest rock she can find and charges towards him.

She swings the rock at his head, but her hand passes through him. He doesn't react. She tries kicking and punching him, only to go through his body like he is made of air. Once she realizes she can't hurt him, she stops. Tears flow down her face. Rogue walks up to her.

"Calm down. He can't do anything to you. You're ok," he whispers into her ear. "He'll never hurt anyone again; we will make sure his tyranny ends here."

She turns and faces Rogue. He wipes the tears from her eyes, and she grabs his shirt and collapses, but he catches her. She pounds on his chest, stomps the ground, and buries her head in his shoulder to cry. After a second, she releases him and kicks the well. The kick rattles the scorpion's nest, and she stumbles backwards, still not having full control of her legs.

Rogue pulls her back when he spots a few scorpions come out of the nest. "Let's not piss those off, please."

They watch as a scorpion walks on Albert's foot and stings him in the leg. He lets out an inaudible yell and brushes the scorpion off. They keep their eyes on him as he bends over to check where he was stung. He is shouting without making any sounds that they can hear. He tries stomping on the scorpions near the well.

Rogue gets Crystal to her feet, holding her arm tight, and escorts her away toward the gemstone mine path. Once they are far enough away from the camp, he releases Crystal's arm. "Are you ok?" He asks her.

KILL HIM, she clicks

Rogue nods. "The hydra will."

She stomps her foot and clicks. NO. ME. MY TURN.

So much for the escape plan. Rogue thinks. "Ok, well we can blow him up."

YES. she clicks. But her face shows she wants to say much more. The clicker shakes with her hand, and she storms off further down the trail and sits on a nearby stump.

Rogue lets out a sigh. "Would be better for us to take the dirigible and leave. But if making sure he dies means this much to you, we'll go with the plan of blowing him up to hurt the hydra."

She grabs his arm with one hand, and with the other clicks. YOU BETTER LET ME, while staring angrily into his eyes. OR I KILL YOU TOO.

"Consider our mission in progress." Rogue says. They follow the station map to a second path passing the entrance of the gemstone mine on the side of the cliff. The sounds of the forest are peaceful as dawn comes. They arrive at a spot where there are worn rocks, indicating the path goes upward. They start to climb, discovering that the path continues toward the cliff face. Rogue follows the map of the camp which indicates a bridge to the skyport is nearby. "You doing ok so far, Crystal?" He checks behind him.

She nods and pats her bad leg.

The sound of a waterfall grows louder, and Rogue spots the semi-collapsed bridge. But someone did start repairs, and a thick support beam is laid across. They have to make sure the beam doesn't roll when they walk across the ravine, which is about a hundred feet above the river the waterfall is raging into. "Let's place some heavy rocks next to the thickest beam so this won't roll on us." Rogue walks back down the path and finds a small, rugged boulder.

Crystal also grabs one and brings it over to the beam. Rogue takes some debris and jams the boulders in place on either side of the beam, then they stand on it to test their handiwork. Thankfully the wood stays still as Rogue begins crossing the ravine. The ravine is almost fifty feet wide. After getting across safely, he turns around to find Crystal is only a few feet behind him.

They continue up the path, which leads to narrow crevices between the rocks. Beyond the crevices, the path is only a foot wide on the side of the cliffs. When they reach the end, they jump down to an opening where the ground is flat. Before them is the base of a tall wooden structure that hugs the cliff face going all the way to the top. "Ok, this should take us to a tunnel leading into the skyport chamber of the gemstone mine." *Assuming this building doesn't fall apart. Looks in rough shape up close.*

They try to open the door of the structure, but find it shut tight and locked from the inside. Crystal drop-kicks at the door with all her might and breaks the latch.

"Well, that's one way to open a door."

Crystal grabs her leg as if she really hurt herself.

When Rogue touches her on the shoulder, she clicks. PAIN.

Damn girl. The moment you can walk, you try drop-kicking a solid oak door weighing three times your body weight? Yeah, wonderful idea. "Here, you're not walking up any stairs now. I'll carry you." He carries her into the building, then leans a bench against the door to keep it closed. Rogue rolls up the left leg of the jumpsuit as far as he can to take a look while she's sitting.

Crystal grabs at her shin and starts to breathe hard.

"No broken skin. We'll have to keep an eye on this. On a scale of one to ten how bad does your leg hurt?" Rogue asks. *The last thing I need is for you to break any bones. You do that and I'm just taking off, and we're going to a hospital, end of story.*

FOUR, she clicks.

He grabs the leg and twists it to the left, then right, seeing if she has more pain in either direction, hoping she didn't break a bone. "Is it worse if I do this?"

She shakes her head.

Rogue checks the next room and discovers an electric elevator where he had assumed they would find stairs. "We can ride up," he tells her. *Well, least I won't have to give her a piggyback ride.*

She nods, and he helps her over to the elevator. She sits down on the bench inside while he looks over the controls. As they rise, the light grows stronger from outside through the gaps in the wooden planks.

MORNING, she clicks with a small smile on her face.

Rogue chuckles a little. "Yes, good morning," he says back with a smile. Realizing around this time yesterday is when he got shot down. *What a wacky day.* The elevator stops at an entrance to a mine shaft. "This should be our stop."

The Stanley Pit is a massive room and the hole itself is like a bottomless pit. Given how deep it goes, the electric lights don't reach the bottom. Ned and Hunter walk slowly and steadily along the perimeter path circling the pit. Natural light comes through several natural holes in the ceiling, showing dawn approaching. "Sunrise is coming," Hunter comments.

Before Ned can reply the ground shakes, but not in the way like the hydra walking causes. "What's that?"

"No idea." Hunter tries to keep his footing during the strong tremor. They stand up against the wall. The path is not narrow, but they don't want to risk falling.

They wait for a minute and press on after nothing new happens. They find themselves unable to speak again and the unnatural silence returns. Hunter looks behind them as the Shadow Figure from before moves behind Ned, pointing a bony finger at him.

Ned turns around and sees the figure right behind him and takes several steps back, almost bumping into Hunter. The figure stays still and silent. The air around them freezes as cold as ice. The lights flicker and again fade into darkness.

Hunter turns up the lamp to discover a huge dark mass moving in the pit itself. Ned taps on Hunter's arm and signals towards the elevator at the end of the room.

Hunter nods and follows Ned. The dark mass inside the pit begins to take a more solid form, making them go from walking to full-on sprinting. The mass forms a shape like the hydra. When they reach the elevator, their hands pass through the metal.

They exchange glances and try to speak but they can't.

Hunter backs away from Ned, who turns around to see the fake hydra behind them. Suddenly, it evaporates into a dark cloud like a dense pale blue smoke or fog. The Shadow Figure emerges from the cloud. The lights come back on brighter than they should be, and the pit is full of a pile of bodies. They are wriggling as though there aren't any bones in them, and the pit contains thousands of them.

Then comes the grotesque sound of skin and flesh flopping around.

The electricity goes out again, and turns back on to how the room appeared before.

Hunter lets out a breath, he can hear himself. "What the hell is going on, is this part of the wake?"

"They must be the hydra's victims," Ned replies.

Hunter leans against the wall and bumps his arm on the sharp rusty metal. "Oh, hey! Now the elevator is here for us."

"Let's go." Ned tries to rush inside. In doing so he runs into something gooey and falls backwards but something grabs his neck.

Hunter stays still inside the elevator as Ned runs headfirst into the Shadow Figure.

The figure tightens its hold on Ned's neck and lifts him up. Ned is too petrified with fear to retaliate or move or try anything. The figure uses its other hand, grabbing Ned's left shoulder, and squeezes hard. Ned tries to shout from the pain, but no noise comes out. But the clear, crisp sound of his bones breaking is deafening. The figure stops and gently places Ned down to wallow in silent pain. It looms over Ned, excreting a liquid which forms into a cloud to rain a pitch black liquid onto Ned.

Hunter is unable to do anything and stays still. A deep and long growl comes from across the pit. The same growl preceded the zombies that attacked Albert's group earlier. Ned gains enough control of himself to cling to the elevator door, scrambling to climb in. Hunter gets to the controls and pulls the levers to go up. The cloud is still raining black stuff over a completely distraught Ned as they move up. Below them Hunter sees a black mass cover the pathway they arrived on.

The cloud stops pouring on Ned and disperses. "Ned?" Hunter reaches over to shake Ned's shoulder.

"Not. Going. To. Be." Ned's voice gets weaker.

Hunter pays attention to the elevator and waits for the sign to brake.

"Okay," Ned continues, almost inaudibly.

"Stay with me man, I need you to pilot the dirigible," Hunter begs. He passes the brake sign and starts to stop. Ned's eyes are now jaundiced. Another shake in the ground causes Hunter to check above them. A massive shadow cuts off the light coming in from outside. He tears some fabric off his shirt, trying to make a rudimentary face covering. The elevator stops a foot below the platform. Hunter opens the gate and throws Ned up onto the ledge and climbs up himself, only to find Ned pointing behind him.

Hunter turns around as the four heads of the hydra come down the holes in the ceiling. Each head emits a strong, pale-blue mist this time, and Hunter holds his breath. The hydra stares at Ned as three of the heads retract. The last one opens its mouth, expecting Ned to jump in.

Ned faces Hunter. He can feel himself getting weaker, and the thought of sacrificing himself crosses his mind. But before he can do anything Hunter grabs his arm, lifts him, and drags him further down the mine shaft.

"Don't you dare think about jumping!" Hunter makes sure he doesn't breathe as he drags Ned into the mine shaft and gets him up on his shoulders. He sprints towards the bend until the hydra is out of sight. He feels a draft coming from wherever they are going and hopes he isn't going outside. Finally, Hunter is forced to breathe, having reached his limit. "Ned?"

Ned lets out an indecipherable moan.

Hunter puts him down and looks at him. Even in the dim light from the mine's electric lights he can tell Ned is losing the fight.

Then Ned turns his head to face Hunter and smiles in a sadistic way.

Hunter backs up a few feet.

Ned inspects his shoulder and uses his uninjured hand to grab a piece of bone sticking out from where the shadow crushed him. He pulls the bone clean out and begins chewing on it like a dog.

Hunter moves away as tears roll from his eyes at the sight. "Oh no, not like this."

"Hehe. Hee. Hehehehee" Ned replies. "Not like this," He mimics with a weak voice, but in a disturbingly cheerful tone. "Oh no. Heh. Hehe. Not like this. Hunter does not approve of how I died! Not his choice. What is his ideal choice? I wonder."

Hunter keeps backing away, keeping an eye on Ned.

"Yes, run, run like a pantsless little prick," Ned says as he gawks at Hunter with a sinister evil smile on his face.

Hunter turns around and sprints down the shaft. Not far ahead he passes the point where no electricity is active, but a light shines from the other end after he rounds a bend. When Hunter gets closer to the light at the end of the shaft, he finds a bridge that's been haphazardly repaired with wooden planks nailed together across two long beams. Hunter crosses over and spots a barrel of tools nearby.

He takes the heaviest one, a sixty-pound sledgehammer and starts hitting the beams several times. Each swing moves the repairs closer to falling off. A strong tremor knocks Hunter off his feet, and the whole bridge collapses into the gap. After the bridge falls, Hunter looks up to find Ned sitting cross-legged on the other side.

Ned keeps staring in Hunter's direction with a smile on his face. "Fly to die, die to fly. Fly away way boom," Ned sings in a gruesome tune while flopping his arms from side to side.

"Sorry Ned." Hunter holds back tears as he swings and throws the sledgehammer as hard as he can to try to hit Ned.

The hammer hits him straight in the face, decapitating Ned in the process. Ned's body oozes a bright glowing orange liquid instead of blood. The body evaporates into a transparent state.

Hunter walks to the stairway at the end of the ridge he is on, coming to a cavernous chamber at the top. Once he gets up to the landing, he stops to turn around and say goodbye, but finds the Shadow Figure standing next to Ned's body, which is solid again.

Rogue enters the chamber and glances out the opening in the cliff wall. *This is an amazing view of the valley and the camp. No wonder I didn't find this when I first landed; I wasn't looking for a massive hole in the cliffs.*

"You again?" Hunter asked.

Rogue turns around and sees Hunter. "Oh hey!" *Oh Shit.*

"You're not a figment of my imagination, are you?"

"How can you tell?" Rogue asked. *Wait, where's his shotgun? I can take him in a fistfight. Possibly. Well, I can, but this might suck.*

"Because I see the girl too."

Crystal doesn't have a visceral reaction to Hunter as she did to Albert or Mack. Nonetheless, she stands behind Rogue, grabbing his shoulders.

"It's ok, I won't let him hurt you," Rogue whispers to her. *Man, I'm unoriginal. Said the same thing several times today like the words help somehow.* "Stay behind me until we figure out if he's friend or foe."

"Look, I'm unarmed this time." Hunter raises both of his hands.

"Ok, fine, but you gotta admit, it was a fun charade back there, and you believed me." Rogue can't help smiling. *Alright, time to come clean and find where this goes.* "So where are your buddies?"

"Ha ha, funny. I'll give you points for originality. As for the others, I don't know where they are." Hunter comes off combative at first and changes to becoming solemn. "Except the one who died in the mines a moment ago."

"Albert?" *Strange, what happened to him? Looks like he lived through a nightmare.*

"No, Ned. I think Albert is still in the Camp. Have you run into Mack yet?" Hunter asks.

"The guy in the other mine, Hydra ate him." *I guess he did go traitor on them.*

"No kidding?" Hunter isn't upset to learn of Mack's fate. "Well, this sucks for me. I need a pilot."

"I gather that." Rogue takes a breath and decides to reveal he overheard the grand scheme. "I learned about your plan to use the Hexogen from my cargo to take down the hydra."

Hunter has a wild look on his face, like he got smacked with a frying pan or something. "Hold up, your cargo? Is your name Rogue Whip? How did you learn about the plan?"

"One of the many people named Rogue Whip. While you guys were hallucinating, I could walk about unnoticed. Well, except for the charade I pulled."

Hunter shakes his head and laughs nervously. "Wow, no kidding. You're the wrong guy. Talk about a mix up." The reality hits Hunter. This guy isn't a sixty-year-old composed military spy who is used to adverse conditions. If this stranger Rogue holds a grudge, it won't bode well, but so far he's remaining calm and composed.

"Yeah, I can't wait until we get a chance to put our hands on Albert; I'm going to let Crystal kill him. From what I heard, giving her the chance should not be a problem."

Hunter raises his eyes for a second, and he eases up, this wrong Rogue hasn't lost his cool or nerve. "No, it ain't. Well, morally. And she has every right to be the one to pull the trigger on him."

Crystal looks at Hunter in confusion. Then she recognizes him. She only managed to catch a few glimpses of him in the events leading up to this. She starts clicking frantically.

"What is she saying?" Hunter realizes she will be the one to choose his fate if he can't outrun Rogue.

Rogue tries to focus on her clicking but she is almost too fast. "She says not to trust you because you're one of Albert's guys."

"Former. To be clear, I never did interact with Crystal or her father. Never touched either of them. Unlike his normal goons, I'm a specialty hire. Decided after the hydra got involved that this job isn't worth the pay. I'm a gun for hire, not a super soldier. You pilot this thing and I'll chalk this up to being the highest bidder. Although I did turn traitor on him. So, do you need help?"

STAY AWAY, Crystal clicks while pointing at Hunter.

Rogue scrutinizes his face as he speaks. The man comes off as honest, and seems to be telling the truth about his intent. "Works for me, and, if you can work with us, you may not be under the toxin deep enough to become a dead weight. And make sure you stay away from Crystal. I'll give you fair warning, she is a real ball breaker. Already put a crack in mine."

"Hey, don't joke. I witnessed what happens to people when the hydra's wake becomes an endgame," Hunter says. "And I'll respect her space. The instant I make a wrong move toward her, you can kill me."

"Are you ok with this?" Rogue checks with Crystal. She nods but keeps a scowl on her face. "Deal is sealed."

Hunter looks over the dock with the dirigible. "So, the miners left a ride here, huh."

Rogue turns his attention to the room. A dirigible is indeed docked in the launch bay. *You gotta be kidding me! This is decked out better than most of the fleet I operate. Granted this won't cross the Tradewinds and will be slower than cold syrup. But this aircraft is meant to lift ships out of the water or other insane heavy objects. This thing can lift a fully loaded train.* "This is more than capable of lifting my entire cargo many times over."

"The dude Mack talked to said this is a smaller one." Hunter is impressed with how small it does seem to appear compared to most airships.

"Well, whoever said that doesn't know the first thing about dirigibles. Gas balloon with no gyroscopes, and the best winches money can buy. This thing's designed to transport massive weight, I'm guessing machinery that can't be brought here by train."

"But, that's good, right?" Hunter reacts as though this is the first good news he's gotten all day.

"Yes; although this one is slow moving. If we end up against the wind, we can walk faster than this will go when loaded." But speed isn't important to Rogue. This can do the job.

Crystal folds her arms and goes to the bridge of the cabin, opening the door and walking in. She surveys the entire valley and sees the hydra moving across the camp towards the phosphorus mine. She clicks. SOS.

Rogue checks what she's pointing at. "Now is a very bad time to launch this thing."

"So, we gotta wait for the hydra to go to the far end of the valley?" Hunter asks.

"Yep. In the meantime, you and I will make sure everything is ready to go." Rogue is more than happy to have an extra hand to help out.

"Also, we need to barricade the entrance to the actual mines," says Hunter.

"What for?" *Barricading the mines? Why would we waste time on barricades?*

"Let's say for anyone unfortunate enough to avoid being eaten by the hydra, the hydra's wake deals with those affected in other ways." Hunter replies. "Also, we need sharp weapons. Knives don't require reloading."

Rogue shrugs, begins looking around, and stumbles across a crate labeled SECURITY CONFISCATIONS. "This looks promising." He breaks open the top. Inside he finds a few small revolvers and a short-barrel shotgun. "They don't like anyone keeping weapons around here." He lifts the hilt of a knife to find an elaborate short sword. "Blades indeed don't need reloading." He takes some wide swings, learning that the sword is a balanced weapon, not a ceremonial piece.

"Use your elbow and wrist," Hunter recommends to Rogue from the far end of the platform. He glances down and feels his stomach churn seeing that Ned's body is no longer on the other side of the ravine. "You get more power out of the shoulder, but the other joints in your arm offer maneuverability which outweighs the advantage."

"You mean like this?" Rogue takes a fencing stance and makes some lightning quick parrying moves with the skill of a professional.

"You're familiar with sword fighting?" Hunter asks.

"Took a few classes back in my grade-school years. Mom was a famous expert fencer, so I didn't have much choice. But to gauge balance, a full swings help." Rogue feels a sense of pride, while having a sword in his hand. "How about you?" Rogue stops to admire the rising sun as dawn breaks the horizon.

"I'm familiar with the basics and I'm good enough to be able to run away." Hunter can tell Rogue isn't an amateur.

Rogue chuckles at the remark. In the distance he can make out a faint, mechanical noise. "Hey, are you guys expecting company?"

"No. Why?" Hunter soon hears the noise too. "The hell?"

Crystal comes out of the cabin, hands Rogue a pair of binoculars and points towards the upper right corner of the skyport bay.

Rogue looks. "More of Albert's men are coming, another set of the same aircraft you came in on." He hands Hunter the binoculars.

"Two helicopters. Must be a back up team in case Albert wasn't back in time. He's rich. Affording these rescue parties isn't a problem. I understand Albert well enough to say we should expect them to be very well armed."

"Poor suckers have no clue what they're flying into." Rogue adds.

5: LINES IN
THE SAND

Albert can now see the entire camp, including the station. In the lobby, he reads the note. "Most interesting." Then he discovers the key imprint in the dust, telling him a key is missing. Moving slowly and quietly, he approaches the first room, which is the only one with a doorknob to appear recently used. He swings the door open and runs inside with his hand under his suit vest. "So now!" he shouts while barging in. Then he glances around and finds no one here. "Empty. How anticlimactic."

He searches the kitchen area to find the pantry is well stocked. "Well, well, so Rogue Whippy keeps a secret, does he? A secret base in a Hydra's territory.

Disgusting," he says with a grimace and makes his way to the bed. "Oh, you old fool. You cannot escape me forever. Hydra or not, I will find you. I will most certainly find you, and when I do, I will hack off your prick and have a chef cook up a unique dish and feed your flesh to your own daughter. And I will proceed to do so many more gruesome things to you both," he says as he dances around the room.

He peers at Rogue's kit lying in the corner. "Oh, let us become acquainted with one another on a more personal level, shall we?"

Albert opens the kit and dumps everything out on the table. Then he throws the pack down and stomps on it. After taking a moment to briefly glance over the contents, he isn't amused. "This is nothing like what I expected. As though he is not a spy of any kind. No tools of the trade, weapons, or ammunition. Strong dedication to being convincing."

Then he spots Rogue's identification papers. When he opens them, he finds the face of the ghost he encountered yesterday. "Well now wait, hold on. No, this is incorrect. None of this information is correct. This is not the Rogue Whip I seek to kill. My informant did not dare screw this up! The incompetent imbecile! When I return, I will have his whole body carved for plant food as he takes the current place of my enemy! This blunder has cost me too much to contain."

The reality hits Albert. They chased down the wrong person. He sighs in disgust. "Well, he is *a* Rogue Whip. Not my rival, but he will have to suffice. Failure. I must analyze this colossal failure of information. A failure! If the information was more accurate, then I would have avoided the jeopardy of succumbing to a hydra. I am so angry. I am actually starting to speak using commoner slang!"

He searches through the rest of the stuff and discovers the tea collection. "My, my, this fellow has excellent taste. Maybe I cannot hate him as much now. Elvador's Diamond label tea? I daresay I may come to terms with forgetting the accident with this very fine fellow altogether. This tea cannot be purchased in stores and is reserved only for royalty and the most elite society. A simple cup is legendary for calming the nerves. This pilot is providing me a grander service than my own men do."

He hears the sound of helicopters approaching. "Ah, my search party," Albert says with a giddy tone and a smile on his face. "I must compose myself. I have been on the brink of madness for a whole day now. A perfect cup of tea should assist with the matter." He proceeds to boil water using the wood stove.

Outside on the airstrip two helicopters land on the opposite end from where the first two are. The middle doors of both swing open and two teams of heavily armed men come out. The helicopters wind down as the engines are turned off, and the pilots immediately jump out to begin post-flight checks.

"Find Lord Albert and wait for his orders," one of the men with an oversize hat carrying the biggest assault rifle, shouts.

"Captain, I found him." The man next to him points at the window where Albert is waving at them.

"Indeed, I must be going soft on you guys. Head into the camp station and await further orders. Pilots, keep the choppers hot," the captain orders.

Hunter, Rogue, and Crystal all watch with binoculars from the skyport inside the cliff. "Those are some major-league toys," says Rogue. These helicopters have rocket launchers and turret guns. "Special forces assault weapons and the works. They came ready for war."

"I know this group. Fireteam Dark. Albert's personal infiltration team. Did some work with them. Of all the people under his organization the most reasonable ones came down. We might be able to convince them to help us bomb the hydra. Their captain is a bit of a loose cannon though." Hunter identifies Captain Westly from the obnoxiously large hat. "Come to think of it, they were with us when we shot you down, Albert waved them off because of the storm.

Must've gone back to refuel and used Mt. Hade to find our location."

"A dozen new fresh meals the hungry hydra gets to eat. They'll be lucky if they turn around and leave." *I hope they leave. If they do, then we can cancel this whole bombing run and use this dirigible to go straight to the mining hub and go to a real hospital. Deal with Crystal's disappointment later after our lives are safe.*

Almost on cue, a tremor is felt.

HYDRA FOOD, Crystal clicks.

"Whelp, least we got a front row seat to the entertainment." Hunter chuckles.

"No plans on defecting back again?" Rogue turns to face Hunter.

"Hah, it'd be a waste of time. The moment this hydra comes, they will turn on him on their own." Hunter's expression is confident.

"It was at the lake in the valley a minute ago. With the injuries from its fight with the harpy bear I doubt it got far and helicopters are a great noisy dinner bell. We'll have to find out how your prediction pans out." *Why do I feel like we won't be leaving until we kill the hydra and Albert? This is insane. We aren't in any condition to fight anything.*

Half of the men assemble in the lounge while the others secure the perimeter. Shortly afterward a small tremor shakes the ground.

"Whoa." One of them reacts to the tremor.

"Just a tremor, Pattel." The captain smirks at the soldier.

Then another tremor, and another, each growing stronger.

"Quakes don't shake this way sir," another says.

They are all up and looking around.

"Cover the windows and doors. Something might just be passing through," the captain says in a stalwart tone.

"Captain Westly," Albert says as he enters the room.

"Lord Albert is present!" one of the men proclaims before Albert can say another word.

"Those are no mere tremors, my dear Westly. A four-headed hydra lives in this valley. Welcome to Camp Tor."

"A hydra?" The captain's smirk turns into concern.

"Get your asses in here!" the two men in the lobby shouts together at everyone outside.

"Close those doors!" Albert demands. "Lock them! No one must breathe!"

Rogue and Hunter watch the hydra approach the camp from above the phosphorus mine entrance. Several of the soldiers start shooting. "Well, so much for getting help. They'll have to survive first."

The hydra roars at the group surrounding the station. Many of them split off and head in different directions, going to the forest and other buildings. The monster makes short work of those who try to reach the office. The soldiers fire their weapons at the monster's faces. Using each of its heads, it snaps them up. It attacks a man trying to escape through the lounge door.

Another soldier runs off into the valley and aims a huge weapon at it. When the weapon fires, a flurry of grenades is unleashed, exploding on impact. Smoke billows around the hydra's body and at first it seems stunned. But then it turns all four heads towards the tiny soldier and they roar in unison. The soldier is reloading when a head lunges towards him.

After the head swallows the grenadier, the sound of a helicopter catches its attention. The weapons of the aircraft are aimed at the wounded leg. A quick-thinking pilot inside uses onboard machine guns attached to the helicopter to attack. A few rockets are also fired. One of them explodes on the wound where the harpy bear tore into the leg. The explosion causes a shower of blood to spurt out.

"Now that's a great shot." Rogue throws his fist in the air.

"Hell yeah!" Hunter matches Rogue's enthusiasm.

With a roar of pain, the monster moves to shelter its bad leg from the attacking helicopter, which is firing its turret gun at the bad leg. The soldiers hiding by the refinery start firing as well. The helicopter's mounted guns make no obvious impact on the animal as it raises its tail, revealing giant retractable spikes the length of its body. It sweeps the new helicopters off the airstrip into the valley with a swing of its tail, destroying them both and killing the pilot.

The other pilot runs toward the forest to join another three men. The hydra is right behind them, emitting massive plumes of the wake, which covers the ground in a thick layer. A moment passes before the echoes of gunshots and small explosions mix with the hydra's roars. Then the gunfire slows down, until only one weapon is firing. Then silence. A loud series of triumphant roars fills the air.

The victorious hydra returns to camp and roars at the two helicopters the first group, with Lord Albert, came down in. After nothing happens, the curious hydra rubs a head against one. The motion knocks the vehicle over. The beast realizes they're nothing more than machines, and loses interest. It turns its focus to the station and lets out more ear-splitting roars. Even from the skyport they are earsplittingly loud.

"Damn, they pissed the monster off." Hunter stops watching when Crystal joins them.

"They did." Rogue gets up. "Alright, we should do something."

"Keep out of sight." Albert hides behind the reception desk. "This thing is patient. Hours long patient."

"This explains why you didn't come back to the manor." Westly can't believe they flew into this trap.

"Who is here? Sound off one at a time, please." Albert wants to know who he can rely on.

"Pattel!" the black man by the lounge door replies. Pattel is a younger recruit, and newer member of Albert's security detail. He is tall and thin, and carries a simple assault rifle. To his left is Walker a rugged white man with brown hair and beard in his mid-thirties. He comes off as the typical soldier type.

Before leaving the helicopters, Walker put on a mask used for combat in polluted areas. He suggested everyone do the same, but no one listened at the time. The soldier grimaces through the mask. "Walker, sir." He is armed with a light machine gun and has mangled scars on his arms. His modified uniform accommodates extra ammunition and tactical equipment of various kinds. Walker glances behind him to the burly soldier carrying a sniper rifle.

"Thebes," the sniper calls out. He is a short white guy with a few broken teeth and an accent with over-pronounced vowels.

"Stoutarm." one of the two men in the lobby replies. He has light brown skin and reddish-brown hair, carrying a regular assault rifle. He is fresh off a discharge from a combat police force, for medical reasons. In his late twenties, he is a body builder. He joined the unit a little before Pattel.

"Jades." the last one announces. He is heavier set than the rest of the group and older. He is the only member present who was part of the team when Westly became a captain for Albert.

"And Gort's team was all outside. And the two pilots, damn." Westly assumes everyone outside is dead.

"Picked a real fine day for a picnic, sir. I love our surprise guest;

very classy and original," Thebes jokes, causing some chuckles.

"I will light your ass on fire, throw you out the window to amuse myself, and feed you to the beast." Westly is in no mood for jokes. The situation is more urgent than Thebes is crediting.

"He would probably survive, since he tastes like hot flaming shit. Smells like it, anyway." Jades makes a few of them chuckle again.

Westly rolls his eyes and shakes his head. How did he allow so many idiots to come with him? "Go fuck yourselves; outside." The men all react to the insult like children. Given how they just lost half the unit outside, Westly thinks this behavior is disrespectful. "You assholes laugh it up while our friends outside were just murdered. The basic human fuck is wrong with you? We suffered a major attack in case you missed the last two minutes. No, really; I will kill every one of you myself for the disrespect."

"In all seriousness, Lord Albert, how many people from your first team are still alive?" Thebes changes his tone after picking up on Westly's unusual intolerance for banter.

"I have not the faintest idea. I assume most of them are dead by now. Lads, the legends about the hydra's wake are true. The toxin will make you madder than the fairy tales describe." His uncharacteristic tone makes it clear he fears this animal.

The team is silent. "That's not funny, My Lord." Albert's fearful voice shakes Westly to the core.

"No, it is not. To be quite frank this place is proving to be an inescapable death sentence. My men outside have learned this to be true. And I say this to level with each of you, this is a foolish place to come." Albert takes a moment to look all of them in the eye as he speaks.

"I don't understand one major detail here. Why doesn't that thing smash the buildings down? When they're outside this hydra doesn't play around." Hunter walks over to the dirigible cabin, seeking out Rogue.

Rogue is rummaging among some equipment in the confiscation crates and comes across an old flare gun. "This might work."

Crystal pulls her hand out of another crate and holds up a flare designed with a delayed burn and a loud whistle. Perfect for distracting giant animals without alerting them to where you are.

"I'll bet we can trick the hydra into getting off their case. Let's just hope it doesn't give them a false sense of hope." Rogue said. He grabs the flare from her and tries to undo the barrel, which is stubborn. But he manages to load the flare after using more muscle.

He walks to the edge of the skyport. The ground is around three hundred feet below. He aims the flare gun at an angle towards the valley and pulls the trigger. The gun makes a small thump. A tiny trail of smoke shows the flare's trajectory vanishing as quickly as it appeared. Then a bright red flare erupts in the sky much further out than Rogue expects.

The popping sound is followed by a screaming whistling noise, that grabs the Hydra's attention. It breaks off from the station to investigate where the flare landed.

"Well, well, there are other survivors." Westly spots a flare through the windows on the lobby side of the building.

Pattel opens the door to get a better view.

"No!" Albert screams.

But it's too late, the pale blue mist makes its way inside.

"Do not breathe, whatever you do," Albert says. Then he discovers more coming from the other side as well. The two soldiers had wanted to check for any survivors of the attack and see the wreckage of the helicopters better. "You poor fools." Albert shakes his head in disappointment.

"What should we expect from this hydra's wake?" Walker is glad he kept his mask on the entire time.

"Severe hallucinations, and trans-dimensional paranormal effects have been my humble experience here." Albert's explanation sounds like fantasy even to himself, as he speaks. "Also, those survivors you mentioned? Rogue Whip's daughter is on the loose out here, or dead. I have no idea. Also a man who shares the name Rogue Whip, but is in fact not our target, turns out to be who we shot down yesterday."

"Are you saying this entire situation is because of faulty information?" Westly can't fathom the idea.

Albert switches tones to his usual self, full of rage. "To top this off, I am robbed of the pleasure of taking my revenge on Gort. This is all his fault! The incompetent fool! He led me to a CEO Rogue Whip, thirty years younger than the spy Rogue Whip. The man is an unrelated individual who owns a shipping company, and I had him shot out of the sky and chased him here. This whole shit show is a misunderstanding and an unforgivable failure of intelligence. But the younger Rogue has perfect taste in tea, so I refuse to hate him."

Everyone on the team gawks at Albert with their jaws dropped. "What's the escape plan?" Westly gives Albert a long stare.

"Well, if you can locate the remaining helicopters, we can use those to evacuate. But I also need to verify that this businessman pilot will not go on to expose me. I must be certain this accident does not leave this valley. Additionally, the daughter of the Rogue I wish to maim and torture, may still be alive. Find her, so I can assure she is properly abused to a slow and agonizing death. Only after accomplishing those objectives, will I be willing to leave."

"I hope your ears caught the details, fellas. Fishing trip dead or alive, dead by the hydra, alive otherwise before we can punch our tickets out of here," Westly calls out.

"With that said, I am aware Dusty is dead. I am unaware of the fates of Ned or Mack." Albert continues. He then faces Westly. "If you come across Hunter, our agreement is to be terminated post-haste." He kept his voice quiet enough for only Westly to hear.

Westly nods. "Consider it done."

Pattel, Walker, and Thebes all study a map Walker pulls out of his pocket. "Camp Tor features two mines, a gemstone and a phosphorus. Half a dozen barracks, general store, refinery, office, and a couple other generic buildings. These mines are old and huge." Walker reads aloud for everyone's benefit.

"You three sweep the mines; we'll investigate the buildings." Westly points at the men gawking at the map.

Rogue keeps watching as three men leave the lounge and make a bee line for the phosphorus mine.

"Did the stunt work?" Hunter gives Rogue some coffee he found by the break area of the skyport.

"The hydra will think so." Rogue takes the cup and blows some steam away. One of the four heads is staring towards the camp but it stays out in the valley. *I can tell from here it had no expectation of needing to fight. A surprised hydra, maybe shocked, can't tell. But either way, damned thing sure fights like a weapon.* "Three of them are heading over to the other mine. And I couldn't count how many are inside the building."

"I counted six." Hunter spots Crystal inspecting the coffee he set down on a crate for her. He keeps his distance. "I'm sure I counted only six. The ones who got munched on dropped their weapons. Those will help."

Crystal picks up her cup, takes a sip, and spits her coffee out, walking off to find sugar. I HATE BLACK COFFEE, Crystal clicks while she walks, getting Rogue's attention.

"Yeah, the ground is littered with guns. Still, we can't launch until there's nothing to pose a threat to the dirigible." Rogue is quick to point out while taking a generous sip. *This coffee is a bit strong.* "Man, this stuff will wake the dead."

Hunter chuckles. "I can go down and check if any of the survivors are potential allies to our cause. Many of them will not handle the hydra's wake well."

"And if not, you have them and a hydra to contend with. Having a firefight breaking out isn't the best idea." Rogue sounds skeptical despite Hunter's confidence.

"You're right, but the other option is to camp up here and let the toxin do its thing. These guys aren't creative enough to escape its wrath, but who knows how long that will take?" Hunter is sure he spotted Walker in the group, which means he has allies down there.

"Four leaving the station. Albert is among them. That can't be good." Rogue said. "The hydra also destroyed every helicopter except the one I found the ignition plate for, which I accidentally left in the station. As long as it stays intact, we will have a ride to Heart."

"Let's hope they didn't find the plate." Hunter can't shake the sense of being useless up here. He scans the valley and spots something. "So, as for planting this bomb, there's a pond by that cluster of trees to the south. Might be a decent place to set the trap."

After searching for a moment, Rogue spots the place Hunter is talking about. "That's perfect. We can lure its heads there and force the body to pass over the bomb. Now we gotta move everything into place. Nice find!"

"Moving ten tons of stuff isn't going to be an easy task."

"That's the easy part. My dirigible is equipped with a military-grade hazard cargo container. No way a simple fire got through. We'll fly this dirigible to the crash site, then use the chain system to hook up my cargo hold, and haul it to our spot. Then we lower the cargo. We'll need time to prepare a detonation system. That will be the difficult part. They don't ship Hexogen in a way that makes it easy to turn it into an active bomb for obvious reasons." He tries to recall how the Hexogen is packaged.

"You want to prep a bomb in the field? That's not viable either." Hunter is right; doing so is suicide.

"Well, we can build a container in this cargo hold and make a more controlled ignition system. Either way, we'll have to open all the containers and dump the powder into the new one we build. But between you and me, I gotta tell ya, that's going to be very time-consuming."

"Ok, what if we take our time, bringing the bomb here to assemble in a way that makes sense?" Hunter's suggestion sounds reasonable.

"That's a good idea, but if we bring it all here and you're wrong about those men down there, it's not going to end well for us. I think the hydra is going to make this as difficult as possible too," Rogue answers. Then a lot of clicking behind them makes them look back.

NO BRING HERE, Crystal clicks as she walks over to them with a fixed cup of coffee.

"So, what's the next best option?" Hunter crosses his arms and stares out over the valley again.

"Well, this thing has a small crew cabin. We can stock up with food and supplies, and take our time during the periods of daylight until we're finished making the bomb at the crash site. Problem is we'll be sitting ducks, and anything territorial will easily take us down. So, we need weapons to defend the dirigible."

"If we are taken down, we're done," Hunter said, cutting Rogue off. "So, we're short on manpower. I'll keep watching for anyone in their camp that I can guarantee is willing to help out."

"I don't like the plan, but yeah, I'll admit we're out of options that don't rely on everything going right for several days straight." Rogue glances over at Crystal, who is upset at the idea of more of Albert's men being around. "This is the only way to kill Albert and this hydra in one go," he assures her.

She nods, understanding the three of them can't carry out this major operation on their own.

Albert peeks out the window as the hydra moves its fourth head away, spotting prey moving across the valley. "About time the monster decided to give us some space. We need to leave this place to accomplish my missions."

As he and Westly walk out the lounge door, Westly stops and looks around. "What the hell?"

Stoutarm and Jades follow and close the door behind them. The bewildered expression on Westly's face turns to panic. "Boss?"

Jades examines the unnerved look on Westly's face.

"What happened to the buildings?" Westly is horrified by the sight before him. He turns around and discovers the station is the same state. Nothing but a charred frame.

"Let me guess, charred frames?" Albert is amused by Westly's expression, remembering how he, Mack, and Hunter felt when they landed.

"Yes, but how is this possible?" Westly walks through where a door stood less than a second ago, as if it never existed. "This is unacceptable." He spins around again, he finds himself alone.

Albert shakes his head as Westly realizes he can't locate anyone. "Damn, the captain is gone to us." He turns to face Jades and Stoutarm. "Well, what do the two of you see?"

"Jades, Stoutarm? Lord Albert?" Westly shouts as he wanders around the area. "Where'd you lunatics go! Guys, sound off! This isn't funny!"

Stoutarm walks over and waves his hand in front of his face. Westly steps forward and walks through Stoutarm. "What the hell! What the goddamned hell?"

Jades steps back. "What the fuck!?" He can hardly believe what he just witnessed with his own eyes.

"This is the kind of shenanigans the hydra's wake is putting us through constantly." Albert contemplates how normal the paranormal is becoming to him.

Stoutarm and Jades exchange a glance and look at Albert. "What do we see? Good question." Stoutarm turns the safety off on his weapon.

"Ain't about what we see anymore," Jades says, as the click from his rifle indicates he has turned his safety off too. The two men raise their assault rifles toward Albert.

"We didn't sign up to come get screwed over." Stoutarm makes sure to aim between Albert's eyes. Before either can pull the trigger, a loud roar distracts them; they both look over their shoulders to check on what the hydra is doing.

Albert uses the distraction and runs, hoping he will vanish from their sights since they are now traitors. "You boys crossed me. Not the wisest idea." He looks up to see the station vanished for him as well. "Well, thanks for the tea, dear lad. I suppose I will join the group in the gemstone mine."

"Welcome to the greatest mind fuck you'll ever experience." Hunter smiles, watching Westly walk through Stoutarm with the binoculars. "That's what I hoped would happen, Albert's lost his men's loyalty."

"How so?" Rogue picks up his binoculars and checks out what's happening. He watches Albert sprinting away from the others.

"The weird stuff is just getting started, and they were quick to turn weapons on him." Hunter let out a chuckle.

"Sure didn't take much. Alright, go ahead and do what you can to bring them up here. But before you do, can you help with these platform ties?" *Well I'll be damned! Hunter knows what he was talking about.*

Pattel enters the entrance of the phosphorus mine first. "Clear."

Thebes comes up from behind, taps his shoulder, and moves deeper into the shaft, walking straight through the stairs to the raised platform on the loading station inside.

"What the hell?" Pattel and Walker said at the same time.

"What?" Thebes turns around to face the two behind him.

"You walked through the platform like a magic trick. You've got a wooden platform up to your waist." Walker walks over to try to figure out what is going on.

"There isn't anything here." Thebes gives them a confused look.

"The hell there ain't." Pattel shoots back.

"You two are trippin' or something." Thebes shakes his head.

Walker tries to walk over to Thebes but hits the wood and trips. "Shit."

"What the hell!?" Thebes starts backing away when he sees Walker lying in midair a few feet off the ground.

Pattel walks up the steps to the platform and right past Thebes, who is gawking at them. "Guess to you I can walk on air, right?"

"That's some bullshit." Thebes rubs his eyes and paces in a circle. "Am I going crazy?" He closes his eyes then reopens them to see the wooden platform. "I. What?" He puts his arm through the wood and tries to grab it but can't.

"Well, Albert did say if we got hit with the hydra's wake, we'll be running into paranormal stuff." Walker speaks in a composed and calm voice. "So, he's not losing his mind; we have a loading platform here, and he doesn't. Let's deal with the fact that this is the way reality works for now."

"No, I see it now! It's like I'm a ghost, or this wood is an illusion or. What the what? How the hell are you so calm about this?" Thebes is freaking out.

"I've been to these mining camps before, and I've seen how people stranded in this forest suffer some adverse fates. Many vanish in the first week or so of us coming back. That's how miners first learned to operate on a very short schedule. The miners understand a lot about the Hydra, but the conglomerates tend to keep details quiet." Walker does his best to speak slow enough not to overwhelm them with detail. "I've spent a few winters here before. But that's over a decade or so ago in my younger days."

"So, this hydra's wake thing. How do you recover? What's the cure?" Thebes never imagined anything like this exists.

Pattel jumps on the wood. "It's definitely solid wood here." He keeps jumping a few times falls through. "What the hell?"

"Hah! Now you have no wood! No wood for you!" Thebes points and laughs.

"Wait, if that happened at random like that, what if it becomes solid while I'm still standing in it?" Pattel asks.

Thebes screams and runs to the side out of the platform. "I don't wanna find out!" He trips on the railway track. "Ouch."

Pattel looks up at Walker, who shrugs. "Probably best to not find out right?"

"I don't think so," Walker answers.

"Please tell me there's a cure for this!" Thebes shouts.

"I've never heard of anyone coming back from this. People aren't found too often, nor do they survive long enough for miners to return. It's rare when anyone does, and I've only ever seen three people who were found at the start of the mining season. I can't recall what happened to them," Walker explains.

"Is that why you chose to wear a mask?" Thebes regrets making fun of Walker over that back in the helicopter now.

"Hence, why I made the recommendation to everyone on the flight down."

Pattel nods. "I'm sure glad I listened."

"Stoutarm and Jades wore theirs too, I think." Thebes tries to calm down, stops pacing and controls his breathing. "So, Westly and I will be enjoying this fun house bullshit?"

"You only put yours on after we left the station. So it's not going to do you much good now. Most filters only last a few days before they become useless." Walker says to Pattel. He doesn't like breaking the bad news. "It only takes one breath."

As they go deeper into the mine, they hear a faint hoo-hah from outside. "On top of a hydra we have those to worry about too?" Pattel aims his weapon at the entrance.

"Looks to be the case. Gotta love the Deep Forest Province." Thebes stares at his rifle and wonders if he can fight back against anything trying to attack him. "All sorts of aggressive animals in this place."

"At least we have the firepower to handle this animal." Walker motions for them to move further.

The ground shakes harder than when the hydra is near.

"I vote not being underground when tremors are shaking everything," Pattel says as he turns and heads for the mine entrance at a jogging pace.

Stoutarm and Jades reach the gemstone mine. "I don't like how the mines are our only cover from the stupid hydra." Jades checks over his shoulder to make sure the area is clear.

"Shouldn't have taken the masks off when we did." Stoutarm is pissed at himself for thinking Walker was playing a prank.

"Well, who the hell figured Walker of all people knew what he was talking about? Superstitious bastard." Jades aims his rifle down the mine shaft as they enter.

"Stop complaining. A hydra is not the only man-eating animal out here." Stoutarm shoulders his weapon and moves up next to Jades.

Jades gives Stoutarm the middle finger and walks forward a few steps into the mine. "Spooky as hell in here." They turn on the lights attached to their rifles.

"All I know is, if I get my hands on Albert, he's a gutted man." Stoutarm kicks at some burned firewood on the floor. "I can't believe he shot down the wrong guy and chased him into this mess."

"Are you saying that only because we got dragged in, or because working for Albert is ass?"

"Both are acceptable reasons. I'll miss the pay though."

Jades looks behind them out of habit and sees a shotgun floating in the air. "Shit's getting weirder here." Then he aims his rifle and fires at the shotgun.

The bullet hits the shotgun but doesn't cause any damage, ricocheting into the wall.

Albert found Hunter's shotgun where the refinery was before

entering the mine. As he gets a few steps in, the shotgun feels like it's hit by something. He can't see anyone, so he shoulders the weapon. "Whose there?" He glances up and down the shaft.

"Please tell me you're seeing this." Jades backs up from the floating shotgun, which is now pointing and moving around as if someone shouldered it and is now searching around.

"Well, you don't see that every day." Stoutarm takes a closer look at the weapon waving around.

"I shot the stock and it didn't leave so much as a mark." Jades is surprised and confused.

"Wait, isn't that Hunter's custom?" Stoutarm asks, after the gun passes between them.

"Hunter? The mercenary Albert adds on from time to time?" Jades lets out a sigh, and lowers his weapon.

"That's the one." Stoutarm turns his safety back on.

"Why would he be going deeper into the mine?" Jades can't help but wonder.

"I'm not interested enough to find out." Stoutarm said, sitting down against the wall. "Ah dammit, which way is out?"

After walks to a chamber "This mine is growing on me." Albert finally calms down and hears something making squishing noises coming his way.

"Betrayed the Lord he did," a voice whispers.

"Ned?" Albert calls out. "Ned, dear lad, are you there?" He runs down the shaft, hoping the pilot is alive.

Upon entering the chamber ahead, Albert doesn't find anyone or anything. "Must not be able to see him." The room is small, and resembles a junction for going to different faces. Rows of benches are lined up in front of a wooden board. He sits down on one of the benches, hoping not to fall through. When he doesn't, he feels a wave of relief.

"All I wanted to do this week is enjoy my pastime of torturing those who do me wrong. Is that too much to ask?" Albert asks the empty room rhetorically.

"No," the whisper replies.

Albert doesn't hear the response. "I take delight in watching the reactions of people when I destroy them slowly and while they are awake to feel every experiment. Experience my unique process, and very much pay witness to their demise. Some people call me evil, convoluted, and a rather creative array of unpleasantries. But the narcotic sensation that resembles a high I enjoy from these heinous acts are worth more than they comprehend to me."

"Alby," another whisper comes.

Again, Albert fails to react. "And I must admit this: women are fun to torture, but they ruin everything by making my pleasure end too quickly. Hell, I find breaking men to be far more desirable. Taking their strength and pride and will away. It is more satisfying than the copious amounts of repetitive and unoriginal things one does to women. Women understand to give in, and the limits of how much fun I receive is based upon my own creativity. I compare this to playing with myself, and after the first few moments the intimacy gets dull. But I love seeing expressions on the face of every man when I show them their hacked-off reproductive member. They are engaging and creative in their responses, which adds genuine value to the whole experience."

The Shadow Figure looms behind Albert during his monologue.

"Wait, who is here?" Albert feels a presence. He glances around in a panic, but finds nothing. Then he looks down. A head rolls up and stops between his legs. "A severed head? How macabre." He sounds unimpressed, and the shadow figure doesn't react.

"Pick me up." Ned's voice echoes in the chamber around Albert.

"Fine then. Whose skull am I in the gracious presence of?" He picks up the head by the hair.

"Hello Alby!" Ned's head says with a wheezing high-pitched and scratchy voice.

"Oh, you. You must be dead I assume." Albert raises an eyebrow as if he has just picked up a piece of trash.

"Well don't come off so dull or bored about it. How rude." Ned is insulted.

"You must understand, out of all the things I can hallucinate, you are not exactly scary." Albert places the head on the bench nearby.

"Oh, I am not here to scare you, but to warn you. Hunter seeks to kill the hydra, and use you as bait to lure the foul beast to its death."

"Now that, dear boy, is juicier information than your dripping gooey neckline." Albert smirks. "Can you bleed away from my suit, please." Albert places the head further away. "Acceptable."

"Well, if the hydra don't die, you end up eaten or turn into a possession. I will admit the idea sounds like a perfect plan C. Fact is, Hunter is the only one of us, aside from you, still alive from our group."

"Damn, Crystal is dead?"

"Well, I should think so. You left her naked and tied up like a simple snack."

"That hydra keeps eating the people I want to murder," Albert says.

"The nerve of the stupid beast. Animals should know their place," Ned replies in a sympathetic voice.

"How does the buffoon intend to kill this hydra?"

"Well, it's good you're planted on your ass because I'm going to spill a lot of things you aren't aware of," Ned said as his eyes widen, and a menacing smile forms slowly on his face. Then his head starts to roll, Albert catches him and holds him in place.

"I may respect you more in death than I ever did in your miserable life." Albert makes sure to hold Ned's head away from his body to prevent his suit from getting blood on it.

Hunter observes several of the items in the skyport starting to vanish around him. "Not now. Not again. Hey, Rogue!"

Rogue walks right past him and approaches the cargo hold of the dirigible. "Oh cool; he got all the ties loosened perfectly. Hey, Hunter! You still here?"

"I'm right he-. Forget this. Apparently, I'm hydra woke again. Huh, hydra woke, that's a good one. Wait a sec, if this happens to people, I wonder if the other animals that aren't eaten and manage to somehow survive end up the same way?" Every time he blinks, more things vanish. Then he closes his eyes for a moment and reopens them to an empty room. Even the blockade to the stairway is gone.

"Ok, this is a problem again." Hunter walks the path Rogue and Crystal used to arrive and follows the shaft. He decides to leave the gemstone mine for now, until the wake affects him less. "I would love to understand why the paranormal bits are stronger and weaker at these random times."

He comes around a sharp bend, almost running into the Shadow Figure. Hunter's heart starts pounding hard enough to be audible. The figure stays still as the shadows on the walls return. They all point further down.

Hunter shimmies past the figure, doing his best not to touch it on the way. When he gets to the end, he locates a place where an elevator should be. "How do I get down without breaking my neck?"

He feels a hand on his shoulder, but before he can turn around, he gets shoved off the edge and begins falling. He screams until he hit the ground. To his surprise, he only feels a thud, no pain. No broken bones, as if plummeting a hundred feet to the ground has no effect on him. After a moment he looks above him. He can't spot the platform above him. "Ah, crap. What happened?" There's a noise behind him, and he turns to find someone approaching the clearing.

Westly swears he heard someone screaming. "Hello?" He approaches the small clearing from around the cliff-side trail.

"Westly?" Hunter gets to his feet and brushes himself off.

"You!?" Westly smiles. This makes Albert's wish easy. "So, you're not dead."

"Well, not entirely yet. Surprised the fall didn't do me in." When Hunter looks back up, Westly has his rifle pointing straight at him. "The hell is this?"

"Fun story. Albert ordered a hit on you before you guys left. Figures you are taking the freedom of being a freelancer too seriously for his contracts." Westly is going to enjoy every moment of killing Hunter.

"No big secret. I haven't taken him out yet, and he didn't have me done in while Mack was around." Hunter stays calm and tries to reason with Westly.

"Well, I'll be more than happy to rectify your failed suicide attempt." Westly turns off the safety and puts his finger on the trigger.

"Pull that trigger and you'll never escape this place. I guarantee it." Hunter doesn't even raise his hands.

"I know we can't deal with a hydra but I'm sure we will find a way out. We'll lose a few people in the process but that's the way things go." Westly decides to humor Hunter with this final conversation.

"Funny; knowledge is far more powerful than guns here. Do me in and you lose some critical need to know intelligence. Which does alter the circumstances on the ground. A drastic enough alteration that could provide you and your men with a real opportunity to survive this endeavor long enough to rescue Albert." Hunter opens his arms as if daring Westly to shoot.

"Hunter, Albert draws the lines in the sand." Westly can't shake a funny feeling about Hunter's bluff; considering for a moment to hear him out.

"Albert doesn't have a way to kill this hydra so we can escape."

"And you're less likely to be able to pull such a feat off." Westly tries to convince himself that Hunter is bluffing, but the expression on Hunter's face shows he's serious. "You're confident in this plan of yours?"

"Did Albert mention that the dirigible we shot down has ten tons of Hexogen in its cargo hold?" Hunter asks.

Westly lowers his rifle a little. "He may have failed to mention some minor details." He stares out at the valley. Westly is familiar with the explosive applications of Hexogen and is quick to put the pieces together. "Impressive. I suspect you need assistance moving the material somewhere you can lure the hydra, and make your kill using an improvised explosive device. Simple plan, bad logistics. Where is the crash site?"

"Forty miles behind me down the Backfin Cliffs. A big smoldering spot at the base marks the wreckage. You can follow the cliff face all the way to the cargo." Hunter points his thumb over his shoulder while talking.

"And the lure?" Westly puts away his weapon; Hunter's plan surprises him.

"Flares. The test shot I fired got you guys out of a tight spot." Hunter knows better than to talk about using anyone as bait because Westly would force Hunter into this role.

"It sure did go after the flare like a dog to the sound of a whistle," Westly says nodding. "So, given we're still supposed to kill you, what incentive do you have for coming to us for help?"

"I help you guys escape. You give me an hour's head start when we arrive at Heart." Hunter extends a hand.

"Gotta admit, your plan sounds solid to me. I guess I can agree to those terms." Westly shakes Hunter's hand. "I might even tell Albert you are why we all survived."

"So, you understand, you die, or you end, in a state of empty misery," Ned finishes.

Albert is distraught by the details Ned has revealed. "This news almost makes me a willing participant in the demise of this damn thing." Shadows begin to line the walls. "These are the souls you mentioned previously, I assume."

"Yes, and they are willing to let you be, if you commit to assisting us by killing the foul beast." Ned replies. "But our current master would be most displeased, so their will is limited, as is mine."

"The duration of my life seems to have little meaning now. I dread feeling as though my existence is lacking purpose. To be the worm on the hook in my end. Is this my very fate?" Albert rubs tears of agony from his eyes. The emotion is a new sensation for him. After a few moments of silence, he stares at the Shadow Figure before him. "Specter of the beast, why are you here?"

"He is the alternate dimension manifestation of the hydra's mind. He controls these souls to an extent. And those worthy of corruption for more corporeal uses such as myself. My master is not happy I told you as much as I did. But you're crying, and it very much appreciates that you are feeling pain, I am of more use to him than his other resurrected puppet who is on the loose." Ned's head continues.

The figure does not move, but projects a shadow on the wall growing four heads. Albert watches as the shadows of the souls move away from the figure's projection. They fear it. The lights fade out and the mine turns dark. "Bloody hell."

Then a pair of lights shine at the end of the shaft closest to him; two small bright lights, and the sound of footsteps.

Stoutarm and Jades walk in with their rifles up. The two walk in step with each other, moving quickly and quietly. They reach the chamber and check the several adjacent shafts. "Which way to the Stanley Pit and skyport?" Jades pulls out a map and holds it in front of the light. The map is too faded to read.

"I don't have the faintest idea anymore. We're lost in this labyrinth." Stoutarm turns an about face and keeps an eye over Jades' back.

Albert freezes as one of them shines a light around the room. It stops at Ned's head. "Hey, isn't that one of Albert's pilots?" Jades voice trembles at the sight.

"Was; we gotta be careful. There might be some animals calling this place their home in the off-season here to avoid the hydra." Stoutarm makes sure not to glance at the head a second time.

A stomping sound comes from one of the other shafts.

Everyone stares down the noisy shaft but doesn't see anything. The sound keeps growing louder and louder.

Albert grows tense as Ned's mangled body appears and walks toward them.

The two soldiers exchange glances. "We should've seen whatever it is by now," Jades whispers.

Albert watches Ned's body pass between the soldiers and walk over to the bench. The soldiers realize the noise has passed by them, and they start to check the room for any signs of the source.

The decapitated body picks up its head and jams it on top,

making a gross liquid popping sound.

"What the hell!?" Stoutarm says as he and Jades witness Ned's head levitating into the air. Ned's eyes open wide and he smiles. "Friendlies! Welcome Fireteam Dark!"

"I'm out. Nope! Fuck that shit!" Jades sprints away. Stoutarm is right behind him, but keeps facing the room keeping his rifle aimed at Ned.

"Your men are rude Alby. Master wants their insides on the outsides." Ned comments.

Albert trembles at the shape of Ned, which smiles at him while the light from Stoutarm's rifle fades as they move farther away. Albert starts to follow the two men, as Ned keeps his sinister smile on Albert, licking his lips.

The lights in the shaft come back on, filling the area with dim lighting, just bright enough so that one can make out where the walls are. But Albert picks out Ned's outline in the chamber. The body raises both arms forward and up. The elbows bend down, and its hands grab the head. And lift it up.

"Alby! Tasty Alby!" Ned's new voice says. "Feed me!" he shouts as his body holds the head in one hand, the other behind his back. "Hehe," Ned cackles. His body throws the head at Albert with incredible speed. "WEEEEEEEE!"

Albert ducks just in time to avoid the head. It passes through the spot where his own head was a split-second earlier. Albert looks back, as Ned's body lowers its arms and starts walking towards him. The sound of it walking is more of a gooey crunch now.

The noise is so unique and gut wrenching, Albert himself finds it disturbing. He turns around to find the Shadow Figure's outline holding Ned's head in one hand, and stroking the top with the other. Albert runs away.

"Alby! Kiss me loving like!" Ned demands.

Albert turns around to find the body is now running towards him. He sprints away before the body can catch up.

"I'll give you a good head. Best you ever had!" Ned shouts, as Albert dashes past the Shadow Figure.

"No need." Albert checks behind him and finds that he is outrunning Ned.

The body stops at the Shadow Figure, takes the head and puts it back on. "Alby! I'm a coming to eat you dead!" Ned adopts a seductive tone as his body resumes walking toward Albert.

Albert pushes his way between Stoutarm and Jades.

"Albert?" Jades asks out of surprise.

"Whatever you lads do, do not go that way!" Albert points down the mine shaft while continuing to run. He doesn't care if those two can see him for the moment.

The soldiers point their weapons in the direction Albert ran from, and keep backing up. "Damn, old geezer is out of sight already." Jades is shocked to see that Albert is actually scared of something.

"He never runs. From anything. We need to hustle." Stoutarm tries to keep calm.

Jades stops when the lights come back on in full and the shadows emerge around him. "What the shit?" He says, right before noticing Stoutarm is no longer next to him. "This is not funny, man."

A deep growl comes from in front of him, followed by squishy sounding footsteps. The sound seems to come from what must be dozens of things. Then the smell of decaying flesh hits Jades. While noxious and very strong, it doesn't faze him, Albert's lab is worse. He begins moving backward slowly.

Shadows of what resemble several people emerge from the floor. Whatever they are, they're covered in a black oily liquid, oozing from all over their decaying bodies. Jades aims at the head of the nearest one and fires a round in panic. Nothing happens and the bullet appears to go through without contact. He fires another shot at the torso of the creature, with the same result; the second bullet passes through without touching it. Jades turns and runs.

Shadows appear all around and step from the walls, turning into these gooey human-shaped things. They make no effort to grab at Jades as he runs past them. They all stare at him without making a move. Then, the silence becomes deafening. He can't hear his breathing, his footsteps, and he tries to say something, but he can't speak. He feels like he's drowning. He stops when he loses his breath and sinks to the floor. The figures stay still, lining the sides of the shaft.

In one unified move, they take a step forward and the light goes out. The sound of their step echoes for a moment and, when the silence returns, the lights turn on and this time the figures are gone. Jades can hear himself breathe again. "Ok, this is just a bad dr-. On second thought, I won't say anything."

"Just a bad what?" Stoutarm asks, catching up to him.

Jades shoots a glance behind him, and Stoutarm is standing there. "The wake, the shit. How the hell is this place not a quarantined military zone or bombed to the ground yet?"

Stoutarm grabs a canteen from his belt and holds it out to Jades. "Dude, you took off like a mad man after popping two caps into the wall back there."

"No. I saw. I experienced something. The hydra's wake is messing me up." Jades takes a swig from the canteen and spits the liquid out as if it's disgusting.

"Pull yourself together man. What happened?"

"That does not taste like water."

"I should hope not. Filled it with coffee," Stoutarm said. "Come on man, on your feet. You're embarrassing."

"That isn't coffee either." Jades has a thick oily liquid dripping out of his mouth.

Stoutarm cringes at Jades' face. "What is drooling from your mouth?" Stoutarm does a double take at the coffee Jades spat on the ground; it looks like coffee to him.

"Crap is like gasoline or over-used motor oil." Jades sees a chamber up ahead. "Let's figure out how to get out of here. I'll take my chances with the hydra one on one."

"That's suicide."

"No, staying in here is suicide. I will blow my own brains out if we stay in here any longer." Jades points the rifle at Stoutarm and then lowers it when he gets a hold of himself. "Sorry. Out there is being murdered. I'd like to think I am not so weak as to do myself in."

Stoutarm listens to the shaky words coming out of the shivering man's mouth. Whatever he endured was enough to shake the man to his core. "On your feet, soldier. We're moving on." Stoutarm tries a stern tone and, after a moment, walks on.

Jades gets up and follows him. He wipes the drool from his mouth. On his sleeve the liquid looks like a coffee stain instead of an oil stain.

"There ain't nothing in here." Pattel kicks the dirt as they regroup at the entrance to the phosphorus mine.

"Yeah, fine by us," Thebes adds.

"Well, there was that odd metal wall." Walker still feels static in the hairs on his arm.

"I didn't like it. Place gives me the creeps," Thebes responds.

"Hey, you two notice anything odd about some of these buildings?" Pattel scratches his head, while staring out at the camp.

The other two look in the direction of the camp, and Thebes finds that all but a few buildings are burned down to their wooden frames.

"Well, sure is odd as hell." He rubs his eyes to make sure he isn't seeing things.

Walker shakes his head. "What changed now?"

"Yo, half the buildings are gone, like they burned down centuries ago," Pattel says to Walker.

"Ok, well, everything looks to me like the way it did when we landed. So, you guys pick a building that's there, and let's regroup before the hydra comes back. I'm not going to check out the other mine during the eclipse."

"Well, the station is gone." Thebes checks around for any massive animals nearby.

"There is a barracks we can use." Pattel points at the nearest one.

"Alright, lead to the one you're picking." Walker pats Thebes' shoulder to have him take point. They're on their way to the building when a strong tremor knocks everyone off their feet. "I don't know where the hydra is! Move now!"

They sprint and reach the front door of the barracks which is already wide open. Walker slams the door shut out of fear. After he does, the ground shakes hard again.

The hydra lowers a head near the door.

"The hell. How did none of us see it right there?" Thebes scrambles to move away from the windows.

"If I didn't see it, I doubt you can. So, stay down, and shut up." Walker hides beneath the windowsill.

They stay out of sight and notice the blue mist coming in through a few windows which have been left open.

Walker tightens his mask to the point that it starts to pinch his face.

Pattel puts his mask back on, and Thebes grabs a nearby blanket as the hydra lets out a series of growls.

Hunter peers from around a tree as the hydra surrounds the same barracks that he, Albert, and Mack used yesterday.

Westly stands next to him and whispers, "I guess we know where my men are."

The hydra turns one head from the building and shifts its focus on Westly.

"How the fuck did it hear that!?" Westly turns to face Hunter, but he isn't there. "Ah crap."

Westly drops his rifle and prepares a grenade in each hand. The head gives him its full attention and starts moving towards him. Westly throws the grenades at the wounded leg. Both hit the hydra's shin, detonating on impact.

The hydra is not fazed and lowers another head down to inspect what happened. Sniffing at its shin, it follows up by growling and making its anger known. All four heads emit an ear shattering roar.

Westly has only enough time to start running before the hydra lowers one of its heads, coming down over the top of him with an open mouth. Westly arms another grenade he doesn't throw and, as the hydra closes its mouth, the grenade detonates, setting off all the ammunition and other grenades Westly possesses.

The head opens the mouth again and exhales a plume of smoke, but Westly's remains are gone.

Hunter sits at the base of the tree with a front-row seat to the attack. He had no time to blink, seeing everything go down as fast as it did. The exhaled smoke smells of digested and rotting flesh, mixed with the explosive residue. It is the most putrid smell he's ever experienced, and it takes everything for him not to puke. He checks above him to find another one of the heads is staring at him.

Hunter can't hold back anymore and vomits.

The disgusted hydra closes its eyes and gags from watching Hunter puke, turning its head away before throwing up itself. Then the hydra walks off to the lake in the middle of the valley, running once it gets clear of the trees.

Hunter is grateful the monster is running away. When he glances at the enormous pile of vomit and semi-digested people and animals, he throws up again. "Oh god." He tries to breathe. "Oh, so gross. Oh! It saved my life, but that's too much." Then he runs over at the barracks. He has difficulty running as his stomach begins to hurt from puking. He realizes he hasn't stopped to eat in over a day.

"Hydra has a low tolerance gag reaction. I will never be able to unsee that." Walker pounds his chest and tries not to vomit into his mask. When he peers out the window again, he spots Hunter sprinting towards them. "Heads up, we got incoming."

"The hydra is coming back?" Thebes asks.

"No, Hunter is running this way." Walker opens the door and ushers Hunter in.

"I knew Westly was bad, but even a hydra couldn't keep his enormous ass hat down." Pattel jokes.

Hunter enters the building. "Thank you." He says as Walker offers him a canteen.

"That is disgusting." Walker looks away as Hunter swishes the water in his mouth and spits on the floor.

"Let's never mention this again. And I'm sorry about Westly." Hunter coughs as he speaks, then takes a sip of water to swallow.

"The hell was he doing with you anyways?" Walker asked.

Pattel raises an eyebrow, and exchanges glances with Thebes, since they're unable to interact with Hunter.

"I guess he's there for real." Pattel scratches his head, watching Walker.

"Are you alone here?" Hunter asks Walker.

"Guess so," Thebes says back to Pattel. "I mean, I hear him, but I guess he doesn't see us. What a lousy scumbag."

"No, Thebes and Pattel are here with me," Walker replies.

"Oh, it's fine. I don't doubt they're here. Everything I've endured over the past day. Uh yeah no, the eyes lie," Hunter continues. "Thanks for the water. Give me a sec, and I'll explain everything." He takes a trip to the lavatories.

Albert reaches the entrance of the gemstone mine and decides to check out the camp to see if any buildings returned for his use.

"Alby, don't go." Ned's voice calls out from behind him.

Albert runs outside as fast as he can.

"No!" Ned shouts when he reaches sunlight.

The ground shakes as though the hydra is moving fast. Albert glances back and finds Ned standing at the edge of the mine. He pounds on what sounds like a solid wall.

"You'll be back, or you'll be eaten," Ned taunts.

"I will not dare walk in there again." Albert rushes for the rock crevice on the other side of the clearing.

"You'll be back and eaten. Or you'll just be eaten. I cannot wait for nightfall. We will come play outside."

Albert squeezes through the crevice and heads towards camp. The only building he can see is the refinery. "Fine, that will do for me."

As he approaches the refinery, he sees the hydra by the lake in the valley, as the eclipse starts to block out the light. "Maybe I will be a party to your demise." He enters the building. "What am I saying? Suicide? Such an end is not my style at all. Blowing up a super monster and registering the first kill of a hydra on record is incredibly attractive. But the cost is as high as costs can be. Oh, foul creature, you do drive people to their darkest demises."

In the building, he discovers the airplane from the airstrip sitting near one of the bay doors. "How did that get in here?" he ponders aloud, walking around some machines to approach the plane. Then he inspects some nearby equipment. "Refining and packaging equipment. Useless. I require fabrication equipment." He peeks out the window and can now see the maintenance shop across the camp. "Now this is a most interesting development."

Albert walks back over to Rogue's plane. "I assume they were thinking of modifying this plane to carry more fuel. Reaching Heart would be easy if done right. What a grand gesture from life, that I started my humble career as an aerodynamics engineer, haha!"

6: DEEP FOREST FLIGHT PLAN

Walker relays every word of what Hunter says to the other two during what feels like a horror story. The daily eclipse is darkening the sky again. "That's some messed up stuff."

"So, three people aren't affected by the hydra's wake. Hunter is only slightly affected; I am definitely affected. Thebes will be tripping all over here soon." Pattel sums up.

"As I understand it, yes," Walker acknowledges.

Thebes sits quietly with his head down on a bunk a few beds away. Walker and Pattel glance over. Everyone is coming to grips with the full depths of the situation.

Walker claps his hands and gets up. "The way I figure, we need to escort the airship to the crash site safely, right? The hydra aside, it doesn't look like an easy task. If the dirigible flies too close to the tree line it will be a target for archons and other nasty flying problems."

Hunter nods. "Honestly, I hadn't gotten that far into the plan."

"We're in," Thebes is quick to say. "We have enough firepower to hold off smaller threats. Also, if we can find Stoutarm and Jades, and regroup, we can give Rogue the time he needs to make the bomb more effective."

Walker nods. "I agree. Hunter, lead the way to the skyport. I'd like to meet this wrong target Rogue Whip. This will be interesting."

Thebes and Pattel grab their weapons and regroup by Walker. "Let's get some payback!" Thebes shouts.

"If none of the infrastructure is available for anyone, whatever you do, do not hide in the gemstone mine. Do what you can to run to the phosphorus mine." Hunter advises.

"Hey, I heard him," Thebes responds to the sound of Hunter's voice.

"Same here. Does the eclipse alter the effects?" Pattel chimes in.

"I don't know," Hunter answers, "but I'm glad to hear you guys."

Walker checks out the window next to the door. The hydra is barely visible. "Ok, hydra's on the opposite side of the valley. Let's move quickly and quietly. Hunter, take point. Stay sharp, weapons down."

Hunter leads them over to where Westly dropped his weapon and picks it up. "Damn, awesome weapon."

Walker nods. "Yeah, he spent a small fortune on the stupid thing. Albert mocked him for days after he bought it."

"I can't let this beauty rot in the mud." Hunter checks the rifle over, and turns the safety on.

Then they follow the trail leading toward the gemstone mine. Ahead of them are two lights in the distance. Hunter and Walker stop. Walker turns the light on his rifle on and off in their direction. The lights flash back.

"Must be Jades and Stoutarm," Walker says as they rush over.

"Oh hey, everyone's still alive," Jades says, with a sigh of relief.

"No, I'm not seeing Westly's hat," Stoutarm observes, as they wait for the group to come up to them.

"Hunter?" Stoutarm and Jades say at the same time, as his identity becomes clear to them in the darkness. The others right behind him.

"It's been too long, guys!" Hunter smiles, and opens his arms.

"Yes, indeed. Not the best place to meet, though." Jades gives Hunter a fist bump.

"Yeah, Albert picked a perfect place for a wasted picnic." Hunter is relieved to see the group is made up of former soldiers and fighters rather than guns for hire.

"Come with us. We're going to hunt a hydra. We'll give you details when we reach the skyport." Walker says.

"Take out the hydra?" Jades echoes with disbelief.

"With what? The grenades we have probably won't tickle an itch on that thing." Stoutarm matches Jades' tone.

"True, but ten metric tons worth of Hexogen might do more than tickle." Walker's reply leaves Jades and Stoutarm silent.

They're surprised at the news. "Hexogen? Laboratory made explosives? Where the hell around here are we going to find laboratory refined super explosives? Let alone ten tons of the stuff?"

"Crash site from yesterday, forty miles down the cliffs that way. The dirigible we shot down yesterday had Hexogen in its payload," Hunter cuts Jades off.

"Say what now!?" Jades can't believe his ears.

"Well, shit. Talk about a firecracker, for sure." Stoutarm raises his eyebrows at Hunter. They follow along, as Hunter leads them towards the rickety building along the cliff.

From the ledge, Rogue watches Hunter lead the men through

the cliffside passage. He spent the time since Hunter vanished building an ignition system and container for the bomb inside the cargo hold. "Crystal, lock the cabin tight, please. Stay out of sight until I give the all clear." he calls out.

Crystal is staring at him from the airship cabin. His expression says everything to her, and she locks the doors.

Rogue leaves the overlook and goes over to meet the group. By the time he reaches the landing the elevator is already moving down. *Aw, crap. Got here a little too late. Well an execution squad is coming up. Either mine or the hydra's.*

When the elevator arrives, he finds the six men inside. "Y'all are packed in there like sardines." He puts his hand on the cable release lever, out of their view.

"Ha, you're funny. If memory serves, we got a job to finish." Hunter decides to get back at Rogue for playing with his mind yesterday.

"Which job?" Rogue asks, Hunter's tone makes him think twice now.

"Thought you needed some help with hydra hunting." Hunter says, before the door opens.

"You're the wrong guy, so the only other major target down here would be the hydra." Walker realizes this stranger doesn't trust them, and for good reason.

"You could've said something," Rogue said to Hunter.

"I phased out. Thought I would do something productive while being half a ghost," Hunter says back.

Rogue chuckles, and motions for them to come with him. "We got everything ready, and as long as no one shoots us down, the only thing we need to be wary of is the other forest animals."

"You don't say! Well, a fireteam of well-armed mercs is fantastic for pest control." Walker cracks the joke to put Rogue at ease. "Fireteam Dark at your service."

"I can't argue with that. Though make sure you don't shoot us down," Rogue fires back.

The group reaches the skyport dock. "Ok, first things first, I want to know who can see who." *I hope this will be easy. If not, we'll deal with communication as problems come up.*

"I wore this mask the whole time, so I'm confident I'm not affected by the wake." Walker readjusts his mask using the straps.

"Excellent! By sheer luck, my copilot and I are immune. Should be seven of us here. If you can hear me, raise your hand." Rogue is hoping not to have any communication problems.

Everyone raises their hands.

"Well, this is lucky," Jades remarks, as he sees everyone's hand raised.

"You're telling me." Hunter wonders what's making the toxin effects so weak at the moment.

"Maybe because the hydra is on the far side of the valley. The further away we are, the less we are affected?" Thebes' suggestion puts the newer group at ease, making them forget what Hunter said about Joe and the coma victims.

"Sounds possible. I can't say for sure though. But we're going to momentarily add forty miles distance, which should help," Rogue explains. "Alright, everything is ready to go. Fold down the doors on the cargo hold. Inside is a container I built, a metal grid hooked up to a battery on a switch. The grid will produce enough of a spark to detonate the Hexogen. Don't break anything, and prep the rest for your needs. Be aware, it's going to be a massive bomb when we come back."

"Alright, you got your orders. Make some adjustments in the hold for firing positions and a comfy ride. We leave when he gives the word," Walker orders.

The men break off and start familiarizing themselves with the setup. Rogue turns toward the cabin, and Crystal unlocks the door to let Rogue, Walker, and Hunter inside, immediately running to the back room before they open the door.

"You are familiar. We've met before, right?" Rogue says to Walker.

"Yeah, I was a little shocked when you were at the elevator landing. You were part of an emergency evacuation that came to my rescue a few years back."

Rogue studies Walker's face for a moment, trying to remember. "Ah yeah, the Mt. Suda eruption. Now I remember." *Suda's eruption was so many years ago. Barely got my pilot license back then. Now that was a disaster of a trip.*

"Wait, what?" Hunter is surprised they know each other.

"This fly boy pulled my team off an erupting volcano after a rescue operation went south. We got hired to rescue some stubborn rich folks out of their homes before Mt. Suda blew up. Got them out, but half my unit found themselves stranded when the volcano began going off in full. This guy was returning to his port of call when we flagged him down. He had the balls to go to the island and bring my stranded men home."

"Yeah, I lost my aircraft back then too. That was an awesome blimp." Rogue is bitter as he recalls the accident. *I dropped my entire life savings on the down payment for that thing. Had it not been for the military insurance, my company would have died back then.*

"But you saved everyone's lives. I'll take the win." Walker can tell Rogue is still uneasy with him.

"How'd you end up in the service of Lord Albert?" The last time they met, Walker was in a real military unit. *From serving his country to serving pure evil. What the hell man?*

"Highest bidder. He always reserved us for follow-ups and evacuations. Never got involved in his dirty work unless he paid more than we knew what to do with. Made my peace with-" Walker trails off mid-sentence. "Well, if we survive, I'll buy drinks and finish up later."

Seen that face more than my fair share of times. "Sounds good to me." Rogue pats Walker on the back.

Hunter listens with his jaw dropped. "Wait, you're how Gort picked up on him?"

Walker tenses up and shoots a glare at him. "I can't speak for Gort."

Hunter is puzzled. Then he begins piecing the events together in his mind. "He deserves to know."

"You weren't present when it happened," Walker says, with a stern tone.

"Guys, if whatever you know that I don't is a potential problem, make it not a problem. Shut up, behave, and we'll hash this out over drinks on Heart," Rogue says, matching Walker's tone and energy.

"Fine, but I think he dragged you into this."

Hunter's comment strikes a nerve in Rogue.

He holds himself back after taking a deep breath. "Like I said, we'll finish this on the finest craft in Urza's Meadworks." *Come one Rogue, keep it together. Someone needs to be the adult in the room here.*

"Alright." Hunter raises his hands and drops the issue, heading over to the cargo hold to help out.

Walker shakes his head and looks at Rogue, who leans against the pilot's chair. "If I had to guess, I'd say you ran into a spy who shares my name, right? From everything I've learned about Albert, nothing is a pretty picture. And while he paid well, he's nothing short of a monster and you decided to do something about it. Somewhere between when you put your plan in motion and Albert put his plan in motion, things fell apart."

"You summed that up pretty well. Obviously more to the tale, but it's best left for telling when we aren't taking on monsters of this caliber." Walker feels bad, because if Rogue Whip the spy had done his part, this Rogue would never have been shot down. Either that, or Captain Gort simply assumed only one person in Yeraputs bore this name, and didn't do any real research.

Walker had suggested looking into the CEO as the possible target, knowing full well he wasn't, and that the difference was obvious. All he meant to do was buy time for the spy to rescue his daughter. But those things happened a year ago. The whole Rogue Whip ordeal should've been dealt with long ago. What took Albert this long to act? Walker had forgotten about the events until Albert said the name in the station. The poor woman has been in Albert's hell for over a year.

"I agree. And I happen to know more about the hydras too. It'll be difficult to prove, and I feel like I'm going mad saying this, but there are a lot more hydras inside the remnants of Shell."

"Are you serious?" Walker snaps out of his deep train of thought.

"Have you gone into the phosphorus mine yet?" Rogue asks.

"Yeah, it's huge, empty, and smells like phosphates. Why?"

"Did you visit the mystery wall at Face Eighteen?"

"The freaky metal thing? Yeah." Walker is not entirely surprised the mysterious wall is related to hydras.

"Found a way inside and discovered an unusual storage facility for them. Has all the knowledge about them one can ever need." Rogue takes a breath. His side feels sore. He focuses on calming down and reducing his heart rate before continuing. "Shell has some secrets, and this particular artifact may be among the deadliest. But the bottom line is this: despite the power of this bomb, the hydra may still survive. All we can hope to do is some serious damage. Cripple it enough to let a rival apex predator have a shot at finishing it off."

"Doesn't surprise me much. There was an advanced race of people on Shell before Yeraputs happened. And this hydra being right here makes that believable. Did you say we might not kill the damned hydra? Are they immortal or something?"

"More or less."

"We're talking a massive bomb capable of destroying an entire medium-sized towns in one go." Walker doubts Rogue comprehends what they're going to make.

"We'll pay a visit to the artifact, after we blow a hole in the damn hydra, and figure out what's next. This animal is highly evolved." *I became the overnight Yeraputs expert on hydras. What a wild life I'm living.*

Walker shakes his head. "Did you tell Hunter this?"

"People have been unreliably appearing and disappearing at random around here. Although we aren't affected by the hydra's wake, they are, and they can still disappear on us. So, no, haven't had the chance yet."

Crystal comes out from back room with a piece of chocolate in her hand.

"Crystal?" Walker asks with a shocked expression, forgetting that Hunter told him about her being here.

She throws the bar away and starts clicking rapidly. YOU. WHY HERE? The more she clicks the harder she breathes and the madder she becomes. Her free hand forms a fist.

"Crystal, are you ok?" *Girl is ready to blow a fuse.*

"This doesn't make any sense." Walker replies.

"Crystal, what's wrong?" Rogue gets in front of her. "Crystal, look at me, not him." *The sight of him is setting her off. This is getting out of control fast.*

HE TRICK ME, Crystal clicks. She lunges at Walker. Rogue catches her to stop her. She lunges harder, trying to break free of Rogue's grip. When she isn't able to reach Walker, she throws her clicker at him.

"Crystal stop, please." *I need her to not make this difficult.*

She couples her hands and puts as much force into elbowing his side several times with her uninjured arm as hard as she can. Rogue uses his strength to hold her back. Squeezing her upper arms and blocking her view of Walker. "Hey, Crystal, focus on me. Walker, can you step out now? Please." *Damn, she definitely broke a rib or two. I can't take too much more of this.*

Walker nods but doesn't move. "Yeah, you're right. We don't have the time." Seeing her puts a knot in his gut, and he's unable to stay composed. "Crystal, I'm sorry, I had no idea what Albert was planning."

"Walker!" Rogue shot back.

Crystal gives Walker the middle finger and spits at him.

Walker comes to his senses and leaves the ship. "Hunter, you could've warned me she was here!"

"You're an idiot! I did tell you she is with him! Dumbass!" Hunter shouts back.

Crystal tries another lunge as he leaves, but Rogue's grip is too strong. When the door closes, she drops her forehead on his shoulder crying and stops struggling. He lets go and strokes her back. Her face is red with anger, and tears flow from her eyes. She stomps on his foot and kicks him in the shin while headbutting him in the chin. He lets go of her as she backs a few steps away. He locks the door, then gives her back the clicker.

"You're safe. The nightmare of Albert is over," Rogue reassures her. *Damn, girl is a pro at fighting.*

She throws the clicker at him. It bounces off his chest, and she picks it up and repeats throwing it at him several times. Then she breaks down in tears again, putting her head on his shoulder with her fingers digging into his sides. Her whole body shakes uncontrollably.

He gently wraps his arms around her, and she starts pounding on his chest out of frustration, this time with less force, not to hurt him, but rather, letting it all out.

"You're ok Crystal, he's gone."

After a few moments she stops pounding and just cries.

WHY YOU STOP ME? She gives him a devastated expression.

"Hurting Walker won't do any good. Not now. When the time comes, you can break every bone in his body or tear his leg off, but not now, please."

I KNOW., she clicks. BUT HE BAD. HE NOT STOP ALBERT.

"He didn't stop Albert?" She clicks a lot of code in a short span, and he finds it difficult to keep up.

FROM TAKING ME. AND WHAT HE LET HAPPEN TO MOM.

"Oh, I'm sorry, I had no idea."

NOT YOUR FAULT. She stares down at the ground for a second.

Rogue hugs her and holds her tight. She hugs back after another long pause.

IM SORRY. She hopes her attack on him doesn't push him away. At the same time, she wasn't ready to have an encounter with Walker and lost complete control of herself.

"Don't be. I can take it from you. You can pound on me all you need to, until this is done." *Well, I can't. Everything hurts. But she needs the release. Damn, girl, you got power. Or a fighting spirit anyway.*

WHAT NOW? she clicks, leaning her weight on him.

"Well, I'm not going to kill Walker. Please don't ask."

She shakes her head. I WONT. After a long pause, she tilts her head up and looks him in the eye. HOW I HELP KILL HYDRA?

Rogue searches around the cabin for an answer. *How about not pummeling me again. Gotta give her something important and easy to do to keep her focused.* He stares at the pilot seat and console. "Well, I do need a copilot. I can teach you everything about flying. You think you can learn to fly?" *Gives her a purpose to focus on which is everything. And I understand this stuff like the back of my hand. Yes!*

She wipes her tears off and nods. THAT HELPS. Flying the ship is the last thing she anticipates doing, but it sounds more interesting than doing nothing. And, more importantly this keeps her close to him and away from everyone else.

"Ok, so first we'll do some preflight checks, and I'll show you how to take off." He speaks with a gentle tone. *Talk about a light-switch change of emotion.*

"Damn it gets cold here." Thebes straps a crate to the floor to sit on.

"The Inner Shell is lovely this time of year. Gotta love this place." Pattel starts cutting into the cargo hold side wall to make a shooting window.

"So, you've worked with the ship's captain, eh Walker?" Jades asks.

"Years ago. The finest pilot alive on Heart. Lives for dangerous missions like this one. He's famous for flying into rough places," Walker replies. "We're in the best hands possible."

"Considering we're coming from the same team who shot his ass down yesterday?" Pattel sounds skeptical.

"I think he'll forgive us when we buy him some drinks. And bring the hydra down." Walker focuses on helping Pattel cut holes.

"Whoa, who's the super fine babe?" Stoutarm walks toward the cabin to introduce himself, never one to ignore an attractive woman's presence.

Walker and Hunter catch sight of Rogue and Crystal leaving the airship. "She's off limits to everyone. She's our copilot, I think. The captain will drop your ass on the hydra's head if you look at her funny." Walker realizes Stoutarm is a potential problem.

"Damn, captain got himself the sweetest damn copilot in Yeraputs." Stoutarm stops walking but lets out a wolf whistle, unable to contain himself.

"Really? Control yourself," Hunter says to Stoutarm.

"All in favor of throwing Stoutarm overboard when we are up high enough, say Aye!" Thebes shouts from inside the cargo hold.

"Fine, I'll put it back and zip up." Stoutarm gets back to work when he sees Rogue covering Crystal's ears and escorting her further away, giving the group a glare.

Hunter pulls Stoutarm to the side. "Just to be clear, that's the daughter of Rogue Whip the spy. Fresh out of Albert's yearlong grasp."

Stoutarm raises an eyebrow and glances back at her. "Thanks for the warning."

Rogue begins a series of preflight checks; Crystal keeps close to him, and he shows her everything he is looking for and what to do. While standing in front of the dirigible, they discover the ship's name. I.S.V. *INSPIRED DREAMS*. "Huh, Inner Shell Vessel Inspired Dreams." Rogue reads aloud.

The group stays busy cutting holes in the walls to shoot through and adding some makeshift seats to ride on. The container Rogue built for the bomb looks like an improvised swimming pool.

Walker and Hunter check the view from the overlook while everyone is working on their projects. "You realize I didn't tell Albert about this guy. All I wanted to do was buy some time by distracting Gort," Walker says.

"Ain't no coincidence in my mind." Hunter doesn't care. What happened in the past makes no difference to the fact that they are all here now.

"Gort suspected a mole in Albert's security. Small-minded bastard got a name from his connections. As soon as I learned the name and Albert's plans, I mentioned his company to give the spy time to rescue her. Clearly Gort didn't investigate the matter far enough. If he did, he'd have learned I was wrong." Walker needs to get this off his chest.

"How well do you know this pilot?" Hunter gives him a curious glance.

"He comes in handy when you need to reach nature's more dangerous places. Managed to leave an impression on me after our first meeting. But on a personal level, not well." Walker shakes his head. He can't forget the hurt look on Crystal's face.

Hunter shakes his head disapprovingly. "That's a short tale."

"Well, there isn't much to say." Walker speaks in a flat tone. "Let's check in on how things are going."

Hunter and Walker go into the cabin. "Must still be on the platform." Hunter can't help but notice that Walker stays by the door.

The door across from them swings open and Crystal walks in. Hunter nods at her while Walker turns away. She looks down and rushes to the back room. Rogue comes in right behind her. "We're all set to go on my end."

"Wonderful. I'll ride with the rest of the hallucinating folk." Hunter steps back out, patting Walker on the shoulder as he moves past him.

"How are we looking?" Pattel asks Hunter, as he steps on the docking ramp.

"Captain says the ship is ready to fly." Hunter jumps off the ramp, stumbling when he lands.

"We're as ready as we can be." Pattel gives a thumbs up.

"Awesome. Tell them, and we'll mount up. I'm riding with you guys," Hunter says, as he heads over to the cargo hold.

"Captain, sir, we're green for launch when you are," Pattel shouts through the door.

"Great work. We're off in two minutes. Strap in." Rogue says to Pattel. Crystal comes in from the back room with a metal pipe in her hands giving Walker a glare.

Walker backs up against the wall and glances at Rogue for another intervention. "Um, Rogue, a little help please."

Rogue shakes his head. 'Unbelievable. Hey, Crystal, how about you launch us, please." *Where the hell did she get a pipe?*

She taps the pipe, threatening Walker, but sets it down and gets into the pilot's chair in front of the console, brushing her hair behind her as if she's in charge.

"You got this. Keep steady, just like I showed ya." *She's a quick learner. When things settle down, I'm going to have to train her and get her a pilot license. She'd be awesome.*

"You're letting her fly?" Walker panics.

"She's going to launch the ship, yes. If you'd rather my hands be on the controls I'll give her the pipe back." Rogue makes sure to stand between them. "Besides, she deserves a part in taking down the biggest, meanest pair of predators in Yeraputs."

Everyone is on board the cargo hold and getting settled in. The spools of rope holding the dirigible down loosen until they're lifting off the platform, pulling on the cable attached to the bottom of the airship which is connected to a rolling guide that follows a track leading out of the cliff wall. The lifting force makes them move forward.

Rogue pushes a few buttons on the center console and the lights outside turn off. "Let's hope we can avoid getting its attention until we're higher up." He also pulls on the lever to close the bird cage around the cabin. The guide rolls forward, leading them out of the chamber. This is louder than Rogue anticipated.

"Oh shit." Walker covers his ears.

"Too late to stop now." Rogue nods, reassuringly to Crystal, who's facing him with a terrified expression. "You're doing great! Keep going!" *And we're going to die. The whole valley can hear us.*

She nods and keeps her hand where he told her. They start to move more quickly, and the super loud squeak becomes a quieter grind.

The hydra on the far side of the valley remains motionless. "Doesn't care for now." Walker grabs the side railing tighter.

The guide reaches the end of the platform and releases the dirigible. It sways a little but keeps moving forward. Crystal walks up to the front window and glances down and around. IT WORKS, she clicks.

"It does." Rogue smiles at her. *I gotta curb my pessimism. This will work, we're going hydra hunting, even though we're making so many stupid all or nothing choices now.*

"You sound reassured." Walker can tell Rogue has a newfound confidence passing the point of no return. He's all in, which means they all need to be.

"We are about to make a very unstable bomb after a half day crawl in stressful conditions. Doing this while relying on a heavily armed crew, while they're having problems keeping their heads because of the worst toxin known to man. This is so unnerving, so I'm rolling with the plan, and hoping everything works. On a ship named *Inspired Dreams,* no less." Rogue's face is confident, but his voice is shaky and nervous.

"You bet. We're embarking on a mission where everything can go wrong faster than we'll be able to fix." Walker states the obvious.

"The volcano at least had some predictability," Rogue shot back with a chuckle.

"In comparison, I guess," Walker acknowledges.

Rogue checks the giant mirrors on the sides to make sure they clear the chamber before adjusting the ballast to gain some altitude. "Gotta be the smoothest isolated launch I've ridden in years. Crystal, you got a knack for this."

"Oy, if you find things ain't right, put your weapon down." Pattel shouts to everyone. "Last thing we need is for one of us to bring this thing down in this forest."

"So far, not so bad." Hunter shivers from the blast of freezing air.

"The shit show hasn't started yet." Pattel checks to ensure his rifle's safety is on.

"Considering I only see two people in here aside from me. Oh it's started," Hunter shoots back.

Pattel glances around. "Seeing everyone but Jades and Thebes."

"I see Jades." Hunter smiles at Jades, waving when he turns around.

Jades shakes his head. "Who the hell is cracking jokes at me?"

"No one. Only doing a sight check," Hunter tells Jades.

"Right." Jades looks around. "I'm only seeing you and Stoutarm."

"This sucks, not knowing a damn thing after we all got in this crate. We turn our heads and people vanish. Like trusting your brothers-in-arms when you aren't sure for certain if they are next to you or not." Stoutarm hates the situation and wants this day to be done with.

Jades chuckles. "Stoutarm appreciates the quiet time."

"I ought to push you off, but knowing my luck, I'd go through you and fall overboard myself." Stoutarm is red in the face with anger and takes a deep breath.

"Thebes? You alright?" Pattel finds Thebes sitting on his crate like a statue.

"I can see everyone." Thebes sits still, looking out over the forest. "We're so disorganized. If any flying beast makes for us, we'll be ill-equipped to properly deal."

"Archon, curious about us," Jades announces from the other side of the cargo hold.

"Archon port side," Thebes echoes.

"Got a clear shot." Pattel turns his safety off and aims for its body.

"Must be the same one from yesterday. It's skittish. Let's not waste ammo unless it gets too close." Hunter says, even though he can't see it from his point of view.

The dirigible aims for the crash site and ascends. Rogue takes over and gains some extra height. After he pulls on a few knobs, he discovers that they are, for the moment, traveling with the wind. He lets the ship drift, so he doesn't have to turn the engines on yet. Another few minutes pass before an animal is curious enough to inspect them.

"An archon?" Walker says looking out the port side window.

"They're not as uncommon as people believe." Rogue feels more at ease as the archon circles around the front.

"Aren't they dangerous?" Walker aims out the door.

"They're more curious and inquisitive than anything else around here. I've seen them go as high up as the Tradewinds. They like to check out all manner of aircraft. If anything, I'll take the free added muscle." Rogue's explanation encourages Walker to put down his weapon.

"This forest giving us a break? Don't make me laugh." Walker backs away from the door.

"Shut up, or karma will tip the scales the other way real quick." Rogue has never had any issues with archons, and they are excellent at keeping nuisances away from slower airships like dirigibles and blimps. *They just look scary, so people give them a bad rap. Heck I remember one hitching a ride on my ship a few months ago, just resting on the top of the balloon and chilling.*

The archon circles around a few times, giving them a wide berth. It breaks to land in the forest.

IT GONE, Crystal clicks.

"That didn't last long, but I'll take its lack of interest in us. Maybe everything else will be as uninterested." Rogue can only hope.

BEAUTIFUL, she clicks.

"Indeed, they are. Nature's kings of the sky." Rogue replies.

"The hydra is taking note of us," Walker says looking out the other side of the cabin.

"We're well out of its reach for now. I'll keep the ship as steady as I can, and if everyone back in the cargo hold behaves, we might come out of this alive," Rogue advises.

"Well, the hydra is looking our way, but doesn't appear interested, yet," Walker clarifies. He still doesn't feel comfortable having its attention already.

"Doesn't mean anything."

WHY NOT HIGHER? Crystal clicks.

"Because I'm letting the wind do the driving, so we move more like a natural thing just passing through." Rogue works the controls to make sure the dirigible stays level to the horizon.

"You call this thing natural?" Walker can't help but chuckle.

"Do you think it cares?" Rogue shoots back, while making minor adjustments.

All three of them glance in the direction of the hydra. Two heads are up and pointing their way, studying the airship. The heads turn back down to the ground as it appears to lose interest.

"And now the wind is against us." Rogue starts making more adjustments as they begin to yaw.

GO UP PLEASE, Crystal clicks. She's terrified of the hydra and begs Rogue to do something.

"Alright, we'll go up." Rogue tries to stay positive and adjusts several levers. The ship starts to tilt upward slightly.

"This is too slow for my liking." Rogue can't help but say it out loud. *And this thing costs more than half my fleet. This is nuts for free floating. No real control whatsoever. Note to self, don't buy one of these.*

"Is the engine busted or what?" Walker agrees. The speed is making him anxious.

"The engine is noisy. We want to be a few thousand feet up before turning the engine on. For now, to go up we are on the base fan, which eats through battery power. We've got maybe an hour of this left before we start to drift. Which we could do all the way there if the wind cooperates. But using the battery means we'll have to use the engine at some point." *Gotta play the steady and patient game.*

Hunter and Pattel both let out a sigh of relief.

"Man, this is nerve-racking!" Hunter exclaims.

"We're what? Five hundred or so feet up?" Pattel looks down and spits.

"No clue. Way high up is all I know." Hunter refuses to look down. This rickety setup is giving him a fear of heights. "I don't think it can reach us up here, though."

"Well, distance isn't a factor. I'm seeing fewer people now." Pattel says, glancing around.

"What are you going on about?" Hunter asked.

"The strength of the hydra's wake." Pattel clarifies.

"Must be how awake the hydra is." Hunter adds. "So, when it wakes up completely, the fun resumes I guess."

After about half an hour Rogue starts pressing on a few levers near the back of the cabin, which rumbles with the sound of a fueled engine. "Twelve hundred feet up, Let's start moving for real."

"How long till we reach the crash site?"

"We'll get there when the eclipse ends. But keep an eye on our monster friend and let me know when it decides to stand." Rogue returns to the navigating panel and grabs the wheel. "I have a visual on the site from here though. The forest is still smoldering."

Walker and Crystal look in the direction of the hydra. "It's awake, but heading away from us. Something other than us at the other end of the valley has its undivided attention. Something big but I can't make out what it is."

"Full grown harpy bear. Last night the two of them fought an all-out war. Must be back for a rematch." Rogue recognizes the same set of roars they listened to from the prior night echoing towards them.

KILL IT, Crystal clicks.

"If only." *I can tell from this far away the bear doesn't look right; something's off about it.*

The rest of the trip towards the crash site takes several hours but is uneventful. The daily eclipse is ending, and daylight again shines into the region.

"Man, my poor ship." Rogue stares down at the giant pile of ashes and debris. The fire burned a wide area around the wreck, but the cargo hold is indeed still intact.

"I'll give props to whoever built your ship." Walker glances down at the wreckage, wondering how in the hell Rogue survived.

Crystal examines the trail of debris on the clifftop. The cabin is destroyed at the base of the cliff. She replays the flashback of him being shot down, but adds in what she's seeing here to fill in the picture. She glances over at Rogue and studies his face. Being back here isn't bothering him.

"Don't joke, this thing cost me more than a few sacks of shiny coppers. It better hold up to a little fire." *Nice things never last long.*

Hunter looks down at the crash site as they approach. "Sure is miserable, compared to yesterday." The cabin half must've fallen overnight.

"Here comes the second act of the fun part." Thebes tries to sound cheerful. Before approaching everyone verifies they can interact with everyone again.

"Yeah, I knew being away from the hydra would be a drag but the experience sucks so much more than that; I feel so weak." Jades is glad he isn't the only one, but the sensation is debilitating.

"This might be a challenge. We got here a little faster than we expected." Pattel tries to ignore how tired he's feeling.

"Speak for yourself, man." Stoutarm sounds as if he is out of breath. "I can barely move."

Rogue turns the engine off, releases an anchor and pulls on a handle to let some air out of the balloon, resetting the handle as they begin to sink. He turns on an air intake and heater to stop them from landing, managing to lower the dirigible to roughly twenty feet above the ground.

"Walker, need you with them to help load the damn thing. Climb down the anchor line. I'm not landing this thing."

Walker nods and heads out the door as Rogue lifts the bird cage. Then Rogue pushes a lever on the panel, lowering the cargo hold using the wench system, but nothing happens. "Uh oh." Then he feels the ship shake and a loud thud follows. *Shit, wrong lever.*

"Oh crap. I knew something was gonna happen," Hunter says as he sits back up.

"Asshole, we didn't shoot him down." Jades rubs his back from the fall.

"Well, I kinda did." Hunter reaches for the back of his head to check for blood. He hit the ground hard.

Everyone gets up after being dropped on the ground.

Walker shakes his head. "Nothing ever goes according to plan! Thebes, Jades, perimeter. Everyone else, crack open the old hold, grab some boxes and let's make ourselves a big-ass IED."

Hunter approaches the charred metal container that is the remnants of Rogue's cargo and touches the side. The metal is cool. He checks around for a way to climb in.

"The latch is likely melted. Climb up and over! There's nothing on top." Rogue shouts from the cabin.

Hunter finds hand and foot holds and climbs in. Sure enough, there's nothing on top, and inside are a few layers of ash from the balloon cloth and a pile of metal cases in the center. "How heavy are they?"

"I think two hundred pounds each."

"Normally this wouldn't be a problem." Hunter walks up to one and brushes the ash off.

"What about the locks?" Hunter tries lifting the container, but in his weakened state they're way too heavy.

"Can we shoot them or something?" Walker's suggestion isn't

the best idea.

A loud cracking noise followed by several bangs catches everyone off guard as Jades and Stoutarm pull off one of the panels of the cargo hold.

Hunter nods with approval. "Awesome! Why didn't I think of that?"

"We can't throw two hundred pounds. Not when we are losing our breath like this." Stoutarm is panting and getting sweaty.

"Found your old toolkit!" Thebes holds up a jaw cutter used for escaping from metal debris.

"Quieter and safer than shooting them open. Bring those here," Walker commands.

Stoutarm and Hunter haul the first case out and over to the bomb container. They cut the lock and open the case to find wooden braces wrapped around glass cylinders. The Hexogen is in sealed metal and glass containers that twist open. Walker picks one up. "So, ten of these a case, how many cases?"

"A hundred? Give or take a few." Hunter groans realizing how long this process is going to take.

"So, a thousand canisters to go through. They're lighter, so break open the cases and walk the smaller canisters here and dump them in the bomb. Let's be as quick about this as we can. We're clearly going to be here a while," Walker suggests.

Rogue watches as they work through the canisters. *Not bad so far. This might work.*

Crystal sits in the corner up against the cabin side, staring into space. She's having a hard time accepting that she's working with some of the men who helped Albert kidnap her. This is surreal for her, and she's wondering why she and Rogue didn't take the vessel out of the valley when they had the chance as Rogue suggested this morning. She crosses her arms and tightens up.

"You ok?" *This morning she's a firecracker, now she's falling apart.*

NO, she clicks and scrutinizes him, still somewhat angry with him for stopping her from attacking Walker. And at the same time feeling bad for giving him a beating. All the way out here they can still hear the hydra's occasional roar.

TWO MONSTERS. She faces back out the window, staring at the horizon.

Rogue takes a seat next to her. "Well, one monster and an animal. I'd be ok letting the animal live. We are kinda trespassing in its home. The real monster, though? No, this world needs fewer of those." He joins her in staring out over the forest.

NOT YOUR FIGHTS. WHY? She bats an eye to study his arms next to her. They are still covered in bruises from yesterday.

"They are my fights now. I don't think Albert will pay for replacing the ship he shot down, my medical bills, and the lost cargo. Or restore my company's reputation after a failed delivery. Gotta kill him since he isn't going to pay otherwise. I'm a businessman at heart. The hydra is a bully to everyone, so might as well kill two baddies with one boom." He tries to lighten the mood and is rewarded when she cracks a small smile.

WHAT ABOUT ME? Yesterday and this morning, she felt the high of being rescued like in some fairy tale. Now her feelings are coming out in the open, and she does her best not to react until he says something.

"Well, I remember you said you can't go home."

NEVER RETURN HOME, she interrupts.

Wow, talk about blunt. "Because you have difficulty communicating?" *What the hell did I let come out of my mouth? Goddammit.*

She gives him an angry glare. This is a sore spot for her, and she nods as tears flow from her eyes.

"Well, tell ya what. When we return to Heart, you can stay at my place. I won't make fun of you. Besides, after this whole thing, having someone to talk to about this will help." He scoots over and wipes the tears off her face.

MEAN IT? she clicks. Her heart skips a beat.

"I'm getting used to how you communicate, so it works for me. And I can provide you with a safe and quiet place to recover. Where I live, people are happy."

MY HOME SAD. Her thoughts turn to her home. Before Albert, living without a voice made her feel like a freak or an object. Society treats mute folk like trash.

Rogue nods as her smile fades.

ALBERT DESTROY FAMILY.

"What about your dad?"

HE CAUSED IT.

"Ok, what about your mom?"

SHE GONE. The emotion drains from her body.

"Oh, I'm sorry."

ALBERT DID THAT TOO. As their conversation progresses, she seems numb. Her body language comes across as though she's dead.

"This nightmare is over. And we'll make sure he doesn't cause more." *Man, I'm going to need years of therapy after this. Talking to*

Crystal alone is proving to be a traumatic experience.

THANK YOU FOR HELPING. Her hand is the only body part moving and her clicking is slow.

Rogue forces out a laugh trying to break her empty expression. "Well, this is a variety of new experiences for me. But I think you're worth it." *Aw screw me, wrong word choice.*

WORTH IT? She snaps to life at the remark, makes direct eye contact, then raises an eyebrow and crosses her arms.

"Well, worth helping out. You're priceless, and I should shut up. What I mean is, you're important to me. I value you as a person, a human. I like you, and I'd like to know more about you other than the nightmare. I did kill someone for you. And I stink at this." *Please don't hit my nuts again.*

She gives him a puzzled glance, but inside he gives her hope. Some words he spoke echo in her head. She is important to him, she is valued. Saying them is one thing, but he meant them. YOU WANT ME?

"I want to learn who you are. Absolutely. And I'll wait as long as you need to open up." Rogue admits. *I don't know you. Well, I guess I know about the worst part of your life and feel committed to helping you. Who knows? Maybe the best parts of you are worth the trauma and punches to the nuts. Crap, I kinda boxed myself in here. I suck at relationships.*

ARE YOU SURE? The reality of how little she knows this stranger starts to hit her. This guy can't be as bad as Albert, and they definitely met under some wild circumstances. But what if when things are normal, he's a pervert like every other man? At the same time, everything out of his mouth gives her hope.

"I can't be that bad, can I?" Rogue can tell she's lost in thoughts with mixed feelings. *I can remember wanting to be a hero since I was a young kid. And here I am being one to this woman. The look in her eyes says as much. Hope I don't want to be her hero for the wrong reasons.*

She shakes her head. A small smile appears on her face. She's trusting him this far. Which is more than she can say about anyone else alive, including her father.

"So, what do you think? You ok with coming to my place?"

ONLY IF NO SEX. She's clicking while pointing a finger at him. She needs to be clear about this, because the thought scares her. This was the one thing Albert and his men didn't do to her during captivity, because she has the disability. Even before then she's faced this problem her entire life.

Rogue chuckles. "Of course, I mean, I might ask you out when this is all over, but I promise, you'll be safe. No one will touch you. Not me, not anyone. You'll have a room all to yourself with your own stuff. I'll make sure of that." *Dammit, stop talking. I have a one bedroom apartment in the largest city around. With this disaster I can't afford a house. Well, maybe, when we return to Acinvar, I'll call in some favors. I'll find a way to keep my word somehow.*

DEAL, she clicks with the biggest smile he's seen. Finally, she eases up and for once is calm. She puts her hand on his side where she elbowed him.

"I'll be alright. I'm strong. And you're strong too, stronger than you know. But if you need to let everything out, I'm here for you." *Bought by a damsel in distress's smile! Now I can't break her trust, or I will become a monster that I myself would hate.* He holds his hand out to her. She gives him a hug.

The noise of some trees cracking in the near distance catches his attention with birds flying out of trees.

Thebes and Jades aim their weapons at the shaking trees. The rest of them take cover in the cargo hold. A tall, slender, furry animal approaches some smoldering bushes. It has long bony spines along the length of a long tail, and bony plates covering its shoulders and hips. There are two massive horns on its head. "It's not a carnivore," Thebes says lowering his rifle.

"No, but check out those spines along the tail." Jades keeps his weapon shouldered.

The animal bellows at the group, then resumes sniffing the charred wood and ashes. It grunts several times before deciding to move away. Several others deeper in the trees approach.

"I don't know what they are, but they don't like the burned forest." Thebes takes the safety off the rifle to be cautious.

"We're clear!" Jades turns around, failing to find anyone. Nor can he see the dirigible or the wreckage. He's alone. "Shit!" He decides to stay put, knowing they still have a ways to go, won't leave anytime soon.

A small rustling in the bushes startles him. He faces the forest and finds a creature resembling a mauler, but its eyes glow a bright green. The creature is quickly joined by several more, coming out from behind tree trunks. They move with their eyes focused on him.

Jades raises his weapon.

"What's he doing?" Walker watches Jades aiming at the animals.

"Jades stop!" Thebes runs over to grab Jades.

Too many of them appear for Jades to count. They take one

step forward in unison. Then another, closing in on him in a slow, coordinated fashion. His weapon starts to move on its own, pointing down, and the hallucination stops. Thebes comes into view, standing in front of him with his hand on the barrel of the rifle, pointing away to the ground.

"You ok, man?" Thebes slaps Jades' arm.

"No. I'm not. Ghost maulers. Glowing green eyes." Jades shakes his head.

Walker signals to the rest of the team to keep working. They are now a little past halfway in making the bomb, with a routine they're managing to work through a case a minute.

Thebes shakes his head. "Damn, man. You almost shot the animals after they decide to ignore us."

Jades tries to remain calm as Thebes' eyes develop the same glow.

"Everything ok?" Walker can tell Jades isn't alright.

"Only a jump scare." Jades glances over his shoulder back at Walker, and discovers that Hunter, Thebes, Pattel, and Stoutarm all possess glowing eyes. Walker, Rogue, and Crystal do not.

Thebes backs off. He can't believe Jades came so close to aggravating the passing herd. "We'll be back to normal when we kill the hydra."

"I remember what those are. Aurochs," Jades says as they move back into the trees.

"Aurochs, you say?" Thebes, for a second thinks Jades is making stuff up.

"The menagerie near my old school had them." Jades rubs his eyes as the aurochs keep moving along.

"You had a menagerie where you grew up?"

"Yeah." Jades glances around and discovers everyone is gone again. "Oh, screw me." He resists the urge to shoulder the rifle again. The forest lights up with green eyes again, this time too far to away figure out what they are, but they are larger this time.

Jades closes his eyes tightly. "Nothing can hurt me because nothing is there." A moment passes before he opens his eyes again to check if the group has reappeared. Instead, huge teeth and an open maw are in front of him. The tongue is covered in sharp, backward-facing spines like razor teeth, sticking out only inches away from his face.

Jades raises his weapon to his shoulder but realizes that nothing's moving. After some tense breaths he backs up a few steps, discovering the hallucination is hovering in the air. No animal is attached that he can see. And as he steps to the side, the mouth becomes invisible to him.

He turns to find scratch marks in mid-air. Claw marks made by something like a small sized bear or large cat. Jades inspects the marks and tries to touch them. His hand passes through them as if they aren't there. The second time he can feel an invisible wall.

"Jades!" Thebes shouts, but Jades can't locate him.

Walker keeps an eye on Jades, as Thebes' hands go through him. "Can't do anything about him, not now." Walker calls out.

"What if we leave him?" Thebes is expecting the group to help him rescue Jades.

"So be it. We kill this hydra and come back and find him. After we knock the hydra down, we won't be going home until everyone is accounted for."

The rest of them give Walker a variety of concerned expressions.

"Jades! No!" Thebes runs after Jades, who is on the ground moving towards the forest as if he's being dragged by something they can't see.

"Thebes, stop!" Walker calls out, as Thebes runs through a charred tree trunk. "Dammit."

"Let's keep the pace up. The best thing we can do for them is take out the dimensional link by killing that hydra." Hunter shudders and closes his eyes.

Rogue watches Thebes run deeper past the trees after Jades.

WHAT? Crystal clicks. Thebes runs through trees the same way her hand went through Albert earlier.

"The hydra's wake is affecting them all the way over here." Rogue answers.

NO GOOD, she clicks.

Jades is being dragged faster than he can react. He's unable to keep a solid grip on his rifle to shoot the wolf with glowing green eyes. "Let go, you piece of shit!" He screams to no avail.

After a few moments, the crazy wolf drops him and bolts off around a bush and vanishes. Jades sits up to find himself in a small, barren clearing with an opening in the ground. The forest falls silent, with no sounds of birds chirping, or rustling of leaves. A warm flow of air comes from the hole.

Jades gets up and wanders over to the crevice. Below ground is a cave with crystals in the walls. "Seriously? The gemstone mine goes this far?" he thinks to himself out loud. The sound of snapping sticks behind him causes him to spin around.

He doesn't see anything, and forgetting about the mine opening, steps backward. Then he leans forward when he realizes there's no ground behind him and falls to his knees. "Nobody saw that." He pushes himself back up.

The wolf that dragged him reappears from behind a tree. "What the hell?" Jades notices he's being ignored. His new friend focuses on something else coming their way.

The faint squishing sound coming from the cave below grows louder. The wolf growls.

Jades moves to the side of the crevice. The angry wolf keeps snarling, focusing on the opening. "Guess we're gonna deal with whatever is coming." Jades aims the rifle down into the darkness.

A man walks into the light at the bottom. He's half naked, with old, shredded clothes draped around him. The way he carries himself is unnatural and he holds his head down. His skin is blue and purple and black, like bruises all over, and long, knotted hair covers most of his body. The man steps onto a rock and starts to climb. Jades is freaking out over the unnatural movement, as if the man has no bones in his body. "Oh hell no," Jades fires a round.

The bullet hits the man in the head, pulverizing it like a ripe piece of fruit. A bright-blue glowing liquid oozes out instead of blood. The growling stops as the zombie melts into the dirt.

"Is that what you needed?" Jades can tell this wolf is connected to the hydra, like a victim trapped by the wake, same as him.

The growling starts again, and the squishing noise now comes from all around the clearing.

Thebes hears the shot. "Jades!" He's going in the wrong direction. He runs toward the sound through the trees to find Jades.

Jades keeps glancing around as more squishing noises approach them, though he can't see anything yet. Then he hears chanting.

"Hydra's wake!" the chant begins repeating.

"Show yourselves." Jades spins around in circles searching for the source. Then he sees the figures approach the clearing through the trees.

"One of us," the chanting now says.

"Nope." Jades controls his breathing and calms down, then focuses on shooting at them as they approach. The wolf starts attacking them as well.

They do not respond to the weapon as the zombies Jades fires at turn into pulverized messes of glowing blue puddles. The chants stop and the figures evaporate. As does the wolf.

Thebes' body lies next to a tree. Blood leaks from his body and runs down towards the cave.

"Thebes!" Jades realizes Thebes is where he just fired into the forest. "No!" He runs to Thebes' body, finding the bullet exit wounds on the back of his neck. He shot Thebes in the jugular and the throat. There's a sudden cold rising from the cave, and a black, smoking hand appears out of the ground. Jades turns in time to see the Shadow Figure rise above the entrance.

"What is this?" a shrill raspy voice said from inside the cave. Ned looks up and sees Jades and Thebes body. "Friendlies!"

"Ned?" Jades backs away from the entrance.

"Well, more or less," Ned replies. His body is more disfigured than the ones Jades just mowed down. "Come, we can end your misery, and make it fun, scaring halfwits and feeding our master."

Jades watches as the Shadow Figure moves to hover over Thebes' body. "What are you doing?"

"Well, you see, the body isn't blown to bits or eaten, so he can become alive again. Like me. The soul is gone, but who cares? No breathing, no eating, no drinking, no living. Being a terror to all the boys and girlsies," Ned replies as he comes out of the mine.

Thebes moves a hand and coughs up a pool of blood. "Pop us, Jades."

"Oh, he's not done, done. I'll fix him," Ned says with excitement, as he clambers over to Thebes' body.

Jades reaches to the back of his belt for a grenade, arming it as Thebes suggests.

"So, basically, you're in hell." Jades asks Ned.

Ned stands over Thebes' body and faces Jades. "Well yes, and it's fun! Seventh Circle VIP membership included." Ned drools thick oily blood all over Thebes as he speaks.

"Here, catch!" Jades throws the grenade at Thebes.

Ned's body catches the grenade, and the Shadow Figure vanishes. Ned's eyes return to regular white when he identifies the object he caught. "I don't want this." Ned says before the grenade detonates. The added grenades Thebes is carrying make several explosions powerful enough to hit Jades and blow him apart as well.

After the blast, the Shadow Figure returns to see all three bodies blown apart. It spreads some fog around and tries to reanimate the corpses, but is unable to, so retreats back into the cave.

Rogue faces the forest when an explosion goes off. "Guys, we are running out of time and space to work with." He looks down at the group as the roars of several creatures fill the air. A lot of movement in the trees shows the animals are running away in a panic. The birds flying away ignore the dirigible as they head higher, to fly over the cliffs.

"We still have forty cases to go through." Walker is unnerved by the explosion and gunfire.

Hunter drops a canister at the sound of the explosions then faces Stoutarm and Pattel. "You guys heard the explosions, right?"

"What explosions?" Pattel and Stoutarm ask together. They stop cracking open the cases. "Who's gone?"

"Walker, where are Thebes and Jades?" Hunter is sure he knows, but relays the question anyway, since neither Stoutarm nor Pattel see Walker anymore.

"Jades got dragged by something, I have no idea what, and Thebes ran after him."

"Are they ok?" Pattel can tell from Hunter's demeanor the answer is no, but wants confirmation.

"I don't know. All Walker saw was Jades getting dragged off and Thebes running after him. Then a lot of gunfire erupted, and it sounded like they used all their grenades on something." Hunter resumes working on the cargo.

Pattel exchanges glances with Stoutarm and keeps working. "Think they're still alive?" Pattel's voice is solemn.

"I'm worried about myself." Stoutarm sounds unconcerned. "If they lived, I'll buy them a beer; if they didn't, I'll drink to their death."

Pattel shakes his head. "I don't like leaving people behind."

"We're all trained not to. But this is above our humanity. Or at the very least, my humanity." Stoutarm continues. "The hydra is trying to hunt us as food. It's not an enemy nation or some dictator. We're up against a force of nature, and nature leaves the weak behind in order to evolve and grow. The survival of the fittest. Its laws are the leading authority now, and we have to play as a pack while we can."

"We are not animals." Pattel is outraged by Stoutarm's comments.

"Biology says otherwise. Humans are but a single species. We're advanced animals. But animals nonetheless." Stoutarm strikes a nerve with the others.

Hunter shakes his head. "We get the picture. Now come on. We've wasted time."

"Not wasted. I'm busy cutting these locks while chit chatting. We need to bust these open and start running the canisters over. Got a dozen left to cut through." Stoutarm throws a cut lock at Hunter.

Pattel starts breaking the lids off the open cases and handing Hunter several canisters to run to Walker.

Albert finishes refueling Rogue's airplane. "This required far more effort than I should have needed to put forth. Luckily, the maintenance shop has a stockpile of fuel, or this would have been for naught." He looks out of the window to check on the hydra, which is still out of sight, but the ground still shakes from constant tremors as it did during the last fight.

He had locked the doors and windows of the refinery, to hide from the zombies that surrounded the building during the eclipse's peak. The creatures were unable to penetrate the walls and made no effort to smash any windows. Aside from that time, he had no trouble going between the machine shop and refinery.

"It is clear whoever brought the airplane inside intended to install a larger fuel tank and a better engine. The parts and tools were present for the repairs, but perhaps they did not have access to them at the time. No matter. I liked the plan, and while it forced me to recall my school years from decades back, I have, as usual, succeeded in my efforts. Though it would be foolish to attempt to journey to Heart at the end of the day. Temperatures mixing from Heart and Shell in the Tradewinds would tear my hard work apart. I am not an experienced pilot, so I must await a calmer time." Frustrate, he speaks to the empty room. His stomach growls for food.

"Must I suffer so?"

"I wondered who was tinkering away in here." Joe speaks, causing Albert to jump.

"Who is here?" Albert scans the room. "Answer me! I demand of you!"

"Or you can ask politely, or perhaps nicely," Joe responds.

"I am far too irritated to play mind games." Albert can't find anyone and shakes his head. "Oh dear me, I am losing myself."

"I forget how rough fading into this alternate reality is. The rest of the guys were doing fine before they died," Joe says in a more solemn tone.

"Spare me your presence, foul spirit."

"Joe, please, and I'm someone who has managed to not be eaten for almost a year now."

"Why are you in my presence?" Albert searches around, again hoping to see the person. "And I suppose you are unable to show yourself?"

"The last bit is not my choice, I'm afraid. No one can leave here. Stray too far from the Hydra physically and you lose energy and your ability to think. Literally to the point where you lie on the ground empty and paralyzed until the monster gets back near enough to you. again"

The words bore into Albert's heart and sting worse than any pain he's endured before. The hope of getting back is stripped away. He sits in the seat of the airplane and stares up at the wing. "Joe, you say?"

"Yes. You must be this Lord Albert I've heard so much about."

"I applaud your deduction. Where are the rest of my men from yesterday?"

"Well, I think Dusty was the first to go. I didn't catch on to your presence until after you met the zombies in the gemstone mine."

"I know of his fate. Eaten." Albert sounds bored with the topic.

"Let's see; the guy named Mack. A floating knife got him. I think Rogue Whip murdered him. The hydra ate what was left of him."

"Rogue Whip? Is he a young muscle-bound lad or an older, scary military person?" Albert perks up at the mention of Rogue's name.

"I can't see anyone who is not affected by the hydra's wake I'm afraid. But I overheard a lot of talk about him and, the way I figure, he's the only option that makes sense. You guys must have really pissed him off."

"I suppose such a reaction is to be expected when one shoots the wrong man down," Albert says. "At least he is not boring."

"Yeah. Ok, now that's been cleared up, your pal Ned."

"I would rather, no need to explain. Does Hunter live?" Albert is quick to cut Joe off on Ned's situation.

"Yeah, he turned on you. If I remember, that's part of why Rogue killed Mack; Mack wanted to catch Rogue and use him as bait for a bomb to kill the hydra. Hunter voted to off you, Ned voted for you because they couldn't find Rogue but could interact with you. The logic is solid."

Albert is unfazed. "I admired the work ethic that freak often brought to the table, but he often got into my way when it mattered most."

"Your second team didn't last long either. Hydra ate the pompous hat guy, and the rest took off to the skyport at the top of the gemstone mine high in the cliff face."

"As Ned explained to me, before things surpassed the definition of disturbing. If I ever lay my hands on any of them, I will tie them down, and have a thick pole shoved down their throats and out their rectums, slice them to shreds and rub them in seasonings, and then leave them out on a spit for the poor starving hydra."

"Graphic, disturbing, all things inhumane and heartless. You sir are the truest adaptation of your reputation in any man I've ever met." Joe speaks with sarcastically with delight.

"Oh that is no-where near as much as I would do to them with proper preparation time." Albert smiles from ear to ear. "Dear Joe, have you ever tasted the cooked flesh of a woman's milky breast, or a strong man's barbecued ribs?"

"You know what? I'm leaving."

"Such a hidden delight when seared to perfection," Albert continues, as if daydreaming.

"Are you a straight-up cannibal?"

"Why no, of course not, dear lad. But I do enjoy experimenting to find ways to make my torture sessions more intense and egregious. This includes knowing for oneself how to shred a human being apart and make them eat their own flesh, prepared in the best way possible. It adds to the cruelty of the experience if you can give parts of the session a sense of luxury. Or just survive being dissected a few times, as well as being an active participant in the dissections."

"If you say you've eaten a man's junk. I'm going to come through this alternate reality barrier and end you myself." Joe sounds as if he's gagging.

"Heavens no. I maintain my pride." Albert waves at the empty air. "Why, I have certain servants for dining on those. And if I take them at their word, it is best procured by swift removal during an ejaculation. Prepared with a mix of chives, paprika, fresh picked thyme, chopped almost to a powder, white peppercorn, and grilled over cherry wood."

"It is such a wonderful thing I haven't eat anything in I can't remember how long." The sound of Joe's puking follows. "Ok, you were tolerable for a few seconds, but man, I want you dead. But I can't do anything about it."

"How dare you insult my company? After all, you made the decision to pay me a visit." Albert's tone shifts to anger. "The recipe is a beautiful requirement in destroying a man. The shocking surprise when they eat it without realizing what it is until I tell them and show them the proof! Many of them compliment my servants the dish. Hahahahaha. Oh, Joe, I do thank you for bringing this conversation up, reminding me of the joy I received when I would see such faces. Oh, the life I have left to live! If you do come to me in a corporeal form, I have to shake your hand."

"I will mess you up."

"Ah, come now, you brought joy to my world for a moment; do not have me dislike you." Albert is enjoying the conversation.

"That's messed up. I don't know how to respond to you anymore."

"The pure delight of enjoying new human specimens to experiment upon. Made sure to never share them with anyone else so the rest of the world may never know the joys. This reminds me, the mute daughter of my rival may very well be alive, if Rogue had any part of it."

"The woman you guys keep mentioning is a mute?"

"Pathetic one too. Cannot read or write. Now that I am thinking about this, a stronger descriptor is required. I fail in justifying the use of such a vessel. The thing is not worthy, as it has little ability to make service of itself. The full term is useless, and I do daresay offing it would be for the best of all humanity, a favor level act. Any savage wanting to breed a mute is a despicable ideal." Albert explains.

"I disagree, as I never tried the experience for myself."

Albert shakes his head in disapproval. "Fair argument. I shall tie her down for you before feeding her to the monster. Do be mindful, though; it is nothing more than a snack for the beast."

"Thank you? I guess." Joe holds back from saying the many things that to mind. Albert is so he's unsure if he can say them without getting into actual trouble. The idea of confronting the psychopath is terrifying, and Joe isn't up for it. "Well, nice meeting ya. I have to hunker down where I am safe before the hungry hydra gets back. I'll check in when I'm safer."

"Indeed, survival must be the utmost priority around here." Albert replies.

Joe reaches the phosphorus mine entrance when the ground shakes hard and the hydra lands behind him. "I despise you, but that freak in the refinery. He needs to go. He's evil, pure villainous evil!"

The hydra lowers a head into the mine. Joe sprints to stay out of its reach, but the head sits at the entrance of the cave as if it's listening and understands Joe.

"Kill that demented freak Albert. Please. You gotta be able to smash into the building like nothing, so kill him. He want to kill everyone."

The hydra let out a snarling noise, acknowledging it hears Joe.

7: JUNGLE BOAT RIDE

"Alright Rogue, everything is packed nice and tight, and we got the fuse box ready to go!" Walker clamps down the lid to the finished bomb.

Rogue gives them the thumbs up from the cabin. "Took less time than I expected." He pulls on a lever to activate the winches to pull the cargo hold back up. They reel in as they should, and the hold snaps back into place. *Everything's going to plan. This is going well. These are good signs, right?*

Walker glances out at the forest after the hold snaps securely and signals for everyone to climb up the anchor chain. "Alright, we're halfway done now," he shouts to the group.

Hunter climbs the chain, followed by Walker. Stoutarm and Pattel head over but a tremor stops them. Not like the hydra's tremor, but something else big is coming. Pattel and Stoutarm find cover in the wreckage.

Rogue catches a glimpse of a large carnivore in the trees, approaching cautiously. "We gotta go! Port side. Tyro incoming!"

Hunter reaches the cabin platform and pulls Walker up. "Guys, come on!"

Rogue extends a hand to help Walker and keeps an eye on the tree line, discovering the carnivore is hiding. "Are they on their way up?" *If they aren't, I gotta protect us and the ship. Sorry guys.*

"They hid in the old hold," Hunter points out.

"We can't stay." Rogue slams on a button. The dirigible starts to rise after releasing the anchor. "We'll be back for them, but the tyro will tear this ship to bits if we stay here."

Hunter and Walker watch as indeed a tyro emerges into the charred area. The curious beast follows the ship with its eyes as it rises into the air. "Shit." Walker pounds on the window.

Pattel and Stoutarm peek through the cracks of the old cargo hold. They spot the fifteen-foot bipedal carnivore sniffing around after missing out on the dirigible.

"We can take this thing down." Stoutarm nods toward Pattel.

"If we don't screw up, yeah."

They grab a grenade off their belts and lob them near its feet. They hurry behind the hold. The grenades detonate, and the tyro lets out an ear-splitting roar.

"Perfect throws." Stoutarm checks over his shoulder to find the beast on the ground, missing a leg.

"Wait, wait, hold up! Don't shoot. Let this one attract other creatures, while we move away." Pattel stops Stoutarm from raising his rifle.

"How do we return to the ship?" Stoutarm stares at the rising airship.

"We'll walk to the mine camp, following these cliffs, and stay out of the forest itself. Move quickly and quietly. We got this." Pattel faces the direction to camp, while studying the cliff wall.

Stoutarm takes another peek at their ship, which is rising fast. He faces Pattel and nods. "Guess I can't call myself a proper soldier if this is a challenge. Forty miles of fun, right?"

Pattel waves his arms to the airship for them to go on. Stoutarm gives the same signal.

"The hell are they doing?" Hunter keeps tabs as both men start moving along the cliffs.

"They're hugging the cliff base. I bet they're going to try walking back." Walker says.

"This ain't no walk in the park."

"They aren't normal henchmen either." Walker smiles as he keeps an eye on them. "Stoutarm is going to be in his element. They'll be ok. We'll meet them back at camp."

"Neither of those things matter," Rogue chimes in. "Best of luck to them. Walker, let's make hydra hunting easier for them. The cliff wall is covered by dense forest near the halfway point. We need to reach the clear bit of this valley close to daybreak to do this right."

"Sounds good. Hey, earlier you mentioned something about going against the wind on the way back to the valley?" With one eye, Walker heeds Crystal who forms a fist with one hand, and punches the other.

"Crystal, may I make a proposal?" Hunter gets between her and Walker.

She folds her arms and stares at him.

"Look, if you can find within you a way not to pummel him

until after we kill the hydra and Albert. Then I'll hold him down so you can beat the crap out of him for as long as you like. Deal?" Hunter extends his arms to both sides, blocking her from running past him.

"Like hell you will!" Walker turns to Rogue for an intervention.

'Don't look at me. I'll help them." Rogue smiles, then faces her. "I'd call that offer a fair trade."

Crystal puts a finger in Hunter's face and nods.

"This is bullshit." Walker takes a seat near the door.

"We'll revisit the deal later Walker," Rogue starts, then Crystal punches his arm. "Ouch! Damn that one hurt. But as I was saying, partly, I'm hoping to time this so that we can do it in daylight. So, I'm going to take the long way to give us time through the night," Rogue replies.

"Hey, this way you don't have to worry about her until tomorrow. Right?" Hunter looks at Crystal who nods.

Rogue lets out a sigh of relief. "In the meantime, food is in the quarters through that door; I'm guessing it's edible."

At the mention of food, Crystal's stomach growls loud enough for them all to hear, and a sheepish smile grows on her face. She walks into the back room followed by Hunter and Walker, who also have growling stomachs.

"I just *had* to say the F word." Rogue braces for chaos as the two men are with Crystal. Then his own stomach growls, and he rolls his eyes. Walker lets out a scream like he's been kicked in the nuts. Rogue face-palms.

Pattel and Stoutarm jog at a brisk pace, putting the crash site behind them. They keep near the cliff base and jog through the thin trees.

"Hey, you planning to keep this pace up all night?" Pattel keeps up next to him.

"That's the current plan. Maintain a brisk, and we won't freeze." Stoutarm rubs his arms for warmth.

They're able to breathe easier with every step closer to the camp. After about an hour, they take a quick stop near a small pond.

"The wolf has been trailing us for some time now." Pattel glances over his shoulder at a wolf with glowing green eyes.

"Yeah; he also brought a few others, but they're unable to interact with the trees or things without glowing eyes." Stoutarm fills his canteen and takes a drink, ignoring the animals following them at a distance.

"They must be stuck in the hydra's wake like we are. And if they figure out we have a way to set them free, too, I can't imagine we have anything to fear from them," Pattel suggests.

"How would they know? As long as they keep their distance, I'll be a lot less trigger-happy."

Pattel shrugs. The wolf behind them growling. It looks into the forest. The Shadow Figure emerges from behind the tree and begins burning in the daylight. Stoutarm aims at the figure's head and fires a round. The bullet hits the figure, which swirls like a vortex and vanishes.

"The hell is that?" Pattel is dazed by the encounter.

"That's from the gemstone mines." Stoutarm never wants to encounter the figure again. "We gotta keep going."

Pattel grabs Stoutarm and points at some bushes. Another tyro is approaching. This one is smaller though. "Another one got the jump on us. Stay sharp. We'll time our engagement." Pattel gets ready to fire.

Stoutarm takes aim at the head. "Squared up. Ready on your mark."

The tyro charges and leaps high into the air. They're surprised by the height of its jump as it lands right in front of them and tries to bite Stoutarm. The maw goes through Stoutarm, though, like he doesn't exist.

Stoutarm stands still, frozen in panic as the beast tries to bite him several times, only to bite at nothing. It stops after a few tries and sniffs around him. Stoutarm smiles. "HAHA! YOU CAN'T EAT ME!" He points at the confused tyro.

Pattel takes several steps away and the animal turns its attention to him. Pattel raises his weapon, hesitating as the cautious tyro sniffs the rifle and appears to lose interest. Unsatisfied, it walks away with a deep growl.

"Too close."

"Yo, that was a thrill." Stoutarm waves his hands up like a champion. "Never felt so dead and so alive in my life. That was better than the best high I've ever felt in my life."

"You done?" Pattel is aggravated with Stoutarm's goofing off.

"Why? You shit yourself? I know I did. Totally admit I shit my pants in terror. That was awesome." Stoutarm holds none of his energy or enthusiasm back.

Pattel rolls his eyes and shakes his head. "Not to be a major killjoy but heads up. All the glow-eyed critters are gone." He checks around them.

"Who cares? If the dangerous ones can't eat us, I'll live this up, because being a ghost is fun." Stoutarm adds as Pattel begins running towards the camp. "Oh, all right, we'll return to the mission at hand. Sheesh."

They resume jogging along the cliff base. A little further on they discover thick, pale-white strings hanging between the trees.

"Now we're getting to why this forest has a real reputation." Pattel walks through the webs, followed by Stoutarm.

"If these webs ain't gonna touch us, the spiders won't notice us." Stoutarm waves his hand through a web.

"I agree. Must be some monster size spiders, though." Pattel spots a fresh tyro corpse ahead, bigger than the first one they encountered. They stop to check out the carcass.

"That's insane. Gotta be more than just spiders doing this." Stoutarm pokes the corpse with his rifle. It is nothing but skin and bone.

"To be fair, I didn't think tyros could jump like the little one did. Had to be a hundred-foot jump." Pattel continues past Stoutarm.

"Sure did close the gap between us faster than lightning. To think they aren't near the top of the food chain around here." Stoutarm lifts a piece of the skin to discover it's hollow inside. The flesh is gone but the bones and skin are moist with blood. "Whatever ate this, did so not too long ago. Still sort of goocy inside."

"Did not need the image in my head." Pattel starts walking back to the cliffs.

They pick up the pace. A loud, high-pitched shriek comes from deeper in the forest. The shriek repeats several times, and they go from a steady jog to a solid running pace.

"Oh what, you scared?" Stoutarm catches up.

"I don't want the hydra's wake to put us on the wrong side of physics at an inopportune moment. We're on borrowed time, you know." Pattel makes sure not to run into trees or rocks.

"Yeah, I guess you're right." Stoutarm runs into a rock and trips. He lands face first in the dirt and the rest of his body continues. He ends up rolling down a small hill.

"Like that." Pattel helps Stoutarm up. "You ran into that full force. You alright?"

"Ugh, that hurt." Stoutarm waits for his head to stop spinning and throbbing. He gets up and checks around them. "Glowing eyes are back."

Pattel takes a quick glance around. "I don't see them yet."

Stoutarm takes a few steps and sees dark spots moving among the grass and fallen leaves on the ground. "Oh, no."

"What?" Pattel glares at Stoutarm.

"Seeing some things, and last time, this went bad for me and Jades." Stoutarm faces where Pattel is standing and finds he's alone. "Ok, Pattel, you've vanished on me! This is not funny. Ok, stick to the plan. Go to camp. Figure this out later."

Pattel watches Stoutarm appear to lose track of him even though he is ahead of him. Unable to hear what Stoutarm is saying Pattel tries lip-reading. He manages to figure out that Stoutarm is going to keep heading to the mine camp. "Ok, this sucks. I'll stick by you as long as I can."

They continue toward the camp, returning to a jogging pace as the daylight fades away.

Pattel turns on the light at the end of his rifle when he sees the spotlight at the front of Stoutarm's.

Stoutarm spots the second light on the ground. "Oh, thank God he kept up." He stops and uses his light to nudge the other one. The other light nudges back.

"So, he's able to see my light. Interesting." Pattel is thankful the lights aren't affected by whatever is going on. "Well, we got each other; at least for now."

Stoutarm hears another growl from the wolf that's following them.

"What's going on?" The wolf is looking deeper into the forest, away from the cliffs. Stoutarm looks in that direction and sees little floating balls of burning coal.

"Stoutarm!" Pattel's hand appears on Stoutarm's shoulder.

"Pattel? You're back?"

"Yeah. You stopped. What's happening?"

"You don't see those?"

"I see them. I also don't care enough to go check."

The coals form a swirling pattern and the Shadow Figure emerges from the center.

This time Pattel raises his rifle and fires a shot. The same thing happens as before. Where the bullet hits, the figure swirls into a vortex. The floating coals transform from a natural orange to a vibrant yellow and stop moving, spread out near trees. Then they draw closer to Stoutarm and Pattel.

"They're moving too fast to outrun." Pattel shoots at one.

He hits one, which explodes into a bright-yellow glowing powder to reveal a black cat-like creature. The coal-looking thing is on an antenna, like a lure. "We have a situation!" Pattel shouts. The light around them fades into a deep, unnatural darkness. The lights from the rifles can't differentiate the creatures from the background darkness. Finding them is incredibly difficult. "A pack of smoke panthers. Unreal!"

"Engaging!" Stoutarm fires when the others move quickly towards them.

"I can't even see them!" Pattel takes a few shots.

Stoutarm reaches for his belt, grabbing a flare and lighting the area. The creature's contrast and the shadows now make them easier to find as their stealth fails in the flare's red light.

With their cover blown, the panthers begin retreating, and Stoutarm and Pattel stop firing. They take the time to put full magazines into their weapons before moving on. Stoutarm picks up the flare. "Every mile we march is a rougher mile than the last." The dark fades back into the natural dusk of night as the pack moves further away.

"Why are people on the trees?"

Stoutarm looks around and there are indeed shadows of people on the trunks of the trees and the cliff face. They all point towards camp. The wolf growls at them. "Come on, you big furry baby with teeth. They aren't doing anything yet." Stoutarm taunts the wolf.

They continue along the cliff side hoping to reach the camp soon. "Do they do anything, aside from look creepy?" Pattel moves closer to inspect one.

"You need to ask Jades for the full effect." Stoutarm fights to keep the memory out of his mind.

The shadows begin to move with them rather than appearing and vanishing. After climbing over a rock wall, they hear the sound of a river ahead of them.

The shadows on the cliffs point towards the sound.

"We have an active audience." Stoutarm does his best to ignore them.

"Do you feel like we're walking into a trap?"

"Yes and no." Stoutarm keeps heading for the river.

"Yeah, I feel the same way."

They reach the riverbank, finding a shack with a pier and a rowboat are next to the water. A few dim lights illuminate the area. The shadows fade away. "Are we close to camp now, or does the power come all the way out here?" Stoutarm is curious about where they are.

"Hey, this river must go to the lake," Pattel says as he starts shivering. The air is freezing cold.

"In the center of the valley, flat, open terrain, with no scary creatures aside from a hydra between us and camp." Stoutarm resists the urge to shiver, portray the tough-guy type.

The wolf behind them howls, followed by snarling and growls. Their wolf is now growling at them. "Hey, the eyes." Pattel backs away.

They aren't glowing. The soldiers raise their weapons and back up to the water's edge. The wolf doesn't follow but continues to growl.

At the water they about face to wade in. "Cold, cold, very cold." Pattel's teeth start to chatter.

"Man, this will freeze my balls off, and I need those." Stoutarm swims to the other side, where the shack and pier are.

"Is this a good idea? Now we're wet and it's way too cold to stay out here."

"Aw look, a rowboat for two to get warm and cozy in." Stoutarm points with a romantic tone pointing at the boat tied to the pier, patting Pattel on the back.

"I will shoot your frozen balls clean off."

"Relax and lighten up. This place is hell; it is literally looking for any excuse to disorient and kill us." Stoutarm shakes his head. "Let's see if it's warmer inside."

"Why not start a fire? It's not like the real threats here will care if we can spot them or not?" Pattel follows Stoutarm walking towards the building. The window by the door is covered in blood spatter.

"Hey Pattel."

"Let's breach; make sure we're alone." Pattel raises his weapon. They approach the door one slow step at a time. They stop when the lights start to flicker. After a moment they continue. Stoutarm stands next to the door and Pattel stands in front of it. Stoutarm opens the door as fast as he can.

"Wow." Pattel covers his mouth. "This poor bastard died near the start of the mining season."

Stoutarm checks inside and discovers a corpse tied to the chair by the desk. There is a bullet hole on his forehead. "Damn, foul play for sure."

Pattel reads the name badge on the miner's uniform. "Joseph Hardy."

"Pissed someone off big time." Stoutarm inspects the rest of the shack, only to find a ladder leading down into the gemstone mines. "How vast are those mines?"

"I'm not going down." Pattel turns around and heads towards

the rowboat.

Stoutarm has a gut feeling to check out the shaft but follows Pattel to the boat. "Something doesn't feel right with this shaft."

"Something *isn't* right about that shaft. And we're not going to go find out. Gut feelings make us want to go check things out are going to kill us like the cat."

But Stoutarm decides to go back and check out the entrance. Pattel waits "So there; my turn to be the loudmouth chicken shit."

The sound of metal bangs against rock comes from the mine. Stoutarm aims his rifle down. "You gonna help cover?"

Pattel shakes his head. "Dammit." He goes back into the shed and stands beside Stoutarm. They keep their rifles aimed down the hole.

"Whatever is down there, if it's confined to a small place, I'd rather take it out in a shooting gallery, instead of giving it wide open space to play with." Stoutarm waits for a visual.

Pattel shakes his head and starts to walk away. "You moron, let's go!"

"I'm camping here until it tries to come up." Stoutarm kneels and tightens his grip on his weapon.

Pattel grabs Stoutarm by the arm and peeks down the shaft. "The hell?" He lets go of Stoutarm.

"What?"

"I didn't see a mining cart earlier."

"I did. Why?" The banging fades off.

"Well, ok, given the options, that's not the worst way to return to camp." Pattel considers the warm air rising from the mines, which is better than freezing outside.

"The caves of horror or the forest of deadly hungry things." Stoutarm glances up to check the doorway out of habit.

"Our life sucks tonight."

"Fine, let's check out the mine." Stoutarm starts climbing down the ladder. Pattel follows.

The cart tracks lead to a caved-in section. "Well, that way won't work." Pattel tosses a small rock at the cave in.

Stoutarm discovers a network map on the wall. "Are you kidding me? These mines are massive."

"Damn straight. You could house an entire city in here." Pattel takes a moment to look over the map.

"This is not a new map. Check this out. The last check-in date here is from twenty years ago." Stoutarm points out the date written at the bottom.

"If we're reading this right, this way heads out to almost under or beyond the crash site," Pattel observes, looking down the open shaft.

"Yep, and the caved-in way leads back to camp." Stoutarm stares at the blocked shaft.

They check out the rest of the chamber.

"Maybe stopping in here isn't a bad idea. Gives us a chance to warm up." Pattel approaches what must be an office area to the side.

"Fair point. The air isn't cold in here."

"Hey, check this out," Pattel calls out to Stoutarm, as he lifts up an old newspaper.

"Woman saves twenty lives in mine-shaft collapse. Heroically sacrifices self with controlled explosion. Prevents Camp Tor's famous gemstone mine from shutting down." Stoutarm reads aloud. "She's a smoking hot babe too. Shame she died a hero like that."

"Really man, that's what comes to mind here?" Pattel shakes his head and keeps looking around.

"Sue me. She's a babe I could mount all day long. I'll speak my mind unashamed." Stoutarm smirks.

"Well, when you're done with the paper, put your pants back on and let's return to the boat." Pattel heads for the ladder, stopping when he spots something else on the map. He walks back over to read more. "Hey, a rail depot is not far from us, over that way."

"Seriously?" Stoutarm points down the mine shaft. "Let's check the place out. If we can start up a train, we'll have a way out of here, considering the possibility that the hydra broke the last chopper."

The Shadow Figure hovers at the end of the chamber by the cave-in behind them and turns to face the rubble.

"Oh yeah, damned monster did smash three of those." Pattel recalls the firefight from when they landed.

They walk along the open shaft and come up on a chamber containing several massive tools used for carting the loose rock out of the mine. Everything is covered in dust, and several lights have burned out over time. "Ain't no one been down this way since the accident, I imagine." Stoutarm runs his finger across a railing to examine the dust collected. The path is lined with concrete walls leading to an incline.

"Must've been where the real goodies came from." Pattel takes the lead as they follow the constructed path.

Soon they feel a breeze from outside. "Talk about a short walk." Stoutarm takes a deep breath.

"No, a mile, maybe two." Pattel is relieved to take a breath of fresh air.

The corridor opens up into a massive train station with enormous cargo-loading cranes. "This is huge." Stoutarm comment.

"This is bigger than a city hub. This is crazy. How much money is in mining?" Pattel examines the room.

"I'll have to ask Walker what he made in his digging days," Stoutarm jokes.

"Check those out. They abandoned a few locomotives in here."

"Ain't no way you and me can operate one of them on our own. We'd need something smaller than those 4-8-8-8's. Those are meant for hauling all the way to the mining hub. You need two people just to keep the fire lit, need six people to get one going. Beltmon's too. Best damn engines around." Stoutarm sounds like a salesman.

"You know your trains, eh?" Pattel finds Stoutarm's knowledge surprising.

"Eh, my old man was a head locomotive engineer. Got to do any route he wanted. Spent my entire childhood around these things. Would be an engineer myself if he didn't derail on a fateful day. I'll save ya the story and tell ya he survived. The problem afterward was the business politics, making home life hell, and the fiasco turned me off as a young adult." Stoutarm rambles.

"That's actually humane. Especially coming from you."

"Hey, I'm not the worst guy around. Albert gets first prize in that category. I, at least, enjoy my women while they're alive and unharmed." Stoutarm steps around a pile of old trash.

"And that didn't last long." Pattel shakes his head as they move along the platform.

"Everything here is so huge and full of grandeur." Stoutarm checks the remaining rails. "Hold up. This last one; Pattel, come here."

Pattel hurries over. "What is this one?" The train has only a single set of six wheels on the base, with a box-shaped body, not cylindrical like a normal steam locomotive.

"This is something they began rolling out in the military not long ago. A gasoline-based engine, like this was invented less than twenty years ago. And I spy an insane problem. Check the insignia." Stoutarm points at a torn banner.

Pattel spots the gold circle with three black stars, with a diagonal silver stripe going across. "Of all the things we could encounter, what would the Juman military want here?"

"Don't know, but going back to the boat is looking like a great idea. We can't win a major firefight."

Pattel approaches the train and climbs on.

"Are you crazy?" Stoutarm glances around, hoping the room stays empty.

"No, but I did find a crazy note written on the floor in blood."

"What does it say?"

"'Beware the zombie hoard.' A massacre happened in here. Blood is old and dried up. I don't think we'll be fighting Jumans today." Pattel finds the door handle unlocked and enters the cabin. "Nobody is in here, just a lot of dried, rotten gore."

"Yeah, my nose is getting a whiff of death. Can we go now?"

"Hang on, A book's been left out with notes." Pattel walks over to the desk. It's the only pristine surface in the room, and the book appears more like a journal upon further inspection. "Yo, these guys were trying to find the hydra's hibernation lair."

"What? You're kidding! Why would the Juman try something so stupid?" Stoutarm is now interested.

"Something about wanting to weaponize hydra's wake. I'm taking this. Gotta be free money here." Pattel grabs the journal. As he does, the locomotives creak with the sound of scraping metal.

"We're leaving now. Jades and I endured enough in these mines. And you don't want to experience them."

As he finishes speaking, footsteps start echoing in the distance.

Pattel rejoins Stoutarm, and they retreat to where they entered.

"I don't see anything." Pattel searches around as they hear more footsteps getting closer.

They reach the corridor and, when they step into the shaft, the lights turn off.

"Ah, shit." Stoutarm braces for what's next.

The electricity comes back on, and Pattel and Stoutarm find the shadows of people along the walls. This time the people step off the wall, forming bodies as they do and walk around the soldiers. They keep their distance and walk in perfect lockstep. With each step the bodies transform from black, oily figures to having skin. Heavily bruised and pale skin. Their footsteps begin to sound squishy.

"What do we do?" Pattel stops to inspect a zombie. The eyes are jaundiced, and its expression is hopeless and sad. The zombies don't breathe. Some of them are crying.

"Be patient." Stoutarm moves one slow step at a time.

The zombies stop and face away from them.

"Why are their backs turned to us?" Pattel breaks into a sweat.

"Shut up." Stoutarm moves two fingers across his lips.

Pattel can see that one zombie hasn't about-faced yet. She turns to face him and reaches out with a hand. Her skin appears more normal than the rest. "Strangers, free us from eternal hell, before our master makes us suffer more. Free our souls before we kill you. Please help me. The hydra is weakened. Its hold on us is loose. I beg" Her mouth stops mid plea and her hand appears to move involuntarily back down. Her eyes lose all emotion and she is forced to join the others, turning her back on Stoutarm and Pattel.

Each zombie lines up facing the walls and begins pounding on them like trapped maniacs, pleading for help in silence. With the path suddenly clear, Stoutarm runs for the chamber with Pattel keeping up. When the soldiers begin running, the zombies start running after them, wailing and screaming.

"Engaging. I'm sorry, everyone!" Pattel fires at the ones coming after them. The bullets go through them, failing to connect. "Bullshit."

"Stop wasting ammo and run. We can help them, but not here." Stoutarm doesn't lift his weapon.

Several zombies catch up to them and start trying to punch, kick, and bite at Stoutarm and Pattel. But the attacks go through them. After realizing they aren't being touched, Stoutarm grabs Pattel's arm and continues running. When they reach the mine-shaft chamber the figures stop as they hit an invisible barrier at the end of the corridor, making loud, disgusting splashing sounds as they do. Behind them, further down the shaft, the woman and two kids wave and walk into the wall, vanishing.

"Is this what you and Jades experienced before?" Pattel jumps over a pile of rubble.

"Something along these lines, except it only gets more intense from here." Stoutarm trips on the rubble.

Pattel runs for the chamber leading to the shack and pier. Stoutarm does his best to keep up. Pattel stops when he arrives at the ladder going up and checks behind him, Stoutarm is still catching up.

"Sorry, man."

Stoutarm waves his hand at him in a dismissing motion. "No worries. I know." He tries to catch his breath. "Am I seeing things or is the cave-in clear?"

"Yep, sure is, but screw the mine. Rowboat?" Pattel glances at the way to the river.

"Rowboat." Stoutarm nods.

Pattel climbs the ladder, followed by Stoutarm. A new figure is approaching them from the now-clear shaft. Stoutarm doesn't notice and catches up with Pattel. "Alright, hold up. I'm coming."

Pattel gets back to the dock and starts removing old junk off the boat so they have room. Stoutarm catches up. "Motor is dead," he observes

"That's why we're gonna ditch the motor and use the paddles to row out of here."

"Fair enough." Stoutarm chuckles, but then hears the sound of creaking wood behind them. Pattel and Stoutarm turn around to discover a naked woman leaning on the door running her hand up her thigh and waving her finger, asking them to come to her.

"Hey now. I can hallucinate this all day." Stoutarm checks her out.

Pattel raises his weapon. "Is she the woman from the newspaper or the shaft? What's her name?"

"I didn't pay enough attention to the name, but, yeah, her face is from the paper." Stoutarm shakes his head and raises the rifle at her as well. "What do you think?"

"She doesn't recognize what's pointed at her. Most people would at least duck behind the door or something."

"Come back, boys. I'd love to devour you," she says in a soft, seductive tone.

"She's been dead twenty years man. Sorry, but she gotta stay dead." Pattel takes a shot. His bullet goes through her head without touching her and lands in the wall of the shack.

"If that wasn't a fact, I'd be taking her up on the offer." Stoutarm fires another shot after Pattel's did nothing. The bullet finds its mark and the woman falls backwards against the wall, sliding down. Normal blood flows from her head. The two men grab the oars, jumping into the boat and throwing away the rope holding them in place.

When Stoutarm pushes off from the pier with his paddle, the woman sits up.

"Oh great." Pattel panics. "She didn't die, again."

Stoutarm turns around to find her getting on her hands and feet and starting to walking like a dog. "Oh, that's hot. I almost don't want to shoot." He puts the oar down, aims, and shoots her again in the top of the head. The woman falls to the floor and doesn't move. "Hey, can you row while I cover?"

Pattel grabs both oars, mounts them into the brackets and rows as fast as he can.

"She is one pesky zombie." Stoutarm tilts his head when the woman gets back up.

"Brain shots aren't doing crap. Shoot her in the heart or something." They are now entering the current and picking up more speed than he expected.

"Or we can float away with the river. Awesome." Stoutarm says.

They face the front of the boat to see where they are heading and hear a splash behind them. They glance at each other. "Oh, *great*," they both say simultaneously, with matching facial expressions and tones.

Pattel keeps rowing and Stoutarm grabs one of the oars to help. "Low bridge!" Stoutarm ducks under a low hanging branch. Pattel ducks in time, repositioning himself to make sure he can steer them away from problems.

"I can't see anything. Hope we don't sink ourselves." Pattel starts rowing faster. No sooner does he finish speaking than various shapes start to glow bright blue on the riverbed.

Stoutarm and Pattel are wary as the glowing spots form into lifeless bodies. As they do so, the smell of rotten flesh begins to rise from the water, which only grows stronger as they travel further.

"Oh, man." Pattel covers his nose with his sleeve.

Stoutarm shakes his head and plugs his nose with one hand. Every time they inhale they taste weeks-old decaying flesh. "Don't get sick on me now. Cause if you puke, I will puke, and we will crash in the forest of hell."

Pattel shakes his head. "I'm fine, it's not like Albert's lab produces worse."

Stoutarm nods. "Well, glad you feel that way, cause now that we're moving, I gotta take a leak." He sighs loudly as he relieves himself into the river.

They drift around a bend and discover glowing blue bodies standing on the water's surface. After exchanging a quick glance, they keep rowing and pass between the bodies. Every breath they take is filled with the smell of rotting flesh, but it now get stronger as they move on. A large animal's carcass is revealed on the riverbank, with more glowing bodies standing all around it.

The bodies raise their hands into the air in a slow dance. Once their hands are raised, they stop moving. Those on the river, on the right side of the boat, each raise their left leg, while those on the left side raise their right legs. Then they all stomp on the river, each one making a little splash with their foot. The splashing doesn't appear to do anything to their boat or the current. Pattel and Stoutarm wait for them to do something else.

The woman's seductive voice comes from all directions around them. "Soldier boys, where you running to? I need your services."

"Is this some sick joke?" Pattel searches for the source of the voice.

"Gotta be a hydra's wake thing." Stoutarm stays still and closes his eyes.

"The zombies?" Pattel hits Stoutarm on the shoulder.

"Yeah, same with the spooky glowing eyed animals. Somehow they're connected." Stoutarm sighs and shakes his head.

"We're not losing our minds this much, are we?"

The bodies splash the water again. In unison, they move with a shared mind and perfect control. This pattern of marching in place continues for several minutes and gets faster with each step. Once the stepping is a constant marching, they stop. The Shadow Figure returns, rising from the water in front of the boat. Stoutarm and Pattel put down the oars and grab their rifles.

But before they can raise them, the sound of water trickling and splashing distracts them. The glowing bodies begin peeing illuminated orange streams, like artistic statues. The Shadow Figure rises above them and vanishes into the night sky. Without leaving their spots, the bodies start to aim their streams at the men. The soldiers fire at the peeing bodies, which vanish when hit.

After they shoot down most of the surrounding ones, the rest fade off and the river returns to normal.

"What the hell?" Stoutarm runs his hand through his hair and smells strong piss.

"We will never speak of this again." Pattel leans over and washes his head in the water.

"Oi, you two smell like piss." The woman's voice makes both men jump and spin around.

The woman from the pier is hanging on the back of the boat and waves when they spot her.

"She caught up to us." Stoutarm looks at her head. The gunshots have healed although scars remain.

"I see that. What are you?" Pattel fights the urge to shoot her. Bullets don't stop her.

"A horny gal, I guess. I'd say 'I think,' but I can't think. You, sir, shot my twice in the brain. Bad man. But you're super cute, so I'm willing to forgive you. If you take care of me." She points at the scars and gives Stoutarm a mischievous smirk.

Stoutarm smiles awkwardly. "Um, forgive me. It's been an unnatural trip for us."

"Oh, well, your trip will be all good from here on, I hope." She speaks with a cheerful tone and an ear-to-ear smile. "Hey, this water is wicked cold. May I come aboard? Maybe join you two for some fun and adventure?"

Pattel averts his eyes from her. "Who are you?"

"I don't know. I want to know who I am, but I can't remember." She pulls herself into the boat, brushes her hair away and raises her arms to wring the water out.

"Ok, do you know anything about the hydra?" Stoutarm can't take his eyes off her exposed body and studies every inch of her.

"What's a hydra? I keep hearing about them but never get to learn. Is this hydra a new thing? I remember stopping a complete mine collapse in shaft sixty-four twenty-three. But I could've sworn I died, I should have. There's no way I could survive thousands of tons of rock coming down on me. That sounds silly right? Next thing I know, some cloaked ghost thing is standing over me filling my head with thoughts of exploiting you two." She shakes her chest while running her hands through her hair.

The soldiers exchange glances. "This ghost person can bring people back to life?" Stoutarm returns his attention to the woman. "So, you come back to life and the first thing on your mind is banging us?"

"I don't remember being such a pervert in my first life. Actually I distinctly remember hating men. Preferring to spend my time becoming a leader of women in engineering. Wow I can remember a lot about my life except my name." She sounds intelligent and grabs her head.

"Is she alive, alive? What's going on?" Pattel whispers.

"I haven't a clue." Stoutarm whispers back.

"I can't stop wanting you in specific brave Mr. Stoutarm, my hero. So how about we go ashore and have some fun? Maybe you can tell me about the monster hydra and how you're planning to set your trap." The woman's voice sounds forced and possessed as she leans forward and rests her head in his lap, staring up at him, stroking his arms, and laying on her back, opening her legs.

"We never said anything about trapping any hydras." Pattel tenses up.

"How'd you know my name?" Stoutarm asks.

"Oh yeah, the ghost guy said I need to figure out your plans before I'm free to live again. Oh, and I have to kill you if the answers are bad. So, can you two help me stay alive?" She lets go of Stoutarm and grabs her head as though she's in pain. "Why am I saying these things?"

"AH! What is that in her vag." Pattel turns away and spits some bile out from puking into his mouth.

"What's a vag?" She asks.

Stoutarm spots a small hand waving between her legs as the oil from the zombies begins to sweat out of her entire body. "You're not attractive anymore." He shoves her off him.

"Sorry, miss, we're in a hurry." Pattel tries not to vomit more as he and Stoutarm grab their weapons.

"Is something the matter with me?" The woman inspects herself. "Oh, how'd that pop out?"

Both Pattel and Stoutarm nod. "Yes!" They open fire on her before she can look back up, this time hitting as much of her body as they can. She lies limp and motionless in the back of the boat, bleeding all over. Pattel grabs a knife from his boot and cuts her stomach open. "I'm shoving a grenade in this thing. She's too dangerous."

Stoutarm already has a primed grenade to hand him. Pattel buries the grenade in her, and the two men swing her as far as they can throw her. She lands on the riverbank and they two row hard to put some distance between them. "How long did you prime the fuse?"

"Thirty seconds." Stoutarm replies as they keep rowing.

The woman sits up. "That hurt!" she yells before the grenade goes off, blowing her to pieces.

The Shadow Figure rises from the water and heads over to the woman's remains. It turns faces Stoutarm and Pattel, who both have their rifles trained on it. After a short moment the figure evaporates again.

"Definitely the hydra's doing." Stoutarm says as they lower their weapons. "Why did killing her matter to me? Like, that feels wrong now. What if we just tied her up until the hydra died? Then she'd have that second life, no strings attached."

"We are having a hard enough time surviving for ourselves, trying to save her, while she's trying to kill us with paranormal powers would be more than we can handle. And get your head of out of your pants." Pattel runs his hands through his hair.

"We can prove this shadow is part of the hydra now. The damned thing was all over us in the gemstone mines, and every time it showed up, hell came. That woman's gonna be on my mind for weeks." Stoutarm checks behind them to find the bank empty.

After drifting for a moment, they start rowing faster down the river. When they get tired and slow down, they listen to the humming and chirping noises.

"They should call this place the Spooky Forest Region; place gives me the creeps." Pattel shivers when a gust of wind hits them.

A few fluorescent bugs crawl around the trees near the riverbanks. Pattel and Stoutarm observe them, then they come up on a small clearing. Several small animals along the banks are eating the glowing bugs. "How wild. This might be an allusion to the circle of life you know. Imagine how those bugs are important to the hydra's life." Stoutarm stops rowing to admire the view.

"No, ain't nothing here to imagine. Hydra is at the top of the food chain. But sitting back and watching this? Kinda brings nature back into perspective." Pattel glances all around them. "And you know what? Nature sucks ass."

Stoutarm laughs at the remark. "Right when you are getting all sentimental, eh?"

"Screw this shit." Pattel starts rowing harder. "But I will take this over that shadowy thing."

Rogue hears more gunfire and an explosion in the distance. "Those two are making massive headway. Shit, they're close to the valley. How'd they move so fast in this freezing cold? Walker said they aren't ordinary henchmen. Are they immune to frostbite?"

"That sounds like it came from inside the forest, though. Wonder what made them go in so deep?" Hunter looks in the direction of the noise.

"Hydra is probably listening to the dinner bells." *As is every other hungry critter.*

"Let's hope it decides the trees are too thick." Hunter takes a glance at the charts Rogue laid out. "So, what do you propose we do when we set the trap? Finding Albert isn't going to be an easy ask."

"We'll deal with that in the morning. You should go back and get some sleep."

"You sure you don't need company?"

"Nah, some alone time might do me some good." Rogue nods and stares at the horizon.

"Alright. Wake us up when we reach the drop zone." Hunter walks into the rear of the cabin.

Rogue waits about an hour or so and turns the engine on to move faster. He keeps an eye on the door which doesn't open when he gets the fuel engine going. *Alright, time to turn on the engines; batteries are almost drained, and we need to recharge. The others should be asleep by now, so they can get their rest. Come dawn, this is going to be a blast. And we're over the valley now. Which happened faster than I hoped.*

Rogue tries to study the terrain below them, but he is unable to see much, so he decides to fly in a circle to pass the time by. He remembers visiting the facility, and how the corridors seemed to lead him down under the valley.

Those containment facilities are intended to withstand the force of an oncoming planet. Finding a shallow place to plant our bomb on will be a priority.

Using the containment facility to stop the bomb's energy from going down will be a major bonus, making sure the full force goes up. That would be better than letting the ground absorb the blast. They might as well use physics if they can.

The door from the back opens and Crystal comes out, closing the door behind her.

"Oh hey. You catch some decent sleep?"

BAD BED, she clicks as she stretches.

Rogue laughs. "Oh yeah. I bet."

MOTOR LOUD. Now she's rubbing her eyes as she goes to sit by the front.

"Yeah, I tried to wait until everyone was asleep before recharging the batteries using the engine."

LEG HURT BAD. The pain in her leg does feel worse. Rogue looks exhausted.

"Worse than earlier?" *Maybe she'll stop attacking everyone else now.*

She nods and walks over, forcing herself not to limp. YOU NO SLEEP?

"No, this thing requires constant piloting. Gotta stay at the controls to make sure we stay afloat." *Normally flying this long is a breeze, but I'm pushing my physical limits here.*

She rubs her arms and touches Rogue on the shoulder. WHY YOU CARE FOR ME?

"Well, I may have crashed more than my fair share of times. But this crash is different. Not just being shot down. Even then I assumed crazy wind shears took me down, it was the way I woke up. I push people away to keep my focus on growing my company; on being a cool boss. I get my kicks when I can, but my life needs to be more than a shipping company and tea with friends."

Crystal stares at him with mixed feelings.

"Finding you in the mud, I wanted to help out and be a hero for someone for once. When you started to trust me last night and this morning, you filled a void. Seeing someone look at me the way you did. And I'm not going to lie, you've captivated me."

YOU LIKE ME BECAUSE IM BROKEN. She's reserving judgment, but his word choice is poor.

Rogue flinches and shakes his head no. "I did say it like that, didn't I? Well, no. No way. I mean that in a different way. I don't know how to convey all the feelings I have developed for you. Sorry, I am terrible at this." *Think before you speak. Treat it like a business meeting. No don't, because this is personal. Aw, screw me, I'm hopeless and flustered.*

YOUR EYES SAY MORE. She lets out a smile.

Rogue makes eye contact. "I like you. A lot. And these feelings I have for you could grow into real love over time." *Why the hell didn't I say this from the start?*

Crystal's shakes her head and crosses her arms. NO LOVE YET. TOO SOON.

Rogue nods. "I am going to fast. I'm sorry."

I DON'T KNOW WHAT TO FEEL. She stares out the window into space.

"Neither do I, if I'm being honest. I'm feeling the most unstable I've ever been in my life."

She glances over to see him making adjustments on the panel. WE SAVE EACH OTHER? She puts a hand on his. His skin is freezing, the cabin is cold, but his hand is like ice.

"I think that's a good starting point." Rogue smiles, trying to dismiss her concern. She starts rubbing his hand to warm him up. *Wow, she's hot. She's attractive hot, and temperature hot. Or I'm freezing worse than I realize. This can't stretch any longer than today if I'm gonna survive.*

HOW I FLY?

Rogue chuckles. "Well for now all we need to do is keep making small turns of this knob here to keep level to the horizon. If we don't, the whole ship can tilt and sway."

Crystal nods along as Rogue shows her the gyroscope and the knobs. She stares at the pipe from earlier next to Rogue.

Rogue spots her staring. *I forgot to throw that away.*

THEY ARE BAD MEN. She points to the back room.

"Did they touch you?" Rogue tries to contain an instant rush of anger.

NO. THEY JUST BAD, she clicks while looking down at the floor, letting out a sigh as she tenses up. Rogue offers her a hug and she shakes no. TOO SOON.

Rogue feels relieved. "I know. They'll be gone when this is over." Then a light shines on the dirigible from the ground. "The hell?"

Pattel catches the faint noise of an engine. "Hey, you hear that? They must be overhead."

Stoutarm turns the light on his rifle on and points up., moving it around until he finds the dirigible way in the sky. Then he turns his light off. "Won't blow their cover more than needed."

"Good to know they're still in the fight."

Albert is taking in the view of the night cities on Heart from the window when he spots a small white dot at the edge of the forest. Then, he notices an airship above the valley. The light is gone as quickly as it came on. "So, they have their bomb, I assume."

"Hey, look, Camp Tor! We pulled it off." Pattel points at the lights coming from the buildings in the mining camp, which become more visible as they clear the trees and the riverbank flattens out a bit.

"About time. This is the worst jungle boat ride ever." Stoutarm drags the boat to the shore.

"Those two idiots are ringing dinner bells." Rogue walks over to the cabin window to search for two lights on the ground. They turn off as he spots them. "So much for secrecy. Bravo, though, for getting through the night alive." He searches the valley for any sign of the hydra, but can't find anything. It's too dark.

The two soldiers walk in a crouch across the field, using several small crevices they make sure to hide in while crossing. Most are wide enough for them to go into, but the hydra will have to eat a mouthful of dirt with them if they are attacked.

"Ain't as flat as it appears from the camp." Pattel stumbles on uneven ground.

"Or the river." Stoutarm checks back over his shoulder.

The crevice they are in widens a bit and Pattel walks into the middle of the gap. The sound of his footstep changes from a soft crunch to a louder clang. He looks down and turns on his light. The floor is unnaturally flat and only has a thin layer of dirt.

Pattel uses his foot to clear the area, revealing the same kind of metal he encountered in the phosphorus mine at Face Eighteen. "That's interesting."

"What is this?" Stoutarm puts his hand on the metal, feeling the static.

"Something made the miners scratch a face out of their plan. A solid metal of some sort. Never seen anything like this before." Pattel clears more of the dirt.

Stoutarm helps. "Is this thing under the entire valley?"

"Sure would be interesting."

Rogue spies on them from above with his binoculars and sees the metal reflect their lights. "Well damn. This is perfect." *This is exactly what we need. Below ground level too. Couldn't ask for a better spot.*

"Should we tell the others?" Stoutarm stops clearing dirt after a sizable patch is exposed.

Pattel is already looking up. "I think they've been watching. Look."

Stoutarm discovers one of the outer spotlights being turned on and off in short and long intervals. "What are they?" he starts to ask before realizing what Rogue is doing.

"M. C." Pattel says

"Morse Code," they say in unison.

"Grab your rifle and point up. That way they should be the only ones to see us," suggests Pattel.

Rogue waits as a small but powerful light from a rifle comes back and replies in code. COPY.

The two watch as the spotlight codes. CAN BOMB FIT THERE?

"Can it fit in here? Why?" Pattel looks around.

"That doesn't make any tactical sense. This is a terrible spot."

"I'm going to tell him it's a bad idea." Pattel starts flicking his light.

YES. BUT BAD SPOT.

"Well, no, I agree. That's not ideal, but that metal helps." Rogue thinks out loud as he replies with the light. DENSE METAL. SEND ENERGY UP.

"I understand where he's coming from." Stoutarm stomps on the metal. "This makes more sense now. Maximize the impact of the blast going upwards. When something explodes, energy is sent in all directions. This weird metal is dense enough to not absorb energy going down. Damn, he's smarter than we are."

"Or he knows something about this metal we don't." WE PREP SPOT. Pattel codes. "Let's clear and prep the spot for our trap. Close off the crevice behind us and in front of us with grenades at sunrise, if the hydra isn't too close."

"Dude, we ran out of those," Stoutarm says.

"I don't think Walker did." Pattel points at the ship.

Albert keeps an eye on the light flickering from the dirigible. "What in the blazes is going on with them? Trying to become a target for the hungry creatures of the night?" He walks away from the window. "Blinking their light irresponsibly. What idiots."

A crashing noise at the other end of the refinery scares Albert. "Ouch!" Joe shouts. "Hey, wait, that's the first time I bumped into anything in months! WOOHOO!"

Albert rolls his eyes. "You clumsy fool."

"Hey when you phase out to an alternate reality for as long as I have, you become used to being able to walk through everything," Joe explains. "But this means I can grab some shovels."

Albert gawks as a few shovels lift into the air from the barrel of tools Joe knocked over. "Why do you need three shovels?"

"Oh, nothing. Digging graves is all. Hey, I can't lock a door from the outside so, this door here will need your attention."

Albert observes the door near the shovels open up on its own. They move through, and the door closes. "Why would he need so many shovels for graves? No matter, time for me to enjoy some genuine shut-eye."

The floating shovels move from the refinery into the valley. Joe can't see the men in the crevice but knows where they are. He can feel it in his dimension. This allows him to detect the beams of light from the dirigible and whatever causes those ones on the ground.

"Hey Pattel, how are we going to dig up this crap?" Stoutarm asks.

"You don't even have one grenade left?" Pattel tosses a canteen to Stoutarm.

Stoutarm takes a drink before replying. "Must've given you my last one to use on the sexy zombie."

Two shovels land near them. "Thought you folks would need some help."

"Joe?" Pattel recognizes the voice from the phosphorus mine and looks up to see a third shovel floating in the air. While Walker and Thebes checked the mine out, he had hung around the entrance and met Joe.

"Who's Joe?" Stoutarm raises an eyebrow at Pattel.

"The local ghost this hydra hasn't managed to eat yet." Joe replies, like a smart ass. "So, if I heard things correctly, you guys have this super bomb?"

"They do above, yeah."

"Our hydra is out of the valley for now, so if you want to lower your bomb, now is a great time to set your trap," Joe suggests.

"How do you know?" Stoutarm glances at where Joe's voice is coming from.

"I can locate it, even through solid objects. It's eating the harpy bear it killed earlier." Joe's voice comes off as smug.

"They want the bomb lowered?" Walker glances over at Rogue.

"I guess they're ready." Rogue goes to the pilot controls and begins descending.

"Where is the hydra?"

"No clue. I lost track a while back." Rogue turns the engine on and the outer lights. *Here goes nothing.*

"This hole is in a wide, flat field." Walker throws his arms up in frustration. "Are they mad? This is no-where near a decent spot."

"Check out what they're standing on. That metal thing is ultra-dense. Put the explosion on top and the dirt can't absorb the energy, sending the power of the blast that would normally go down, up instead." Rogue explains.

"Ok, so how do we lure the monster to the trap" Walker puts his hand to his chin. "This bomb is useless if we can't do that."

"The escape plane I used to fly to the camp. If someone uses my plane to guide it over and someone else hidden nearby activates the detonator on time, this is still doable." *If the person flying can get enough of a head start. That hydra can outrun the plane. I'll keep that bit to myself for now, though.*

"What do we do about Albert?" Hunter glances at Rogue.

"Why not straight up kill him when this is all done with?" *Assuming he hasn't somehow died from that nasty arm bite yet.*

"Fair point," Hunter accedes

The door to the rear of the cabin opens and Crystal comes out, yawning.

"Oh, don't do that. Those are contagious." Rogue yawns himself. Hunter chuckles.

Rogue keeps a close eye on the altimeter until he is a hundred feet up. *I can't see a thing outside.* "Ok, guys, I need you to help me position the cargo hold."

Hunter and Walker nod and go to open the doors on the side of the cabins.

"You guys enjoy your walk in the park?" Walker shouts at the men below, and gives them an enthusiastic wave.

"Up yours! Tonight sucks!" Stoutarm raises both arms with middle fingers extended.

"Rogue, go that way a bit!" Hunter points.

Rogue turns the guide wheel and lets the propellers move them over the spot. "I don't have the anchor anymore, so I'm going to start lowering the container." *Now that I found the correct lever, the hold won't drop like last time.*

"Do the winches work now?" Walker hopes not to have a repeat of the drop at the crash site.

"Yeah, figured them out." Rogue pulls on the lever to lower the winches rather than release them. *Much better this time around.* The cargo hold descends from the dirigible.

"Joe, the hydra isn't coming, right?" Pattel searches the horizon, but the sky is too dark.

"No, it hasn't noticed us yet," Joe informs them. "That's a huge bomb."

"Ten tons of Hexogen." Pattel smiles.

"I heard the details, but seeing this thing up close is intimidating." Joe sounds terrified.

"Stop!" Hunter, Walker, Stoutarm, and Pattel all shout in unison.

Rogue pulls the brakes and stops the cargo.

"Can this thing pivot?" Walker shoots Rogue a glance.

"Not like a helicopter, no." *What do they think a dirigible does? Hover?*

"Guys, we need to guide this in the hard way," Walker shouts to them.

"That is not going to be easy," Rogue admits. *More like impossible. You guys realize how much this airship weighs?*

"Hunter, let's go down with rope and show them what we're made of," Walker says and Hunter nods.

Crystal grabs a coil of rope from the front of the cabin, hands it to Hunter. He in turn tosses the coil to Walker, who ties it to the handle outside the door. "Untie this when we get down, please." Walker says towards Rogue.

He nods as Walker throws the rest of the rope. "I got it, you guys."

"Awesome. We'll rappel down. Easy-peasy," boasts Walker.

"How far off am I?" Rogue keeps an eye on Crystal, so she doesn't kick Walker off the ship.

"Around thirty feet away, give or take a few. Do what you can to keep this thing here, and we'll try something else."

"You can pull all you want but the ship won't budge. Air buoyancy doesn't negate the fact this whole vehicle weighs an insane amount." Rogue begins moving forward, "I'll try a three point turn to move closer."

Rogue executes the maneuver. The container comes much closer to the opening in the ground.

"Damn you're good at this. Stop here!" Walker shouts before Rogue goes over the spot.

Rogue slows the dirigible to a crawl. *This is impossible to navigate with pinpoint accuracy. I like mine better; this is more of a blimp than a dirigible.*

"We need to guide it down, but that's perfect." Walker ties one end to a railing in the cabin.

"Best of luck up here," Hunter says to Rogue as he rappels down to the others, followed by Walker.

"From here on out, you guys do all the work." Rogue gets off the chair to pull on a few levers near the door.

Crystal waits until Walker is halfway down before starting to untie the line, hoping to cause him to fall.

"Crystal, you're better than that."

She gets upset and gives him the middle finger. She yanks hard, untying the knot, and releases the rope, clapping her hands as though she's finished taking the trash out.

Walker gets to the ground before the rope comes loose and falls around him. He grabs one end and jumps towards the cargo hold. It doesn't shake as much as he expected. He then pulls some rope in until the halfway point is in the center of the container. Then he starts tying knots on rails. Once finished, he jumps out the other side with the rest. "Ok, we got this. Let's lower all the way."

"Bring the bomb down nice and easy!" Hunter waves his arms to signal lowering to Rogue.

Rogue activates the winch motors at the slowest they will go. The airship begins to rise with the winches a little.

"Perfection!" Hunter gives Rogue a thumbs up. "We'll detach this, and then you guys go stand by at the skyport."

Stoutarm and Pattel get into the hold and began unhooking the cable clamps. Three of the cables come off easily but one hook gets bent and stuck.

"Dammit," Stoutarm shouts.

"I got it." Pattel aims at the clamp and shoots it. The cable snaps and the dirigible lurches upwards violently for a second.

Rogue waits for the lurching motion to stop before letting some air out to slow their ascent. "That is a bad way to do it." *At least give me a warning to adjust the ship, so we don't crash. We all still need a way out of here.*

Crystal is clinging to the wall at the back of the cabin. WE CRASH! she clicks.

"No, we won't, I promise." Rogue turns the outer lights off and retracts the winch cables. "And Crystal, now we're free of them, I need to ask. Do you want to finish this or should we fly to safety and run away?"

Crystal stares at Rogue. He's right, they should leave while they can. They should've run sooner. But she is very curious to see their bomb go off. WE STAY.

Rogue nods and smiles. "I'll move this thing to higher altitude, and we'll keep a look out from here."

The ground shakes from a tremor. "Well, hydra has decided to go back to the far end of the valley. We can reach the camp if we run now." Joe's voice is followed by the sound of running footsteps.

"We're finished and everything is in place. Let's make for camp, and deal with Albert in the morning." Pattel tosses a shovel.

"I'll stay with the trap." Walker is going to make sure Albert doesn't attempt anything stupid. "If things are coming in and out for you guys, this won't work well."

"Suit yourself," Stoutarm says as he and Pattel climb up to the surface. "While you're here, try to close off the crevice."

Walker jumps down into the cargo hold with the bomb. "With what?" He spots three shovels leaning up against the wall. "Never mind."

Stoutarm glances around. "Camp looks awesome. Lots of buildings."

"I see half of them," Pattel calls out.

"I can see everything," Joe adds in a superior tone.

"Quiet." Hunter shushes Joe.

The ground shakes more, and the group sprints towards the camp.

8: LIGHT THE FUSE, RUN LIKE HELL

"Ugh, this shaking makes the simple task of sleeping impossible." Albert says as he starts to get up from the couch he is lying on. The sound of a door opening makes him move quicker, and look towards the door.

"I left my shotgun in here, and Mack's revolver should be here too." Hunter heads in, and holds the door as Pattel follows him.

"That's all you guys brought?" Pattel stops near the entrance to admire the machines in the building.

"Well, this trip started as a manhunt for one dude who lived through a nasty wreck, not a war or firefight."

They walk right past Albert. "Can you two not tell I am standing here? How rude." They do not react to Albert. "I suppose not. Too bad, your doom awaits you." He raises Hunter's shotgun and fires, but the shot goes through them both.

The wall cracks outward from a sudden hole in front of Hunter and Pattel. "I guess we aren't alone." Pattel says glancing over his shoulder.

"Albert must have our weapons." Hunter preps Westly's rifle.

"Yes, I do. Well deduced for something not being in your face." Albert comes up behind them, about to grab Hunter, but remembers the moment Rogue Whip grabbed his neck and became visible. Exposing himself is too risky, Hunter will be too difficult to overpower in a straight fight.

"I think that's called friendly fire, Albert." Pattel takes a peek at the hole.

"Oh, my boy, there is no mistake. I intend to kill you all." Albert shoots at Pattel.

"Ooh, felt the wind on that one." Pattel smirks and moves to the side, away from Hunter. "Well, he officially tried to shoot me. Guess I'm not a traitor anymore, because this is gonna be payback."

"Useless weapon!" Albert throws the shotgun, which fires upon hitting the ground. The shot grazes his leg. Albert clutches the wound and falls, letting out a scream of pain.

Hunter and Pattel look around at the machinery.

"Last time, this place was nothing but an empty warehouse for me. None of this stuff was here." Hunter says, as they move to opposite ends of the refinery.

Albert stands up and runs after Hunter. "I shall be the death of you."

"Hey, I found a plane in here!" Pattel calls to Hunter. "Someone added a bigger tank and engine to this thing."

"Oh no! No, you do not dare touch my work!" Albert spins away from following Hunter to run towards the plane. "That belongs to me!"

"Yeah, Ned and I were going to upgrade it early on." Hunter peeks behind the larger machines in the room. "Wait, did you say Rogue's plane has been modified?"

"Yeah, come check this out." Pattel inspects the airplane. Someone did a lot of work.

Hunter turns around and sees Albert running. "Found him!" He aims Westly's assault rifle at Albert. "Freeze, you ungrateful bastard. What do you think you're doing, shooting at us?"

Albert stops in his tracks and turns around to find Hunter aiming right at him. "Well, well, look who we have here."

"For once I have a job for you. You're gonna help me kill the pesky hydra." Hunter said.

"Oh, heavens me. You sound rather confident, perhaps too overconfident." Albert shouts back, giving Hunter his full attention.

"Hunter? Where'd you go?" Pattel walks around the corner of a big machine and straight through Albert.

"How fortunate. The fool cannot join us." Albert uses the opportunity to hide behind a machine, while Pattel blocks Hunter's line of sight. The shotgun isn't far away and crawls on his hands and knees to retrieve it.

Hunter moves forward, taking small steps. "Yeah, thing is, we're chasing the wrong guy, and he's agreed to help us dispatch this hydra. Which shows adoration for you, staying fixated on you when you're within sight. At the risk of sounding daft, we need you to lure it over the bomb we've made from the crashed dirigible. The hydra blows up and dies; and we all walk out of this nasty nightmare and go home. Take the night off, and go after the right bastard tomorrow."

"You speak as though I will live through this venture." Albert tries to control his breathing and slow his heart rate. The extra blood flow is making his arm and leg hurt.

"That's the current plan. Being the bait doesn't mean going down the throat. This does mean, though, that you will be chased for a few thrilling seconds." Hunter approaches the machine behind which Albert ran to hide. When he glances around the corner, Albert is gone.

"Thrilling. Bizarre word choice. Why so cautious?"

"Well, out of respect for your abilities My Lord. The hydra's wake altering us gives me pause to everything, so you'll have to pardon me." Hunter spots the plane and observes the modifications made, with the bigger tank and engine. "I see you've been putting as much work into this whole thing as we have. Using this plane will be a perfect lure. You should be able to grab its attention and fly over the trap with hydra in toe."

"I am quite proud of my work," Albert says as he checks on how many rounds remain in the shotgun. The gun is empty now. "Despicable."

"Thebes and Jades are gone." Hunter says, trying to keep Albert talking, so he can find him.

"The hydra eat them?"

"No, they ventured off into the forest, and we never saw them again after a massive explosion."

"Ah yes, the Deep Forest is an unsafe locale for humans," Albert continues, as he tries to keep out of Hunter's line of sight.

Pattel exits through a door near Albert, distracting them both.

Hunter turns to face the sound of the door. "Did you run away? That's not very sportsman like of you."

Albert stays quiet where he is, hoping Hunter will approach the door.

Hunter circles around the machines, being careful to stay quiet. To his surprise, he finds Albert crouching behind a machine looking at the door. "I guess we are playing against each other."

Albert closes his eyes and smiles at hearing Hunter's voice behind him. "I guess there is no denying that I intend to kill you."

"Yeah, Westly made your intentions quite clear. So, I guess helping bring the hydra down is a hard sell, huh?"

"There are admirable perks, although the major downside is, as you have made clear to point out, it requires being within close proximity to the business end of the beast. Not the most reassuring part of the plan. And the meager reward is to what? Live?" Albert tries to assess how to escape Hunter. He's too weak to properly use his personal weapon without the element of surprise.

"I have Crystal in an easy to access spot. The reward will be, as you often say, the journey to torture them and reaping their torment for your pleasure. I do believe this would be cause for celebration with your newest experiments."

"Why do you reek of kiss ass?" Albert is delighted to learn about

Crystal's still being alive, and Hunter isn't wrong; there are some new things he's been waiting to try. "You almost tickled the joyful little spark in me. Valiant effort, truly."

Hunter lowers his weapon. "Don't make me do this the difficult way when things are hard enough as they are," Hunter changes his tone.

"Ah, there is the threat I expected. And what will you do? Shoot me? I shall bleed out. I have come close to doing so twice on this venture, in fact. I appear to be hard-pressed to survive another major wound. Given my advancing age, and lack of physical stamina and all." Albert glances down at his leg, no longer able to ignore the pain from the grazing wound on his leg.

"Tempting, but I can knock you down, stand on your back, and tie you up. You don't have the physical strength to take me on." Hunter takes note of Albert's injury. "The hydra is going down. With you the mission is easier, but without you it's still doable. Either way is the same to me and I don't have concrete feelings about who I have to kill at this point to succeed."

"Now you are starting to sound as hardheaded as myself." Albert controls his rage and stays analytical.

"You're right; you make a good mentor." Hunter closes some distance between him and Albert while staying cautious.

Albert pulls Mack's revolver from his vest and points it at Hunter, who aims the rifle at Albert. They stare at each other with hatred. "So, what now?"

"Are you willing to help us kill the hydra?"

"Now you ask politely. No. The beast can eat you all." Albert fires the revolver. The shot goes through Hunter without hitting him. "Oh, for the sake of a fuck." He throws the gun, which itself hits Hunter, bouncing off him and falling to the ground without going off.

Hunter kicks Mack's revolver away. "Are you done with your little temper tantrum?"

"Are you finished hallucinating yet?" Albert gets to his feet and rushes Hunter.

Hunter lifts the rifle up and plans on knocking him out with the stock, but the weapon and his hands goes through Albert.

Albert punches Hunter in the gut, following up with a kick in the groin as hard as he can. The pain in his leg makes standing unbearable for Albert but somehow, he keeps himself on point.

Hunter watches Albert hit and kick him, but he is weak and his strikes don't hurt. "Care to try again?"

Albert spits on Hunter and runs away through the wall, going outside. "The hell?" Hunter runs to the door and searches outside but Albert is nowhere to be seen.

The tremors stopped during the fight, and Hunter does not realize the hydra is in the camp. And is now looking straight at him. He slams the door shut and runs deep into the building, hiding behind some machines as its heads peer through the various windows. "Dammit!"

The Shadow Figure rises from behind a nearby machine and points at Hunter. Inside the refinery, the lights turn off and back on. The machinery vanishes. The curious hydra moves two heads near the doors to block him in.

Hunter searches frantically for a way out, and discovers none of the heads are guarding the open bay doors.

The Shadow Figure rises to the ceiling.

The hydra roars again and takes a step using its bad leg, which is torn all the way to the bone now. Its second fight with the harpy bear did an incredible amount of damage.

Rogue watches from the dirigible and glances at Crystal "Got the flare gun?"

Crystal shakes her head and keeps searching.

"We gotta figure a way to distract that thing." Rogue is getting jumpy from not being able to help. *That leg has taken a severe pounding over the last two days. The rockets from yesterday, and maybe the fights took a bigger toll. If we're lucky, that's its weak spot.*

Pattel watches the confrontation from the lounge. "Damn, Hunter is in a situation." He walks over to the door and searches for where Albert ran to hide. "Where'd Albert go?"

Stoutarm is in one of the barracks and can see the equipment in the refinery vanish when the lights flicker. "Gotta get him out of there." The door to the station swings open and Pattel comes out.

"Hey you!" Pattel fires a few rounds from his rifle at the bad leg. "Nya, nya!" He about faces and slaps his rear. "Oh shit!" He jumps back through the door when he receives its full attention.

"You lucky bastard." Stoutarm watches Pattel's stunt. Then he notices what's going on inside the refinery as Hunter is trapped with the Shadow Figure. "And he's an unlucky bastard."

Hunter runs as fast as he can towards the bay doors. Taking his chances with the hydra is better than what happened to Ned. He escapes outside as the black liquid pours all over the floor. He somehow manages to avoid being touched. The hydra is now focusing on the station.

Hunter crouches and walks to the side of the building, trying to stay hidden. "Too close. Oh, not good."

Stoutarm turns around to find Albert right behind him and jumps. "Oh, man! You scared me half to death!"

"What a shame my presence failed to bring you to your full death. I need your help with something."

"Sure. What's the deal?" Stoutarm has just finished speaking when a sharp, stabbing pain tears through his gut with a soft, metal, grinding sound.

"I need to feed the monster. And your fresh guts might be a tasty treat, ripe for distracting." Albert stares into Stoutarm's eyes with a smile.

Stoutarm manages to punch Albert, knocking him to the ground. He reaches the door until the blood loss affects him. Whatever Albert used to cut him goes too deep for him to survive.

"You managed to move a surprising distance while letting me have you on such an interesting leash." Albert holds up Stoutarm's intestines, which he grabbed before being punched. He is squeezing and pulling on them. As Stoutarm screams, Albert laughs like a maniac.

Stoutarm reaches for a grenade from his belt but then remembers he doesn't have any. He faces Albert. Rushing him and grabbing him by the neck, he head-butts him. Then he drags Albert out the door. "Hey! Hydra! Look what I got for you! Snack time sale! Two for one bite!"

"No, you fool! Only you are to come out here."

Stoutarm fights against the incredible pain and holds Albert with an iron grip. He can feel himself getting weaker. His vision is getting blurred. But he can make out the hydra is moving towards him. Right then, he closes his eyes and loses consciousness.

Albert breaks free of Stoutarm's grip and lunges as far from him as he can.

One head eats Stoutarm's body, while another launches at Albert, who manages to reach the door to the building. The hydra's head stops at the open door with its mouth open. Exhaling a foul breath into the barracks and following up with an ear shattering roar.

Albert takes a glimpse down the throat of the beast. "Oh, heavens me."

The angry hydra growls and lets out another roar toward Albert. The other three heads stare at him through the windows.

"How can this building cause you to stop? If you wish to eat me, come and take me, you insufferable creature! Oh, my head. That bastard Stoutarm. Spit him out this instant! I want to murder him again. I demand you resurrect him like Ned!"

The hydra roars again and fills the air with its abhorrent breath.

"On second thought, do keep your breakfast down, please. Where are my manners? If you will excuse me, I must vacate the contents of my stomach," Albert says politely, as he has difficulty enduring the stench.

Hunter uses the distraction to reach the station. "Thanks for the save!" he tells Pattel.

"I can't believe what he did. Albert fed Stoutarm to the monster." Pattel pulls the curtain down. "Bastard lives."

"Yeah, saw the whole thing go down as I walked over. Should've shot him when I had the chance."

"What else are we gonna do?"

"That plane you found can annoy the damned monster like a pesky fly and lead it over our bomb." Hunter catches his breath.

"So, why'd you leave the refinery again?"

"That building is not a safe place to hide," Hunter replies with a terrified voice.

A dark spot appears on the floor between them. The Shadow Figure rises from the spot and points at Hunter. Hunter shoots as soon as the Figure materializes, which vaporizes when hit.

"You gotta be kidding me! That thing again?" Pattel backs up to a wall.

"The hydra's manifestation in the alternate dimension or some bullshit. The scariest part of the hydra's abilities. I don't remember everything Mack said, though." Hunter sits down and takes a few breaths.

The hydra returns its focus to the station, roaring constantly.

"So loud!" Pattel shouts, while he and Hunter hide and cover their ears.

Crystal hands Rogue the flare gun. *That took too long.* Rogue preps the gun and fires out over the valley. "Get your ass off them!" He fires a second flare.

The hydra spots the flares and follows the smoke trails to where they came, locating the dirigible and roaring at them.

The Shadow Figure appears behind them and moves around, letting out a plume of wake toxin inside the ship.

WHAT? Crystal clicks.

Rogue searches for the source of the blue mist. "Hydra's wake? In here? From what?" Rogue spots the Shadow Figure in the corner of his eye. "What the hell are you?"

WE DIE? Crystal runs to Rogue.

"No, we're immune to this stuff. Remember the medicine I gave you two days ago? I can deal with whatever this thing is." Rogue moves to the center of the cabin.

Crystal nods and clings to him hiding behind his back, and burrows her head into him.

Upon hearing Rogue say those words, the Figure's reaction is to point at Rogue and vanish.

The hydra runs to the area under them, covering the distance from the camp to the middle of the valley in less than a minute.

The hydra's roaring catches their attention. GO UP, Crystal clicks.

As the Shadow Figure vanishes, Rogue glances at the hydra sprinting toward them. "That thing can still run like that? We're a half mile up. No way something so giant can jump this high." *At least,*

I don't think a hydra can reach us. They keep watching as it lowers its body while running and lurches upwards. It reaches an incredible height, and the hydra's heads come closer to the dirigible than Rogue thought possible, but luckily, they are still out of its reach, barely.

Crystal digs her hands into Rogue's sides, squeezes him hard, and screams. Rogue turns around, and holds her tight for a second.

"That sure did come a lot closer than I gave it credit for." Rogue rushes to the controls, turning on the air intake and heater to gain some extra altitude, just in case another jump has more oomph. *Note to self; underestimating any aspect of this hydra will kill us.*

The falling hydra lands with a thud, sending shock waves through the ground as it roars in pain.

That sound, the snapping sound. Did it break its leg? Rogue takes note as the hydra stumbles and roars. The Shadow Figure is emitting blue mist over the broken leg. "Overconfident hydra overdid it. I think it broke a leg."

GOOD! Crystal clicks. She shudders in Rogue's arms, trembling with fear. So far she has managed to observe from a distance, but getting some action was nothing short of terrorizing.

Rogue holds her head to his chest. "We'll survive. I promise." *We're done. Sorry guys, this ship is leaving.* Rogue turns the engine on, so they can overcome the wind. They hear a sputter and a series of metal bangs, and the ship falls silent.

Crystal's tears are soaking his shirt. She opens her eyes to find him keeping calm and wiping away her tears. How can he stay so stoic and calm?

Of course, we lose compression in a cylinder; now of all times. At least we still have battery stabilizers and vertical control. "We're still going to survive this, Crystal. As long as we stay together and don't give up, we'll be alright."

Pattel sits up. "Man, I fell flat on my ass with that one." The Juman notebook falls out of his pocket and slides on the floor away from him.

Hunter pushes himself up. "Better than landing on your face." He walks over to the lobby area. The dim light of predawn is starting to grow stronger.

"I don't think that's the bomb." Pattel brushes dust off himself.

"No, definitely not. I think the hydra tried to grab the airship." Hunter caught a glimpse of the monster landing before the tremor hit and knocked them both down.

The handle on the door at the back of the station by the lounge jiggles like someone is trying to come in.

"You locked the doors, right?" Hunter aims his weapon at the door.

"Yeah."

Hunter peeks out at the valley, observing the hydra's attempt to stand back up and stumble. "Its leg is worse now. I can't imagine it's going to be moving so fast anymore."

"About time we score a win of some kind." Pattel checks how much ammunition is left. "I burned through almost everything I brought."

"Got half a clip left in Westly's rifle." Hunter replies, doing the same thing. "Think Stoutarm's rifle has anything left?"

"No clue, He was more conservative than me last night so, maybe. The other weapons laying around might have ammo too."

Albert is unable to enter the station, so he kicks with every ounce of his might, despite the throbbing pain in his head and the sharp stabbing pain in his leg. This just makes him feel more pain. "I will take frivolous pleasure in murdering you all!" After a second, he turns to try entering from another side when the Shadow Figure appears before him. "And what do you desire of me?"

The Figure begins shrinking to the size of a normal person. "What do I desire of you?" It shouts back in an echoing voice that morphs into Albert's by the last syllable.

"Do not mock my words. You are far more intelligent than that." Albert tries to walk past to the door.

The Figure takes Albert's physical form and sticks his arm in front of Albert.

Albert backs up. "Oh, dear me no, do not do that." He falls backwards, scrambling to back away from his impostor. The impostor takes a step forward as he starts to run away, slipping on the mud.

"Kill you all. I desire!" The impostor uses Albert's own voice.

Albert closes his eyes and trembles in fear.

A floating pipe hits the Albert impostor from behind.

It turns away from Albert and smiles. "Well, well, what do I have here? The runaway puppet who failed me. I will take your second life away."

"Uh-oh." Joe's voice replies.

"I see you." The impostor faces where Joe is.

"Oh, good, well can you see my Pyrecone baby?" Joe shouts. A huge plume of flame erupts out of the empty air from Joe and engulfs the impostor. "I'm putting some hydra brains on the barbecue today!"

"I have you, pest!" The imposter stares at Joe through the flames from his flamethrower. It's arm forms a long blade and impales Joe.

Joe screams in agony but still doesn't become visible. But his blood is flowing like a river down the imposter's arm and forms a pool of blood on the ground.

After a short moment, a whip-like sound cracks the air, and the impostor's blade arm is severed.

Albert takes off, running in the opposite direction, while putting something under his coat.

Pattel and Hunter get outside to find an Albert impostor covered in flames. They see a blade slice through its arm, which vanishes immediately after being severed.

"The hell did Albert do?" Pattel barely saw Albert move and a silver flash tore through the impostor. "I've never seen a weapon like that before."

"Oh, right. That's why I wasn't keen to be too close to him in the refinery." Hunter is watches Albert running towards the office as both of them scurry back inside the station.

The impostor returns its attention to Hunter and Pattel, looking through the window.

"Heads up," Pattel said as the impostor comes through the wall and window and enters the lounge.

The Shadow Figure is reverts to its original form.

Before Hunter can move, Pattel fires a shot from his rifle. But the bullet stops in mid-air and drops to the ground. "I don't think we can shoot this thing."

The Shadow Figure's cloak retracts to reveal a shiny black skeleton hand. It touches a wall. Instantly, the station transforms to the charred ruins they encountered before. The Shadow Figure's head reveals itself to have a skull of a hydra, and is joined by three more.

Another burst of flame shoots out at the Figure, but stops as the flamethrower is disengaged. "Take that," Joe's voice says, while drawing his final breath. His body appears after he died. Pattel recognizes him as the same man from the river shack.

Hunter and Pattel open fire while backtracking, even as the bullets stop mid-air and drop. "The phosphorus mine! Go!"

They stop firing and sprint for the mine. The buildings begin exploding into flames. Flying burning debris crashes all around them and flies through them. While they aren't hit by the debris, they can feel the heat.

The impostor form reappears ahead of them, cutting them off from the mine. Pattel ducks under the impostor's arm blade and runs past. Hunter stops in front of it and tries to work out an escape.

Albert runs out of the office ruins. "Everything is exploding! Fire everywhere!" He screams at the top of his lungs. The imposter turns its attention towards Albert, reverts to its usual form, and sinks straight into the ground, forms the all-too-familiar dark spot and moves right beneath Albert. A ball of smoke rises up. Albert runs out of the smoke, coughing.

Hunter laughs. "The last person to ingest anything coming from that being was Ned. It did not turn out well."

Albert freezes and stares down at his hands, admiring them.

"What happened with Ned?" Pattel has stopped running towards the mine.

"He turned into a zombie." Hunter smiles, and can't believe Albert is being dealt with so easily.

"Does it look like that's what happening to Albert?" Pattel aims at Albert.

Hunter waits a moment. "Um, I don't know. Let's try this." Hunter raises the rifle and fires on Albert. The bullet strikes Albert in the side of the head but fails to harm him.

"Did Ned become superhuman when this happened to him?" Pattel starts backing away.

"More like squishy zombie abilities." Hunter's smile fades. This is nothing like Ned's transformation. "No, this is different."

The Shadow Figure re-emerges and appears more transparent, fleeing to the hydra in the valley. The surrounding buildings rematerialize.

"Ha-ha, our fellow hydra did do itself in trying to jump at the airship." Albert says, while inspecting his arms and hands. "I shared its mind and thoughts during its attempt to consume me. The projection now goes to heal the animal, the master, or rather, the true form. Ancient, and designed to exist in many dimensions. What an animal! Designed with so many powers and abilities. What we have experienced from this hydra's wake is but a small fraction of the vast array of its mechanisms and uses. Such as the fact that to be able to corrupt me, I required being strengthened, so I could survive the corruption process. Healing me fully and giving me the strength and stamina of youth and multiplying those attributes. The process of conversion was interrupted before it could be initiated, but not until after I have enjoyed the healing and strengthening powers. What most fortunate luck, would you not say?"

"We need to find a way to bomb the hydra's ass now." Pattel shot a glance at the hydra.

"In due time, dear boy. A task I can now do on my own, for the poor animal must be put down humanely. But now, who to kill first? The backstabbing traitor, or the other traitor who owes me a refund for every service he's provided? Oh, dear me; this decision is so black or white."

Pattel opens fire on Albert, landing several rounds in his face. "The fuck you say!?"

Albert's face is severely deformed, but he shakes his head. "Now, that was unkind of you. Guess you are first. Shall I end you with elegance or gratuitous violence?"

Pattel stops, when he notices Albert shaking his head, looking down. Remembering Albert's weapon, he runs for the phosphorus mine. He turns around after gaining some distance. Seeing Albert does not move, changes his mind and runs to the maintenance shop.

"More hide-and-seek?" Albert smirks and sprints towards Pattel. "You will fail to find any refuge from me inside any building."

Hunter glances over his shoulder, thinking of the plane and luring the hydra over the trap. The refinery is an invisible charred frame, and Rogue's plane isn't in sight. He glances back toward Albert and Pattel to discover that they're missing. "Shit." Hunter kicks at the ground and decides to run towards the Machine Shop where Pattel headed.

Pattel slows down to let Albert gain on him. When he is close enough, Pattel stops and pulls a roundhouse kick, hitting Albert in the head, knocking him off his feet, and sending him stumbling back a few feet.

Albert begins to pick himself up, but is stomped on by Pattel until Albert's neck audibly breaks. "Oh, so that is what this feels like?" Albert responds to the sensation. He laughs, catches Pattel's foot and shoves with all of his might. Pattel is thrown back all the way to the shop and crashes through a window. Albert's face is healing again. "I think those wonderful abilities are still empowering me."

Pattel gets off the floor and searches around. "How the hell does anyone fight something like this?" He sees Albert walking toward the door. The layout is an open floor plan with tables and machines laid out in the same way as the refinery. "This is a bad place to fight."

Albert waits for his neck to heal, before approaching Pattel. "The sensation of my neck snapping back in place is worse than when you broke my neck to begin with."

Pattel checks his rifle and finds it's jammed with two rounds left. "Seriously?" He starts to clear the jam when the door swings open.

"Toys down, everyone. Let us return to work; chop, chop now," Albert says, with the biggest grin on his face.

"Don't be so elated." Pattel grabs a hammer from a nearby worktable, swinging at Albert. The hammer goes through him.

Albert grabs the handle, yanks it out of Pattel's hand, and swings back at him. The hammer goes through Pattel as he tries to block with his arm. "Useless tool."

Albert throws a punch at Pattel, hitting him in the face and knocking him back against a table. Pattel moves to the side to avoid getting kicked in the head and gets back to his feet. He waits for Albert's next attack, but Albert pulls the weapon he used on the Shadow Figure out from under his shirt. Pattel backs up against another table and rolls backward to put distance between them. Albert rushes to a button nearby and slams his fist on it. "Know your surroundings, dear boy!"

Pattel lets out an ear-splitting scream of pain as the table saw activates and rises up into his back before he can roll off.

Albert grins and turns the saw off. "Run away. If you can. I'm feeling a little too generous in the heat of this moment."

Hunter barges through the door. "Pattel!"

"Ah, you came when I needed you most. How sincere." Albert smiles and walks toward Hunter.

Walker watches as dawn rises and the hydra roars in pain. Damned thing actually broke its leg trying to jump at the airship. "If only you had broken your leg closer." He plants another flag in the mud. He is marking a perimeter to let him know when the monster is centered over the bomb.

There had been a lot of gunfire going off in the camp, but everything has stayed silent for the last half hour. While the injured hydra isn't moving, he decides to make a run to figure out what's going on at camp. Crossing the valley is easy enough. When he feels the tremors start again, Walker discovers the hydra is getting back up, roaring and limping towards Camp Tor.

Walker runs to the station and gets in before the hydra arrives in the camp. He hears a gut wrenching scream from near the middle of camp. Several more loud screams follow the sound of metal being pounded. "Pattel!" Walker bolts out of the lounge to find Pattel impaled to the ground with a thick pole through the chest. Albert is swinging a hammer, and driving down the pole.

All four hydra heads are above the station watching, and growling.

"You Hungry?" Albert shouts at the angry hydra, pointing at Pattel.

Walker keeps to the wall of the station, trying to stay out of the hydra's line of sight.

Next to Pattel, Hunter is tied up and motionless. Another pole with a sharp point lies at his feet.

"You bastard," Hunter groans.

Albert spots Walker. "Ah Walker, I'm delighted to see you again!" One of the Hydra's heads turns to locate him.

"We're done! You're going to die, asshole!" Walker aims his machine gun at Albert, but he's too far away for a clean shot.

The head returns its focus to Albert.

"They wanted to kill me. I am of the fine opinion that, if I am to perish, my underlings must join me!" Albert shouts hysterically. He faces the growling hydra. "Can you believe the humiliation? They acted to murder their master. Traitors, the lot of them!"

Walker glances up to find that the hydra appears to be listening, and isn't happy.

"I give them a life of luxury and easy jobs, money for enabling their hobbies. And when the going gets too difficult for them, they are worthless. And, to elaborate, they are worse than worthless. They become an active problem."

The Shadow Figure emerges in front of Albert in impostor form. "Only I decide who lives or dies."

"I fear not, hydra. That divine power is mine alone," Albert retorts.

"As your enemy says, you die next," impostor says, before vanishing again.

Hunter manages to untie the knot behind him, rolls over and tries to sit up. Albert runs over and hits him in the back with the hammer. The hydra moves one of its heads and glares at Albert aggressively.

Albert holds up Hunter's body, and the closest hydra head stops inches away from Hunter's face. "I see." Albert spits on the hydra's nose.

Another head comes to pull the pole out of Pattel, who remains motionless and without a sound. The four heads growl towards Albert.

"I suppose we're going together, Albert." Hunter can barely move after being thrashed around by Albert.

"You fool! The idiot made it clear that only I am next, which is a shame for you, and myself, I suppose. I will be most damned that I have to use your still breathing carcass for a shield."

Hunter chuckles. "What a good boy," he says with an exhausted voice, letting his body stay limp to make lifting him more difficult for Albert.

"You cannot possibly know its gender, you moron." Albert backs up towards the refinery.

"Hydra, I got this side. Cover the other." Walker raises his weapon with Albert in his sights, moving around the side to flank him. One of the head's nods in acknowledgment. Walker tries not to let the hydra intimidate him. "Hydra said you die next; but it didn't specify how." Walker takes a kneeling stance to steady his aim at Albert.

In the instant Walker has a clear opportunity, the hydra takes a step to assist Walker in pinning down Albert and roars in pain. The heads turn toward its leg. The roar is so loud that Walker is forced to look away and cover his ears.

Albert takes the opportunity to drop Hunter and run away. Walker takes a few shots at Albert, but they don't stop him. When Albert is hiding, Walker grabs Hunter, dragging him to the station.

The hydra resumes the hunt, after regaining focus, and discovers everyone is taking cover again. It moves to Pattel's body, and eats him whole, doing the same to Joe. Then it limps out to the valley, letting out several ear shattering roars as it goes.

Rogue watches the whole thing unfold from the dirigible. "That's gotta be the coolest, most terrifying thing I've seen it do." *Walker, you have titanium balls the size of galaxies.*

Crystal jumps up and down. NOT DEAD, she clicks, repeating the two words many times.

"Easy." Rogue put his hand on hers. "This isn't over yet."

"Walker, hey; you gotta go back to that bomb. Be ready to detonate. I'm going for that plane." Hunter says. "And watch yourself. Albert has unnatural abilities now. And he brought his favorite sword. It's wrapped around his chest."

Walker nods. "Take the time you need to take off safe, alright?" Walker leaves the station. Daylight now lights everything up, and the hydra is by the lake getting a drink of water and resting.

Hunter takes a peek at the refinery. "Shit, I can't. Damn those charred frames."

Walker crosses the valley as quickly as possible to reach the crevice. He grabs the fuse box detonator, and walks out to a crevice further out and jumps in. He is about a quarter mile from the bomb, hoping he won't blow himself up. After arming the detonator, he pops his head up and peeks at the hydra, which so far hasn't noticed him.

The sound of a small engine comes from the airstrip. "Here we go." Walker keeps his eyes on the plane.

"Oh, bloody hell-" Rogue said, with a concerned tone. "Albert is in my plane. I'm willing to bet he's coming for us."

Crystal watches out of the window with binoculars, while Rogue gets to the controls and lets air out to descend.

"We're gonna go lower. If he decides to pop us from up here, we go straight down." *Did not expect this possibility. We're a massive target, and he's suicidal.*

Crystal goes to the box where she got the rope and opens it. "If you find anything useful in there-" he starts to say and stops when she pulls the sword out that Rogue found in the confiscation box earlier.

"I don't think he'll board us. That would be insane." *Though ramming us with a plane to take us down isn't a sane thing to do either.*

Walker panics as the dirigible starts to sink fast. The airplane is heading for the ship rather than going for the hydra. "Oh no, is that Albert?"

HE COMING! She clicks almost too fast for Rogue to interpret.

Rogue keeps watching out the window, as Albert heads straight in their direction.

Albert smiles as he heads towards the airship. "The beauty of this new strength will guarantee only my survival of the crash this time." He has also made a rudimentary grappling hook to try boarding them if he needs to. As he approaches, he takes note of the two hydra heads watching him.

He decides to fly into the cabin instead. He can see two people inside. Crystal is indeed alive, and he wants to hit her dead on. The two heads stay locked on Albert. The Shadow Figure appears on top of the wing and places its hand on the plane, causing Albert to fly through the dirigible, instead of colliding with it. Rogue and Albert exchange glances as he flies past him.

Crystal is clicking out of fear, making everything she's clicking incomprehensible. She cringes when Albert passes through her, falling to her knees.

Rogue looks down at the hydra, which returns to focusing on its broken leg.

"This is not going as planned." Albert observes the figure above him. "Ah, so you control what happens to whom. I will smite you, foul creature." The hydra's painful cry again summons the Shadow Figure back.

"Alright, let's see if this will work." He grabs the grappling hook, deciding to try latching on to the balloon or a structure cable. He circles around and gets close, dropping the hook over the dirigible. He becomes excited when his hook grabs into the cloth and has a firm hold. "Finally." He maneuvers around to pass right above and jump on.

Rogue spots the rope leading from his plane and picks Crystal up off the floor. "Crystal, keep pulling on this lever to release air and take us down, but do this slowly. Our lives are in your hands now. And I trust you. You got this." Rogue takes the sword. "Now he's trying to board us, and I'm not going to let him."

WHERE YOU GO? she clicks, as she tries her best to keep focused on what he says. She places her hand on the lever and holds it down the way he showed her. Albert's flyby is still fresh in her mind, but she tries hard to focus.

"Perfect, keep your hand just like that. I'm going to cut his rope before he boards us." Rogue opens the cabin door and climbs a rope ladder leading to the top of the ship.

Albert makes a clear pass over and jumps out. The small plane flies on its own, to eventually crash somewhere in the valley. Albert manages to land on board, and, because air is being let out, the balloon isn't very firm, which lets him land with ease. He throws away the grappling hook.

"You're out of your mind!" Rogue reaches the top, to discover Albert standing there.

"Ah, the legendary Rogue Whip wannabe. I do apologize for this whole misunderstanding. My sources appear to have been wrong. A rare occurrence I must assure you." Albert says.

"I'll bet. Now get your ass off my ship." Rogue stands on the supports for better footing.

"How rude. But I did shoot you down so I shall ignore it. Give me the girl back so I may resume my plan and I will spare you." Albert holds his hand out.

Rogue bats the hand away. "Your reputation would be tarnished if I live. Now jump off or I will throw you off."

Albert nods and walks away a few steps. "You are correct. Guess I will kill you now, burn your company and legacy to the ground, and feed Crystal your carcass."

Rogue forces himself not to react, and stays focused, brandishing the short sword and adopts a staggered stance.

"A challenge? Dear lad, have you no sense of style?" Albert takes off his suit vest. A metal band is wrapped around his torso. Albert grabs the handle and pulls it out. There is a metallic scraping sound as the weapon unfurls from his body.

"An urumi." Rogue changes his stance to standing straight and holds the sword to his side. *Mom, I'm about to make you real proud. This guy has no clue what he's up against.*

"Single blade urumi. Well done. You know a thing or two, I will grant you that." Albert waves the flexible sword around, while building momentum into the blade.

Rogue follows Albert's hand leading the six-foot blade as it flails around. Albert knows how to use this weapon well. Rogue clenches his sword with a firm grip and spreads his feet apart for a wider stance.

Albert flings the blade at Rogue like a whip. Rogue hits the urumi with his sword at arm's length. It's like fighting a rope that can't be cut. Albert moves his hand down and rotates his elbow, transferring momentum and control into the weapon, then, swings down and to the side like the urumi is a solid blade. Rogue moves his arm away just in time. But before the urumi hits the balloon, Albert swings up and prepares another strike.

Rogue reacts quickly to the opening and charges at Albert, punching him in the face as hard as he can. Last time he managed to send him to the ground. This time he only pushes him back a few steps. Something is different about him. But Rogue doesn't give him time to recover and unleashes several more punches, alternating between Albert's head, chest, and gut, using his sword to keep the urumi blade from moving at him, until Albert regains enough control to make a swing.

Albert misses but ends the barrage Rogue unleashed and forces him back. Rogue takes several steps backward to move out of the immediate range of Albert's weapon. "Damn you are a competent fighter," Albert shouts in anger.

Rogue waits for Albert to make a move. *This is going to be far more difficult than I expected. Experience matters with urumi's, and he has plenty.*

Albert keeps swinging in a crisscross motion defensively. He uses his open hand to wipe his nose and discovers he is bleeding. "I will dissect your corpse as payment."

Rogue maintains his stance and stays quiet, not giving Albert the satisfaction of an answer. *Come on, make another mistake. I dare you.*

Albert moves to attack Rogue, who dodges the blade's path and holds the sword between him and the blade in case Albert tries to make it stiffen and move laterally again. Albert is proving to be a master, who has decades of practice with this unique weapon.

Albert instead follows through the initial swing, and brings his blade back down, forcing Rogue towards the balloon's edge. "You handle yourself better than most, but you are begging for another opening. You cannot dance around me forever." Albert makes a few lateral parries, forcing Rogue further to the edge, making a wide swing, hoping to force him off.

Rogue dives forward to avoid backing too far where he can slip off. He rolls and regains solid footing, able to rush at Albert from the opening at his side.

Albert is too slow to redirect the urumi and catches Rogue's sword blade with his bare hand. It cuts though the palm down to the bones. Albert ignores the pain and wraps his fingers around the sharp edges to try yanking it away from Rogue, who's already starting a haymaker punch and hits Albert's face.

Rogue prepares to take advantage of Albert's loss of footing after that hit when he stumbles backwards. Albert swings around blindly, forcing Rogue to keep his distance and cancel his next move. Albert uses the space to return the blade's swinging to a circular motion, giving him time to rise to his feet and resume the crisscross pattern again at incredible speed. He advances towards Rouge to force him off the side.

The dirigible's balloon makes a lurch as more air escapes and the floor sinks under their weight; the urumi's blade hits the cloth and gets stuck. Albert put so much force behind the swing that when it stops, he almost lets go of the handle.

Rogue jumps right at Albert with the sword extended. Albert drops his urumi and uses both hands to grab the sword this time and manages to shove himself away. Rogue lunges down and grabs the urumi, wasting no time in throwing the weapon as far as he can off the ship.

Albert can no longer ignore the pain from having his hands sliced open. The loss of blood is taking its toll. He closes his eyes, loses focus for an instant. As he does, a sharp pain crawls across his neck.

Rogue slashes Albert's neck and then runs the blade into his gut and up the chest cavity. Albert's expression shows the severe pain he is feeling. Rogue leaves the sword in his stomach and kicks him to the side of the balloon, where Albert slides off and free-falls to his death.

The dirigible is still high up and Albert stares straight down as he plunges the hundreds of feet to the ground. "Good show, mate." He opens his arms while plummeting. A shadow crosses beneath him. Massive teeth appear in his peripheral vision and close around him; leaving nothing but endless darkness.

Walker watches as the plane passes over the dirigible and glides off, barrel rolling out of control and crashing in the distance. The hydra gets up and heads for the sinking dirigible. After a minute or so a body falls from the airship and the hydra is there to snap it out of the air. It's too far away to be able to tell whose body it is.

In spite who fell, the hydra is conveniently positioned across the field with the bomb between itself and Walker. He gets up out of the crevice, grabs a flare, igniting and waves it around then lights another one.

At first, the hydra doesn't react, waiting for the ship to fall to an attackable height. "I need its attention." Walker sits down and aims his weapon at the monster's broken leg. He puts his machine gun into full auto mode and empties the entire clip. One of the four heads checks in his direction and is soon followed by the other three. It lets out an ear shattering roar and begins to run at Walker.

Rogue hears gunshots from the valley below. He watches from the top of the ship as the creature runs for flares about half a mile away. "Oh shit!"

Crystal is watching the same thing and stares from the window in the side of the cabin.

The ground shakes with every step the titan-sized creature takes, acting like a confident predator, moving with incredible speed and a certain elegance. Rogue sits down to bear witness to a legendary animal's final moments.

Walker waits for the heads to pass by the flag marker he put down and counts one second before flipping the switch on the fuse box.

An enormous flash of bright red flame engulfs the hydra's body. The instant after, a massive plume of smoke blankets the area as fast as the flame appears. Shock waves and the sounds following shake everything. The airship shakes violently when the shock waves hit.

Walker is covered in dust and smoke, after getting knocked backwards off his feet.

Hunter ducks, and the glass windows shatter and falls like rain around him. The buildings rattle and the ground shakes like a major quake is happening.

The hydra lets out a final shriek, before falling silent somewhere in the smoke.

Crystal hides behind the cabin's wall as the whole ship shakes violently.

Rogue is knocked off the balloon and lands on a piece of rigging by the side of the cabin. Wrapping his arms and legs around the poles, he clings for his life.

Several seconds pass before everything stops shaking, Crystal looks out the cracked window to find Rogue hanging on to broken rigging.

"Wow." Hunter glances out the destroyed window.

"Damn. That's crazy," Rogue says when the smoke clears enough to see the aftermath.

The hydra's body is half obliterated and has been thrown some distance from where the blast originated. Most of the dirt covering the containment facility is gone, as a massive sheet of the mysterious metal is exposed. The heads remain motionless. Two of them are severed from the obliterated part of the body.

Hunter comes out of the station running out across the airstrip. "Yeah! Woohoo! Take that!" He starts doing a victory dance.

Rogue climbs down the rigging and back into the cabin. "Crystal, are you ok?"

Crystal wraps her arms tightly around him. ALL DEAD! She throws the clicker and jumps up and down.

"Got them both. No more monsters." He looks down at her face and stares into her eyes. Her smile is the biggest he's seen from anyone. *I can't believe we did this. We pulled off the impossible. And wow, this is how a genuinely happy Crystal looks? Uh oh, the ground is coming fast. Not good.* "Find something to grab. This landing is going to be rough."

A few moments later the dirigible crashes with a thud. Hunter is running across the valley towards them. "Guys, we bagged a hydra!"

Rogue and Crystal come out of the cabin. Crystal is gripping her leg as Rogue carries her. The hard landing and the explosion made her pain worse. "Where's Walker?"

"Where's Albert?" Hunter asks back.

"Killed him myself. Come on, let's find Walker."

Hunter nods. "But damn, check that out. We killed a hydra. We're gonna be famous."

Rogue chuckles. "Let's hope the monster stays dead."

"Hope? Do you see that thing?" Hunter points at the half of the body still intact.

"Hydras regrow heads if you tear them off. What if the damned thing regrows the missing half and spawns four new heads?" *I hope I'm wrong.*

Hunter stops and the smile fades off his face. "That's some disgusting ass, you know."

"I know, but if it doesn't move for a while, I'm sure we'll make a fine profit off the scientists who will be all over this thing." *Ugh, man, I feel worse than I did after waking up from the first crash.*

Hunter laughs. "Rich and famous, I like the sound of that. Hey, hydra, stay down forever, will ya?"

The flare Walker lit is still burning, and Rogue heads for the smoke. "He should be around here!"

THERE! Crystal clicks and points to a spot a little further away from the blast site.

Rogue and Hunter head over. Rogue reaches there first. "Aw shit, man."

Walker wakes up to find a large rock jammed in his leg. He lifts his head when he hears the others approach. "Did I kill me a hydra?" he groans.

"You only scratched it, and we're going to die," Hunter replies sarcastically. "No, man, you annihilated the damned monster." Hunter jumps into the crevice, next to Walker.

"Oh, good." Walker sounds weak and is breathing hard. Rogue sets Crystal down and starts to lift Walker out of the hole he is in and lay him flat on the ground.

"You got a boulder in your leg." Hunter tries to keep the leg steady as Rogue helps move him to the flat surface.

"Oh damn, I really did a number," Walker says looking over at the hydra's body. "I'm pumping so much adrenaline I can't feel my leg."

Crystal walks over and stares at him like she's going to hurt him, and smiles.

"Rogue, you don't happen to know how to fly the helicopter?" Hunter points at the remaining helicopter the group came in on.

"Yeah, I do. Keep him steady. I'm going to bring it here, and we'll head to Heart. Then we're going straight to a hospital in Acinvar." *I ain't flying anywhere else.*

Rogue picks Crystal up and heads for the station. "I'm going to grab my stuff. I have no intention of ever coming back here." When they reach the airstrip, he sets her down on the tarmac.

Crystal taps on his shoulder. When he turns around, she punches him in the arm, hard.

"Ouch. What was that for?"

YOU STOLE MY KILL! she clicks, giving him a scowl, then smiles.

Rogue can't help but laugh. "Oh, yeah, you're right. I'm sorry, but he boarded the ship."

She follows him into the room.

The place is wrecked. Someone clearly ransacked his stuff. He repacks what he brought and finds Crystal lighting the wood stove with a solemn expression. "You hungry?" Rogue goes help her.

Crystal shakes her head and starts throwing the cables and gag she was tied with into the fire. She stares at them as they burn to cinders, and closes the stove to let the fire die off. She stares at her hands and then rubs her wrists.

Once Rogue has everything, they go to the helicopter. On his way out of the Lobby he kicks a journal across the floor. He looks down and picks it up. Figuring the journal might have fallen from a shelf during the events he sets the book down on a table.

Crystal takes a deep breath the moment they're outside and stares at the sky, at Heart. I'M FREE, she clicks.

"Yes, you are." Rogue inspects the helicopter to see if the blast damaged it. The glass on the canopy cracked during the shock wave but Rogue is sure he can still fly. None of the gears or major cogwheels appear to be out of place and the engine looks unharmed. "This will be fun." *I'm not sure if it will hold after that shockwave but we don't have any other choice. Add the cracked windshield and I am having difficulty breathing, fun indeed.*

Crystal is hesitant to climb in at first as a feeling of apprehension stops her.

Rogue holds his hand out to her. "I'm not leaving without my new copilot."

She closes her eyes and climbs in. Rogue takes off to go get Hunter and Walker.

After Rogue lands near Hunter, he helps load Walker into the middle cabin. When they open the cabin, they discover two boxes inside with raw gemstones. "Did you guys plan on stealing gems?" Rogue pops one open and lifts a gemstone.

"Hey, can I pocket some please?" Walker reaches out for one. Rogue hands him the one he picked up.

"I didn't know these were here. Damn, they're shiny." Hunter opens a compartment behind the back seats to shove them in, clearing room for Walker.

Once he's loaded on, Walker lies still on his back.

"The gravity shift in the Tradewinds is gonna suck with how battered we all are. Make sure he stays pinned to the floor during the zero gravity shift." Rogue hands Hunter their weapons.

"Hey, it's over, Walker. We'll get you fixed up." Hunter sits next to him as Rogue closes the doors.

Rogue lands at the Airdrop West Hospital in the mega city

of Acinvar on Heart. He climbs out and tells the swarm of nurses rushing at them that they are all badly injured. Hunter exits the passenger compartment with dried tears all over his face and a solemn expression.

Rogue and Crystal watch the nurse team rush off with Walker's body on a stretcher as they walk over to Hunter.

"He went on the way here. Quiet and peaceful." Hunter wipes his eyes and stands next to them.

Rogue nods. "We'll give him a proper sendoff."

All three of them give the stretcher bearing Walker one last glance.

"But hey, we did it." Rogue says as Crystal hangs on his arm.

WE DID, she clicks.

"Think I understand Morse Code now," Hunter grumbles.

"Oh yeah? What did she say?"

"Not a clue, to be honest." Hunter says, causing them to laugh. "So, uh, the things in the back of the chopper, What are we gonna do with them?"

Rogue glances back at the helicopter. "Umm, we'll figure that out later."

The head doctor comes up as nurses bring wheelchairs for them. "Is everyone accounted for?"

"Everyone who survived is here." Rogue coughs up some blood after speaking, and they each sit in a wheelchair.

"Let's take you inside and have everyone checked over." The doctor is impressed that they are all able to walk given how banged up they appear.

AFTERMATH

Rogue walks into his office after the successful maiden voyage of his biggest airship. Crystal is right behind him. "Just gotta grab a few things from here and we'll head home." He says to her.

Crystal looks at the desk and spots an unopened letter in the middle. STRANGE, THAT WAS NOT THERE BEFORE YOU LANDED. She uses sign language to tell him.

Rogue glances at the desk when she points. "The door was locked, you have the only key... strange indeed."

Crystal closes the door and locks it and sits down next to the desk and her jaw drops on seeing the wax seal.

Rogue is quick to catch on to the sudden unnerving of her body language and stops picking up papers to go inspect the letter. He stops for a moment when his brain registers what he's seeing. "What in worlds do they want?" He mutters.

Crystal shakes her head no.

"It's just paper. Besides, the tyrant king died a few years ago. I'm curious." Rogue opens the letter and pulls out the contents, a single handwritten page.

Crystal picks up the envelope and glances inside to find it empty.

"Dear Mr. Whip, I am contacting you with a plea for help. Specifically, I require the aid of anyone who can travel between Shell and Heart without suspicion. But for the cause of reuniting the royal family of Darmoro. It is likely public knowledge that the late king exiled most of the family as punishment. And his heir, King Barret Roberts is attempting to reunite the family as part of his attempts to undo the actions of his father and begin the journey to restoring our nation's once respected stature. A long road lies ahead of us and with no allies, private or public, this task has been difficult. I hope this message finds you well and that you will at the least hear my request. Signed Archebald Van Fisc, Viceroy to the Darmoro Royal Court." Rogue reads aloud then hands the letter over to Crystal.

Crystal snatches the paper from his hand and reads it over herself.

Rogue opens the door. "Hey Jessie, did you place a letter on my desk?"

"No, why?" A woman from the main office replies looking up from her desk.

"I did." Hunter says while sitting at an empty desk.

"Hunter? Thought you were out hunting down Albert's network." Rogue replies.

"I am, and was asked to deliver that as a favor for trading information. I'm here to ask you to oblige so that we can further dismantle the connections. And oddly enough remove high value prizes from the field at the same time, those who were exiled are worth a lot to several countries. For unpleasant reasons as you can imagine."

"What in the hell are you guys talking about?" Jessie asks, as she can't help herself from overhearing the conversation.

Rogue lets out a deep breath. "Crystal, it's your call."

IM STAYING HOME THIS TIME. BUT IF IT HELPS TAKE DOWN ALBERT'S PEOPLE, PLEASE HELP HIM. She signs quickly.

Rogue chuckles nervously. "Jessie, close out my personal schedule and fill in with pilots who want some overtime. Sounds like I might be performing a few rescue missions depending on how things pan out."

Hunter nods. "One rescue. There's only one family member who isn't accounted for and the viceroy learned where they are. Although, unfortunately he can't get there."

"Dare I ask where?" Rogue asks.

"The Underlands, Outer Shell. Exiled to a town called Retundro Pass." Hunter answers.

"Even for us, that's going to require pulling major strings." Jessie comments.

"Getting into the Underlands is impossible politically. There's a major civil war going on. We go in flying Acinvar flags, it's not going to go well." Rogue replies, and then leans up against the door like he has an idea.

"I know that look; sounds like there's a 'but' coming." Jessie says, crossing her arms.

"They still allow for special permit flights for heavy commerce reasons. I have an idea on how to get one but, I'm not going to like it." Rogue says.

"What could you possibly need from there?" Jessie asks.

"A combat racing locomotive. From the company with the best parts. Beltmon is still in operation there somehow. But putting this in motion means visiting an ex of mine." Rogue comments.

"I thought you and Wyonna are on good terms still? Wait, are you going to buy her a whole new train?" Jessie gets excited. "Does this mean we can bet on our favorite team for a change? I mean, don't get me wrong, it's fun to provide emotional support but it'd be nice to see them actually win a time or two."

Crystal gives Rogue an intrigued look.

Hunter gives Rogue a pat on the back. "I had no idea I was going to be doing something so drastic to you. Maybe there's another way?"

"None that are easier or that can provide the country with a large influx of cash they can't and won't refuse." Jessie starts digging through a file cabinet at her desk.

"We are on friendly terms; but you know, I'd rather go Hydra hunting. Less complicated." Rogue comments.

An elderly man walks into the office wearing formal attire. The sight of him makes Crystal close the office door on Rogue and she locks herself inside.

"What the?" Rogue reacts.

"Hi, welcome to Rogue Whip's Tradewinds Crossing, what can we do for you?" Jessie asks getting back to her desk.

"My name is Rogue Whip, and I'd like to speak to Mr. Whip."

Jessie gives Rogue, the owner, a sideways glance as he and Hunter both drop their jaws a little.

"Somehow I figured this was going to happen sooner, rather than later." Rogue replies, approaching the spy.

"I hear you're going to the Underlands. This will make your trip a little easier. Less questions to ask and less attention gained in asking them. Consider it a thank you for doing what I couldn't." He pulls a small piece of paper out from his jacket and hands it to the pilot.

Rouge looks down at the paper and unfolds it to find an address for Nickel Point in the Underlands.

Thank you for reading Hydra's Wake. Don't forget to leave a rating and review!

ABOUT THE AUTHOR

Daniel Jones

Hydra's Wake is the breakout novel from Daniel Jones. Born in California USA, he grew up in a military family and lived in several places all around the world; including Japan, Germany, New Mexico, USA, and England. Along with being the oldest brother of three and a child of the 90's, Daniel is an Eagle Scout; an accomplishment he takes great pride in.

He currently lives in Maryland, USA with his wife Robyn. They has a passion for nature and animals and Daniel can often be found wandering local parks, zoos, or aquariums in his spare time when he isn't working on his next project. Some fun trivia about him is that his favorite colors are dark green and teal, his favorite animals are Leopards and Rhinos, and if Hydra's Wake is any clue, his favorite movies are creature features.

Be on the lookout for the next exciting novel from Daniel Jones: Frost Wake!

SPECIAL THANKS

This novel is self-published. There was a lot of work and effort that has gone into making this project a reality. While Daniel Jones did write Hydra's Wake, he also used several services to make the novel what it is today.

Ivan Zann - Book Covers Art
Cover Art Illustrator

Phillip Newey - All-Read-E
Copy Editor

Pamela Wilson - The Picky Bookworm
Proofreader

Thank you to everyone who participated in this journey!

Made in the USA
Monee, IL
11 March 2024

d15ccb02-c702-4e6e-8385-6fdf92450a08R01